What the critics

Best selling erotic romance e-book of 2000!

Voted favorite futuristic for 2001 by the host of AOL's Romance Fiction Forum!

Selected by Romantic Times Magazine as a reader's favorite in the Feb 2002 issue!

"[This] world is like Feehan's Carpathians (without the blood), Anne Rice's Sleeping Beauty (without the discipline), and Dara Joy's Knight of a Trillion Stars... all rolled into a hot and unique world." - *Karen McBride*

"*The Empress' New Clothes* is a delightfully sexy and funny romance. The author has created an entire new galaxy and race of people that will capture the attention of any science fiction fan. While this is a highly erotic novel, it does not fall into the trap of many erotic romances of lots of sex and little plot or story. Highly imaginative with captivating dialogue and a fast pace...I recommend *The Empress' New Clothes* highly." - *Terrie Figueroa, Romance Reviews Today*

"This is definitely women's Erotica with a capital E. This story is a combination of romance, erotica, futuristic fantasy, science fiction, a bit of mystery, and a LOT of humor. You have to view the whole thing as an outrageous romp, and don't expect it to fall neatly into the rules for any particular genre." - *Bookaholics.com, Sensual Romance*

"The author creates a place of fantasy with her vivid descriptions, and her attention to details is wonderful. The characters, each in his or her own right, draw the reader in, giving glimpses of themselves, carving a place of their own. THE EMPRESS' NEW CLOTHES, the first in Ms. Black's, Trek Mi Q'an series, is superb. Starting off her series with a bang, THE EMPRESS' NEW CLOTHES contains everything a reader of erotic, futuristic romance could ever imagine." - *Michelle Gann, The Word on Romance*

Books by Jaid Black

Death Row: The Avenger Π
Death Row: The Fugitive Π
Death Row: The Hunter Π
Dementia Σ
The Empress' New Clothes Σ
Enslaved Σ
God of Fire
The Hunted (anthology)
No Escape Σ
No Fear Σ
No Mercy Σ
The Obsession
The Possession
Seized Σ
Sins of the Father
Things That Go Bump Σ
Tremors
Vanished
Warlord

Π Death Row Series
Σ Trek Mi 'Qan Series

ELLORA'S CAVE
ROMANTICA PUBLISHING

Ellora's Cave Publishing, Inc.
PO Box 787
Hudson, OH 44236-0787

ISBN # 0-9724377-0-3

Edited by Martha Punches.
Cover art by Darrell King.

Warning: The following material contains strong sexual content meant for mature readers. *The Empress' New Clothes* has been rated NC17, erotic, by three independent reviewers. We strongly suggest storing this book in a place where young readers not meant to view it are unlikely to happen upon it. That said, enjoy...

The Empress' New Clothes

Written by

Jaid Black

To my parents for their unwavering support of me.
To my best friend Aparna for being proud of me.
To my fans at jaidblack.com for encouraging me.
And to Crissy Brashear for always believing in me.
This book wouldn't have existed without all of you.

Chapter 1

Kyra Summers took a soothing sip of the herbal tea, then serenely passed the cup along to her best friend Geris Jackson. Geris accepted the cup placidly, took a calming sip, then sedately passed it along to the next person in the meditation circle.

Once the cup had made the full round, the extremely tranquil leader of The Smiling Faces and Peaceful Hearts Meditation Retreat, Mrs. Blissful-she actually went by that name-smiled at the group. She reminded Kyra of a Stepford wife. "Is everyone feeling soothed?" Mrs. Blissful asked melodiously. "Are our faces smiling? Do we have peaceful hearts today?"

Geris frowned. She shot an icy glance over toward Kyra and gave her an "I'm-really-gonna-kill-you-for-this" look. Kyra absently noted that nothing about Geris's frown looked serene. She could only hope that Mrs. Blissful didn't catch her best friend's slip. Otherwise she'd probably make them do some sort of weird extra credit project. Like move into Mister Rogers Neighborhood indefinitely.

Mrs. Blissful closed her eyes and breathed in through her nostrils and out of her mouth. She raised a balmy hand into the air and let it meander back and forth in a gentle swaying motion. "Let us breeeeathe. Let us find the peeeeeace."

The paying retreaters followed the instructor's lead, albeit a bit skeptically. They closed their eyes, breathed, and tried like hell to find the peace.

Kyra's group consisted of she and Geris, plus four others. Next to Geris sat Fred, the fifty-year-old CEO extraordinaire whose physician ordered him to The Smiling Faces and Peaceful

Hearts Meditation Retreat after his last triple-bypass. Mrs. Blissful had denied him the use of his portable fax and cell phone, but Fred had already been caught breaking her rules a time or two under the guise of "making sure they still worked". So far Fred hadn't found the peace.

Next to Fred sat Prue, a forty-three-year-old homemaker and mother of five who had a slight nervous breakdown after her eldest son disclosed his homosexual orientation to her last fall. Trying her best to be a supportive mother to her son and his new husband, she came here to find the peace. Since it was typical to see Prue crying at any given time you happened to glance in her direction, she probably hadn't found it yet either.

Next to Prue sat Lord Jameson, a thirty-year-old English aristocrat. No one knew precisely what in the hell was wrong with him, but if his relentless scowling and infinitely puckered lips didn't give his secret away, then the negligent bags under his eyes certainly told his story-he needed to find the peace.

In between Jameson and Mrs. Blissful sat Arthur, a monk. Who would have thought there was anything in a monk's life that could be stressful enough to send him packing to this place? But, well, there he was. A monk who needed to find the peace. If Brother Arthur's nervous twitches and incoherent mumbling were any indication, he too was yet to find it.

Peace, it seemed, was an elusive thing.

Kyra breathed in through her nostrils and out of her mouth as she listened to Mrs. Blissful's breezy voice chime out tranquil instructions. This was her and Geris's third day straight at the camp and so far she was no more serene than she'd been when she'd first arrived.

Perhaps this retreat she'd talked Geris into attending with her hadn't been one of her more lucid notions. It had seemed like a good idea when the EAP at work had first given her the pamphlet filled with information on the camp. It had seemed the perfect way to leave the stress of the past year in the city behind her as she found her peace in the Catskill Mountains for a week. Now she wasn't so sure.

Ah well, no matter. She and Geris were here now. Might as well make the most of it.

Kyra closed her eyes and breathed, trying desperately to find the peace. She felt like a drowning woman going down in the currents, grabbing in desperation onto a passing twig for help, praying it would hold her afloat.

It occurred to Kyra that finding the peace was stressful business.

* * * * *

"I still can't believe I'm wasting an entire week of hard earned vacation time at this godforsaken place." Geris scowled at Kyra from over her plate of salad greens and-oh boy!-vinegar dressing.

Kyra looked up from her own helping of rabbit food long enough to frown. "Why must you put down all of my ideas? It's highly annoying."

"I didn't mean anything by it." Geris waved her hand in a dismissive gesture. "I was only teasing." She leaned in closer to the table and caught her best friend's gaze. "You do remember what teasing is, right? You know, that thing we did before you turned into the Morticia Adams sitting before me today?"

Kyra winced. She didn't care to think on how appropriate that nickname was at the moment. She set her fork down on the tabletop with a sigh, then closed her eyes and rubbed her temples. "I'm sorry Ger. I know you didn't mean anything by it. I don't know what's gotten into me lately. I feel like I'm losing it."

Geris reached across the table and grasped Kyra's hand. "Baby, you've got to move on," she told her quietly. "It's been a year."

Kyra opened her eyes. She bit on her bottom lip and nodded. God did she ever need to move on. Her younger sister Kara had been missing for a year as of yesterday. And it didn't look like she would be coming back-ever. "It's just so hard to accept, Ger. I mean, Disney World of all places! Who the hell falls off of the Pirates of Penzance ride never to be heard from again?" She groaned. "Shit like that just does not happen."

Geris squeezed her hand. "I'm here for ya, honey. Just like always."

Kyra blew out a breath, blowing a wine red curl out of her line of vision in the process. She squeezed Geris's hand back. "I know, Ger. I know." She sat up straighter in her chair and expelled a humorless laugh. "God I'm terrible! You've all but put your life on hold to care for me this past year and I thank you by criticizing every word that comes out of your mouth." She shook her head. "How do you put up with me?"

Geris grinned. "It ain't easy." Her smile faltered as she squeezed Kyra's hand again. "But I am sorry. You know, about putting this place down. I won't ever-"

"No!" Kyra insisted, shaking her head vigorously in the negative. "Things need to get back to the way they were. I need some sense of normalcy again."

And truly, having Geris watch every word she uttered around her was *not* normal. They had been best friends since early childhood and because of that fact, they had always shared an easy camaraderie that some friendships, no matter how close, couldn't claim. Most of the time they knew what the other one was thinking before they even spoke.

Geris nodded. Nothing else had to be said on that issue. "So," she asked, effectively changing the subject, "is this fun-filled, not to mention appetizing"-she looked to her plate and frowned-"excursion to Green Acres helping you *at all*?"

"Not really."

She looked up from her salad. "Oh? Why not?"

Kyra shrugged her shoulders. "The breathing is boring. I find that instead of relaxing me, it only gives me time to think about all of my problems."

"So think about other things."

"Like?"

Geris chuckled. "You know how we have to breathe during the massage exercise?"

"Uh huh."

"I breathe deeply all right. And the whole time I'm breathing I pretend I'm getting rubbed down by Denzel Washington and Mel Gibson instead of those two ole bitties who massage us."

Kyra lifted an eyebrow. "Both of them, eh?"

Geris grinned. "That's right. Just one won't work. There's something about the Washington-Gibson combo that can make a woman breeeeeathe. Girl, in those moments I have *found* the peace!"

Kyra laughed. A musical sound to Geris's ears. "Oh Ger, you're so bad." Her eyes shuttered as she nibbled on her lip. "But I think I'll try it next time. Do any other combos work or only the Washington-Gibson one?"

Geris shook her head. "Only Mel and Denzel, baby. I call it the Mel-zel technique."

Kyra grinned. "Then the Mel-zel technique it is!"

"Good." Geris chuckled.

Two days later, Kyra admitted to her best friend that her Mel-zel technique had worked wonders. Oddly enough, Geris been correct on that other score as well-the technique was no good in any other combination. Only Mel and Denzel worked. Mel had to massage her left side and Denzel her right. It was an amazing discovery! Not to mention a rather, well, weird one.

Fresh from the massage room, and therefore still sporting their white spa robes, Kyra and Geris helped themselves to two china cups filled with herbal tea and found a table to sip from them at. They were joined by Prue, the housewife with the gay son, and Jameson, the forever scowling English lord.

Geris glanced over to Jameson and quirked an elegant eyebrow. "Jamie, baby, you look almost chipper this morning."

Kyra looked away before she laughed. The English nobleman was forever frowning. How Geris could tell his one mood from the next was beyond her. But she could. And it was obvious that Jameson didn't mind at all. In point of fact, he probably welcomed it, as it had become glaringly obvious to one and all that the married aristocrat had developed a minor crush on her best friend.

But then who could blame him. Geris Jackson was exquisitely beautiful. She was long and sleek and sported flawless mahogany skin. Just as Kyra imagined that the Egyptian Queen Nefertiti had probably looked in her heyday.

Geris's jet black hair hung down to the center of her back in micro-braids, surrounding the face of a woman who could give a super model a run for her money. Light brown almond-shaped eyes. Full red lips. The woman was exquisite.

But out of all of her attributes, it wasn't her face that Ger cared about. She took pride in her hair instead. She hadn't cut it once in her entire life and swore she never would.

Kyra had never cut her curly wine-colored tresses either. Long hair and above-average height was the only thing she and Geris shared in common from a physical standpoint. In every other way, their looks ran along opposite ends of the spectrum.

Where Geris was dark skinned, Kyra sported the pale, creamy complexion that all women in her family possessed. Thankfully, her ivory coloring went well with the wine red hair and silver-blue eyes that were the stock and trade of the females of the Summers clan.

Their shapes were different too. Where Geris was perfectly, fashionably toned with her pert C-cup and regally sculpted body, Kyra was fuller and more lush of hip and breasts.

They were two women, two best friends, who society labeled "beautiful". Different, but beautiful. And the miracle of miracles to all outsiders was the fact that neither woman felt it or really even believed it. But that was ever the way of American women. The grass is always greener in someone else's pasture, and the mirror always casts a better reflection in someone else's bathroom.

Kyra brought her humor under control and turned back around to face Jameson and Geris. She inclined her head to the British gent solemnly. "Indeed Jameson, you look as though you are finally finding your peace."

Jameson scowled-nothing out of the ordinary there. "All this bloody nonsense about finding one's peace has been a waste of precious pounds." His scowl deepened. "I declare, I feel no more at peace than I did when first I arrived."

Geris clucked her tongue. "Jamie, you need to relax, baby. You need to breeeeathe. You need to find the peeeeeace."

Kyra would have laughed, but Prue picked that particular moment to burst into a bout of tears. She pulled a hankie from out of the pocket of her robe and swiped at her eyes. "I'm so sorry. But I think Jameson is right. I can't find the peace either. And I've only got two days left to find it!" She burst into tears again.

Jameson scowled. Well, more than usual.

Kyra reached over and patted Prue on the hand. "It will be okay." She flicked her gaze toward Geris and grinned. "Perhaps we should introduce Prue here to the Mel-zel technique."

Geris smiled back. "Not a bad idea." She raised her brows and regarded Jameson. "I'd teach it to Jamie here, but I doubt it would work the same wonders."

The English lord inclined his head. "And what technique is that, Miss Jackson?"

Geris's almond eyes lit up. "Honey, let me tell you something..."

Chapter 2

Sand City on Planet Tryston, Trek Mi Q'an Galaxy, Seventh Dimension, 6023 Y.Y. (Yessat Years)

Zor Q'an Tal, High King of Tryston, Emperor of Trek Mi Q'an galaxy, Guardian of the Sacred Sands, and the most feared man in six hundred galaxies and seven dimensions, popped a cheesy doodle into his mouth. He munched thoughtfully for a moment as the cheesy concoction turned into a paste-like substance before slithering down his royal throat. 'Twas nigh unto disgusting, he quickly decided.

Frowning at the Chief Priestess, he telekinetically summoned a bejeweled flask of *matpow* from the royal high table to wash the hellish paste down with. The Chief Priestess watched His Majesty grasp the flat bottle out of the air and drink from it, the muscles in his throat working in time with his swallows. As he drank, two naked *Kefa* slave girls massaged his massive shoulders from behind.

The Chief Priestess's lips curled wryly. Were she but a few hundred years younger, she would be flat on her backside, begging the High King to her take her here and now, audience or no. She grinned at her own musings. By the goddess, the future High Queen was a lucky wench indeed! But then what female humanoid wouldn't desire the privilege of being mounted by a warrior such as The Excellent One every day and night?

Hair as black as the darkest swamp night on Tryston's tenth moon.

Eyes as blue as translucent *gista* stones.

Skin as golden brown as the valuable *vesha* rawhide.

Seven-feet-four inches and three-hundred-seventy pounds of thick, powerful muscle.

Yes, the future High Queen of Tryston and Empress of Trek Mi Q'an was fortunate above all others.

The High King finished drinking from the flask, then motioned for the bottle to take its place back at the raised table. That accomplished, a third naked slave girl wiped the remaining droplets of matpow from his mouth.

Zor turned to the Chief Priestess. His voice was deep and rich, rumbled and dark. "What else have you brought me from this primitive, first dimension world?" He looked behind her to make certain she was alone. "You mentioned my betrothed, yet do I not see my future High Queen at your side."

The Chief Priestess nodded. "You know as well as I that although my visions almost always come to pass, there have been the unfortunate few times where I have been wrong, sire."

He grimaced, remembering that one fatal time all too well. He drew Muta, the slave girl that had just dried his face of the matpow, to his side. Kneading her blue buttocks with his large hand, he motioned toward the Chief Priestess with his other. "And your point?"

"You must go amongst the first dimension primitives to collect her yourself, if she is indeed your Sacred Mate. Only a Trystonni warrior can perform the necessary tests to surmise if a woman is his by the law."

He nodded. "That is true, Holy One. And do you deem this trip to the first dimension worthy of your High King's time?"

The Chief Priestess met the gaze of The Excellent One. "I do."

Zor nodded, satisfied. He turned to his brother Dak, the King of Ti Q'won-Tryston's fifth moon-to command him. "You will accompany me on my quest, brother."

Dak inclined his head. He turned to his first man and bade him to prepare the gastrolight cruiser for their departure. That accomplished, Dak scratched his head as he turned on his heel to face Zor. "I best bring Kita with me. My friend gets a mite put out when I go questing about without him."

Zor sighed. He would endure the *pugmuff's* presence during their journey for his brother's sake, gaseous creature or no. Besides, they would be gone no more than six moon-risings. The *pugmuff's* gas passing could set his eyes to stinging only so much within six days time. "So be it."

Zor turned his face toward Muta's chest and suckled on the plump blue nipple she offered him. The naked slave girl ran her fingers through the master's thick black hair. He pulled her onto his lap, his shaft fiercely erect.

The eager *pugmuff* drew Zor's attention away from his lusty intentions. Kita jumped up and down gleefully, snorting his excitement of being included in the quest out of his uppermost arse.

Zor buried his face in Muta's breasts to ease the vile stench that rose up as a result of Kita's overly zealous snorting. He glanced toward his brother and grunted. "You will allow the *pugmuff* nothing with beans in it whilst we are on our quest."

Dak nodded, his own eyes stinging. "Aye, brother. No beans a'tall."

Zor slapped Muta playfully on the buttocks. She was the favorite amongst his playthings. "Wait for me in your chamber. I will attend to you before I leave."

Muta rose from the High King's lap to do his bidding. The remaining two *Kefa* slave girls followed on Muta's heels, in case the master was feeling especially lusty this moon-rising.

Zor turned to the Chief Priestess. "I thank you, Holy One. You may leave the Palace of the Dunes and retire to your dwelling."

The Chief Priestess inclined her head. "I shall return to greet the High Queen, Your Majesty. Until then, I bid peace and prosperity unto you."

"And I unto you as well."

She vanished at those parting words, fading into the mist the same as she had come.

Zor stood up and clapped his brother on the back. "Be ready within three hours time. We depart as soon as the cruiser has been stocked and refueled."

Grinning, Dak raised his eyebrows. "I look forward to questing with you, brother." He cast a meaningful glance toward Muta's bedchamber door. "And 'tis high time you settled down."

Zor grunted. Whether from agreement or disagreement none could say. He inclined his head to Dak and Kita, then made his way down the hall. His footsteps were as loud and commanding as the rest of him was.

Upon arriving at his destination, Zor telekinetically summoned open the chamber doors with a faint flick of his wrist. He stilled, his staff growing agonizingly hard at the sight that greeted him.

Three *Kefa* girls. One of blue. One of green. One of red.

All lying on Muta's bed.

All with their legs spread wide apart.

All ready for his thrusts.

The corners of Zor's lips curled wryly. 'Twas good to be High King.

Chapter 3

By the last day of the retreat, even Prue and Jameson had found their peace. Albeit, not to the great degree that Kyra had, but nevertheless, they'd found some. Prue still cried on occasion and Jameson still scowled, but the Mel-zel technique had managed to work wonders on both of them.

Not that Jameson was happy about that fact. He'd scowled more than ever since he'd tried Geris's breathing technique and found that it actually worked. Apparently the aristocrat had decided immediately thereafter that he was going straight from this spa to one of those testosterone-laden masculine retreats in the woods where men beat on drums and get in touch with their inner animals.

Hey, to each his own.

Kyra and Geris, both clad in tee-shirts and jeans, shook hands with their fellow retreaters and wished them well. "Thank you so much for everything you've done, Mrs. Blissful. I feel like a new woman." Kyra smiled warmly at the serene instructor. She released her hand and picked up her duffel bag. Her and Geris's suitcases had already been loaded into the trunk of Geris's BMW by the retreat's staff.

"I'm glad to have been of service to you, Miz Summers. Please feel free to return to our little getaway any time you're in need of our assistance."

Kyra inclined her head. "I will."

Five minutes later, the two friends ambled slowly toward the car, both of them feeling rejuvenated, both of them actually sorry to see their week of meditation come to an end. Geris spotted her Beamer toward the left of the outdoor parking facility and indicated with a wave of her hand that they needed to switch directions. Kyra repositioned her heavy duffel bag, hoisting it over her left shoulder to give her right one a rest. She nodded and followed.

Geris nudged Kyra playfully in the ribs as they walked. "Girl, that wasn't so bad. I really had a good time toward the end of the week."

Kyra snorted. "Too bad it took us over half of our vacation to ease into it." She grinned, displaying neat white teeth. "But I agree. I had a good time too. And I've realized something important."

"Oh?"

She nodded. "I've finally realized that stressing myself out over Kara's disappearance will not bring her back. I *will* continue looking for her, but wasting away in sorrow isn't going to do either of us a lick of good." Kyra took a deep breath and shrugged. "Kara would expect me to stay strong. I am the big sister after all."

Geris smiled. "She looked up to you, honey. Always did."

"I know."

Geris hesitated for a brief moment before finishing her thought. "Kyra, I never said this before because I didn't want to give you false hope, but I think you've healed enough to deal with it now."

Kyra arched a wine-colored brow but said nothing.

Geris sighed. She pulled Kyra to a stop and swung her around to face her. "We're going to see Kara again. I just *know* we are! I can feel it." She shrugged her elegant shoulders and grinned self-depreciatingly. "How and when I have no idea, but I'm certain we will," she mumbled.

Kyra chuckled, then beamed a smile back at her. "Me too."

That settled, the women resumed their stroll towards the BMW. Geris found her keys in her purse and detonated the locks on the car's doors by remote. She opened the trunk and threw her duffel bag in to join their suitcases, then motioned for Kyra to do the same.

"You know what sounds good, Ger?"

"What?"

Kyra waited for Geris to slam the trunk closed and look at her before responding. "Pizza!"

Geris's eyes lit up. A week of rabbit food made pizza sound like manna from heaven. "Ooooohhh! Good idea!"

"I saw an Italian bistro down the road when we first drove up here. Let's stop there on our way back to Manhattan."

Geris grinned. "Girlfriend, you've gotta-" Her eyes rounded. She stopped, her smile faltering as she glanced over Kyra's shoulder. "Deal," she whispered.

Kyra wrinkled her nose at Geris's wide-eyed expression. She spun around to see what her best friend was gaping at. And then she swallowed-roughly. Her own silver eyes widening, she did a little gaping herself.

Good grief.

Two men were watching their every move. Two huge, gigantic, barbaric looking men. One was blonde, one was raven-haired, and both of them possessed eerie blue eyes that seemed to glow. The barbarians stood well over seven feet in height and were as thickly muscled as they were tall.

The men were bare-chested, sporting nothing in that region except for a single gold medallion with beautiful, sparkling stones imbedded into them. The gold and stones contrasted brilliantly against their richly tanned skins. Black leather pants and black boots completed their ensembles.

Kyra's jaw dropped when she realized that the bigger, dark-haired man was eyeing her up and down like a woman for hire. He was smiling at her as though he boasted some esoteric knowledge she hadn't been made privy to. She tried to look away, but found to her dismay that she couldn't. She continued to stare at the giant as she whispered under her breath to Geris. "We better go. I don't like the look of those guys."

Geris gulped. "Sweet Jesus, the blonde one is oglin' me like a piece of candy." Worry was evident in her tone, but she didn't break his gaze.

The women stood there, still as statues, waiting to see how this scene would play out. They were to find out all too soon.

Kyra gasped in shock as she felt her clothes coming undone. She shrieked as her shirt and jeans were ripped from her body by forces unseen and went hurling through the air, leaving her totally naked in the barbarian men's presence.

Kyra's scream snapped the spell the blonde man had held over Geris. Geris whipped her head around to regard her best friend. She gasped. "Girl, what in the *hell* are you doing! You're butt naked!"

A shiver ran the length of Kyra's spine, hardening her nipples into tight points. "He did it," she breathed out, unable to break the dark-haired man's eerie gaze. "He did this to me."

"He's nowhere near you!" Geris pointed out hysterically.

Kyra nodded like a marionette. A bead of sweat formed on her brow as she concentrated on breaking the hypnotic hold the giant had on her. She didn't know how it was possible, but she knew beyond a shadow of a doubt that the hulk standing but a few feet away had done this to her.

Another chill shot down her spine as she took in the expression of triumph he now garnered. Her eyes widened and both women gasped as the man let out an ear-piercing war cry, pounded on his chest, and sprinted toward them at top speed.

* * * * *

Zor and Dak came to a halt as they spotted the two gorgeous wenches heading toward some type of boxy, metal contraption. Both women were exceptionally lovely, with their long tresses and rare skin colors. Where the free women spread throughout Trek Mi Q'an galaxy, and especially planet Tryston, tended toward skin tones similar to their own, these wenches were fashioned of translucent shades of *sekta* pearl and deep onyx.

Dak's eyes feasted upon the black-skinned wench. His staff was nigh unto bursting at the mere thought of burying all of his ample inches inside of her. He groaned with disappointment, remembering that he was here to help his brother find his Sacred Mate, not to cater to his own desires. He held the wench's stare captive without even realizing he had done so.

Zor immediately honed in on the fiery-headed wench. All of his senses, both physical and metaphysical, locked in on her. She was the one. She had to be. There could be no other. Never had his senses stirred so. Never had his very blood seemed to boil at the merest glimpse of a woman. His shaft was erect to the point of broaching pain.

The *sekta* pearl wench was alerted to his presence by her friend. When she turned around to see what the onyx woman was gaping at, Zor captured her gaze and held it. He smiled with a predator's satisfaction as the first test of a Trystonni warrior's Sacred Mate was confirmed. No matter how hard she tried, and the *sekta* pearl wench was indeed trying with all of her furious might, she could not look away from him. She was imprisoned. She had to be his.

So this 'twas what it felt like when a warrior found his Sacred Mate. Zor had heard other warriors describe the sensation, but had never been able to relate to it. By the goddess, there was nothing more pleasurable or more painful in all of existence.

But then, it would have to be. How else could lusty Trystonni men forsake the beds of all other wenches when there were *Kefa* slaves and bound servants in abundance, clamoring for a warrior's attention? *Kefas* were engineered to be pleasure givers, yet all three hundred of his slaves held no appeal at all after seeing the woman who was to be his *nee'ka*.

Zor continued to hold hostage the gaze of his High Queen. He moved on to the next phase of the testing, praying to the Sacred Sands that this wench was to be his by the unbreakable, holy law. He channeled all of his energies, summoned all of his many powers, and focused them upon the task of removing her clothing.

'Twas only upon himself or the warm body of a Sacred Mate that a Trystonni warrior could manipulate inanimate objects. On all other creatures, the living body prevented the telekinetic summoning of the inanimate. Why 'twas so, none could say. 'Twas as much a mystery as why the holy sands could heal.

Oh aye, he could have confirmed she was his by removing naught but a piece of jewelry or another lifeless object upon the wench's body, yet did her clothing offend him sorely. 'Twas not the garments a warrior favored upon his woman.

As the wench's clothing was ripped from her well-curved body, Zor experienced an erotic elation that was indescribable in its intensity. He all but spilled his life-force, so pleasurable was the feeling.

She was his.

By the goddess, she was his!

In keeping with the ancient tradition of claiming a Sacred Mate, Zor let loose a triumphant roar, pounded upon his chest, and charged forward to lay claim to his bride.

'Twas time to take his High Queen home.

* * * * *

Kyra all but peed her pants at the sight of the gargantuan man barreling down upon her. And she would have peed them, if she'd had on any pants to pee in, she thought grimly. His gigantic muscles were flexing as he charged toward her like a raging bull in Pamplona.

Good god the crazy barbarian was going to kill her! Right here in the parking lot of The Smiling Faces and Peaceful Hearts Meditation Retreat. She idly considered the fact that this was not a very serene way to die.

Somewhere in the back of her mind, Kyra realized that Geris was screaming. She also understood that her legs were being held as entranced as her gaze was by the dark-haired brute. Kyra couldn't move if her very life depended upon it.

A bead of moisture trickled down her forehead when she vaguely considered the possibility that her life probably did depend upon it. Believing that a fact, she tried again to free herself from the invisible chains the giant had lassoed her with.

It was no use.

She was a dead woman.

* * * * *

Zor came to a sudden halt in front of his Sacred Mate. His ears nigh unto bursting from the shrill screams of the onyx wench next to his High Queen, he took a moment-careful not to break his Sacred Mate from the trance in the doing-to glare at her friend. The noise immediately stopped. The wench fainted.

Casting all of his energies back upon his woman, Zor held up the bridal necklace he had brought with him from Tryston and clasped it about her neck. 'Twas done. Their bond could never be broken.

Smiling down to his wee wench, who looked as perplexed as she was mesmerized, Zor lifted her up into his heavily muscled arms. She would sleep for hours once he released her from the trance. Or so other warriors had claimed. Taking no chances, he held his Sacred Mate tightly against him, kneading her pearly buttocks as he looked into her eyes and let the spell break.

She gasped. Her wide, silvery-blue eyes fluttered and she fell into a deep sleep.

Chapter 4

Dak revved the gastrolight cruiser down from hyper mode to a normal gait. 'Twas tricky steering indeed, the first wormhole he encountered that led from the primitive first dimension into the next one. Once he was satisfied that the majority of obstacles were behind them, he glanced over to Kita, who was seated next to him in the navigator's chair, and grinned. "Aye, my friend, the onyx wench was beautiful indeed. My cock nigh unto exploded just gazing upon her."

The *pugmuff* made a few snorts that released a noxious odor into the air. Dak frowned as he considered the two-arsed, yellow and red spotted creature. "Calm down, my friend. You are burning my eyes yet again."

Kita ceased his snorting. He spoke to Dak in a series of clicking sounds that the King of Ti Q'won understood. Dak smiled. "Believe me Kita, I have asked myself the same question over and over again in the last few hours since we departed first dimension earth." He shook his head and sighed. "I should have performed the test to see if 'twas possible so fine a wench was mine."

Kita's clicking picked up in speed. "I don't know if I shall return to test her," Dak slowly admitted, "I must give it some thought."

Kita snorted incredulously. He clicked something sarcastic that made Dak scowl. "I know I am not well known for my thinking on such things, yet must I consider the matter before such a journey is taken yet again." He shrugged. "Besides, 'tis my duty as her new brother to help our High Queen settle in."

Kita clicked rapidly, warming to the change in topic. Dak grinned. "Aye, the High Queen is as comely as my brother boasted. Even more so, mayhap."

The *pugmuff* gestured animatedly with his hands as he continued to click away. "Aye," Dak answered, "Zor is with her now." His eyebrows rose. "Waiting for her to wake up I would imagine."

* * * * *

Zor lay on his side upon the raised bed, his elbow propping his head up whilst he studied the form of his sleeping Sacred Mate. She was nigh unto perfection, his woman. Pearly *sekta* skin, fire-berry hair, plump breasts capped off with translucent pink nipples, and a patch of fire-berry hair between her thighs that could cause any warrior to spill his life-force at the mere sight of it.

That thought made him frown. He liked not the notion that other warriors would desire her, yet could it not be helped. She was a rare skinned beauty indeed. No man would dare seduce the *nee'ka* of the Emperor of Trek Mi Q'an and High King of Tryston, yet would he still feel better once the joining was accomplished.

Zor ran a large hand over his wench's breasts. He tweaked a plump nipple, grunting with satisfaction as it hardened for him, then bent his head to suckle from it. The feel of it against his tongue was too much. He groaned as his shaft hardened and lengthened, deciding 'twas probably best not to tempt his self with what he could not have until they reached the palace.

Zor released her nipple, a slight popping sound echoing in the quiet bedchamber aboard the gastrolight cruiser as he did so. He realized with a yawn that he was nigh as fatigued as his wee High Queen. Questing and mate claiming was a tiring business.

Unable to resist, his hand trailed a path down her taut belly and grazed in the fiery pelt between her legs. He played there absently as he rested his head on her breasts and settled in for a nap.

'Twas bliss.

* * * * *

Kyra awoke as a devastating orgasm slammed through her body. Breathing deeply to calm herself, she made to get up so she could figure out what in the hell was going on. And then she realized she couldn't. Somebody's heavy body was sprawled across her own limp one.

Kyra closed her eyes tightly, afraid to look down, terrified to see whose body had hers pinned to the bed. After all, the day's events were coming back to her. The giant men in the parking lot. The hypnotic gaze of the dark-haired man. Her clothes ripping off and flying to only God knows where. Geris's screams. The barbarian charging...

She opened her eyes, realizing she needed to know if said barbarian was the one responsible for capturing her and bringing her sleeping body into wakeful climax. Good grief, had she been raped?

No! It wasn't possible! She frantically reassured herself that she'd feel at least some tenderness between her thighs if she'd been brutalized. But that didn't mean she wasn't *going* to be raped. She gulped, wide-eyed and mortified by the idea of it.

Summoning every ounce of willpower and courage she possessed, Kyra swallowed roughly and chanced a glance down her body.

It was him.

And he was sleeping.

Kyra gawked at the brazen man's audacity. He was asleep, yes, but even in slumber he was manhandling her. His mouth was latched onto her right nipple while his fingers idly stroked the hair between her legs like some exotic pet. The tips of his meandering fingers occasionally came into contact with her clitoris, sending tiny pulses of heat through her belly.

She frowned. It was obvious to her now how she'd been brought to orgasm. Good grief! The man could accomplish while asleep what her ex-boyfriend Todd had been unable to do while awake.

Not knowing what to do or even what to think of this bizarre situation, Kyra studied the profile of the giant slumbering at her breast. He was a frightening looking man, handsome but terrifying at the same time. And yet, the more she watched him the less fear she harbored of him, and the more connected she felt toward him. It was a strange sensation. Definitely creepy. She wanted to be afraid of him, realized even that she should be, but for some strange reason she simply wasn't. Annoyed with him-very, but not afraid.

His thick black hair was silky and past his shoulders. She noticed for the first time that it was braided in a series of three rows off his temples, then flowed down his neck in the back. The more she studied him, the more handsome he seemed to become. Dismayed by that realization, she decided to try and wiggle out from beneath him and slink away unseen.

Kyra made the smallest of movements, desperately trying to inch her body out from under the giant's. The barbarian apparently reacted to her every move. He grumbled something incoherent in his sleep, latched back onto her nipple, then began to lazily suckle from it again. Heat shot from her breast to her belly, inducing her to stifle a groan. This was no good. The hulk was a stranger to her!

Kyra breathed in deeply, then made another attempt at relocating her body out from under his large frame. Only this time she shifted her hips instead of her chest.

Bad move.

Or good move, depending upon one's vantage point.

The slight arching of her hips served her no purpose other than to make the giant's access of her pelvic area more available.

He mumbled again, continued to lave and suckle absently at her nipple, and on top of that, he was also now stroking her clit directly.

Kyra whimpered as an exquisitely arousing tendril of sensation washed over her. This just wasn't right! Here she was, pinioned under a strange man in a strange bed and not only was her body reacting to him, but her emotions were as well. She abhorred force of any kind. Rape was not something to be trivialized. But then this man hadn't raped her. And somehow, she knew he wouldn't.

Dismayed by her body's innate acceptance of this stranger, her mind struggled to maintain some semblance of normalcy. Things like this just didn't happen, Kyra told herself. Men like this just didn't happen.

She glanced over toward the giant's face, then sucked in her breath. He was now awake. Wide awake and peering at her. His haunting blue gaze made all the weirdness of the different puzzle pieces of this situation click together. She gasped.

Men like this didn't happen because he wasn't a man. He wasn't even of her kind, her species.

Wide silver eyes met glowing blue ones. Kyra's jaw dropped open.

The barbarian was not a human.

* * * * *

Zor shifted slightly to prop himself back up on his elbow. He grinned down into the bewildered silvery gaze of his *nee'ka*. He continued to lazily stroke her fire-berry pelt, enjoying the intimacy of touching his High Queen. Soon, they would join. But before the Consummation Feast, Zor thought it important to learn more of the woman who was to be mother to his future sons. He decided that her name was a good place to start. "Greetings unto you, Sacred Mate of Zor Q'an Tal. By what name do you go?"

Kyra closed her gaping jaw shut with a click of her teeth. Good grief! The giant was claiming she was the mate of some Zor character! She'd have to set him straight on that one. Perhaps that was why he'd captured her to begin with. Maybe he was trying to gain revenge on this Zor guy and, thinking her to be his wife, kidnapped her as a form of vengeance against him. At least that's how it always happened in medieval romance novels. "Kyra," she breathed. "Kyra Summers."

The giant shook his head. "'Tis Summers no more, *nee'ka*. 'Tis *Q'ana Tal* now. Kyra Q'ana Tal. Sacred Mate to Zor Q'an Tal, High King of Tryston and Emperor of Trek Mi Q'an."

Kyra's jaw fell back open. What in the hell was he talking about? "Y-You are mistaken," she blithered out. "I am the Sacred Mate to no one." She shook her head frantically, hysteria bubbling up inside of her. "I don't even know what a Sacred Mate is!"

Zor continued to stroke the pelt between her legs even as his agitation grew. He narrowed his eyes into menacing blue slits, causing his *nee'ka* to gulp. "You dare to lie before me and deny that the claiming was made?" His deep voice rose in decibels as his anger flamed. "You dare to tell me that I did not seize your gaze, *that I did not summon the inanimate from your body?*"

Kyra had no idea what A had to do with B, but she sensed that she had best tell the giant that she dared no such thing. "I do not deny it!" she sniffed. "But I don't understand how that makes me the Sacred Mate of this Zor character either!"

Zor visibly relaxed. 'Twas not a denial. His *nee'ka* was merely ignorant of the Trystonni way. He smiled again as he continued to stroke her, grazing his thumb over the swollen nub between her thighs. She gasped. He ignored her. "Those are the tests a warrior of Tryston performs to know if a woman is bound to him by the holy law." He shrugged dismissively. "You passed the test, thus are you now my Sacred Mate."

Kyra's eyes widened at that announcement. "You mean you are-"

"Zor," he interrupted.

She shook her head to clear it. "And you are a king?"

He took offense at that. "I am more than a king, *nee'ka*. I am High King to all of Tryston. Not to mention Emperor of Trek Mi Q'an."

"I see." In truth, she didn't see. Kyra was beginning to fear that she'd just been abducted by a seven-foot-plus alien with delusions of grandeur. She blew out a breath, inducing a tuft of fire-berry hair to skimp across her forehead and off to the side. Whether her breathing was growing labored from Zor's crazed proclamation or from the fact that he was rubbing her clit, it was difficult to say. "Then what does that make me?"

Zor leaned down and adoringly kissed the tip of Kyra's nose. "It makes you my High Queen and Empress." He nipped lovingly at her chin, then laved the dimple in it with his tongue. "It makes you my Sacred Mate." He lowered his head further, grazing at her nipple with his teeth. "It makes you *mine*." He suckled her peak thoroughly, causing a groan to escape from the depths of her throat.

Kyra tried to push his face away, but the gesture had the same effect as a butterfly batting at a brick wall. She couldn't believe what he was doing. Nor could she believe all the nonsense she was hearing. No woman goes from being a tax accountant to a High Queen all in the same day. This was just too much. "You m-must be m-mistaken." She groaned as Zor trailed kisses from her breasts to her belly. "I wouldn't make a v-very good High Queen," she insisted. "I—*oooh*!"

She sucked in her breath as Zor's head disappeared between her thighs. She briefly considered the possibility that she would need another week at the meditation retreat when this was all over.

Chapter 5

Zor grunted as he raised his head from between his *nee'ka's* legs. "What in the name of the holy sands are you doing, woman?"

"Meditating."

He grunted again. "What is 'meditating'? Some bizarre notion of primitive first dimension pleasure?"

Kyra opened one eye to glare at him through, but continued her deep breathing. "I do it to relax." She closed her eye again, breathing in through her nostrils and out of her mouth. She conjured up an image of Mel Gibson and Denzel Washington kneading her shoulders into blissful relaxation. She smiled serenely.

Just when Kyra thought she had reclaimed control over her raging nerves, Zor let out a bellow that could have made a hungry predator halt in its path and forsake its prey in favor of scampering away. Her eyes flew open in shock. "Wh-What is it?"

The giant drew himself up to his knees and glared at her with unmis*taka*ble menace. "The red stone within your bride's necklace sings to me," he hissed.

Kyra's eyes bulged out. She glanced down to see the necklace in question, the one she hadn't even realized she was wearing. It was there all right. It didn't appear to be singing, but it was indeed glowing red. "So?"

Zor's nostrils flared to wicked proportions. His face reddened in anger. "Your emotions have desired mating with another man!"

Kyra's eyes widened. "They've desired no such thing!"

Oh Geez, this was awful! The necklace told him if the image of another man popped into her head? First things first, she'd have to lose the damn piece of jewelry. "I was merely envisioning having my shoulders massaged. I do this during meditation to relax!"

He growled something imperceptible then smacked his fist into the palm of his other hand. "You will think of no other touching you but me! I am your High King and Emperor! I am your Sacred Mate!"

Kyra took advantage of Zor's focus on her "sin" long enough to slip out from under him and sit on her knees to face him. She crossed her arms over her breasts to shield them from his view. Puckering her lips into a frown, she scowled at him. "I agreed to nothing!" she fumed.

He slashed his hand tersely through the air. "That matters not. Still are you mine!"

"I don't even know you!"

Zor grunted. "You will know me well in two moon-risings. Our bodies will join at such time."

Kyra's jaw dropped open. Unfortunate though it was, gaping was not an uncommon event while in the barbarian's presence. "I will not be forced into having sex with you!"

"'Tis your duty by the holy law to submit to me and give me heirs. Do you refuse to honor our bond, you will shame me before our people." He shook his head, not understanding. For the first time in Zor's forty-two Yessat years he felt vulnerable. "Would you do this thing unto me?" he asked quietly. Well, as quietly as a bellowing High King gets.

Kyra winced. The hurt on his face was evident. Just when she was working herself up into a good and proper tirade, the big oaf had to go and ruin it. And why should she feel guilty? She was the injured party here! She was the one who had been stalked, stripped, wedded without her knowledge or consent, then kidnapped!

And yet, there it was...guilt. It was the oddest thing. Why would she feel it? Had the bizarre wedding ceremony fused them together in some freaky mental way? "I would never shame you," she heard herself say, though somewhat frigidly.

Bewildered and angered by the fact that she'd made even that much of a verbal concession, Kyra pinched her lips together tightly and threw him her best disapproving old-maid frown. "I don't even know you, Zor." She thrust her chin up stubbornly. "This just isn't the way things are done where I come from."

He inclined his head, ignoring her haughtiness. "I have gathered as much, which is why I am trying to be tolerant." Zor slashed his hand through the air. "Yet will I not allow you to envision other men whilst relaxing, whether this is a primitive first dimension custom or no."

Kyra narrowed her eyes. "I wish you would quit referring to my people as primitives!" It occurred to her that this should be the least of her concerns at the moment, but oh well. Insult was insult.

Zor glared at her. "I would have your word."

"Huh?"

"I would have your word. You will entertain visions of no man but me." He crossed his massive arms over his equally massive chest. "Vow it now, *nee'ka*."

Kyra sighed. She rubbed her weary temples and closed her eyes. "Whatever." She fluttered her hand dismissively through the air, exposing a breast to view. "I vow it."

Zor grunted. He reached out for his beautiful *sekta* pearl's chest and flicked one pink nipple with his forefinger. "Remember, woman, I will know do you lie."

Kyra opened her eyes. Her hands flew to the bridal necklace, oblivious of the giant's intimate caress. "I want this thing off of me! And I want to go home! *Now*," she bit out.

He shook his head in the negative. "This I cannot do."

"*Why not?!*"

He shrugged. "Which question do you ask? Why can I not remove the necklace or why can I not return you to the primitive first dimension?"

"*Both*! And I'm not a primitive!"

Zor sighed. Truly his wench was a trial. "Kyra, *nee'ka,*" he crooned soothingly, "not even death can remove the bridal medallion from around your neck. 'Tis the symbol of our eternal bond."

Kyra gasped incredulously. She remembered the giant wearing this very medallion when she'd first spotted him. Since his own neck was now bare, she could safely assume the necklace she was wearing was one and the same. "I don't see one of these things around your neck anymore! Why must I endure having a full-time baby sitter who tattles to you about every little 'emotion' I have when you don't?" Again it occurred to her that, considering her current circumstances, this was a trivial matter. But again, insult was insult.

Zor grinned. Ah, but his Sacred Mate was an amusing wee wench. "Because you are a woman and I am a warrior."

She gasped again. Truly, Zor thought her face was red enough to start a fire off of.

"You call that a good reason?" she screeched.

He chuckled. "Aye."

"I want to go home!" Kyra became aware of his hand caressing her breast when she tried to cross her arms over her chest again. Huffing, she threw his hand off of her body and assumed her most forbidding arms-across-the-chest stance. As a tax accountant, she typically reserved this pose for IRS agents she had to deal with. She realized it probably had somewhat less of an effect while naked. "I want to go home I said! Now!"

Zor rolled his eyes toward the ceiling, praying to the goddess for patience. "Your home is now in my bed. And my bed is on planet Tryston in Trek Mi Q'an galaxy of the seventh dimension." He forced her hands from her chest and resumed toying with her nipples. "Let us belabor the point no more, *nee'ka*."

Kyra scowled at the big oaf. She tried to shove his hands away from her again-she was in no mood to be turned on-but gave up when he didn't so much as flinch. It was like trying to move a mountain with her pinky finger. "My home is on earth. All of my friends are there."

Zor bent his neck and flicked his tongue across one rosy peak. She sucked in her breath. "You will make new friends."

Kyra tried to push his face away. It did no good. "I like the ones I already have."

He sighed. "By the tit of the *heeka-beast*, you know how to kill a fair mood." His eyebrow shot up. "You needs be with me. I am your High King, your Emperor, your-"

"Sacred Mate," she finished for him. Kyra rolled her eyes. "Yeah. Yeah. Yeah." She sighed.

Zor released her nipple to growl at her. "Worry not, you will come to love me. We have been destined. You will realize soon that you need me."

She arched a fire-berry brow. "Oh? And why do I need you?" she asked grandly, splaying her hands to the sides.

Zor frowned. Why must his wench be from a primitive world where they understand naught? Why must he explain everything to her when all would be revealed soon enough through the joining? He was weary of arguing.

Zor's eyes flicked toward the bridal necklace Kyra now wore as he immersed himself in thought. He wanted to end this exasperating conversation once and for all. But how to-

The answer came to him. He smiled slowly. He peered at the ornate piece of jewelry once again while he formed a plan of attack. For once, his *nee'ka's* ignorance of Trystonni ways would work to his advantage. He would demolish all reticence against him, his home, and his touch until the time arrived when his Sacred Mate no longer desired to leave him. "Your bridal necklace."

Kyra scowled at the mention of the odious, tattle-telling thing. Her eyes narrowed with grim disapproval. "What about it?"

Zor searched his brain for a quick lie. "'Tis, uh, possessed of my life-force."

She sighed. She had been stripped, kidnapped, and wedded by some mammoth alien. And worse yet, the big dumb oaf rarely made sense. "Your life-force?"

He nodded. "That is correct. My life-force." Zor ran the fingers of one hand along the stones within the bridal necklace as he sought Kyra's gaze. "But it doesn't last long. Therefore the bejeweled symbol of our union must constantly be replenished with my life-force."

Kyra rubbed her temples. The man was giving her a headache. "What in the hell are you talking about!"

Zor shook his head as if the telling pained him greatly. "Without my life-force in you to replenish it, your necklace would die. If it dies, you die with it, *nee'ka*."

Kyra's head shot up. Her eyes rounded. "D-Die?"

He shook his head vigorously in the affirmative. "I fear 'tis so."

Her jaw dropped open. "How do we replenish it?"

Ah, Zor thought, *suddenly his Sacred Mate thought in terms of "we"*. A good battle tactic he'd just executed, if he did say so his self. "'Tis, uh, replenished every time we mate."

"Mate? We have to mate or I'll *die*?"

"That is correct."

Kyra's silvery gaze narrowed suspiciously. "How often must we mate?"

Zor wasted no time in taking advantage of her ignorance. "At least once every moon-rising."

Kyra held her suspicions, but then again she had no reason to doubt his word. What she knew about suicidal bridal necklaces was about as much as she knew about Zor, which was next to nothing. So she swallowed-roughly. She'd often heard that sex could kill, but she'd never before realized the same thing could happen with abstinence. "What happens if we don't mate every day?" she asked hesitantly.

Zor regarded her grimly. He was pleased to note that he could actually make his face pale on cue. "The bridal necklace will strangle you," he whispered hoarsely.

Jaw agape, Kyra's hands flew to her neck. She clicked her teeth shut. "Good grief! That's deplorable!"

Zor sighed. He reached out and stroked his *nee'ka's* mane of fire-berry hair. "You see now that I think only of you?"

Kyra nodded her head absently. "Y-Yeah."

She chewed on her lip as she contemplated what he'd just said. They had to have sex-every day no less-or she would die. A part of her didn't believe it, but the primal survival instinct within her, the piece of her being that would do anything to stay alive, realized she had no choice but to take Zor at his word.

Kyra reminded herself that, big oaf or not, she had no reason to doubt him. He had told the truth about the bridal necklace's "singing"-she *had* been thinking of another man, though not in the way her alleged Sacred Mate had imagined. So why doubt his word now? What choice did she have but to believe him?

Kyra begrudgingly confessed to herself that she could think of worse fates. Whether or not the barbarian exasperated her, she *was* attracted to him.

Huh? No! No! No! She absolutely was not attracted to him!

Oh god, yes she was.

Kyra clapped a hand to her forehead and moaned dejectedly. She didn't understand what was happening to her. Her mind hadn't accepted Zor, as well it shouldn't-she scarcely knew the man-yet her body and emotions had already quit resisting. What had he done to her?

Kyra drew in a deep breath and released it. There was no point in belaboring the issue. For now she would have to go with the flow, or at least until she found a way back home.

A frightening thought occurred to Kyra at once. Her eyes bulged out as she regarded him. "Shouldn't we mate or something now?"

Zor's shaft thought so. It perked up at the mere mentioning. Unfortunately, ritual deemed otherwise. "Nay. We will join for the first time when we reach Tryston."

"But you said that wouldn't be for another two days!" she screeched. "What if I'm dead by the time we get there? I really think we should have sex now!" Kyra was taking no chances that she'd wake up a corpse.

Zor smiled with a hunter's satisfaction. He might be stretching the truth to get his Sacred Mate into bed willingly, but once he got her there she'd never choose to leave it. Of this he was certain. "Nay, *nee'ka*. Your bridal necklace will not need my life-force every moon-rising until the joining has taken place."

Kyra considered that piece of information for a moment. "Then perhaps we shouldn't join to begin with. Then it won't need your life-force at all."

Zor's smile faltered. His wench was too smart for a primitive. He thought quickly, rebounding like a true High King. "It, uh, it still needs my life-force. But it can go for three full moon-risings once it's clasped about your neck. After that, if there is no joining..." He let his words trail off ominously as he slashed his finger across his throat and made a hellish gurgling sound.

Kyra winced. "Good grief. We'll make it to Tryston in time to save me?"

He nodded.

She expelled a breath of air. "Thank god for that."

Satisfied he'd accomplished what he'd set out to do, Zor stretched out on the bed beside his Sacred Mate and pulled her down to lie on his chest. He ignored her shriek of dismay. "All of this talk of death has worn me out. Let us sleep, *nee'ka*, then we will rise and I shall feed you. You will also meet my brother 'ere we eat."

Kyra huffed incredulously as she was pulled down onto Zor's Herculean chest against her will. He situated her body against his flat, heavily muscled stomach, then began to knead her buttocks. Gasping, it irritated her even more when she glanced up at his face only to find him smiling dreamily, his eyes closed. She felt like Fay Ray to his King Kong. A barbie doll the odious brute had found and refused to give up.

Sighing dramatically, Kyra gave up. She lowered her face to the area of his chest above his heart and let it drop the rest of the way with a telling, no-nonsense thud. "All right, you win," she said wearily. "I'll go to sleep. But first, I want to put some clothes on."

Zor grunted. His eyes remained shut. "You will always remain naked whilst alone in my presence, yet will I allow you the dress of Trystonni women whilst in the company of others."

Kyra sighed. The man was infuriating, but she was suddenly too overcome with the enormity of it all to continue fighting with him. Sleep might not be such a bad idea. Perhaps when she woke up she'd have the energy to argue with High King Kong about her attire, or lack thereof. "Has anyone ever told you what a jerk you are?" she asked bitterly. Kyra couldn't resist one last jab. "Well?" she inquired shrilly, "have they?"

When his only answer was the faint sound of snoring, her nostrils flared in agitation. Harrumphing, Kyra gave up the fight. She nestled her head into the valley between his neck and shoulder and closed her eyes.

She was very tired, Kyra soon decided. This had been the most trying day of her life. Yawning, her body went limp against Zor's.

A few seconds later, Kyra Q'ana Tal fell asleep to the feel of her husband caressing her buttocks with whisper soft touches. Somewhere in the back of her mind lurked the distressing thought that she'd never felt more at peace then she did while being held in a certain barbarian's arms.

Huh? No! No! No!

Oh god-yes, yes, yes.

Chapter 6

"You call this clothing! I can see right through it!"

Kyra frowned at her Sacred Mate in the holographic mirror aboard the gastrolight cruiser's main bedchamber, then resumed her perusal of the wanton image she presented. Good grief! Even if she lived to be a hundred years old, never in all of her life would she grow accustomed to dressing so scantily.

And *all* women of Tryston were attired like this? Geez. The place was probably Hugh Heffner's dream come true.

Zor leaned down and kissed the back of her shoulder. "You look more beautiful than any woman I have ever beheld, *nee'ka*."

She scowled at him for good measure-and because she felt like it-then turned back to the hologram mirror. Her teeth sank into her bottom lip. "Zor, I cannot wear this. I feel like an idiot in it."

"Women are permitted no attire but the *qi'ka,* my hearts. You must wear this."

Kyra spun around. "Zor, I insist-" She stopped mid-tirade. Her jaw dropped open. She gaped at him for a suspended moment. "Wait a minute. Why did you just call me your *hearts,* as in plural?" Thinking better of it, she closed her eyes and held up a palm to silence any forthcoming explanations. "Never mind. I'm certain I don't want to know." Shaking her head to ward off insanity, Kyra took a deep breath and whipped back around to face the hologram mirror again.

Good grief! How could she wear this!

The outfit, if one could indeed stretch the meaning of the word enough to call it such, consisted of two pieces of sheer fabric. The first piece was similar to a strapless bikini top and was tied together in a knot in the valley between her breasts. The second piece of material was a sarong skirt that started just below her navel and cinched together in a knot on her left hip, exposing her entire left leg and flowing down to just above her sandaled feet. Her midsection was completely bare.

Even this, embarrassing as it was, Kyra could have lived with, were it not for the fact that the material was virtually see-through. The *qi'ka* Zor had selected for her today was of a silvery translucent silk, apparently to match her eyes. Although the outfit offered minimal protection, it was still transparent enough for anyone looking at her to make accurate guesses on her nipple and pubic hair color. Good grief! Even she could see the wine-colored shadow between her thighs!

Kyra's shoulders drooped dejectedly. "I'm not feeling so well. I think I would prefer to eat in here tonight," she muttered.

Zor reached toward her in sympathy and patted her bottom. She yelped. "'Twill be alright, *nee'ka*. 'Tis best do you get used to wearing the *qi'ka* whilst in my brother's presence, else will you feel that much worse if you must wear it for the first time in front of the whole of our people."

Standing behind her, he reached around and rubbed Kyra's left thigh. "Here, there is only my brother King Dak and his friend Kita the *pugmuff* to see you. When we reach Tryston, hundreds upon thousands will wish to meet their High Queen."

Kyra shuddered at the very thought. A chill raced down her spine, inducing her flesh to goose pimple and her nipples to harden. She didn't want to think about that.

Forcing herself to think of less terrifying things, Kyra met her husband's gaze in the hologram mirror. "Why do women dress like this on Tryston?"

Zor craned his neck down to kiss her temple. He reached around her body and stroked her nipples through the sheer fabric. "Because it brings a warrior pleasure."

She closed her eyes and sucked in her breath. The sensations his hands were producing were exquisite. She didn't want to enjoy his touching, but did.

Qi'ka-somewhere through the haze of pleasure, it dawned on Kyra that the literal translation of the word meant "my pleasure". She now understood that when a Trystonni said "my" it implied "warrior's". *Qi'ka-my pleasure,* or *warrior's pleasure.* That knowledge irritated her immensely.

Determined to be as disagreeable as possible, Kyra tried to dislodge Zor's hands from her breasts. He didn't budge. "Is everything on Tryston made for a warrior's pleasure?" she asked acidly.

Zor answered her unashamedly. "Aye." He continued to play with her nipples through the *qi'ka*'s top. "Such is the way of all things on Tryston, *nee'ka.*"

Nee'ka-my desire, or *warrior's desire. Nee'ka* was interchangeable, also meaning *wife.*

"And what of your women?" Kyra pressed on, her eyes glazing over from the physical stimulation. "What of their pleasure?" she asked quietly.

Zor laved the outside of her ear with his tongue. "A warrior lives only to please her back."

Kyra sucked in her breath. She closed her eyes and let her neck go limp, falling involuntarily back against the middle of her husband's chest. Fighting off her arousal wasn't working. "Oh."

Zor groaned as he continued to fondle her breasts and nibble seductively at her ear. "By the sands, how I cannot wait to join with you," he breathed.

That much was indeed obvious. If his thickly whispered words didn't give his desire away, the fierce erection pressing into her back did. Kyra hated to admit it, but when Zor kissed and caressed her like this, she felt the same way that he did. She comforted herself with the assurance that it was only because she needed his life-force to prevent death by strangulation.

Zor turned Kyra around in his arms and peered into her wide, silver eyes. She gasped, placing her hands on his massive chest in a self-protective gesture meant to ward him off.

Understanding the confusion that all new brides not raised on Tryston harbored when faced with the natural conflict between their bodies need to join with its recognized mate and the mind's abhorrence at lusting for a warrior unknown to them, Zor didn't take offense at Kyra's attempt to dislodge his grip on her shoulders. But neither did he give credence to it. Cupping the back of her head in his large hands, Zor lowered his mouth down to his *nee'ka's* and drank from her lips.

Kyra whimpered as a jolt of heat coursed from her lips down into her belly and onward to her groin. As if they possessed a will of their own, her arms wrapped themselves around her husband's waist as best they could manage, then she parted her lips to invite him inside.

Zor accepted. He plunged his tongue hungrily into his Sacred Mate's mouth, wishing 'twas time to plunge other parts of his person inside of her as well. He licked and stroked, plundered and took, arousing his *nee'ka* to ecstasy with naught but a kiss.

Nay, 'twas more than a kiss. All of his hunger, all of his desire, all of his passion was contained within it. Hundreds of years worth of waiting and hoping, needing and wanting. Mayhap she would never understand the significance of what it was that he was feeling.

Kyra kissed him back with all that she had. It had never before been like this. No man had made every cell in her body tingle this way. Only Zor. Only this warrior. As insane as it seemed, it was as if he had been made for her and her alone.

She inhaled deeply when her husband reluctantly ended their kiss. Her reaction to him only served to further confuse her in an already confusing situation. She was embarrassed by her reaction at first, but not after she noticed that Zor was as shaken as she was. His breathing was just as labored, his signs of arousal just as pronounced.

"Ah *nee'ka,*" Zor groaned, kneading her buttocks. "We best stop."

Kyra took another deep breath. This was just too much. "Good idea."

Zor smiled down at her. He ran his hands through her fire-berry hair then tilted her chin up to gaze into her eyes. "What are you thinking?"

She shrugged.

"Tell me."

Kyra wrinkled her nose. "Honestly?"

"Aye."

She shrugged again. "I was sort of wondering how it is that I can both understand you and speak to you in a tongue that is not of my own language." She squinted her eyes a tad. "How can that be?"

Zor traced a finger over her bridal necklace. "The moment I clasped it about you, you understood. The symbol of our union makes it thusly."

Kyra grimaced. "Don't remind me of this awful, murderous thing."

A pang of guilt surged through Zor. He quickly brushed it aside. "You asked."

She nodded at that. "I suppose I did."

Zor bent his neck and brushed his lips against Kyra's once more. He wished he hadn't lied about the bridal necklace. He wanted her to have pride in it, not a fear of it. He vowed to make amends after they were joined. "There are at least ten times as many warriors as there are free women in Tryston. Thus, warriors must often mate outside of our race with women who do not speak our tongue." He fingered the bridal necklace again. "This helps with that."

"I guess it would."

"Can we greet my brother now, *nee'ka*?" Zor squeezed her buttocks as he continued to knead them.

Kyra sighed. She loathed the idea of parading around all but naked, but saw little choice in the matter. Zor was right.

Better to get used to it in front of his brother and his brother's friend than to have to get used to wearing the *qi'ka* surrounded by the tons of people she was bound to encounter on Tryston.

Besides, this Dak character was probably used to seeing women dressed like this. Most likely he wouldn't notice anything at all about her body. "Okay," she agreed, though somewhat reluctantly, "let's go."

* * * * *

"By the sands, sister, you have magnificent breasts."

Kyra cringed a little lower in her seat at the golden crystal table. So much for Dak not noticing anything at all about her body. She glared at her alleged brother-in-law, hoping she could summon him into silence.

No such luck...

Dak inclined his head to Zor. "I vow brother, our High Queen's nipples have the look of ripe *taka* fruits."

A gurgling sound emitted from Kyra's gaping jaw. She wanted to die.

Zor's chest puffed out arrogantly. Instead of defending her honor, the big oaf looked pleased by his brother's words. The ogre actually reached toward her and flicked one of the *taka* fruits in question back and forth with his finger. "The tasting is much sweeter, brother."

Kyra glared at the man who called himself her husband, but he didn't notice. He and his brother were too busy laughing lustily at each other like the lechers they were. Even the *pugmuff* creature was enjoying himself at her expense. Kyra fanned her hands in front of her eyes, nearly fainting from the smell that accom*pani*ed the bizarre creature's snorting sounds. Good lord and she had thought she'd seen it all. A being with two asses, one of those asses where its face should be, of all things!

Zor scowled. "By the goddess, Kita! Control your mirth." He pinched his nose closed with his thumb and forefinger. Kyra noted that the whites of her ogre husband's eyes were burning red.

Good! As far as she was concerned, he deserved it for speaking of her as though she was a newly acquired toy. And for kidnapping her. And for dressing her like a lingerie model. And for-*bah*! She could go on all night.

Kyra picked up her eating utensil, a golden crystal fork-spoon object, and shoved a piece of meat into her mouth. She chewed vigorously. The meat was pretty damned good, she begrudgingly admitted.

The conversation picked up and actually became somewhat enjoyable after that. Zor and Dak asked a lot of questions about her homeland and she gave them all of her answers. She tried not to notice when Dak's eyes occasionally wandered to her breasts. In return, the warriors responded to all of the questions she had about Tryston and what was to be expected of her there.

To Kyra's dismay, though she couldn't say why she cared as she didn't plan to be there any longer than necessary, she soon understood that women weren't expected to do anything on Tryston besides pleasure their warrior when summoned and breed his *heirs*. What a meaningless existence if ever there was one. She and Zor would have to speak on this more when they were alone.

Not that she planned to stay on Tryston. If she could find a way to remove the bridal necklace, she would also find a way to go back home. But still, a little of the feminist movement could go a long way on this planet from the sound of things.

The conversation carried on even after the meal ended. Zor draped his arm across Kyra's chair and listened to his brother fill him in on the political situation within the colony he ruled. Zor nodded occasionally, scratched his chin now and again, and listened intently. Throughout the whole of it, his massive left hand continually stroked and tweaked at her left nipple in a leisurely manner.

At first, Kyra had become embarrassed. In fact, she had come close to tears at one point. But then she took a hard look at her brother-in-law Dak's oblivious expression and she realized that he truly thought nothing of Zor's fondling. Even the comments he had made about her breasts had been uttered without malicious intent. She honestly wondered if either man even realized she had been embarrassed by his words.

She doubted it.

Good grief! What would Tryston be like? An image of couples screwing each other on the street popped into her head. They probably did it anywhere they felt like it with no regard for what others were witnessing. This was just too much. She was a tax accountant for goodness sake!

Sighing, Kyra picked up her golden crystal goblet and drank from the sweet, glowing turquoise wine it contained. The drink was exceptionally tasty. Later, she would inquire as to what kind of fruit could possibly exist as to make a glowing wine from its berries.

For the present, however, all she wanted to do was go back to her room and think. Kyra was more overwhelmed with emotions than she had ever been, even in the grueling first days right after her sister Kara had disappeared.

So many questions needed to be answered, but confiding in Zor wasn't something she felt up to doing at the moment. She needed rest. She needed to meditate. And more than anything else, she needed to find a way to remove the bridal necklace and go home.

She just wished that leaving Zor behind *felt* as good as it sounded.

Chapter 7

"What is the matter, my hearts?"

Kyra took the time to pinch her lips into a frown and glower at Zor before she pulled the soft pelt of *vesha* hide up to her chin and flopped over onto her side. The big dumb oaf had lived up to his word, making her remove her already scant clothing the moment they were ensconced behind closed doors.

She'd show him. She would never get out of bed again if that's what it took. She'd stay under the *vesha* pelt forever.

And damn it-what was it with this hearts business? Why the plural? Kyra was afraid she knew the answer to that, which only brought more questions to mind. How many of Zor's organs, for instance, came in pairs?

Good grief. As long and wide as his erection had felt at her backside earlier today, she could only pray that a certain male organ was too unique to be replicated. She'd never survive this joining business otherwise. "I'm tired. I've had a long, difficult day and I need to rest."

Kyra closed her eyes and sighed as Zor began stroking her hair. She hated how nice his fingers felt against her scalp. The lecher was simply too easy to grow attached to and comfortable with.

Zor softly ran a finger across her cheek. "You are angry with me."

It was a statement, not a question, but Kyra treated it as such. She opened her eyes and glared at him from over her shoulder. "You kidnapped me! Of course I'm angry with you!"

"Why?"

Kyra blinked. She blinked again. "Why? *Why do you think?*" she wailed.

"If I knew this, would I ask?" Zor bellowed. He tersely ran his hands through his hair and grunted. "Sacred Mates are a trying lot!"

"T-Trying?" Kyra sputtered. "*Trying*?" She held the *vesha* hide securely over her breasts as she swung around on the bed and sat up on her knees. "You don't know what trying is! So let me tell you something about *that* state of being, oh exalted High King! Trying is being kidnapped by a man who heralds from a planet you didn't even know existed!"

When Zor opened up his mouth to retaliate, Kyra forestalled him with an upraised palm. "Trying is being told you've been wedded without remembering the wedding! Trying is being told you have to prance around in see-through clothing everywhere you go and when you're not wearing that you have to be butt-naked!"

She ground her teeth together and narrowed her eyes. "Trying is being told you have to make love with the very man who did all of these things to you or else you'll die a violent death of strangulation from some godforsaken necklace!"

Kyra flopped back over onto her side. She closed her eyes and took a deep breath. "Trying is being told that you will never see your home again," she dejectedly whispered, "and that you will never laugh with your friends again. That," she shakily concluded, "is trying."

Zor drew in a steadying breath. Her words had stirred him mightily, yet did he know he would never let her go. He couldn't. She was his Sacred Mate. If there was no Kyra, there could never be any other *nee'ka* for him either. He had waited forty-two Yessat years for his wee one, four-hundred and twenty years in terms of the primitive time-keeping dimension from which she heralded. Nay, he would never give her up.

Leastways, a High King needs an heir. A High King therefore needs his High Queen. "I am humbled by your sorrow, my hearts. Truly, I do not wish to be the cause of your pain."

"Then let me go home."

"I cannot. It is done. You wear the unbreakable symbol of my troth."

When Kyra didn't respond, Zor stood up to take his leave. 'Twas probably best did he leave her to her thoughts that she might adjust to the changes in her life in her own fashion. "We can talk later, *nee'ka,* for I understand your need for time. But 'tis best do you understand this..."

Zor walked over to the side of the raised bed and sat down next to his Sacred Mate. She was curled up in an unconscious attempt to comfort herself. He gently drew her chin up and peered into her scared silver eyes. "'Tis for the better do you accept your fate, *pani,* for I will never let you leave me." He sighed. "I say this not to frighten you, but because I would have truth between us always."

Zor leaned down and brushed his lips against Kyra's. And then because he couldn't resist one last glimpse, he lowered the *vesha* pelt to her belly and gazed at her breasts with longing. Slowly and reverently, he reached out and brushed each nipple with the pads of his thumbs.

Glowing blue eyes and wide silver ones connected. "You belong to me. Now and forever." After one last kiss to her lips, he stood up and strode toward the doors.

Kyra watched him walk away, staring at the doors even after Zor had disappeared through them. She clutched the *vesha* hide and shivered.

Moaning like a mortally wounded animal, she fell back on the bed and cried for the first time since the entire ordeal had begun. She cried for the loss of Geris, for her sister Kara who might come back home only to find her gone, now missing without a trace.

Deep inside, Kyra realized that Zor wasn't lying. He had only stated the reality of her future. There was no more Geris. There was no more Kara.

Kyra would never see earth again.

* * * * *

"For the love of the goddess, I cannot fathom why the High Queen would desire to return to so primitive a land." Dak frowned thoughtfully as he watched his brother drink his fifth share of matpow. "'Tis nigh unto disgusting, that place called earth."

Zor grunted. He slammed the goblet of spirits down upon the table, then summoned it from his sight. "I am in agreement, yet is it my *nee'ka's* place of birth. She carries many a fond memory of her life there."

Dak's eyebrows rose. If any of her memories were of the fair onyx wench, he could understand why Kyra missed the dreadful place. Still, 'twas not the time to consider his own lusty appetites. His brother needed support. "She will come around once she realizes she cannot return to this land of primitives, brother. Do not dwell upon it until your head gets the ache."

"Who said my head had the ache?"

Dak rubbed his temples and closed his eyes. "'Twas merely a guess. My brain is already feeling it from all of this talk."

Zor frowned. He crossed his massive arms over his equally massive chest and scowled at his brother. "You get the ache from no more than breathing."

Dak's eyes flew open. He pounded one large fist insolently on the tabletop. "Do not condescend to me! I am trying to be of help to you!"

"I know." Zor's eyes flickered shut briefly, mentally reining in his tongue in the process. "You are a good man, a good king, and a good brother, Dak. I had not the right of it to take out my troubles on you with cruel untruths."

Dak nodded, appeased. Actually, he was more than appeased; he was also surprised. Never before had Zor apologized to him thusly. "I thank you for that, brother." Uncomfortable with such a show of affection from a warrior so normally unemotional, he waggled his eyebrows and grinned. "Now, what do you say to a game of *tipo*?"

Zor snorted confidently. He was as content with the turn in topic as was his brother. "As father once said, a king and his credits shall soon part."

"When did he say that?"

"I believe after our mother once departed the palace for the shopping stalls."

* * * * *

Kyra rifled through the vast supply of *qi'kas* that Zor had brought with him from Tryston as bridal gifts to her. If it wasn't for the fact that the attire left her all but naked, she would have been able to better appreciate the exquisitely soft, satiny bolts of garments that came in so many precious colors-colors no human eyes save her own had probably ever seen. The hues were shimmery, translucent, and utterly indescribable in any tongue known to her except Trystonni.

Kyra held up the *qi'ka* Zor had asked her to don and studied it. The closest color she could phonetically come up with from her own dimension to describe it with was black. And yet it wasn't. She smiled to herself. If she ever had the good fortune to send a message of some sort back home, she wouldn't have the first clue as to how she would go about expressing the things she saw in this world.

Kyra briefly debated with herself over whether or not it was worth it to defy Zor and wear a *qi'ka* of another color. In the end, she decided against it, thinking it was best to pick and choose her battles with care. It wasn't as if any of the other *qi'kas* offered more protection against roving male eyes. Every last one of these outfits was as obscene as she didn't know what.

Kyra took a deep breath, then mentally resigned herself to the fact that she might as well get over her reticence because her shyness was having no effect whatsoever upon Zor. He hadn't been moved in the least by her proclamation that she wished to wear clothing from her own home, in her own style. "Nay," he had declared, "I would not be embarrassed in front of my people by such loathsome, peasant attire."

"But why this *qi'ka* in particular?" she had asked. "Why not the silvery-blue one from yesterday, then?"

"Because of your valuable skin."

Kyra had shook her head slightly, not comprehending. "My skin is valuable?"

"Aye."

"How so?"

"'Tis a rarity in Trek Mi Q'an to possess a female with skin like a *sekta* pearl. The dark *qi'ka* goes well against so distinctive a skin, my hearts."

Ah. So this was the Trystonni version of showing off one's mate. Odd that skin color would be a point of praise. "Forget it!" she had argued with a fluttering of her hand, "I'm not going to wear it!"

Zor had looked hurt, but he had relented with an incline of his head. "Wear whatever your hearts desire, *nee'ka*." And with that, he had left her alone. Again.

So now Kyra stood before the holographic mirror, trying to tell herself that she didn't look one hundred percent scandalous in the black-like *qi'ka,* and that she absolutely was not blushing from the roots of her "fire-berry" hair-whatever in the world that was-to the tips of her toes.

Kyra needed to get over her embarrassment, wanted to get over it even. She had spent the majority of the last three days moping about the bedroom and feeling generally put upon. It was growing dull. She wanted to get out of this godforsaken room.

However true it might be that she was indeed put upon, it was against Kyra's nature not to at least *try* to make the best of a difficult situation. That was why she had gone to that meditation retreat in the first place. Funny, but her time with Geris now seemed like a lifetime ago, when in fact she had left her side barely three days past.

She blinked her eyes several times in rapid succession to ward off the tears that threatened to spill whenever the image of her best friend's face popped into her mind. It was time to regain control of herself.

Kyra did a quick study of her attire in the holographic mirror. Her eyes widened when she noticed that the shimmering stones in her bridal necklace looked...*sad*? She shook her head to clear it. How could a necklace have emotions? How could it look so dismal?

Ah well, she could figure that piece of the puzzle out later. She was hungry and wanted to eat before they landed in Tryston, which Zor had assured her would be within three earth hours. Slipping into a matching pair of shimmering sandals, Kyra headed for the doors.

Chapter 8

"Will not the High Queen be dining with us this moon-rising, brother?" Dak put the question to Zor as he picked up his crystal fork-spoon to eat with. He noted the tension, the almost depressed manner of the High King, but said nothing of it. He knew his brother would be naught but embarrassed were he to remark upon the state the Empress had driven him to.

And why would Kyra wish for such a thing in the first? Did she not realize the honor that had been bestowed upon her? Did she not understand how many droves of females of varying species had trekked to the galaxy of warriors to see if they would be fortunate enough to have the fates proclaim them High Queen, the Sacred Mate to the Emperor and High King Zor? Dak harrumphed. 'Twas obvious the wee wench was daft.

"I do not think she cares to partake of the evening fare with me, brother." Zor stood up to fetch a bottle of matpow from the raised table across the room, then strode back and fell into his seat.

It was telling to Dak that Zor hadn't used his powers, but had seen to the task physically. Only a warrior whose spirits were unduly depressed would deign to do such a trivial task as that.

"By the goddess," Zor confided to his brother with a shake of his head, "'tis safe to say that my *nee'ka* loathes me."

"I wouldn't go that far. I'm very mad at you, yes, but loathe you, no."

Zor and Dak turned their heads in unison at the sound of that smoky voice. Zor's eyes lit up, glowing with approval and an emotion he chose not to dwell upon o'er much. He was, after all, a warrior. Not the type to have his hearts swoon at the mere sight of a wench, Sacred Mate or no.

As Kyra sauntered more and more into Zor's line of vision, he gave up and admitted to himself that his hearts were nigh unto bursting with joy. His woman had donned the dark *qi'ka* embedded of expensive, shimmering stones. She had bracelets clasped about either of her upper arms. Not only did she look more beautiful than he could say, but Kyra was honoring him by wearing it.

Zor knew she didn't realize it, but the hue of the *qi'ka* not only complimented her rare skin, it also proclaimed her to one and all as Q'ana Tal, a woman of the immediate line of the Emperor and High King. It was no matter that she sported it unawares of its deeper meaning; the fact was that she was indeed wearing it.

"Welcome, *nee'ka*. I would be honored do you join us." Zor stood up quickly, motioning for her to be seated in the chair next to him.

Kyra's step faltered for a disbelieving moment when Zor telekinetically pulled the chair out for her to sit down in, then pushed her in toward the table with an absent flick of his wrist. She had all but forgotten that he could do things like that. The reason for that neglect didn't escape her notice-she most likely hadn't wanted to remember. It made Zor too different from her. Not that there was anything familiar about the entire situation. "Thank you."

"You are welcome."

Kyra smiled shyly up to her husband when she realized how truly content she'd made him by coming into the dining chamber to eat with him and Dak. His eyes were glowing a brilliant, happy blue.

A brilliant, *happy* blue?

Understanding soon dawned. Kyra quickly glanced down to her bridal necklace to confirm her suspicions. Sure enough, the macabre piece of jewelry looked happy now. Somehow, some way, the necklace was able to convey Zor's emotions to her. A frightening, but nevertheless interesting discovery.

"So," Kyra asked, smiling hesitantly, "are we having any of that glowing turquoise drink tonight?"

Dak's eyes shot up from their lazy perusal of her breasts. "Turquoise drink?"

She nodded, pretending not to have noticed the direction in which her brother-in-law's eyes had been glued. "That drink that was brought into me at dinner last night."

Zor chuckled. "'Tis called turquoise in your dimension?"

Kyra met Zor's eyes and gave him a tentative smile. "We don't have drinks like that on earth. What is it called on Tryston?"

"Matpow."

She nodded. "May I please have some?"

Zor never let his eyes stray from his *nee'ka's* face as he flicked his wrist and summoned the bottle of matpow to pour some of its contents into Kyra's goblet. "You may have all that is your desire, my hearts." He cleared his throat, realizing at once that his whispered words had tumbled out sounding like a man besotted. "There is matpow aplenty," he amended in a darker, manlier rumble.

Dak, however, wasn't fooled. He beamed a smile in his brother's direction, winking knowingly at him when he caught his eye.

Zor grunted. "We will arrive in Tryston the soonest," he muttered. "We best eat."

Kyra nodded her approval, then spent the next two hours thoroughly enjoying the delicious meal that had been prepared by a gadget of some sort that cooked meals just like the machine had on *The Jetsons*.

Kyra tried not to blush when Zor's fingers brushed over her nipple. She reminded herself that this was the way of things on Tryston, so it was therefore nothing to feel self-conscious about.

Zor's fondling was done without thought, after all, as if it was merely a gesture of affection that all warriors did to their Sacred Mates when near them, much like stroking one's cheek or holding their hand.

Kyra managed to convince herself of that fact clear up until the point when her husband's arm left the back of her chair and settled onto her leg. Soon, his fingers made a trail up and down her thigh, then into and under the sheer skirt of the *qi'ka*. Kyra began to understand why the left side of every *qi'ka* skirt was slit up to the knot. It was called easy access.

"Do you really think the Tron insurrectionists will be daft enough to attempt to overthrow the warriors I have placed within their colony?"

Kyra couldn't believe how nonchalantly Zor had put that question to Dak while she was sitting next to him praying his fingers weren't about to leave the puff of curls between her legs to venture further down to-*ohhh good grief.*

"Aye brother, I believe it. They are an odious bunch of thieves, the lot of them."

Kyra listened to Dak's reply with half an ear. Her pulse was racing, her nipples were growing thick and hard. She could only pray that Zor ceased stroking her clit before she climaxed right here at the dinner table.

She attempted to shove his hand away. He didn't so much as flinch.

"Then I will send more warriors."

Kyra knew her breathing was growing increasingly labored. She realized with all certainty that her eyes were glazed over with need, hazy from the sharp knot of pleasure that was twining in her belly. Her gaze shot up to Dak's face, hoping that her brother-in-law had no idea what Zor was doing to her. She should have guessed. The men were embroiled in their political discussion. Dak hadn't spared her even a passing glance.

"There is no need. The warriors already on Tron can see to the rebellion."

Zor nodded. "'Tis true."

Kyra inhaled sharply, knowing an orgasm was quickly approaching and not having the faintest idea of how to stave it off. Zor's fingers had gone from slow strokes to lazy circles, and it was enough to drive any sane woman over the edge. She wondered if shouting at him would stop this embarrassing scene from playing out, but doubted it. Besides, it would only draw Dak's already captured attention her way.

Kyra could hear their conversation from some far off place in her mind, but she paid it little heed. She was coming. She knew she was coming and there wasn't a blessed thing she could do to stop it.

And then her pleasure reached that inevitable place of no longer caring. Still somewhat aware of her surroundings, Kyra bit down on her lip to keep from crying out.

It hit her. Hard. Relentless.

The twining in Kyra's belly snapped as her climax ripped through her body. She cried out softly, but managed to suppress the desire to scream.

She swallowed roughly, her breath coming out in pants. She couldn't believe it. She refused to believe it. But it was true. She had just had an orgasm at a dinner table-with witnesses present no less. Mortified, Kyra glanced toward Dak to witness his reaction. Her eyes widened.

Nothing.

That was even harder for Kyra to believe. The man was apparently so used to women climaxing at dinner tables that he didn't think it a sight worthy of garnering his attention. Her head snapped over to study Zor. Same thing. He was talking animatedly with his brother, not paying her the least amount of attention.

Good grief. If this was telling of what life on Tryston would be like, she planned to eat her meals in her bedroom alone. Every single one of them. This was beyond humiliating. That the humiliation was her own and no one else's was of no import.

Tryston sounded like a dreadful place. It was Hugh Heffner's Playboy Mansion on a planetary, perhaps galactic scale.

Well, Kyra thought grimly, perhaps what this place needed was a woman to shake things up a bit and refuse to allow herself to be fondled at the dinner table in front of strangers. And then her thoughts were no more, as Zor began the process all over again, and the heat in her belly pooled like fire.

Finally, long minutes later, and after three soul-shattering climaxes, Zor petted the dewy curls at the juncture of her thighs, as if praising her body for reacting to him. Tired and embarrassingly sated, Kyra merely nodded her compliance when Zor suggested that she retire to their chamber for a nap before the gastrolight cruiser made its landing.

"You will need your energy, *nee'ka,*" Zor whispered provocatively into the whorl of her ear. "We will join this moon-rising."

Wide-eyed, Kyra's head shot up. She met her husband's gaze. Furious that all choice had been removed from her, but resigned to the fact that there was little she could do about it without dying a horrific death, Kyra inclined her head regally, stood up, and stalked off toward the bedchamber.

* * * * *

It took three attempts before Zor was able to successfully rouse his Sacred Mate from her slumber, albeit somewhat. Chuckling, he tugged playfully on a tuft of her fire-berry hair, waiting for her eyes to open. "Wake up the soonest, my hearts. Kita has piloted the cruiser atop the landing pad. We descend even now."

"Mishtaayll smska dkfrr." Kyra opened her eyes long enough to mumble an incoherent statement, then rolled over onto her belly and resumed snoring.

"My hearts? *Nee'ka*? 'Tis time to rise, my love."

Zor frowned, uncertain as to what he should do to wake Kyra up. Her sleepy-headedness was his fault, for a certainty.

'Twould have been best had he not brought her to her woman's joy during the evening repast, yet he had deemed it prudent to gentle her to his touch. After all, this moon-rising would bring with it the consummation, and not even a High King could break the holy law in an effort to give his wench more time to accustom herself to her fate. All within the palace would expect to see the stones of Kyra's bridal necklace fully attuned to him on the morrow.

Slapping Kyra on her well-rounded rump, Zor decided to quit humoring his *nee'ka*. Time was of the essence. There was much to be seen to this day in the way of ceremony.

"Ouch!" Kyra shrieked as she flopped onto her backside and glared at Zor. "What was that for?"

He grunted. "I have been trying to wake you for many moments, woman. We are here. 'Tis afternoon on Tryston."

Kyra's expression went from annoyed to distressed in the blink of an eye. Her head shot up. "H-Here?" She gulped roughly, then licked her parched lips. "So soon?"

Zor was mesmerized by the touch of Kyra's tongue to her upper lip. He shook his head to clear it of lusty thoughts. There was time aplenty for that this moon-rising. "Aye." Taking to his feet, he held out a hand for his Sacred Mate. "Come, wee one. Dak and Kita await us at the bay doors."

Kyra scrambled to her knees and shook her head in the negative. She looked her husband up and down, noting that in addition to his black leather pants, he was now wearing a black leather vest-like contraption. If anything, it made him look even more ominous than he appeared while bare-chested, drawing attention to his gigantic, muscled arms. "Please, Zor. I'm not ready. Can't we stay in here for a little bit longer?"

Zor sighed. What his woman's obvious fright did to his resolve was not a good thing. There was no time left to bargain with. Much had to be accomplished this day. "I would that I could, *pani*," he gently informed her, "yet we cannot afford to tarry here."

Pani-it occurred to Kyra that the word meant "infant" or "baby". She frowned thoughtfully. "Why did you call me, *pani*? It's the second time you've used that word. Are you saying I behave like an infant?" she asked stiffly.

Zor grinned. "Mayhap you do at times." At Kyra's offended intake of breath, he chuckled softly. "But no, I did not call you *pani* because you behave like an infant, but because you are one, in terms of age."

"I'm thirty-two," she pointed out reasonably. She splayed her hands out, palms up. "Hardly a child, let alone a baby."

Zor's smile was amused, and if Kyra hadn't missed her mark, condescending as well. "As I said, still a baby."

She arched a brow. "Oh? And how old are you?"

"Forty-two Yessat years."

Kyra snorted incredulously. "Oh yeah, forty-two is so much more worldly and sophisticated than thirty-two." She rolled her eyes and feigned a bored yawn. "Give me a break, Zor."

Zor reached out and stroked his *nee'ka's* mane of hair affectionately. It annoyed Kyra how safe and loved the gesture made her feel. The barbarian could all but anticipate her every need. "You are thirty-two earth years, *pani*,"-he emphasized the word-"whereas I am forty-two Yessat years, the standard by which all galaxies in the seventh dimension measure time."

The very air in the room seemed to stop as Kyra contemplated that tidbit of information. She bit her lip, then reluctantly prodded him for more detail. "How, uh, how many earth years comprise one Yessat year?"

Zor met his Sacred Mate's gaze. "Approximately ten."

Kyra's bottom lip quivered slightly. Zor had a mad desire to suck on it. "Then that makes you..."

"Four hundred and twenty earth years."

"I see." *Good grief*! Four hundred and twenty! She truly was an infant to him. Talk about your May-December romance. "That's amazing," she admitted breathlessly, momentarily forgetting her fear of seeing Tryston. "How long do Trystonnis typically live?"

Zor scratched his chin. Why he always did that, Kyra had no notion. The man was always clean-shaven. "Mayhap two hundred and fifty Yessat years, sometimes as many as three hundred."

Kyra did the math, tallying the numbers in her head. Her jaw dropped open in astonishment. "*Two thousand and five hundred* to *three thousand* earth years? Good grief! You'll be alive and ticking thousands of years after I'm dead!"

Zor looked at her as though she'd gone daft. He shook his head. "Nay, my hearts, 'tis not so."

Kyra peered at him inquiringly, but said nothing.

"You will age like a Trystonni once we are joined."

She gasped. "Really?"

"Aye." Zor frowned as a misguided thought occurred to him. He jabbed a finger in the air accusingly. After all, he couldn't fathom anyone being interested in a phenomenon so well known throughout the galaxies. "You are merely stalling for time with this talk. We must depart this place anon."

He flicked his wrist toward the bedchamber's huge dressing room and telekinetically summoned his Sacred Mate's dark *qi'ka*. When it landed on the bed, he crossed his arms over his leather-incased chest and threw Kyra a look that broached no argument. "Dress at once, wee one. Many of the lesser kings and their *nee'kas* will be here to greet their Empress and High Queen."

Kyra, who hadn't even realized she was nude until just then, did a little arm-crossing of her own. "When did you take my clothes off?" she screeched.

"When first I entered the room." Zor grunted, offering no apology. "I have told you before, but apparently you did not heed me then, so 'tis best do you heed me now: whilst we are alone, you will never offend me by the wearing of garments." He slashed his hand through the air in a gesture of dominance. "By the holy law, I have the right of it to look upon what belongs to me at any time I choose."

Seething with rage, Kyra's face turned a mottled red and her nostrils flared out comically. "Ooohhh!" She clenched her teeth and set her jaw.

Zor merely laughed, thinking his *nee'ka* the most adorable of *pani* brides. Dismissing her antics with a grin and a wave of his hand, he summoned the *qi'ka* upon Kyra's body.

Kyra gasped, then gasped again when forces unseen removed her from the raised bed and sent her flying into Zor's arms. "*Shiiiit*!"

Zor paid her no mind. "Now," her husband chastised in his most patronizing "let's be reasonable" tone, "will you walk to our conveyance or must I carry you?"

"I believe I'll walk." Kyra thrust her chin up to a stubborn angle. "As I've said before, I am not an infant." When Zor began to chuckle, she glared at him, narrowing her eyes defiantly. "Are you ready or not?"

Zor lowered his wife to the ground, then bowed mockingly. "By all means, *nee'ka*, let us go. Your palace awaits you."

Chapter 9

As the bay doors opened and Zor laced his fingers through hers, Kyra absently noted that warriors were lined up on either side of a bejeweled path forged of amazing red crystal that led from the landing dock to some sort of ornate carriage a ways down the road.

Kyra's first thought was that she'd never seen so many huge men in all of her life. She felt like Thumbalina.

Her second thought was that, in the light of day, all of these barbarians could no doubt see what lay beneath her *qi'ka* with zero effort. Luckily, that horrific thought was quickly replaced by a third-Kita must be in close proximity because it smelled like somebody cut one.

Holding her breath, Kyra glanced over to Zor to see if he smelled the stench too. Although her husband remained outwardly calm and emotionless, it gave her grim satisfaction to note that the whites of his eyes were a stinging red, making an eerie contrast against his glowing blue orbs. Furthermore, he had developed a wicked tic in his cheek.

Good!

As the fetid odor relented, Kyra turned her attention back to the perfectly lined up men waiting below. All of these warriors were of roughly the same coloring, height, and musculature. All of them wore the same leather-like pant and vest attire, although the colors were different from Zor's and Dak's.

Kyra recalled Dak mentioning during dinner that colors were significant on Tryston. Only the Chief Priestess of the Trystonni, as well as those of the immediate bloodline of the High King could don the black-like color her *qi'ka* was in.

Dak, for instance, was within his rights to attire himself in black, but down the road when he married and had a son, his son-when starting his own family-could not. His son's sons would wear the color white, the emblem of lesser kings not directly of the Emperor's line of succession. Dak, even after he took a wife, could choose to wear either black or white, as could his Sacred Mate. A little confusing, but Kyra got the gist of it.

Dak had also informed her that as Empress and High Queen, it was Kyra's duty to wear "the night"-his translatorial term for the black-like hue-to all official functions, but it also fell to her to show her support of the various clans by interchangeably sporting their colors as well.

Whatever.

Tired of standing on the landing pad looking like a lingerie model on display, Kyra squeezed Zor's hand, conveying her desire to get it over with and start moving. He grunted, but made no motion to leave. Harrumphing, she gave up. He wasn't paying her any attention now anyway. All of his focus was on the warriors assembled on either side of the red crystal path.

Stifling the urge to dig her nails into the palm of Zor's hand-not that the gargantuan would feel it or care-Kyra waited in awkward stillness until at last her husband broke the silence.

Raising the union of their clasped hands, Zor bellowed his decree. "I give unto you Kyra Q'ana Tal. The High Queen of Tryston and Empress of Trek Mi Q'an."

All of the warriors present, and there had to be roughly a hundred or more, bent down on one knee out of deference to her station. Kyra bit her lip, uncertain as to whether she was expected to bow to them or nod or something. Oh well. If she was supposed to bow, then Zor should have told her, she assured herself defensively.

It occurred to Kyra that squatting on one knee would put these warriors at about eye level with her. As it was, the top of her head barely made it to the top of Zor's abdomen when he was at his full height. The *top* of her head! Good grief.

All at once, Kyra felt overwhelmed by the past few day's events-being kidnapped, getting married without her knowledge, climaxing at the dinner table-it was all too much. She wanted to go home. She longed for the normalcy of manipulating numbers and scowling at IRS agents. Nevertheless, she would settle for simply going to the palace and locking herself behind closed doors.

Then suddenly the group was moving, Kyra and Zor in the lead, Dak and Kita taking up the rear. Speaking of rears, Kyra had an odd premonition that her abominable brother-in-law was staring at hers, getting a great view in this light, no doubt. Glancing over her shoulder, she threw him a look that shot daggers when her suspicion was confirmed. Dak merely grinned, winking unrepentantly.

Kyra sighed. The man was brazen as hell, but hard to stay mad at.

Turning her attention to the red crystal path before her, Kyra was mortified to discover that all of the warriors were ogling her in the manner Dak had. She had thought they would all be immune to seeing scantily clad women. "Why are you allowing them to stare at me like this?" she whispered to Zor.

"Like what?" Zor was taken aback by the hurt transmitted in his *nee'ka's* tone. "All non-mated warriors behold a desirable woman thusly. You should be pleased, as it speaks well of your beauty."

"I'm not pleased," Kyra whispered tersely, her face heated with embarrassment. "I'm humiliated."

It struck Zor just how different his Sacred Mate's upbringing had been from the free women of his acquaintance. Even though he realized that the lusty thoughts of non-mated warriors would never subside, Zor suddenly had the urge to shield his woman from further upset. Kyra would adjust given time. For now, he could do naught less than to help her ease into it...slowly.

Picking up the royal party's pace, Zor squeezed his Sacred Mate's hand to express his respect of her feelings. Kyra threw him a grateful glance, further strengthening his resolve to move them to the Q'ana Tal conveyance the soonest.

Truth be told, now that Zor was mated, he didn't care for other warriors lusting after his *nee'ka* any more than his *nee'ka* desired to be lusted after by them. Her wee body was his, made for his pleasure alone. Still, Zor knew from his own forty-two Yessat years before mating just how lusty a lot the Trystonni were. He tried not to take offense as he witnessed the unabashed perusal so many eyes gave to his wife.

Zor's muscles grew taut with a surge of primal territorialism. He could feel the gazes of his warriors taking in every nuance of his woman's body. From the sparkling stones embedded into Kyra's sandals, to the slit skirt that revealed the creamy *sekta* pearl skin of her left leg and hip, to the wisp of fire-berry curls shielding her mound, to the plumpness of her lush breasts and jutting nipples...

Zor felt all of the stares and was surprised to discover that his first inclination was to whisk Kyra away and lock her in their bedchamber where none save the *Kefa* slaves could see her charms. In the past, mated warriors had claimed he would one day feel this powerful urge, that 'twas natural before securing the woman through the joining, and mayhap even after. Zor had laughed, insisting that no wench could make him feel that strongly for her. How wrong he had been.

After what felt to Zor to be a never-ending sentence in the hell fires of *Nukala*-the reputed winter solstice home of Aparna, the omnipotent dark goddess of war and pleasure-the royal party at last alighted into the Q'ana Tal conveyance. Sighing his relief, Zor patted Kyra affectionately on the rump, then set her down next to him in the front seat of the golden crystal carriage. Dak and Kita took the seat behind them.

Kyra shot him a glance that spoke volumes, her lips curling in disapproval of his proprietary behavior. He merely grinned. "Let us be off."

"Where are we-oh my!" Kyra gasped as the ornate carriage floated off of its perch and took to the air. Suddenly, she was having too much fun to stay angry with her husband. Even the fact that his large, vein-roped arm was draped over her shoulder, allowing him to fondle her breast at his leisure, was lost on her. "Zor this is wonderful!"

Zor grunted with satisfaction, inordinately pleased that his *nee'ka* approved of the conveyance he had purchased for her as a mating gift before leaving to claim her. This was the first he had seen of it. He had to admit the open-top carriage was well worth the eighty thousand credits the crystal guildsman had required as payment. If for no other reason than to see the joyful look that permeated every feature of his *pani* bride's face. "I acquired it for you, my hearts. This conveyance is Q'ana Tal and therefore yours to do with as you will."

Kyra's face beamed brightly. It occurred to Zor that never had a sight robbed him of his very breath until that moment. Her delight was more beautiful than the moon phasing, a stellar phenomena that occurred only once every ten Yessat years.

During a moon phasing, the skies turn to night and every of Tryston's seventeen moons are visible from Sand City for four successive days. 'Twas always a time of great feasting and revelry for the Trystonni, because the moon phasing is what renews the metaphysical powers of the mystical sands. Aye, she was more beautiful even than that.

Kyra simply couldn't believe what her eyes were seeing. Tryston was beautiful, overwhelmingly so. The colors here were so vivid and jewel-like. Even the very air around them seemed to shimmer with flecks of gold.

She peered down from the confines of the floating carriage and took in the sights from below. Now that they were well above what Zor had told her yesterday was called Sand City, she was able to take it all in with perspective.

There looked to be a massive market place at the heart of the city proper, where even now she could see people bargaining for their wares. Surrounding the market, were what had to be homes-thousands of them-in row after row, all of them centered in such a way as to circle the main trading area. And every structure, whether a market stall or a private residence, was fashioned of crystal from every imaginable hue of the rainbow and then some.

Kyra studied the streets, then gawked in amazement. "Zor! Are the roadways paved of gold?"

"Nay, my love, all of the roadways save the one of red crystal leading to our palace are fashioned from *trelli,* which is composed of Trystonni sand."

"Sand?" Kyra's eyes widened in disbelief. "But it shimmers like gold."

"'Tis not like the sand of your earth, sister," Dak called out from behind them, "Trystonni sands are different."

Kita clicked out a few words, causing Kyra to gasp. "Really? That's amazing! The sands heal?"

"Aye," Zor confirmed proudly. "It has many special properties, which is why our priestesses concoct spells to enchant it and our warriors guard it vigilantly from all outsiders."

Kyra's eyes widened in awe as the floating carriage made its way from the city proper and toward a series of glittering sand dunes that sparkled a regal gold. Leading up to those dunes was a road of red crystal, so she knew they were getting closer to the palace.

Kyra didn't care that she probably looked like an eager child on Christmas Eve-this journey was too exciting by half. Knowing that she was probably the only earthling to ever witness the sight only added to her sense of giddiness. "What is the name of our home?" she inquired, squirming restively in her seat as her head darted back and forth, missing nothing and taking in everything.

Zor's hearts thumped pleasurably in his chest. His wee one had called it "our home". She was no doubt unawares of the words she'd used, but no matter. "'Tis called Palace of the Dunes."

"Palace of the Dunes," she murmured.

The conveyance lurched another seventy-five feet upward, preparing to hover past the peak of a mountainous dune that looked to have fifty or more guards posted at the bottom of it. The shimmer in the air surrounding them grew denser. "What are those warriors guarding?" Kyra asked as she pointed to the foot of the glittering dune.

"The only passable entryway leading to the palace," Zor replied. "There is a tunnel carved into the belly of the dune that Trystonnis may pass through when granted permission to enter."

Kyra squinted her eyes thoughtfully. "But if an enemy wanted to breach the castle, couldn't they simply fly over the pass like we are doing now?"

"Nay," Dak answered from the backseat. "The structure of your conveyance was enchanted by the Chief Priestess herself, Kyra, allowing this carriage to glide unharmed through the atmosphere. No man or woman alive is a match for the awesome powers of the Holy One. Did an enemy ship come within a hundred yards of the dune we are now passing over, the very air about us would disintegrate it instantaneously."

Kyra gasped in amazement and not a little awe as she studied the dense, glittering air that became its heaviest at the peak of the mountainous dune that cut the palace off from the rest of Sand City. "That is the coolest thing I've ever heard! I never even saw anything like that on *Star Trek* back home!"

Zor chuckled wryly. He turned around and winked at his brother. "Bloodthirsty wench, my *nee'ka*."

When Dak laughed, Kyra threw them an impatient glance. "You both have to admit, this really is cool."

"Aye, *nee'ka*. Whatever you say, my hearts."

Kyra frowned at Zor's patronizing tone. When Dak's laughter grew bolder at her expense, she favored him with the middle finger without so much as turning around. Apparently the symbol was not only universal, but her lecherous brother-in-law found it amusing instead of irritating. She had meant it to be irritating.

Zor drew Kyra's hand down and kissed it sweetly. Trying to look stern, he gently admonished her for exhibiting so crude a gesture. "An Empress doesn't do things like that, *pani.* You will cause the wives of the high lords to swoon do you do that in their presence whilst holding court."

"Holding court?" Kyra screeched. She shook her head and frowned. "Good grief. I'm a tax accountant, Zor. I don't know anything about holding court."

Zor waved a hand dismissively. "This you will be taught by noble women you befriend, or mayhap by my brother Rem's *nee'ka* if they come visit. Rem is the youngest brother to Kil, Dak, and myself," he explained, "and is the King of Sypar, one of Tryston's lesser moons."

Kyra chuckled. Her head fluttered about in amused disbelief. "Rem is a semi-normal name, I suppose, but what did you call the other one?"

"Kil."

"You actually have a brother named *Kil*? Good grief. I hope he's not as ferocious as he sounds."

"He is, if not worse."

There was no amusement in Zor's barely audible confession, only what sounded like a whisper of remorse and a lot of guilt for what his brother was. The look on his face made Kyra's heart constrict-an empathetic condition she chose not to dwell upon. Clearing her throat, she pointed toward the outside of the conveyance, hoping to turn the topic. "It looks like the enchanted fog is letting up."

The pad of Zor's thumb resumed its brushing motion against Kyra's aroused nipple, telling her without words that his spirits had been restored. Odd that she would care. "Aye. We are almost through the barrier the Chief Priestess erected. On the other side lay the Palace of the Dunes."

Without even thinking about it, Kyra's hand clutched Zor's knee in anticipation. He smiled into her hair, planting a feathery kiss atop her fire-berry head. Fully aroused, Zor inhaled deeply, knowing now was not the time for his lust. "We are almost there, *nee'ka*."

Kyra heaved in a breath of air when the Palace of the Dunes loomed into view. Never, ever had she beheld such a wondrous sight as this. Nestled within a cloister of mammoth dunes of golden sand, was a behemoth castle made of shimmering black crystal. The sparkle of the structure alone was enough to set anyone's jaw to gaping. The beautiful jutting turrets fashioned of colored jewels only heightened the intensity of the effect. The palace was magnificent.

"My god," Kyra whispered breathlessly, "I've never seen anything like it."

Zor slowly nodded his head in agreement, looking at the palace through the eyes of his *pani* bride instead of through the eyes of a man who'd dwelled within the castle perimeter all of his years of life. "You think it worthy of you?"

Kyra's eyebrows shot up in surprise. "Worthy of *me*?" She shook her head. "I'm not worthy of *it*," she mumbled.

Zor felt immediately humbled by her words. He didn't agree with Kyra, of course, but was pleased she thought the palace a beauty. Rem's *nee'ka* had always thought it eerie, ever grateful she was to leave it and retire to her own castle on Sypar.

Zor's hold on Kyra tightened appreciably. Gathering her closer, his right hand continued to stroke her nipple, while his left hand slithered up her thigh and disappeared under the skirt of her *qi'ka*. "'Tis glad I am that you like it."

Kyra's face flushed red. She was about to ask him to stop, then decided against it. She didn't want to call attention to what

Zor was doing-she'd rather wait and have that conversation alone.

And when Kyra realized that he wasn't going to force her to climax, her screaming nerves relaxed again. Zor's hand was staying put, petting her curls lazily, but straying no further. Deciding to save her breath for when it would matter, she put the situation from her mind and focused on the palace up ahead. They were almost there.

A tendril of premonition passed through Kyra's consciousness.

She didn't know how and she didn't comprehend why, but Kyra suddenly realized that she would never be allowed to leave this place. Like it or not, she was gawking at her new, permanent home.

Chapter 10

The Chief Priestess was the first to greet Kyra and Zor upon their arrival. Others were gathered about, looking their fill at the wee High Queen, but spoke not a word. They all realized it was the right of the Holy One to speak to her first. Even Zor deferred to her, offering Kyra's arm to the most exalted mystic among them.

Leading the new Empress and High Queen away from her Sacred Mate and down a fascinating corridor carved of green crystal, the Chief Priestess looped her arm through Kyra's and steered her into a chamber of blue crystal, where the women could speak confidentially.

Kyra marveled at the room around her. The chamber cast off a beautiful blue glow that was noticeable, yet didn't hurt the eyes. Further into the room, tall tree-like plants of sparkling purple surrounded what looked to be a curving pool-like structure of shimmering silver water.

"Shall we partake of the ceremonial bath?"

Kyra's head snapped to attention, having forgotten for a moment that she wasn't alone. She turned to study the Chief Priestess who was even now divesting herself of her dark *qi'ka*.

Kyra wasn't certain what she had been expecting-perhaps someone that looked older and more omnipotent-but a tanned, statuesque blonde with large perky breasts, puffy pink nipples, and the nicest butt Kyra had ever seen, certainly wasn't it.

As if reading her thoughts, the Chief Priestess grinned, her trill chuckles sounding throughout the chamber of blue crystal. The woman was a dead-ringer for Pamela Sue Anderson. "Come," she smiled, "let us take the ceremonial bath together and I shall try to answer your questions."

Kyra slowly nodded. "All right." A little embarrassed to be totally naked in anyone's presence, even another woman's, she took her time undressing. The Chief Priestess waited patiently, giving Kyra time to adjust to the situation. After a short lapse, she was naked and following the mystic into the silvery waters.

"I am called Ari," the Chief Priestess announced over her shoulder. She then took a seat on a soft jewel-like rock within the water. "I would be honored did you call me by my given name. Might I call you Kyra, my High Queen?"

"Yes, of course." Kyra perched on the rock adjacent to Ari's, noting with some degree of shyness that the lulling waters came only waist high, exposing both pairs of breasts to the other's view. She took a deep breath and tried not to look mortified. "What do we use as soap here?"

Ari grinned, causing Kyra to wonder not for the first time just how old the beautiful Chief Priestess was. The powerful woman had the hard body of an eighteen-year-old, but Kyra doubted that anyone who could enchant sand, foretell the future, and cast spells would be so young.

"You are right. I am one-hundred Yessat years."

Kyra gasped. Her eyes rounded tellingly. "But how..."

"I can read your mind." Ari grinned again. "Do not worry over it. Once we leave this chamber and take away your fears, I will not pry into your mind again. I do so now only that you might not doubt my abilities later."

Kyra snorted very un-empress-like. "As if that could happen."

Ari chuckled softly. It occurred to Kyra that the sound of her laughter was as lovely as her body.

"Thank you."

Embarrassed, Kyra bit her lip and turned her head to the side. Immediately contrite, Ari reached out and stroked her mane of fire-berry hair. "'Tis all right. We do not inhibit pleasure on Tryston the way you do on your planet. Nor are women here embarrassed to display their charms."

"So I've noticed," Kyra muttered.

Ari laughed. "Ah. So you did take note of the *nee'kas* of lesser kings and high lords gathered about, did you not?"

Kyra frowned in thought. She remembered one female in particular. The petite brunette sporting a white and completely transparent *qi'ka* she had passed en route to the blue room hadn't seemed embarrassed to be on display at all. She had enjoyed the attention of the lusting warriors, reveling in it even. Kyra envied her, if for nothing else, her ability to be so uninhibited. "Yes, I noticed. Why are they here?"

"They await you to finish your bath that they might dine with you this moon-rising at the consummation feast."

A tic appeared in Kyra's jaw. "C-Consummation dinner? They aren't expecting me to have sex with Zor in front of them are they?"

"By the sands, no!" Ari threw her head back and laughed. When her amusement waned a bit, she shook her head and grinned. An engaging dimple popped out. "Only I will bear witness to the joining."

Kyra clapped a hand to her forehead. "You have to watch? Good grief!"

Ari grasped a hold of her hand and clutched it soothingly. "'Twill be all right, Kyra. Believe me, you will want me there for your first coupling."

"I will? What for?" she asked apprehensively. An image of Zor's manhood rending her in half exploded into her mind.

Ari tried desperately not to laugh, for it seemed 'twas all she'd done since meeting the *pani* High Queen. Biting her lip, Ari shook her head. "You will not be split asunder, my friend, yet for virgins the breaching can be difficult. I will leave once the High King's rod is fully embedded within your channel."

"But I'm not a virgin."

"Have you mated with a Trystonni warrior before?"

"No."

Ari waved dismissively. "You are virgin."

"Good grief." Kyra felt faint. Crossing her arms protectively over her breasts, she shuddered. "Are warriors *that* big?"

Ari licked her lips as if recalling a tempting morsel she'd indulged in on some past occasion. "Aye."

Kyra's only response was a gargled, strangling sound.

Ari chuckled again. She couldn't help but to like the amusing High Queen. "Now to answer your earlier question..."

Kyra wrinkled her nose. Smiling for the first time, she shook her head. "Forgive me, but I'm so overwhelmed I haven't the foggiest notion what question I asked."

"'Tis all right. You asked what kind of soap we use."

"Ah yes. So what kind is that?"

Ari gestured toward the cool, inviting waters the women were halfway submerged into. "The lesser priestesses of Sand City have enchanted all bathing facilities within the Palace of the Dunes. A cleaning substance is in the waters, washing away impurities as we speak."

"That is so cool." Kyra cupped her hands together under the silvery liquid, then splashed the cool water over her breasts. "We don't even need sponges?"

Ari shrugged. "Nay, but we will be washed more thoroughly momentarily. *Kefa* slaves will arrive the soonest to see to that."

"S-Slaves?" Offended, Kyra's hands flew to her hips. "That's deplorable!"

"Not at all."

"How can you say that?"

Ari smiled. She appreciated the fact that unlike every other person in Sand City, male or female, Kyra didn't approach her with kid gloves, fearing to be turned into a *titzi*. "They are not thinking creatures, *Kefas*, merely enchanted ones."

At the High Queen's furrowed brow, the Chief Priestess tried to explain. "I read your thoughts and see your planet's past in them. Making a slave of a *Kefa* is not like making a slave of a human of a different race." She gestured absently. "'Tis like making a slave of a machine."

Kyra bit her lip. "They are machines then?"

"Aye, but not in the way you are thinking. They are not possessed of mechanical parts." Ari sighed, uncertain for the first time in her thousand earth years as to how she could explain her words. "*Kefas* are made of colored sand found in the borderlands. They have been enchanted by priestesses, created with the sole purpose of pleasuring. They have no thoughts, no feelings, no emotions. They do only as instructed. An amoeba on your earth would have more thought processes."

Kyra chewed that over. "And Zor has many of these enchanted women?"

"Over three hundred."

"I see." Her shoulders drooped a bit. The thought of Zor having sex with unreal women shouldn't bother her, but it did.

And then when six naked *Kefa* slaves strolled into the blue crystal chamber and joined them in the waters, Kyra decided that she minded fiercely. They might not have thoughts, but these enchanted women were beautiful.

The slaves possessed bodies that glittered in whatever hue they favored. Standing in the waters with them were two females made of sparkling yellow, two made of glittering red, one made of shimmering lavender, and the last one of twinkling blue. All were beautiful. All were busty. And the priestess looked like Pamela Sue Anderson. This was definitely Hugh Heffner's dream come true.

Gritting her teeth, Kyra motioned toward Ari. "*All* of these *Kefas* have had sex with my husband?"

"Of course." Ari shrugged as if it was of no import. "As is the way of a warrior once joined to his Sacred Mate-as you will be this moon-rising following the consummation feast-Zor will turn only to you for his coupling needs." She smiled, the gesture a soothing balm. "Truly is there no point in angering yourself over females in your Sacred Mate's past, for if you do, you will be mad forever." She shook her head and grinned. "I think the High King has taken to the beds of every of his six hundred slaves and servants."

"Good grief."

Kyra gasped as the blue woman splashed water onto her breasts, then rubbed the liquid into her pores. The feel of the *Kefa's* hands rubbing over her nipples caused them to grow erect. Another pair of hands joined in, paying homage to her vagina. Embarrassed by her arousal, Kyra bit her lip and looked away.

"'Tis a natural reaction to physical stimulation," Ari demurred, as she closed her eyes and basked in the feel of three sets of hands gliding over every crevice of her body. The Chief Priestess' puffy pink nipples turned taut and rouged. Unashamed of her pleasure, she splayed her thighs wide, giving the questing hands of the *Kefas* easier access to massage her intimately.

Ari moaned and groaned, her eyes closed, her lips turned up in a slight smile. This was a woman who gloried in her sexuality.

And when Ari's tremors of pleasure began, Kyra understood what it was about voyeurism that drove adolescent boys and adult men back on earth to purchase risqué movies. There couldn't be a more erotic or arousing sight than watching a woman so beautiful as Ari peak. Her nipples grew thick and stiff as a look of utter bliss passed over her features. Even the pungent scent of her arousal was intoxicating. It wasn't necessary to be sexually attracted to women to appreciate the view aesthetically.

Before she fully realized what she was doing, Kyra splayed her own thighs wide and allowed the *Kefas* to caress her intimately. She closed her eyes and gasped, the feel of so many hands toying with her nipples and pussy difficult to stay immune to. When she felt a mouth latch onto her clit, she shuddered, crying out softly with pleasure.

When Kyra at last opened her eyes, it was to watch six pairs of naked *Kefa* derrieres leave the lulling waters of the pool. Apparently once their job was finished, they took off. Good grief. How embarrassing.

Ari clucked her tongue and made a tssking sound. "'Tis best to get over your shyness, my friend, for you shall peak at every bath. A *Kefa* can do no less." She shrugged. "Leastways, it is common for women to bathe together on Tryston. This is how we bond."

Kyra wouldn't have been surprised if her eyeballs fell straight out of their sockets, they were bulging so animatedly. "By climaxing together?" she screeched.

Ari grinned mischievously. "Can you think of a better way?"

Kyra's unhinged jaw clicked shut. Suddenly she couldn't help herself. She had to laugh. Succumbing to a fit of the giggles, she covered her mouth with her hand. "Let me guess? Those that peak together, stay together?"

Ari's trill laughter sounded throughout the cavernous chamber. "Something like that, my friend."

"What is the cause of all the gaiety in here?" Zor's deep voice boomed out his question as he strode toward the silvery pool.

Standing up, Ari reached for Kyra's hand, then sauntered from the waters with Zor's Sacred Mate in tow. Stopping to stand before him, the Chief Priestess inclined her head out of respect. "We were merely becoming acquainted, sire."

Zor's eyes flicked over Ari's body. "You are looking well, as always."

"I thank you." Inclining her head to Kyra, she smiled. "We shall speak more later. For now, your Sacred Mate and consummation feast awaits your attendance."

Kyra bit her lip, gnawing on it slightly. She didn't want her only friend here to leave. "Won't you be eating with us?" she asked quietly.

"Nay," Zor denied with a shake of his head. "Whereas it is our duty to dine and make merry with those below our station, the Chief Priestess is too exalted to do so. She will await us in our bedchamber for the joining." With that, Zor reached out and plumped one of Ari's nipples between two fingers, causing Kyra's eyes to widen in shock. "You may go, Holy One."

Ari inclined her head. "Peace and prosperity unto you."

"And unto you as well."

Kyra threw Zor a disgruntled look at his touching of Ari's breast, but forgot what he'd done just as quickly. She gasped instead as Ari's form shimmered, then dissolved into thin air. "Good god. How did she do that?"

Zor smiled down to his *nee'ka,* his eyes glazed over with their passion. "I cannot say." Picking Kyra up, he thrust her chest toward his face and suckled on a ripe nipple. "Did the *Kefas* assigned to you pleasure you well, my hearts?"

Kyra shook her head. She didn't want to talk about *that.* She had had a difficult enough of a time discussing it with another woman. "Shouldn't we go eat?" she squeaked out, somewhat flustered as Zor continued to suckle her breasts.

"Mmm. I suppose so." He sucked on both nipples one last time, then reluctantly set her down. "Come. Let us attire you properly before we join in on our consummation feast."

Chapter 11

Kyra made quick friends with the beautiful, vivacious brunette named Tia, who she had spotted in the palace earlier. Tia was a lesser queen and cousin by marriage to Zor. Her Sacred Mate was called Jik and he was ruler of a colony on Tryston three days journey from Sand City.

Tia turned out to be not only extremely open and friendly, but an invaluable educator as well. "Do you see those women that wear the skirt of the *qi'ka* but no top?" she whispered.

"Yes." Kyra frowned, not at all pleased by their presence. One of those topless females, who was very much alive and by no means enchanted, was using her large breasts as a pillow for Zor to lay his head back on. She stood behind his chair, massaging his massive shoulders and laughing at whatever sexual pun some warrior had just made.

"They are not slaves, but neither are they free. They are always great beauties for they are acquired through wars and are then forced into servitude for five Yessat years time." Tia shrugged her elegant shoulders. "Though most do choose to remain on Tryston even when their time is over, seeing to the needs of the non-mated warriors."

"I see." Kyra filed away that bit of information. At least Tia had said the *non-mated* warriors, which completely excluded Zor after tonight. Of course, why should she care?

Kyra scowled across the expanse of the room, noting that the infuriating man was currently kneading the buttocks of two *Kefas* standing to either side of him. First the Chief Priestess and now these slaves. Couldn't the ogre keep his hands to himself? "Why is that topless woman who is not a *Kefa* massaging Zor if those servants only pleasure non-mated warriors?"

"The same reason why a topless servant is massaging my Jik." She grinned engagingly. "'Tis the only time mated warriors play, at consummation feasts."

Ah. The Trystonni version of a bachelor party. Only these non-bachelors allowed other women to pawn them right in front of their wives eyes. "Doesn't it bother you?"

Tia glanced over to where the men at the table across the room were seated, segregated from their women as was the custom at all consummation feasts. That Jik allowed two *Kefas* situated on their knees at either side of him to suckle his engorged cock, didn't even seem to register as a concern to the petite brunette. She shrugged. "'Tis no more than the *Kefas* of our household perform on him in the bathing chamber, for a certainty."

Kyra's hands flew to her heart. "Ari, the Chief Priestess, said once a warrior joins he seeks his needs only with his Sacred Mate."

Tia nodded. "True. My Jik would never mount a *Kefa*, nor any other female bound to him by the holy law. Only me."

"You don't consider that,"-Kyra waved her hand toward the table of men-"seeking his needs elsewhere?"

Tia actually looked surprised. "By the sands, no!" She shook her head and giggled. "Did not the *Kefas* bring you to your woman's joy at bath?"

Kyra had the good grace to blush. Tia had a point, but she still didn't care for the thought of one of those enchanted women performing oral sex on Zor. So when two *Kefas* dropped to their knees and disappeared under the table before her husband, her heart slammed painfully in her chest. It was true she hadn't wanted to come to Tryston to begin with, but damn it, now that she was here and had no choice for the time being but to stay put, she was beginning to think of the man as hers.

Tia sensed the High Queen's hurt. She brushed her hand soothingly across her arm. "Kyra, you are truly upset, are you not?"

She nodded.

"Oh you poor dear." Tia clasped Kyra's hand in her own, thankful that none of the other *nee'kas* gathered around the women's table were paying them any heed. She knew that realization would only further humiliate the High Queen. "Dearest Kyra, do not make more of this in your mind than is there. Look at them. They are but dolls."

Tia chuckled, trying to lighten the mood and make her friend understand. "You would get hurt because a lifeless creature suckles your Sacred Mate? Or even a lowly bound servant such as the one pillowing Zor with her breasts?" She patted Kyra's hand soothingly. "I forget you do not yet know the pleasures that only a Sacred Mate can bring to her warrior. Once you are impaled upon Zor's manhood, you will not concern yourself over the harmless play at consummation feasts, believe me."

Kyra glanced over to the table. She bit her lip indecisively.

"The *Kefas* aren't real," Tia whispered in her ear. "They are but a trick of magic, fooling us into sensing them as actual forms. And the topless bound servants are held in no higher a regard."

"I'm not so sure that's a good thing. They *are* women, after all."

"'Tis the casualty of war. 'Tis life."

Kyra hated to admit it, but when viewed in that light, the weight on her heart eased somewhat. Tia was right. Jealousy over an enchanted female was like feeling threatened over a virtual reality game. And as for the bound servant, Zor didn't appear to notice her beyond the cushioned softness of her breasts. Smiling tentatively, she covered her new friend's hand with her own. "Thank you," she said softly.

"Do not mention it." Tia grinned, searching her eyes. "'Tis only at consummation feasts, which are a rarity leastways, that our men get so randy with the bound servants and *Kefas*. Take heart." She leaned in, lowering her voice to a wisp of breath. "Besides, we will have our turn to prick the tempers of our men."

"What do you mean?"

Tia winked. "In a little while you will see, then again at the gentling will you know."

As Zor bellowed his climax throughout the dining hall, Kyra decided she couldn't wait to find out.

* * * * *

A half an hour later, Kyra discovered exactly what Tia had meant. And she noted with smug satisfaction that Zor looked like he wanted to kill somebody, particularly the non-mated warrior whose lap she was perched on.

"King Dak had the right of it, my High Queen." The handsome warrior continued to stroke her thigh as he grinned unabashedly. "Your woman's berries do have the look of ripe *taka* fruits."

Kyra smiled charmingly up at him. Funny how two days ago, perhaps even so little as yesterday, perhaps even just an hour ago, such a comment would have mortified her. Odd what climaxing at dinner tables and peaking with virtual strangers while bathing could do to a woman's sense of propriety.

Kyra glanced over her shoulder to be certain her odious husband was watching every moment of this scene. Oh yeah. He was. "Why thank you, Cam. How generous of you to say so."

"'Tis naught but the truth." He flicked a *taka* fruit with his thumb, inspiring Kyra to yelp.

Kyra threw the giant a reassuring smile when he gazed at her questioningly. Okay, so she wasn't totally oblivious to mortification.

Another warrior strolled up to where Kyra reclined across Cam's lap and squatted down on his knees beside her. Running his hand over her thigh, he made an appreciative groan. Kyra noticed that the newcomer was fiercely erect. "I vow, my High Queen, I have never beheld such skin as yours."

Kyra glanced across the room. Zor was paying no mind at all to the topless servants rubbing up against him, hoping to entice him, thrusting their nipples toward his mouth. He was looking straight at her. He was in a rage. Good. "Thank-you. What is your name?"

"I am Jek, son of Jik and Tia."

Kyra's head snapped to attention. Her eyes bulged out. This warrior was full-grown! She kept forgetting that people age differently on Tryston than in other places. Still, to think that petite little Tia had a son this age...

Kyra scanned the room and found Tia lying down on a narrow cot not very far away from her. She was proudly thrusting her breasts in the face of a besotted young warrior, giggling as he grabbed her by the waist and suckled them. Another warrior was reclining beside her, stroking her clit and grinning. Jik, a huge man in his prime, was seated across the room glaring daggers at the bold younger men.

Kyra was still amazed that this went on. She was so lost in thought that she didn't even notice when Cam parted her *qi'ka,* exposing her nether lips to the view of every non-mated warrior on the women's side of the dining hall. She semi-registered the fact that Jek's fingers had twined in her pubic hair and were stroking her like a kitty cat.

Tia had explained that this part of ancient custom was done to work the mated warriors up into a frenzy. She boasted that she and Jik always had the best couplings when they took to their rooms after a consummation dinner. It was as if her warrior had something to prove, and of course, Tia was only too happy to oblige him.

The feel of Jek's fingers grazing her clit snapped Kyra back to the present. Realizing she was laying on Cam's lap totally divested of her *qi'ka,* her legs now spread wide for every non-mated warriors' viewing pleasure, she began to grow just a tad apprehensive. And alarmingly turned-on.

"Fire-berries," Jek whispered thickly, "'tis true as well."

"Fire-berries?" Kyra ruminated breathlessly. Clearing her throat, she forcefully brought her tone down to one that sounded slightly less aroused. "Fire-berries?" she inquired more calmly.

"Aye." Nestled between her splayed legs, he leaned over and made one long licking motion from the opening of her vagina to the tip of her clit. He swirled his tongue around before responding further. She sucked in her breath. "Dak claimed your pelt was the color of fire-berries. 'Tis true, I see."

"Oh." To her dismay, Kyra realized she was having a rather difficult time keeping a thought in her head. Jek was talented, she'd give him that.

The next thing Kyra knew, she was surrounded on all sides by towering, aroused giants, Dak included. Even as Cam suckled her right nipple and groaned in need, a handsome warrior she hadn't yet been introduced to flicked his tongue across her left one, drawing the bud into his mouth.

Kyra wanted to scream. She wanted to tell these men she wasn't like this, that she didn't enjoy this. But she couldn't. It would have been a lie.

It was hedonistically erotic.

Lying naked and spread wide as a clan of lusty, handsome men fondled her intimately was more of a turn-on than she could say. It was a thousand times better than the bathing chamber incident.

"Let me be the chosen one, Your Majesty."

Kyra somehow managed to open her glazed over eyes long enough to peer into Jek's turned on, expectant face. "The chosen one?" she breathed out.

"Aye." Jek swirled his tongue around her clit, then suckled upon it as his fingers continued to delve into her fire-berry curls.

Kyra grasped the back of his head, running her fingers through his jet-black hair.

Jek looked up and grinned knowingly. "The non-mated warrior who gives you your woman's joy before the High King breaches you." His mouth dove between her thighs and suckled her thoroughly before coming back up for air. She moaned wantonly. "I have been known to bring as many as ten bound servants to their woman's joy in one moon-rising, my High Queen. My mother has heard the stories. She can vouch for my lusty escapades."

Good grief! Imagine asking a mother from earth to rate how well she thinks her son performs oral sex. This was just too much. And yet Kyra couldn't seem to ask Jek to stop laving at her pussy anymore than she could quit breathing. Her aroused body truly had a mind of its own.

Tia had mentioned that at the consummation ceremony, couples didn't take to their rooms until the warrior had been serviced by bound women and their *nee'kas* brought to their peak by non-mated warriors. The young, randy men looked forward to their part in the tradition, for it was the only time they were allowed to touch a mated woman. Did they come near her at any other time, the woman's Sacred Mate would strike him dead.

"Am I your chosen one?" Jek asked hoarsely.

Kyra gazed at him through lowered eyelashes. She could still see Cam and the warrior whose name she didn't know sucking her nipples like lollipops. The other warriors gathered around her-Dak included-were watching everything, not missing any nuance of the ceremony. Their eyes feasted on her body, devouring Kyra's glossy cunt lips as if they were the ones kneeling between her thighs.

The tantalizing scene of so many fully clothed and erect men gathered around one extremely aroused, naked woman was a heady one. Kyra felt more erotic and deliciously wanton than words could express. Giving it no more thought, she lowered the face of her friend's son between her legs, inviting him without words to bring her to climax.

Jek groaned, his face diving between her thighs. He licked, nibbled, and sucked at her clit like a favorite treat.

From somewhere in the back of her consciousness, Kyra heard Tia scream as her friend's orgasm ripped through her body. She registered the sounds of giggling, and the voice of a man who could only be Jik hoisting his Sacred Mate into his arms and telling her he'd show her what pleasure really was.

She heard these things, but paid them little attention. She was too caught up in what their son was doing between her legs.

Kyra's arms went limp as the feelings of ecstasy grew sharper, more intense. Moaning and shivering, she closed her eyes and simply felt.

Mouths, tongues, and teeth at either nipple. Lips, tongue and teeth sucking on her engorged clit. Another hand rubbing up and down her thigh. Tongues on her belly. Fingers stroking her nether curls. Whispered words of appreciation from the spectators.

It was overwhelming.

Screaming, Kyra's nipples jutted up thicker and harder into the appreciative mouths of the warriors sucking on them as she violently climaxed. Her labia turned a delicious rouge, puffing up to tell Jek without words that he had done well.

And then Kyra was being lifted into the arms of a fiercely aroused High King who had something to prove. She closed her eyes and snuggled into Zor's chest as he made his way toward the bedchamber.

"No warrior will make you scream like I will, *nee'ka*. No warrior."

Her eyes flew open. She suddenly wondered how good of an idea it had been to set off Zor's jealous instincts.

She swallowed roughly. Ari had been right. Kyra was glad she would be there for the joining.

Chapter 12

Zor had wanted to kill the young warriors who had dared to touch his *pani* bride. Between lust and temper, he was so worked up, it became necessary to take a few deep breaths.

His *nee'ka* lay sprawled out upon their raised bed, her arms thrown over her head and her legs wide open for the joining. Her gaze was captured, just as it had been when claiming her, making her unable to resist his will.

Not that it appeared as though she wanted to.

Zor quickly rid himself of his warrior's clothes, then joined Kyra upon the high bed. He situated himself on his knees between her legs, giving his Sacred Mate her first view of his erection.

Kyra gasped at the size of it. It was thick and long and she had no idea how he planned to get it all inside of her. And yet, she was still so primed for Zor's invasion that it was useless to deny wanting him.

Just then, the Chief Priestess's form crystallized next to the raised bed. Naked like she'd been at their bath, Ari sauntered up onto the raised bed and took her place next to Zor. "You've the need to calm down, sire, else you will do an injury to your *nee'ka*."

Zor closed his eyes and drew in a ragged breath. He could smell Kyra's arousal, see with his own eyes how puffed up and ready her engorged pussy was for his staff. It overwhelmed him in a way he was unfamiliar with, making him feel primal, more animal than man. He needed some control. "You have the right of it, Holy One," he shakily admitted. "'Twill hurt her do I rut on her like a *maki* beast."

Kyra sensed what the Chief Priestess was about to do before she did it. Turning Zor's body around to face her, Ari took his long, thick penis into her mouth and suckled him with the skill of a thousand-year-old woman well-accustomed to a warrior's lust.

Zor shut his eyes and groaned, the veins in his neck tightly corded. He grabbed at either side of the Chief Priestess's face, riding in and out of Ari's mouth ferociously. She matched his pace, giving him all that he needed.

Kyra was amazed to realize that instead of feeling jealous of Ari, she was getting turned on by watching the Chief Priestess perform on her husband. It was like witnessing some mystical, pagan rite where she was slated to be the virgin sacrifice. Somehow, Kyra instinctively knew that Ari would never touch Zor again once the joining took place. That only made the scene more erotic, knowing she could watch her fill, delight in pleasures she had only read about in books, never having to worry that they would carry on behind her back when the night was over.

Not that she should care.

But *God*-she did.

Zor released himself into the Chief Priestess's mouth moments later, a roar echoing in the glowing red crystal chamber.

Ari lapped at him until he was dry, then released his penis and made her way over to Kyra's highly aroused body. She smiled down at her as she placed a soft, silk pillow under Kyra's backside, hoisting her hips into the air and thrusting her labia out more prominently. Zor groaned.

Kyra smiled back at Ari, then turned her neck to face her husband. She couldn't believe it, but the man was as fiercely erect as ever.

"Are you sated enough to breach your bride with care or do you still feel out of control?" Ari crawled on hands and knees to join Zor back at the bottom of the bed before Kyra's spread legs.

Zor didn't answer her. His brow was dripping with perspiration as he made an obvious effort to rein in his need to conquer and claim.

Ari turned to Kyra and arched a golden brow, as if asking her permission to ease Zor. Kyra closed her eyes briefly, wondering what was happening to her. She moaned from the anticipation of watching it, feeling deliciously aroused and unrepentantly wanton. It was all the urging Ari needed.

Crawling around Zor on the massive bed and up to where Kyra lay, Ari fell onto her back next to the High Queen and opened her thighs beckoningly. "Come to me, sire. I give myself to you freely for the easing of your body."

With a growl, Zor lifted the Chief Priestess's hips up off of the bed and entered her cunt in one long thrust. Ari gasped, her back arching and her breasts thrusting upward. Oblivious to anything but satiation, Zor fell onto her body, sucking her nipples as he thrust fast and hard. Ari groaned, reaching her peak quickly.

Kyra couldn't get over how entrancing the scene was. She watched, totally spell-bound as she propped herself up on her elbow, liquid heat pooling in her belly. Zor's eyes were closed as he latched onto one of Ari's jutting pink nipples and sucked frenziedly, riding her hard the entire while. The muscles in his sleek, tanned back bulged brilliantly. The ones in his buttocks clenched in a series of contract, release, contract, release.

Ari peaked once, twice, three times more before Zor finally climaxed.

He never let go of the nipple.

And then Kyra knew why.

The process was starting all over again.

For the next twenty or more minutes, Kyra's arousal grew heavier and more urgent as she watched Zor thrust into the Chief Priestess's body over and over, again and again. His eyes never once opened as he drew from her nipple throughout all twenty of Ari's climaxes, spilling himself into her two more times before he felt in control enough to take his bride gently.

And then he stopped.

Thanking the Chief Priestess for her generosity of body, Zor murmured his readiness to proceed with the joining. Both of them took up their prior positions, Zor on his knees between Kyra's re-splayed thighs, Ari next to him.

Reaching down to adjust the pillow, Ari repositioned Kyra's aroused body, shifting her hips back up to their original position, thrusting her swollen labia out prominently.

Zor groaned. "By the goddess, I want you *nee'ka*."

The Chief Priestess ground the heel of one hand into Kyra's mons, causing her to moan. Dipping into her puffed up flesh, she was satisfied with the amount of dew that saturated her fingers when she drew them out. She smiled wryly. "'Tis time." Moving to Zor's side, the Chief Priestess took his large penis in one hand and massaged his buttocks with the other. "Enter her slowly, sire. Ease the way."

Kyra's nipples lengthened considerably in reaction to what she knew was about to happen. The event wasn't lost on Zor. Taking a deep breath, his nostrils flaring, he closed his eyes briefly to rein in his appetite.

"Do you require another suckling, sire?"

"Nay, Ari. I will manage this time." Zor smiled appreciatively, flicking the crest of the Chief Priestess's puffy areola. "Though I thank you."

This time Kyra was glad for it. She was ready to be more than a mere observer. She wanted to participate. Shifting her hips wantonly, she groaned. "Please Zor, take me now."

Growling low in his throat, Zor closed his eyes and ran his fingers through his jet black hair. Droplets of perspiration appeared on his forehead again, making his hair damp. Luckily the three braids at either temple kept the silky mass from falling into his line of vision. "You are prepared to join with me, *pani*?"

"Yes," she whispered thickly.

Zor allowed Ari to guide his shaft to the opening of his *nee'ka's* heat. The Chief Priestess continued to massage his buttocks with her other hand, producing a balmy effect on his otherwise raging need. "Then join with me you will," he gritted out.

Thrusting a quarter of the way into her, Zor stifled an oath at the exquisite feel. He needed to spill his life-force the soonest lest he rut on Kyra like a wild animal in its heat.

Kyra gasped, arching her hips upward for her Sacred Mate's invasion.

Zor grabbed her waist. "Do not, my love." His breathing was labored and sporadic. He could feel his control slipping. "Lie still until my shaft is fully embedded within you."

Sensing his tentative hold on control, Kyra stilled completely. He was huge-just huge. He truly would hurt her if he didn't keep himself in check.

Kyra nodded her agreement, though her hold was quickly becoming just as elusive. "Please hurry," she murmured.

Zor moaned as he pushed his cock further into her. The sticky velvet channel was nigh unto killing him. Never had he thought to need a woman's body like this. He had coupled with more women than he could count, enchanted slaves and bound servants alike, yet never had his control been so sorely tried.

The veins in Zor's neck corded tightly as he prayed to the goddess for control. Thrusting again, he embedded himself until the only part of him visible was what Ari had her hand curled around at the thick base as best she could manage.

Kyra whimpered. Eyes wide, she searched Zor's face. Clearly, she was beginning to feel a virgin's fright. "There is more?" she whispered.

"I am almost completely within your channel, my hearts."

"She is scared." Ari waved a hand toward Zor. "Go no further in just yet." Releasing his staff, the Chief Priestess turned her attention fully on Kyra. "'Twill be more bliss than you can imagine, my High Queen. Let me help prepare you."

Kyra gazed at her quizzically, then looked down to where she and Zor were almost fully joined. Ari used both hands to splay wide the lips of Kyra's puffed up labia. When the Chief Priestess' tongue first touched her clit, Kyra's head fell back upon the pillows as she began to moan in ecstasy.

Zor rocked back and forth within her vagina, going no further than he was already lodged. Ari's tongue swirled and danced, licked and suckled, creating a magic that soon had Kyra's pussy flooding with moisture.

But the Chief Priestess didn't stop. She kept up the pace, nibbling at Kyra's engorged clit, then interchanging it with sucks. Kyra realized that Ari didn't mean to stop until she peaked.

Zor continued to rock back and forth in her tight channel, suppressing the urge to spill his life-force. "You are doing beautifully, Ari." He reached around her backside and began to rub the Chief Priestess' slick folds. "My *nee'ka* will peak the soonest." He grunted as he relentlessly pummeled into Kyra. "Had I known what a valuable service you would be performing in this bed, I would have rewarded you with more cock before the joining."

Ari didn't look up from her work to comment, but Kyra knew she was aroused by Zor's words. She could feel the Chief Priestess's nipples hardening against her belly. She could see Ari's buttocks lifting in invitation to Zor's questing fingers, like a cat wanting a petting from its master.

Zor slipped three fingers inside of the Chief Priestess, encouraging her to ride his hand as he continued to ram into Kyra. "Take your woman's pleasure, Ari. You have earned it well." He rubbed the pad of a finger against her swollen clit as his three embedded fingers continued to delve deeper.

Ari accepted the summons, riding up and down in bliss, moaning against Kyra's clit, vibrating it.

"Oh god," Kyra cried out, clutching the *vesha* hides surrounding her. "Oh god."

"Do it, *nee'ka,*" Zor commanded. "Find your pleasure."

Kyra burst.

Ari exploded.

Zor buried himself in Kyra to the hilt. He removed his sticky fingers from Ari's pussy and licked them clean. Swatting the Chief Priestess playfully on the rump, he grinned when she let out a yelp and flopped over onto her backside. "You have done well this moon-rising." He ran a palm over her breast and squeezed a nipple. "I can see to the remainder on my own."

With an incline of her head, the form of the Chief Priestess shimmered and dissolved.

Zor grunted in satisfaction, turning all of his attention toward his *nee'ka.* Fully impaled, she looked more beautiful than he could say. Zor placed his hands on either side of her head and loomed over her sated body. He made no motion to move within her, just remained still, watching her emotions play out.

Kyra was thoroughly sated, smiling dreamily, her arms thrown over her head, her nipples jutting out devilishly. Zor grinned at the sight. "Are you ready for real pleasure, *pani*?"

Kyra's eyelids fluttered open. Zor kissed them both, then smiled down at her. "You mean there's more?"

He grinned. "For a certainty."

Kyra wrapped her legs around her husband's waist, inviting him to show her what he had in mind. "Then by all means, don't let me stop you," she whispered.

Groaning, Zor withdrew and plunged in her pussy to the hilt once more. Kyra arched her back and gasped, her legs locked tightly around her husband's waist. Peaking instantaneously, Kyra moaned as he delivered a never-ending series of long, thick strokes. "My god," she whimpered, "Zor, oh my god!"

His jaw clenched, Zor kept up his relentless pace. "By the goddess," he ground out, the veins in his neck and arms prominent, "your wee cunt welcomes me like none other's."

Kyra screamed as she peaked again. Her legs still locked around Zor's waist, she pounded her hips back at him, eagerly anticipating his thrusts. "Do I feel better than your servants?" she asked wickedly.

"A thousand times better," Zor growled.

"Better than Ari?"

"Aye," he snarled as he ground deeper into her pussy.

"Oh really?" Kyra prodded sinfully.

Zor managed to forge into her cunt even further. Closing his eyes against the exquisite pleasure-pain, he hammered into Kyra's channel until it once again flooded his cock with moisture. "Ari's passage is a tight and tempting repast, but yours, my love, was created by the goddess to service me." He thrust harder. "Your channel," he ground out, "is a High King's feast."

Kyra shattered around him, crying out in pleasure. "Give me everything," she begged him, "hold back nothing from me."

"Your pleasure is mine, *nee'ka*."

His nostrils flaring, his muscles tightly corded, Zor grabbed Kyra's hips and pounded into her body with hard strokes. Over and over. Again and again. "I join you to me by the holy law," he bit out, pummeling her cunt mercilessly. "Kyra Q'ana Tal." Throwing his head back, he roared like a wild beast as his climax came upon him and his life-force spurted into her womb.

The stones in Kyra's bridal necklace pulsated rapidly. She didn't have time to make sense of that event before a ceaseless peak overpowered her, maddening in its intensity. The stones blinked in tune with the pulsings of her climax, in tune with the throbbing of Zor's peak. Kyra screamed, moaning in pleasure-pain from so all-consuming a release. It seemed to go on and on, unrelenting in its ferocity.

Zor was roaring-primal, territorial. Like an animal. The climax was as shattering to him as it was to Kyra.

When it was over, her eyelids fluttered open tentatively. She gazed up at Zor like a woman well and truly enamored with her husband. He peered down into her eyes like a man feeling the same intense emotions, a man who knew he would never hold the desire to release himself in any other channel save Kyra's.

Zor pulled his semi-flaccid shaft out of his *nee'ka's* channel. Exhausted, he fell down beside her on the bed, then pulled Kyra on top of his chest and bade her to rest her body there.

Neither of them was anywhere near ready to divulge to the other just how strongly their emotions had meshed in the joining. The new sensations were overwhelming to them both.

Saying nothing, the High King and High Queen of Tryston fell asleep in each other's embrace.

Chapter 13

Kyra woke up an hour later still stretched out on Zor's chest. She sat up on her elbows, studying his face. Sound asleep, he looked so innocent. Not at all like a man who had taken his pleasures with two slaves, a priestess, and a bride all within two hours time.

Grinning, she shook her head. It still amazed her that she, Kyra the sedate tax accountant, had been brought to climax so many times and in so many ways in the past few days. She felt like a new woman. A provocatively wanton woman.

Deciding to explore the bedchamber of the royal apartments while Zor slept, Kyra drew herself up off of him and dropped to the floor. The cool red crystal felt wonderful against the soles of her feet.

Looking around, the first thing she noticed was that the bedchamber was gigantic. It was bigger than the whole of the house she had lived in on earth. Off to one side was a private bathing chamber. Kyra could easily make out the silvery waters lapping hypnotically against the walls of the red crystal pool. They looked inviting. She knew she would be bathing come morning.

Next to the pool were lounging cots made out of some sort of dark *vesha* hide. Why they were there when the bed was just across the room, she had no idea.

On the far side of the chamber a huge storage facility was carved out of the red crystal, housing Kyra's *qi'kas* and Zor's warrior attire. There were also chests of precious jewels and raw materials inside of it.

In another corner of the chamber, what looked to be a mini-kitchen was carved out of the red crystal structure. Walking over to examine it, it turned out to be a refrigeration unit storing bottles of vintage matpow. The sheer look of the ornately jeweled bottles indicated their worth-expensive.

The best part of the chamber, however, was without a doubt the massive harem-esque bed she had been taken on an hour past, the very one Zor was sleeping contentedly upon now. It was raised a great length off of the floor, no doubt to compensate for a warrior's superior height. Black, soft as sin *vesha* hides were used to sleep on and to snuggle up with. Pillows fashioned of a material softer than silk and crafted from every hue on Tryston were scattered about. Large, sparkling jewels were embedded within the red crystal foundation. It was a magnificent sight.

Almost as magnificent as the barbarian sprawled negligently within in. Grinning, Kyra was about to join Zor, waking him up in a most pleasant way, when a beam of shimmering lavender light caught her eye. Mesmerized, she slowly turned on her heel and walked toward a set of doors that opened up onto a balcony.

Stepping through the doors, Kyra caught her breath as she made her way out onto a balcony carved of black crystal. The light was coming from one of Tryston's moons. A lavender moon. It was more beautiful than-

"Who is next?"

Kyra's gaze trailed from where the moon loomed in the sky down to the floor below where a warrior was engaged in lusty play with five naked servants. Squinting her eyes a bit, she realized the lazily reclining warrior was none other than Jek, the warrior who had orally brought her to climax at the consummation feast. Tia and Jik's heir.

"I'm next!" One of the busty servants giggled shamelessly as she impaled herself on Jek's cock and groaned. Kyra felt as though she shouldn't be watching, but couldn't seem to stop herself. It was as if an entire new world of pleasure and desire had been opened up to her this past day and she wanted to learn and to savor all of it.

"I can take on more than just one," Jek boasted. "What other wench wishes for their pleasure?"

A giggling blonde with mammoth breasts impaled herself on the fingers of Jek's left hand. A brunette with equally impressive endowments embedded his other hand within her. A third servant sat on his face, her hips writhing as Jek apparently suckled her clit and hole. The original servant was still riding up and down on his shaft, moaning in pleasure.

Yep, the kid had talent.

Apparently in spades. The fifth one laughed as she managed to find a way to pleasure herself on one of Jek's feet. Calling an evident friend over to join in on the fun, a sixth bound servant ran from the shadows, her breasts bobbing up and down, and found her ecstasy on Jek's other foot.

The erotic scene was making Kyra wet.

Women were attached to every protrusion Jek could claim, writhing and moaning, climaxing over and over again.

Kyra gasped as her body was picked up and she was impaled from behind on a stiff erection. Moaning with arousal, she flung her head back against Zor's chest.

Zor grabbed Kyra's hips, effortlessly gliding her cunt up and down on his staff. "Open your eyes, my wee love," he whispered hoarsely. "Open your eyes and watch the servants reach their woman's joy."

Kyra gasped. Zor was choosing to move her up and down his erection slowly, torturously. Opening her eyes, she peered down at the women below, watching through glazed over eyes as they moaned and writhed, impaling themselves wantonly on every part of Jek's body. Between the sight of such hedonistic pleasures, the slow coupling Zor was giving her, and the tugging one of his hands was giving to her nipples, Kyra felt trapped in a haze of seductive need.

"You are so tight and hot, *pani*." Zor groaned softly as Kyra continued to milk his cock with her sticky heat. "You love to watch, don't you?" At her moan, he tweaked the swollen buds of her breasts. "Aye, I know it. You enjoyed it when I coupled with Ari, did you not?"

"Y-Yes," she admitted breathlessly, licking her lips. "I loved every wicked moment of it."

Zor groaned, rotating his hips in such a way that Kyra gasped. "You are so passionate, *nee'ka*." He picked up the pace of her impaling a scarce fraction, yet it was enough to cause her to moan again. "I am almost sorry that I can no longer desire to spill my life-force in any other channel but yours. Just to see your arousal..."

The scene below was building to a crescendo. Kyra cried out in reaction.

"Do you remember the servant of ample charms who pillowed my head with her breasts at the consummation feast?"

"Yes."

Zor's hips rotated again. Kyra moaned.

"She was a favored of mine before we mated. I fucked her every night."

"Oh." The word came out breathlessly, aroused. The image of Zor coupling with another woman no longer bothered her the way it had before Ari, at least not in fantasy. Now it turned her on.

"And more importantly, there was Muta, the blue *Kefa*." Zor grunted as he squeezed Kyra's nipples and summoned the pace of their joining to pick up. "My pet name for her was the suckler." He rotated his hips. "She brought me to climax five to six times every moon-rising without fail." At Kyra's moan, he continued relentlessly. "Many a moon-rising did I summon them both to my chambers, hour after hour of fucking."

"Oh god."

Zor brought the pace of the mating to a frenzy, inducing Kyra to peak on the balcony. She cried out.

The lusty group below was still going at it, though the servants had now switched positions, each of them taking their turn on Jek's erection.

"Would you like one of my playthings to join us at bath some morn, *nee'ka*?" Zor whispered seductive enticements into the whorl of Kyra's ear as he continued to pound into her from behind. "Would you like to watch Muta suckle my staff whilst Myn the servant attends to my man sac?"

Kyra climaxed violently, an act that almost caused Zor's erection to be milked of its seed. "Would you like to watch them bring me to my man's pleasure, my hearts?"

"Y-Yes," Kyra admitted on the rush of a third orgasm. "Yes. Oh god. Oh yes."

Zor shifted his hips and pummeled her cunt mercilessly as he stumbled with her from the balcony and back to their bed. Without removing himself from her snug channel, he splayed Kyra on all fours, still standing to his full height as he thrust into her mercilessly from behind. "Do you wish for me to summon them on the morrow, *nee'ka*? Do you desire to watch your Sacred Mate suckle plump blue nipples and taste the pink charms between Myn's thighs?"

Kyra met his thrusts, climaxing for the fourth time. "Zor."

"Tell me," he gritted out, the never-ending pounding driving her to her fifth orgasm. "Name your desires, wee one."

"Yes," she groaned, all but sobbing from the overwhelming pleasure. "I want them at our bath. I want to watch them suckle you and you them."

Every muscle in Zor's body grew taut. The images in his mind were vivid. The feel of Kyra's sixth climax was gut-wrenchingly intoxicating. The pull of her sticky pussy was enchanting. "Then on the morrow, 'tis what you shall get." Groaning, he rode Kyra hard.

Rotating his hips, Zor slammed into her a few more times before giving himself up to the pleasure-pain and spurting his life-force into her womb. The stones in the bridal necklace pulsed. His climax intensified, making him roar.

Kyra screamed, bucking beneath her husband as wave after wave after wave of intense, painful pleasure bore down on her. She shuddered and pulsed as orgasm after orgasm ripped through her belly.

Replete, Kyra moaned as she fell face first onto the bed. Breathing deeply, she closed her eyes.

Zor spanked her playfully on the rear. "Do you mean to forsake your duties, wench?"

Kyra's eyes stayed shut as a lazy smile stole over her features. "What do you mean?"

Zor didn't answer her. He showed her instead. Pulling Kyra back up on all fours, he entered her again from behind and thrust wickedly.

Kyra groaned. She decided not to complain.

* * * * *

Kyra awoke the next morning to the sounds of Tia's laughter.

"I see you pleasured her thoroughly, cousin," an amused male voice proclaimed, "her cunt is swollen and she sleeps the rest of the dead."

Zor chuckled. Kyra felt his fingertips brush possessively over her vaginal lips. "Aye. I coupled with her five more times after the Chief Priestess departed. The High Queen is no doubt replete," he boasted.

Laughter sounded throughout the bedchamber. "Are you certain we should awaken her for bath?" Tia asked, lowering her tone. "She looks exhausted."

Kyra didn't give Zor time to answer that. Her eyelids fluttered open, then squinted shut a fraction as she tried to adjust her vision to the new day's light. "Good morn, sleepy one," Zor mused.

Kyra smiled gently up to him. Taking in a deep breath, she took note of her surroundings. She was still in her bed with Zor, both of them naked, but Jik and Tia were here for reasons she couldn't understand.

Kyra was sprawled out on the *vesha* hides with no covering, one arm thrown over her head and one leg bent at the knee, giving a thorough view of her puffed up vagina to her friend and Zor's cousin. Alarmed, but hoping to come off as nonchalant, she smiled up at Jik and Tia, making a move to close her legs from their line of vision.

Apparently oblivious to the awkwardness she was feeling, Zor continued to stroke her pussy lips in front of them even after she attempted to close her legs. Her thighs remained splayed. "Hi. What are you two doing here?"

Jik smiled warmly down to Kyra, his eyes flicking appreciatively over her body, over her cunt. "Zor has invited us to bath, my High Queen. I hope that is to your liking?"

Kyra smiled in return, studying his handsome face. "Of course. And please call me Kyra."

Jik nodded.

"'Tis an honor you give us," Tia exclaimed brightly, grinning down to Kyra. "Thank-you for inviting us to be the first mated couple to bathe with you and the High King."

"You're very welcome." Kyra wasn't certain how she'd honored them, but she mentally shrugged, deciding to go along with it.

Zor cleared his throat. "You and your *nee'ka* start without us. We will join you the soonest, cousin."

Jik inclined his head, took Tia by the arm, and led her toward the other side of the massive bedchamber.

Once they were out of earshot, Zor turned back to Kyra, noting at once that she was studying him with a questioning expression on her face. "Aye?" he asked rather gruffly, afraid he knew what she was thinking.

"I thought..." Kyra bit her lip, indecisive over whether or not to pursue the issue or question her good fortune.

"Aye?"

"I thought you were inviting Muta and Myn to bathe with us this morning."

Zor sighed. To Kyra's bewilderment, his face was actually flushed with what on most people would be called embarrassment. "*Nee'ka...*" He sighed again, then shook his head.

Kyra sat straight up. She rubbed her hand soothingly across his back. "What is it?" she whispered.

"Kyra," he began again, "Trystonni warriors are not like men from your earth, I would imagine." At her raised eyebrow, he took a deep breath and plowed onward. "Once joined, we haven't the desire to seek out the charms of other females." He slashed his hand through the air. "I admit that between the excitement of the consummation feast, the frenzy of the joining, and so on, that I became o'er excited mayhap, but I..." He sighed, groaning comically.

Kyra bit her lip to keep from laughing outright. Placing a kiss on Zor's shoulder, she let him off the hook. "Actually, I'm glad you feel this way."

His head shot up. "You are?"

She nodded. "I think I was caught up in the fantasy of it all, too." Kyra smoothed his hair back from off of his shoulders. "But now that I'm awake, those fantasies you whispered to me last night don't sound terribly exciting. They sound heartbreaking."

Zor grinned, completely relieved. "So you don't want to watch me suckle another woman?"

"No!" Kyra scowled, slapping him playfully on the back. He laughed. "In fact, I want Muta and Myn nowhere near you ever again."

"For a certainty?"

"I'm being serious, Zor." Kyra bit her lip. "I don't want them around," she admitted in a small voice.

Zor nodded, pleased by her possessiveness. 'Twas the way it was supposed to be between true mates. "'Tis done." He leaned down and kissed her sweetly on the lips. "Besides," he mused, "Tryston is a lusty place. There will be many an opportunity for you to indulge in your love of watching others without the other being me."

Kyra giggled. "You make me sound like a pervert."

Zor placed a hand over his hearts in mock hurt. "Never, my love." Grinning, he kissed her again. "So we are agreed. Neither of us, with the exception of the gentling and whilst attending consummation feasts-which I'm thankful are a rarity now that I'm mated-will touch another. And never, under any circumstances, would we join with another. Aye?"

"Yes," Kyra eagerly agreed, very much relieved. She thought to ask him more about what this gentling business was, for Tia had mentioned it as well, but found herself distracted by his grin. She jumped up and kissed him soundly on the lips. "But what about at baths? I thought the *Kefas*..."

"That cannot be helped," Zor interrupted, shaking his head. "You know that, *pani*. But just because *Kefas* can do naught else but to bring pleasure to the one they bathe, 'tis not of necessity to touch them back."

"And you will not use Muta?"

"Aye, 'tis a vow between Sacred Mates. I will not use Muta." Zor waved a hand dismissively. "I will give her to one of my brothers, or as a gift to a favored king or lord mayhap."

After a long moment, Kyra nodded her acceptance of their pact. "All right. I can accept that."

Zor rubbed her thigh, appreciative of their understanding. "Good. Now let us have bath with our friends, then enjoy a morning repast."

"I am a bit hungry."

Zor cradled Kyra in his arms, standing up to walk her to the bathing pool. "Afterwards, I thought to show you more of Sand City."

Kyra squealed excitedly, causing Zor to laugh. "Can we take a floating carriage?"

"Your pleasure is mine, *nee'ka*."

Chapter 14

Kyra had to admit that bathing with others really did help strengthen the bond you felt with them. Of course, that was probably because it was hard to feel shy in front of people you watched climax, or people that watched you climax. She still couldn't believe she'd been so uninhibited during their bath.

When the *Kefas* had sought to massage between her thighs, Kyra had opened her legs wide and enjoyed it, not caring that Jik and Tia were there, or that Jik was hard with arousal from watching her. Indeed, she and Zor had enjoyed witnessing the *Kefas* do the same to Tia. Zor had placed Kyra's hand over his erection and bade her to masturbate him while Tia thrashed about and moaned, peaking violently.

And then Kyra had discovered what the soft reclining cots next to the bathing pool were for. Neither of the warriors could wait to take their Sacred Mates to a bed. Instead, they had taken their women well and thoroughly, pleasuring them at poolside.

Afterwards, the foursome had breakfasted together in the bedchamber on pelts of *vesha* hides. Still naked, they had laughed and eaten and had engaged in a great conversation. Nothing had embarrassed Kyra. Nothing had shocked her. Not even Zor's continual lazy strokes of possession between her thighs.

Kyra shook her head and grinned. She still couldn't get over how drastically her life had altered.

Standing in front of a holographic mirror, she donned the gold *qi'ka* Zor had asked her to wear, stating it was time for her to interchange the colors of what she wore daily. At official functions, Kyra would continue to don black, but every other day she would wear a *qi'ka* of varying color out of respect for Tryston's many clans. Today was for gold.

The gold *qi'ka* was much more sheer than the ones she'd been sporting up until this point. There would be no doubt for anyone just how large her areolas were or what color the pelt of hair between her legs was. Kyra well and truly may as well have been naked.

The bridal necklace was fully empathic to Zor now, conveying and conducting his wishes and desires to Kyra at every turn. She thought it a little bold, since he wasn't wearing anything that conveyed her wishes to him, but since they'd already been down that road and she had lost the fight, she decided not to give it any more thought.

She took one last glance at herself in the holographic mirror, then turned on her heel and left the bedchamber. The pace she set was a brisk one. She was giddy with excitement over the prospect of seeing more of Sand City.

Her expensive jewel-encrusted sandals clicking on the black crystal floor, Kyra waved enthusiastically to every guard she encountered en route from the royal bedchamber to the great hall. "Good afternoon!"

"Peace and prosperity, my High Queen," a warrior called out. Kyra smiled brightly, then turned to him with a quizzical look on her face. She looked him up and down, realizing there was something familiar about the golden-haired, glowing green-eyed man. "Don't I know you?"

"Aye," the handsome warrior confirmed with a grin. "You sat upon my lap whilst I attended to one of your woman's berries at the consummation feast."

Kyra's cheeks tinted scarlet. "Oh," she mumbled, suddenly remembering everything. His name had been Cam. And he possessed a talented tongue. "Cam, isn't it?"

He bowed. "At your service, Excellent One."

Kyra shook her head gently, bemused. As long as she lived, she doubted she'd ever get used to being called a High Queen, an Empress, or anything else she was referred to as around here. "Wonderful. Can you answer a question for me, Cam?"

His eyes flicked over her body. "For a certainty."

"Am I going crazy or wasn't this floor red yesterday?"

Cam squinted as if not understanding, then laughed when reality dawned. "You must have entered your apartments from the south door yesterday, which is led up to by the red crystal. This is the north side, Your Majesty, which is paved of the night."

"I see." Kyra bit her lip.

"If you would like," Cam offered cordially, "I could escort you to His Majesty whilst I better explain the lay-out of the palace to you."

"That would be wonderful!" Kyra enthused. "I'm supposed to meet him in some room where people can refresh themselves with matpow while waiting for their conveyance to be brought around. Do you know this place?"

Cam held out his arm, offering it to her. "For a certainty." As they began strolling down the long corridor, he complimented her on her choice of *qi'ka*. "'Tis beautiful. And it displays your charms much better than yesterday's. 'Tis for a certainty His Majesty will enjoy showing off his *nee'ka* this day, knowing all will see the rare fire-berry pelt that belongs to him."

"Thank-you," Kyra mumbled, her face coloring again.

"You are welcome."

"So," she asked, smoothly changing the topic, "which one is the matpow room?"

"That would be the chamber of gold crystal."

Kyra shook her head. "I don't know how you keep all of them straight."

"'Tis more simple than it seems mayhap." Cam gestured toward the huge great hall as they entered it. Kyra acknowledged the warriors and servants they passed en route with a smile and nod. "This is the heart of the palace and therefore the biggest chamber within it. It is called the great hall, or dining hall, and as you can see, it is fashioned of the same black crystal from which the outside of the palace and the north corridor are made."

"Why black?"

"'Tis the emblem of the Q'an Tal, black." Cam shrugged dismissively. "Mayhap the great hall was kept black like the palace walls to remind visitors of who it is that rules here, since this is where they will spend the majority of their official time."

"That makes sense I suppose." Kyra squeezed the heavy muscle in Cam's arm. "So that would mean that the north corridor is fashioned from black crystal because it leads to our apartments, correct?"

"Aye."

"Then why is the south floor red? Why is my bedchamber red?"

Cam chuckled. "Not much escapes your notice, does it?" At Kyra's chagrined look, he patted her hand and continued. "First of all, private chambers, even royal ones, are built to suit personal tastes, not to serve as emblems."

"So you're saying my bedroom is red simply because it's Zor's favorite color?"

"Aye." Cam caught her gaze and winked. "He's always had a taste for fire-berries."

Kyra shook her head and grinned. The warrior reminded her of Dak-brazen as all hell, but too affable to get mad at. "Back to the original question: why is the south floor red?"

"Because it doesn't officially lead to your apartments, so 'tis not officially of Q'an Tal." At Kyra's confused look, Cam hastened to explain, "The door you used yesterday, the one on the south side, is actually a secret door that very few know of. If the High King has not yet mentioned it, I'm certain he will before any political guests come calling, that you are not permitted to pass through that door when any but family are present."

"Interesting," Kyra mused. She waved to a friendly topless servant named Leha who had brought up her breakfast this morning. Leha smiled back and waved. "So what else is housed on the south side, other than the secret door?" she asked as they continued their promenade.

"Mostly guest chambers of high ranking lords, and also a few theaters."

"Theaters?"

"Aye. Many performers trek to Sand City, hoping to entertain the High King."

Kyra squeezed Cam's arm as they continued walking. "How exciting. What kind of performers?"

"All kinds, I suppose, though most are those gifted in the erotic arts."

"Erotic arts?" Kyra jaw dropped open. She shook her head disbelievingly. "What do you mean by that?"

Cam grinned down at her, then flicked his wrist to summon open a set of heavy double doors. "Women who are well-versed in the bed sport, for a certainty. I remember a performer last year who was able to bring ten warriors to their pleasure at the same time."

"Ten?"

"Aye."

"Wow. Talented woman."

Cam concurred with a nod to his head. "She will be entertaining here again in three moon-risings, I believe." He scowled, then mumbled something about unfair practices.

Kyra raised a fire-berry brow. "Unfair? What do you mean?"

"Nothing, Your Majesty." Cam's face flushed red, indicating he had revealed more than he had meant to.

Kyra halted, stopping in her tracks. She turned around to face him. "Tell me what you mean."

Cam sighed, then shrugged, figuring it unwise to refuse what sounded like a direct order from the High Queen. "'Tis just that when the performers ask for volunteers in the audience, the older, high-ranking warriors always win out."

"I don't understand." Kyra fluttered her hand between them. "Do you wrestle for the honors of coupling with the performers or something?"

"I would that I could!" Cam laughed. He shook his head and grinned. "Nay, the younger in rank never get such an opportunity to best them, for if a warrior of higher standing chooses to volunteer, there is naught we can do but accept."

"In other words, the young warriors get no couplings and the older warriors get them all?"

"Precisely." Cam sighed, clearly agitated. "Older warriors have everything. All of them have at least one *Kefa* assigned to their apartment, and usually several. Younger warriors who come to Sand City to train under the High King and Emperor get none, unless of course, they come from wealthy stock and were gifted with a few slaves by their parents to bring with them."

"Interesting."

"Aye. The only bed sport younger warriors get is when we can entice a bound servant to let us sample of her charms." Cam flushed sheepishly. "I have said too much, Your Majesty." He motioned toward a door. "Come. This door leads to the east wing, which is where the golden chamber is located."

Kyra tapped her chin as she studied a clearly frustrated Cam. The image of a certain busty, gorgeous, sparkling blue enchanted woman with the nickname of the suckler flitted through her mind. She smiled slowly. "We can speak more of the other later. For now, you're right, we should go."

Kyra took Cam's arm, feeling vastly relieved now that she knew what to do with Muta. And if Zor agreed with her wishes, Cam would be feeling much the same way very soon.

* * * * *

The open-topped conveyance they took for the tour of Sand City wasn't Kyra's personal one, but was the official floating conveyance of the High King. Fashioned of black crystal and embedded with rare jewels, it was a grand display of decadence.

"I was afraid my cousin Jik was going to want to tour with us," Zor mused as he cradled Kyra in his lap and nibbled at her neck. "For a certainty, am I glad to have you to myself for a spell."

"Mmmm." Kyra closed her eyes and enjoyed the feel of her husband's lips and teeth grazing at the sensitive spots on her skin. "Me too."

"Speaking of alone," Zor chastised as he flicked his wrist to summon the *qi'ka* from Kyra's body, "did I not tell you to be naked always whilst it is but you and I?" He threw her discarded *qi'ka* into the empty backseat, then resumed his nibbling.

Kyra sucked in her breath, her nipples hardening. "What if we meet up with other people after we get past that palace perimeter coming up?" she asked breathlessly. "They might see me naked."

"So?"

Her head shot up. "So?"

"Feeling shy of a sudden, my hearts?" Zor grinned mischievously, kneading Kyra's *sekta* pearl buttocks as he studied her face. "After peaking with the Chief Priestess in yon bathing chamber, then again at the joining? After peaking with warriors at the consummation feast-which we won't speak of. After peaking for Jik and Tia's pleasure? After-"

"Okay! Okay!" Kyra slapped a palm over his mouth. He licked it and grinned behind her hand. "But seriously, what will others think if they come upon us while I'm naked?"

"They will think you a loyal and respectful *nee'ka.*"

Kyra frowned. That sounded too much like submissive for her liking.

Zor grumbled something about primitive first dimensions, able to read her emotions much more clearly now that they had joined. "It doesn't matter what things were like in your former home. Here, women seek to please their Sacred Mates."

Kyra snorted at that. She crossed her arms under her breasts and scowled stubbornly.

"Oh?" Zor lifted a regal black brow as he reached for one of Kyra's nipples and rolled it around between thumb and forefinger. "And pleasing me has been so bad?"

"N-No." Kyra sucked in her breath. "Not at all."

Zor lowered his voice as the open-topped conveyance made its way out of the enchanted palace perimeter. "Then why would you not wish to please me?"

"I-oh my." His other hand was now busy stroking between her legs. "I do wish to please you," she admitted on a gasp.

"Good girl." Zor turned Kyra around so that her back was against his chest. Opening his knees to spread her legs wide, he freed his erect shaft and impaled her on it. She cried out, her slick folds wrapping around him, accepting him fully inside of her. Zor resumed his intimate stroking, one hand making lazy circles around her clit while the other played with her nipples, and settled in for a lengthy tour of Sand City.

Between climaxes, Kyra managed to see a lot and to ask many questions. She was especially impressed with the enchanted dune Zor had said the priestesses and their male slaves resided in. "How many men does Ari own personally?"

"At last count well over four hundred."

Kyra chuckled. "Go Ari go."

When the conveyance steered back to return to the palace three hours later, Kyra was sorry to see the tour end. She had had a marvelous time, lying in Zor's arms, making slow love with him while they tooled around. She knew every day wouldn't be like this one. He had gently informed her that although he had absented himself from his duties and would continue to do so for a few more days out of respect for her and their new marriage, he would have to personally see to the training of his warriors very soon.

Kyra had nodded, telling him that she understood.

After one of Zor's warriors lifted Kyra up by the waist and deposited her onto the crystal floor of the conveyance launching pad, Zor summoned the *qi'ka* back onto her body. Taking his *nee'ka's* hand, he led her into the palace proper.

Chapter 15

Three days later, while Zor was busy outside training his men, Kyra was ambling around the palace depressed, lost in her thoughts, wondering what Geris was doing this very moment, asking herself if her little sister Kara was still alive. Not having Zor hovering around her forty-five hours a Trystonni day was giving Kyra way too much time to ponder all that she'd lost.

A few minutes later, Kyra happened upon Dak in the great hall. The first thing she noticed about her giant fair-haired brother-in-law was how out of sorts he looked today, not at all his typically cheerful self. Figuring misery loves miserable company, she strolled up to his side and greeted him. "Good morning, Dak."

Dak glanced up from his study of the matpow in his goblet and flicked his eyes up and down the length of Kyra's body. She blushed, knowing that the silver *qi'ka* she was wearing today was as translucent as saran wrap. "Good morn, sister. You are looking exceptionally lovely today."

"Thank-you." Kyra let out a telling sigh. "I wish I was feeling exceptionally lovely today."

"Depressed spirits?"

"Yes."

Dak snorted, gesturing for her to be seated next to him. "Then you have come to the right place." Summoning an empty goblet from the raised table beside them, he filled it with matpow and placed it before Kyra. "Now, tell me your troubles and I will tell you mine."

Kyra smiled. "Sort of like, 'show me yours and I'll show you mine'?"

Dak wiggled his eyebrows. "I have already seen your charms on display, beautiful Kyra, but would oblige you, of course, should you wish to show me again."

"Oh stop it!" She laughed, punching Dak in the arm. He pretended to feel it. Kyra picked up her goblet and saluted him. "To you, for making me smile."

Dak inclined his head, then searched her eyes. "What troubles you, sister?"

Kyra shrugged, sipping leisurely at the goblet filled with glowing turquoise matpow. "I miss my home." She shook her head, frowning. "No, that's not true exactly. I miss certain people from my home, but mostly my sister and best friend."

"Do you want me to go fetch them for you?"

Kyra's eyes brightened. "You could do-"

"Of course, they could never return once brought here."

Her eyes dimmed, shoulders slumping. "I wouldn't take away their choice as Zor took away mine."

Dak scratched his chin thoughtfully. "Do you carry anger toward Zor for claiming you?"

She considered the question. "Odd, but no, not since we joined." She took another swallow of drink, then set the goblet down on the table beside them. "It's strange, but from the first moment I laid eyes on him, even though I was utterly terrified, a part of me always recognized that I was a part of him, that he needed me and I needed him." She ran a hand through her hair. "Strange, hm?"

Dak grinned, shaking his head. "First dimension primitive notions of mating must not be very mentally progressed. What you have just described is the same as any *nee'ka* will tell you she felt upon first laying eyes on her Sacred Mate."

"Like..."

"Two halves of one whole."

Kyra nodded slowly. "Yes, two halves of one whole. I feel that way." Shaking her head, she stood up. She wasn't ready to deal with the implications of that just yet. "Will you stroll the gardens with me while we talk?"

"For a certainty." Rising, Dak took her arm and led Kyra through the great hall. "You should not be in low spirits for leaving that dreary planet, sister. The standard of living here is much superior."

"I told you, it's the people I miss. Remember the woman I was with when Zor took me?"

"Aye." Dak grew immediately aroused at the vivid memory. Her long, braided tresses, her rare onyx skin, her-

"She has been..." Kyra's bottom lip began to quiver. "She has been my best friend since I was,"-she blinked her eyes to keep from crying-"a child." Taking a deep breath, she looked up and smiled unconvincingly at Dak. "Sorry," she murmured.

"Do not apologize," he said softly. Squeezing her hand, Dak asked, "what is the wench's name?"

"Geris."

"Geris," he repeated, letting the sound roll around on his tongue. "And what of the comely Geris? Do you think she would not enjoy life on Tryston?"

Kyra shrugged. "I'm sure she'd come to love it after she got used to it, but that isn't the point."

"Oh?" Dak arched a golden brow as he regarded her. "What is then?"

"I would want for her to have a choice."

Dak summoned open the heavy doors that led out to an atrium filled with plush, exotic plant-life. "And what if I said to you that 'tis possible this Geris is my Sacred Mate?"

"Wh-What?" Kyra stumbled, thankful when Dak steadied her. She swung around to confront him, grabbing both of his bulging biceps. "Is she?" she wailed.

"I do not know," Dak admitted, "but 'tis true I harbor all the feelings warriors are said to possess when they meet their Sacred Mates, but are separated from them by wars or other events."

Kyra shook her head, her brow furrowed. "I don't understand."

"I'm depressed!"

"Oh." Kyra bit her lip, grinning. "But wouldn't you have known when you saw her if she was the one?"

"Under normal circumstances, aye," Dak explained, "yet were we in a dimension we did not know, facing potential enemies we couldn't be certain of." He shrugged, though the gesture was anything but casual. "I was too busy scanning for threats to pay full attention to the comely onyx wench, as now I wish I had."

Kyra wasn't concerned with that. She dug her nails into his arms. "But it's really possible that Geris is your mate? That she belongs here on Tryston?"

"Sheathe your claws, sister." Dak grinned, an engaging dimple popping out. "But aye, the more I think on it, the more convinced I become of it."

Kyra jumped up and down, her breasts jiggling with her excitement. "That would make Geris a queen, wouldn't it?"

"Aye." Dak searched Kyra's eyes as if looking for answers. "Speaking of titles, I am a king and therefore do have a colony I must return to the soonest. So if I go, I needs go anon, sister. What think you of it?"

Kyra blew out a breath, mulling it over. "Would you force her to come here if she turned out not to be your Sacred Mate after all?"

"Nay. I would give the wench a choice if she didn't belong to me, but if she is mine..." Dak slashed his hand through the air, indicating Geris's free will would be nonexistent.

"I see." Kyra released the hold she had on his arms and glanced around the atrium, absently surveying the bounty of plants. She considered how much a part of her Zor was since the joining, how lonely she knew she'd be without him, how melancholy she grew with even a few hours separation from him. This was what Sacred Mates were to each other he had said.

Kyra's mind was made up. "Then go to Geris. See if she's yours." She whirled around, shaking a confrontational finger at Dak. "But if she's not, you give her a choice!"

* * * * *

The troop of traveling performers that specialized in the erotic arts put in an appearance at the palace that moon-rising. The theatre in which the buxom wenches were to perform was packed full of lusty warriors almost a full two hours before the show was scheduled to begin.

Up above in the balconies, the individual boxes were filled with the highest ranking men of Tryston, lesser kings and high lords. Unlike below where there were only chairs for resting on, the private boxes each contained a mammoth bed, where the warriors could watch the performers at their leisure, taking their own pleasures when the mood struck.

As Kyra walked into her box with Zor, she immediately noticed that the private boxes weren't exactly private. The only partition that separated one from the next was a thin jewel-like rope.

Her attention was then snagged by the warrior in the box next to theirs. He was obviously not mated, for there were ten bound servants in his bed, kissing and fondling him all over, including the infamous Myn, who was currently suckling his penis.

Though his eyes were closed, the warrior's features could only be described as harsh. His hair was jet black like Zor's, his skin the deep tan of Tryston men, and his height looked to be on par with her husband's as well. A single jagged scar was slashed across his right cheek, giving him an even more barbaric appearance than Zor. The man gave her the shivers.

"Ah Myn," the warrior praised gruffly, sucking in his breath, "I see you have not lost your skill whilst I was away.

Gret, suckle from my man sac whilst Myn attends to my staff." Without opening his eyes, he turned his head and curled his tongue around the proffered nipple of another servant.

When the warrior climaxed a minute later, Kyra was disconcerted to realize that she was immensely turned on. Zor was right. She really did like to watch.

"See something you like?" Zor whispered provocatively in her ear as he came up behind her.

Kyra smiled slowly, still watching the scene. A servant's bountiful breasts were covering the warrior's face, but as Myn stood up to impale herself on his shaft, she could see that he was already fully erect again. "You're right," she admitted in low tones, "I'm a pervert."

Zor chuckled softly. "I never said that, you said that, my hearts. 'Tis natural to enjoy watching do you ask me."

Myn's huge breasts bobbed up and down as she rode the warrior, which Kyra hated to admit, she did with an enviable expertise. Her moaning picked up as her pace grew faster and more frenzied. This was a woman who clearly knew how to give pleasure.

Zor chuckled as he summoned Kyra's *qi'ka* to the floor. "Yes, *pani,* Myn is an excellent fuck, but not nearly as good as you." He reached around her body and slid the fingers of one hand through her pelt of intimate hair. "You are wet with need, wee one. Let us take to our own bed."

Kyra turned around in Zor's embrace and held up her arms to be lifted. He groaned, obliging her at once. Their tongues met as Zor kneaded Kyra's buttocks, moaning into her mouth as they tasted each other. He had missed touching her body so much whilst at training today.

Music began to play, indicating that the show would soon begin. Zor fell onto the bed with Kyra in his arms, then broke off the kiss. "Lie down facing the stage so you miss out on nothing, *nee'ka*. I will lie behind you."

"Okay." Kyra turned onto her side, reclining on an elbow. She sucked in her breath when Zor's long, thick penis entered her from behind. "Mmm. That feels wonderful," she admitted, gasping. "Would you roll my nipples between your fingers?" she asked provocatively.

"Lusty wench," Zor teased. He drew Kyra up against him in such a way that allowed him to slip his left arm under her, giving that hand access to her left nipple. His other hand reached over the top of Kyra, resting comfortably while he gave her right nipple attention. "Better?" he breathed into her ear. He swirled his tongue around the whorl until she shivered.

"Y-Yes." Kyra rotated her hips, impaling then re-impaling herself slowly on his cock. Now it was Zor who was sucking in his breath. "Do you like that?"

"Mmm Kyra. Aye, *pani*." Zor closed his eyes and enjoyed the sensations his *nee'ka's* cunt was gifting him with. When she thrust back, then rotated her hips in a grinding motion, he groaned. "Ah Kyra. Give me more of that sweet channel, love. Take all of me."

"Zor." Kyra's climax was swift. She let the feelings overpower her, making no attempts to stifle her moans of ecstasy. "Zor," she whimpered.

His thrusts became harder, faster. "Give me more, *nee'ka*. I command more from the body that belongs to me." He rotated his hips and pounded harder. She moaned louder. "Would you deny me?"

"N-No." Kyra met his thrusts with wicked enthusiasm. Knowing that those in the boxes near them could see everything, hear her moans, was an added aphrodisiac. She broke apart, coming violently. "Harder," she cried, thrashing against him madly. "I need more."

"Do you deserve more reward?" Zor asked as he thrust into her faster and harder, pinching her nipples. "Have you sought to pleasure me in all that you do today?" He shifted his hips and ground into her, eliciting another groan.

"Yes-oh god." Kyra bucked up against him, purposefully contracting her vaginal muscles while she gluttonously accepted the fucking he gave her. Her husband's roar told her he liked what she was doing. "Make the stones in my necklace pulse," she begged him frantically, "please."

"You are greedy for my life-force?" Zor inquired through clenched teeth, shifting his hips and thrusting rapidly.

When Kyra came apart and climaxed again, he could take no more. "Your pleasure is mine, *nee'ka*." With one last thrust, he spurted his seed deep inside of her.

The bridal necklace pulsed.

Kyra screamed.

Zor threw his head back and roared.

Wave after deliciously peaking wave coursed through their bodies, binding them further, bonding them forever in a way human words could never explain.

The lights in the theater slowly dimmed and spotlights shone onto the various stages. Zor licked Kyra's ear as the intensity of the waves gently ebbed. "Ah *nee'ka*. Such pleasure you give to me," he admitted in a thick whisper.

At Kyra's contented sigh, he sat up, careful not to remove his cock from her body, and placed her between his legs-still impaled-her back against his chest. "Let us watch the show."

"Yes." Kyra reached up behind her and ran a hand over his jaw.

Zor nuzzled it, then kissed her palm before releasing it. "I've a need of something soft to lean against. Would you mind greatly did I call for a servant to pillow me?"

"No," she admitted truthfully, "not at all."

A few minutes later, the show began and Zor had his pillow. The bound servant massaged his massive shoulders as he lay his head back on her huge silken breasts. Kyra leaned back into the fold of Zor's embrace, his penis fully embedded within her. "Is this too much weight for Leha to bear?" Kyra asked.

"Nay, *pani*. I am careful not to hurt her."

Appeased, Kyra turned her attention to the performers taking the stage. She could scarcely wait to see just what a performance of the erotic arts entailed.

* * * * *

Cam shuffled back to his private quarters, deciding he'd rather not gaze upon the performers when he knew he'd never get to sample from their charms. 'Twas best not to get himself worked up when he had no means for working the lust out of his system, he reminded himself. Indeed, after the High Queen's consummation feast, he had sustained an aching erection for the better part of two days.

Cam's step faltered as he rounded the corridor, surprised as he was to find a bound servant slipping from his chamber. "What do you here?" he asked quizzically, more out of curiosity than concern. No bound servant would have the audacity to steal from a warrior, after all.

The servant bowed, then straightened, displaying her ample breasts proudly. "I was sent from the High Queen to deliver a gift to your rooms. Since you were not here, a guardsman let me in." She smiled, gesturing toward the chamber door. "The High Queen wished for me to convey her regards and tell you the gift is yours to keep."

Cam arched a brow, having no idea what one such as Her Majesty could wish to give to him. "I thank you then."

"Enjoy." The servant smiled flirtatiously, then turned on her heel and sauntered away.

Cam watched her leave, enjoying the sight of her well-rounded backside as it swayed beneath the transparent *qi'ka*. Shaking his head to clear it, he walked through the door of his suite and closed it securely behind him. He looked high and low for this mysterious gift, but saw nothing. Shrugging mentally, he divested himself of his warrior's garb whilst reminding himself to ask the High Queen what she had thought to gift him with on the morrow.

Naked, Cam padded into his bedchamber and plopped down wearily onto the raised bed. He flipped onto his backside, drew his hands up behind his neck to pillow it, and closed his eyes.

Somebody began to caress his penis.

Cam's eyes flew open in surprise.

Sitting on her knees next to him, was an amazingly beautiful *Kefa* with sparkling blue skin and breasts so large they lay fully against her almost all the way to her navel. His erection was rigid and instantaneous. The *Kefa* emitted a small mewling sound, pleased by his body's response. "Who are you?" he asked hoarsely.

The *Kefa* handed him a note, then bent her head and took his cock into her mouth. Cam sucked in a breath through his teeth and ripped opened the piece of parchment that boasted the High Queen's feminine scrawl.

This is Muta. Her nickname is the suckler. Enjoy.

Cam lay the note reverently on the bed as he gazed down at Muta, watching as his large cock disappeared into her voracious mouth. "By the sands," he muttered through clenched teeth, as the *Kefa* performed on him in a way he hadn't known possible.

Over the course of the next several hours, Cam came to understand just how Muta had acquired her nickname. Whereas most *Kefas* would quit the room after bringing the master to peak, a warrior's life-force only seemed to elicit the slave to a heightened desire to suckle.

Two hours later, Cam realized he hadn't yet stuck his rod in Muta's channel. He doubted he would this night, but smiled to himself, knowing she was his and could therefore sample that part of her charm on the next moon-rising, or whenever he chose to do so.

Seven hours and ten climaxes later, Cam began to wonder if 'twas possible to die of Muta's abilities. Never had he been given so thorough a pleasuring. He allowed her to suckle him to peak one last time, then bade her to pillow him whilst he slept.

Cam snuggled up against Muta's breasts, sucking from a plump blue nipple as he fell into the most sated sleep of his life. He smiled, his thoughts turning to Kyra.

Long live the High Queen.

Chapter 16

When Kyra came down to breakfast the following morning, she was to learn that the warrior whose box had been adjacent to her and Zor's last night was none other than Kil, second oldest of the Q'an Tal ruling family.

The two brothers were hugging each other, pounding on each other's backs affectionately, when Kyra first entered the great hall. "Dak will be sorry he missed you," Zor exclaimed, grinning from ear to ear.

"And what of Rem?" Kil asked, his glowing blue eyes so much like Zor's.

"Bah. He is forever on Sypar, where his she-bitch of a *nee'ka* has bade him to stay."

Kil snorted, a gesture that softened his grim features somewhat. "You flatter her with such undeserved praise."

The clicking of Kyra's sandals against the black crystal floor caught Zor's attention. He spun around, smiling upon seeing her, his eyes devouring her body which was clothed today of a transparent blue *qi'ka*. "*Nee'ka,* come." He motioned with his hand for her to join them. "Meet my brother, Kil."

Kyra took a deep breath to steady herself, then strolled up to where the two giants stood. Kil took his time studying her form, his eyes moving over every inch of her body, lingering at her most intimate parts. She pretended not to notice. "Hello. My name is Kyra." She smiled up to him, even though his eyes were still perusing her body.

Kil eventually brought his gaze up to meet Kyra's eyes. He inclined his head, but didn't return her smile. She sensed that smiling was something he didn't do much of. "I remember seeing you last night in the box next to mine. I am Kil."

"Kil has traveled here from Tron where he has been busy putting down an insurrection," Zor explained to Kyra, reaching down to brush the pad of his thumb over one of her nipples. "He is sore tired I would imagine, so we will dine with him in privacy. Can you ask the servants to send a repast up to our suites, my hearts?"

"Of course." Kyra nodded, grateful to have an excuse to get away from Kil's unnerving presence, if even for a little while. She smiled graciously at the men, then turned on her heel and left.

"She is beautiful," Kil admitted. "Even more so now that I can see her in the harsh light of day."

"Aye," Zor boasted proudly, "that she is." He clapped his brother on the back. "I take it you would have no objections to honoring your duty were something ever to happen to me?"

"Nay, I would have no objections," Kil admitted without a qualm, "yet do I not care to think on something so bad as that, jest or no."

"I am sorry." Zor felt immediately contrite. "I forget you are just in from seeing much death. Forgive me, brother."

"'Tis naught to forgive." Kil thumped him on the back, hugging him again. "'Tis naught to forgive."

* * * * *

Kyra learned a lot about Trystonni culture over the private breakfast in their rooms, much of it shocking, leaving her numbed through and through. Due to their laws of succession, for instance, Kyra was supposed to regard Kil as a sort of lesser husband. They weren't supposed to have sexual intercourse, but because she would be given to Kil in marriage if Zor was to die-a thought that terrified her-she was expected to have many of the same intimacies with him that until now she had shared only with Zor.

Her *qi'ka* was removed while in Kil's presence, an event she was told would happen every time they were alone, whether or not Zor was present. Kyra had eaten naked with Jik and Tia in their bedroom before, but that had been as a part of bathing, so hadn't seemed too unusual. This felt unusual. This felt like what it was-Tryston law's way of establishing another male's dominance over her.

Kyra was also expected to bathe with Kil per his request...yet another intimacy given to a male without her consent.

She also discovered what gentling was. Kil and Kyra were to be locked away in the bedchamber together, during which time Kil was required by the laws of succession to bring her to orgasm until she no longer feared him or his touch, thus "gentling" her. This relationship was established as more of a symbol than anything.

Kyra was furious with Zor for not preparing her for so shocking an event. She was also more than a little terrified. Kil's countenance was so severe as to send chill bumps coursing down her spine. She couldn't imagine him being very kind toward her.

There weren't very many positive aspects to this frightening situation, so far as Kyra could see, but a few nevertheless existed. The first was that, during this gentling, Kil wasn't allowed to do anything with her intimate parts besides touch them. In other words, the law permitted him to do anything he wanted with his hands while he gentled her, but his tongue and penis were out.

The second good aspect was that there was a hypothetical end to the situation in sight: once she had been appropriately "gentled", Kil could never gentle her again. She was still required to shed her *qi'ka* when alone with him, and bathe with him upon request, but that was the extent of his privileges once this unbelievably bizarre ritual was done with.

The final positive aspect was that Kil would no longer be given any of the rights of a lesser husband, except for the removal of her *qi'ka,* once Kyra gave birth to Zor's heir. As a result of all she'd learned in the past hour, childbearing had flown to the top of her list of things it was time to consider doing.

When Zor had stood up to quit the chamber using the excuse that he needed to train with his men, Kyra had stood up as well, desperate to leave with him. "Nay," he had whispered in gentle tones, "you must become acquainted with my current heir, *nee'ka*."

"But Zor-"

"Nay, little one." He had admonished her with a shake of his head. "'Tis all right. He will not harm you. But you must be gentled to his touch, lest something happens to me and I can care for you no longer. I would not leave you terrified of the fates."

"I don't want to," she pleaded, tugging at his hand.

"'Twill be all right," Zor insisted, broaching no argument. "Do you remember telling me you enjoyed our time with Ari because it was a part of a ritual as old as time?"

"Yes," she admitted hesitantly.

"So is this *nee'ka*. 'Tis ritual and no more." After explaining that Kil would not be permitted to take his leave of the bedchamber until Kyra no longer feared his ministrations, he turned on his heel and quit their rooms. A guard blocked the door to the bedchamber, making certain she couldn't leave.

Kyra had taken one look at Kil, then flew across the bedchamber and locked herself in the nearest closet. It had taken him an hour to coax her from it, during which time he had reminded her repeatedly that the sooner they began the gentling, the sooner it would be over. Eventually, she relented and unlocked the closet door.

So now Kyra sat perched on a raised table-legs spread open before Kil-allowing him to inspect her body until he'd had his fill, wanting to get the entire thing over with. Grabbing her breasts with both hands, he plumped the nipples and tweaked them, rubbed them and rolled them between his callused fingers, until they were acceptably hard. Much to Kyra's consternation, her traitorous body was growing aroused.

"Spread your legs wider for me. I would know all of you." His voice was a rumble, mysterious and dark, like him. The slash across his right cheek gleamed ominously in the dimmed chamber, giving him a malevolent appearance.

Kyra did as she was bade, her arousal growing more acute. She was discovering another aspect of her sexuality that she wished she had never learned, namely that this game of domination and submission was turning her on fiercely. "Use your fingers to spread your cunt lips," he commanded, "show me what 'tis mine should the goddess decree it."

Kil's eyes feasted on Kyra's swollen labia and engorged clit. He continued to knead her breasts and plump up her nipples whilst his eyes took it all in. The scent of her arousal was intoxicating, beckoning him to sample from what he couldn't have. He knew he would take to his rooms with the servants, mayhap not surfacing for days, once this session in torture was complete.

Releasing one breast, Kil trailed his freed hand down her belly and ran his fingers through her fire-berry patch of curls. "'Tis softer than *vesha*, your pelt."

Kyra sucked in her breath, closing her eyes against the pleasure his words brought to her.

"Nay," Kil reprimanded her, "you will open your eyes and see who it is that brings you to your woman's joy."

Kyra took a steadying breath, then complied. Kil's fingers traced lower, gently rimming the folds of her puffed up labia. She moaned, wanting him to touch her clit, needing him to touch it. "Not yet, lusty one. Almost."

Kil tweaked one of her nipples, then rolled it between thumb and forefinger, over and over, never stopping, glorying in her passionate moans. His other hand rimmed the oval of her sleek folds again, his fingers saturated. "Do you want me to touch your woman's bud?" he asked thickly, his voice hoarse.

"Yes," she admitted without hesitation. "Please."

"Please what?"

"Please touch my woman's bud," she quietly begged, using the Trystonni word for her clit.

"Say my name," Kil growled, tugging on her nipple, then rolling it again. "Tell me who you want to touch your woman's bud."

Kyra groaned, almost climaxing. "Kil," she gasped out, having more and more difficulty keeping her eyes open, "Please Kil, touch my woman's bud."

Kil placed the pad of his thumb on her clit. "Look at me, Kyra. Know who is bringing you to your pleasure." As her eyelids fluttered open, he began to work the pad of his thumb in circles, slow and agonizing. She moaned, peering into his glowing blue eyes the whole time. Her hips thrust up to meet him. "You want more, beautiful Kyra?"

"Yes."

Kil began to rub her clit briskly, causing her to thrash about, moaning. She cried out, splintering apart, as a climax ripped through her violently.

Thinking it was over, Kyra was surprised when Kil hoisted her up into his arms and carried her into the bathing pool. Splaying her wide on a raised rock of soft jewel, he repeated the entire process, forcing her to peak repeatedly, commanding her to look at him the entire time.

An hour later, Kil carried Kyra to a reclining cot by the pool and started his ruminations yet again. A *Kefa* suckled him to his own violent climax as he continued to milk Kyra's body of everything it had to offer him. He touched and rubbed, pressed and pulled, fondled and prodded. He accepted no less than Kyra's complete, whimpering surrender, knowing that when he left this bedchamber, her body would remember and respond to his touch did it become necessary.

Kil brought her to climax a few more times than what was truly necessary, telling himself it was to ensure that the gentling had been accomplished well and good, but knowing it was because he'd never be permitted to have another gentling session with her again after he quit the rooms.

Greedily taking the fill that was his right by the holy law, Kil commanded Kyra to ride three of his fingers while he stimulated her clit with the pad of his thumb. She peaked that way, sobbing from the violence of it, then peaked twice more before he released her.

Kyra slumped against his chest, indicating her trust in Kil to take care of her. He stood up, carried her exhausted, replete body to the bed, and gently deposited her within the soft *vesha* hides. She was sound asleep within moments.

Kil tugged at one of her distended nipples a last time, then quit the chamber, taking to his rooms for his comforts.

* * * * *

On the training fields, Zor's mind was dangerously unfocused. His attention was not on his task, but on what his *nee'ka* and brother where doing together in his bedchamber even now. Deciding 'twas foolhardy to practice the warring arts whilst distracted, he called in an older warrior named Tym to relieve him of his duties.

Zor summoned a bottle of matpow and took to his floating conveyance, riding aimlessly about Sand City for hours, drinking but finding no relief from the spirits.

He could only hope that his brother followed the law and sought no comfort between Kyra's thighs. And he could only hope his wife forgave him for all of it.

'Twas a boggle, trying to figure out how to break a first dimension woman into the ways of a seventh dimension culture, especially when that culture was the dominant one of Tryston. Her new life was so different from her old.

Zor couldn't claim to have firsthand knowledge of Kyra's former planet beyond the few minutes he'd been there, but he had no doubts that it was a vastly different world. Everything there that involved the body was viewed in a negative light, from what Kyra had mentioned.

His *nee'ka* had seemed unnaturally afraid of the gentling, a ritual any highborn woman raised on Tryston would have not only expected, but probably anticipated. Clearly, Kyra had neither anticipated it nor welcomed it.

And as much as Zor wished it were otherwise, he was grateful to the goddess that his wee one wanted no warrior's hands touching her but his. By the sands, how he couldn't wait for this business to be over with, knowing well and good that he would have to bear no more tortures such as this for many moon-risings to come. After the gentling, none other would dare to fondle his woman again, save at royal consummation feasts when all were feeling randy.

A dark, niggling feeling continued to lap at Zor's mind. Since the joining, his mind and hearts had grown more and more attuned to Kyra's emotions with every passing hour. He could sense her embarrassment, her shame in finding pleasure in another's ministrations. He could feel her sorrow, no doubt wondering what other aspects of Trystonni culture she would be forced to endure without prior knowledge.

Guilt ate at Zor, tore at him. He should have better prepared Kyra for this. He should have been more sympathetic of her ignorance to Tryston's ways, teaching her all there was to know, instead of being arrogant enough to think his way was best, to believe that she should learn of it all on her own.

Zor commanded his floating conveyance to return to the palace, an apology forming on his lips. He wasn't certain of everything he would say to his *nee'ka,* but one thing was for a certainty: he would make sure she realized that never again would she have to bear such a thing. He would even relent and go against his people's ways, allowing her to skip attendance at royal consummation feasts if 'twas her desire.

Anything.

Zor would do anything to have his wee one forgive him.

Chapter 17

Kyra awoke an hour later with tears streaming down her cheeks. The events of the last few hours whipped frenziedly through her mind as she scrambled off of the raised bed and donned the blue *qi'ka* Zor had summoned from her body after bringing her to their bedchamber with his brother.

Zor had given her to Kil-given her to him. How could a man who loves his wife give her body to another, most especially to his own brother?

Fat tears dropped like diamonds from Kyra's eyes as she considered the very real possibility that Zor didn't love her at all. To him, she was no doubt just a vessel, a body to empty himself into at night, a body to breed heirs for the Q'an Tal line.

Humiliation washed over her, battering at her, as she fled from their apartments through the secret door and ran down the long red crystal corridor that was a short-cut to the conveyance launching pad.

Did everyone in the palace know what Kil had done to her today? Had the many servants that had wandered in and out during the gentling to attend to Kil told others of her screams, of being brought to heel, of being lowered to begging for his touch? Would Zor be told of the way she had sobbed? Of how she had pleaded for more? Of how violently she had climaxed in another warrior's arms?

Kyra ran through the corridor, her breasts bobbing up and down, tears coursing down her cheeks, stopping to talk to no one. At the launching pad when five of the palace guards had thought to ask her for her destination, she turned on them like a she-beast, ready to strike out at anybody who stood in her way.

"I am the Empress!" she snapped, tears still falling. "I answer to none of you!"

The guards had studied her tears, then looked quizzically at one another. Thinking it no more than a spat with the High King, they bade her to be on her way, signaling to a tower guard to open the hatch.

"Go!" Kyra verbally commanded her conveyance. "Drive to the outskirts of Sand City! I don't care where you go, just go!"

Suddenly, it was all too much. Her new life was too much. Kyra wanted Geris, she wanted Kara, she needed to be with people who understood her, who were raised in her culture, knew what she found acceptable and what she didn't. She was tired of the male dominated hedonism of Tryston, tired of all that it encompassed.

Kyra had grown used to wearing *qi'kas* so displaying her body no longer bothered her, but the rest was too overwhelming to endure. Sex was everywhere, done with everyone. Fondling was as ordinary as breathing. "I'm a tax accountant!" she screamed into the night, laughing hysterically. "A goddamn tax accountant!"

The moon shining tonight was Tryston's dominant red one. The glow it gave off sent color licking at Kyra's features. She gazed up at the moon, hating it because it wasn't yellow, despising it because it didn't belong to earth, to home.

Covering her face, Kyra broke down and sobbed into her hands. She had to find a way out of here. She had to find a way back home.

* * * * *

Zor put off the inevitable confrontation with Kyra for as long as his conscience would allow. Thinking to gage just how bad of a situation he was liable to be walking into, he went first to Kil's rooms to consider his view on it.

Zor was not surprised to find Kil's bed crawling with bound servants, many of whom he had acquired during his last war on Tron, apparently letting the experienced servants teach the initiates what was to be expected of them.

The lusty Myn, whom Zor himself had shared much bed sport with, was currently suckling his brother to peak, apparently not for the first time. "That is seven tongue lavings," Kil roared as he climaxed. He pointed to a shy looking blonde woman with magnificent, huge breasts. "Think you that your channel can give me more?"

The blonde woman cast her eyes demurely to the floor, nodding slowly.

"Come to me," Kil commanded her. "See to my release as is your duty."

Hesitantly, the blonde climbed up on top of Kil and impaled her body onto his. "Ride," he ordered her. "Milk me." He grabbed her bobbing breasts as her hips thrashed about in a series of hard embeddings, pulling at her nipples. She did as she was bade, riding him hard and fast.

"Master," she gasped. "Master." Climaxing around his cock, her tremors set off Kil's own.

Zor smiled wryly. He had never had the patience for breaking in bound servants to their duties, which was why he had always relegated Kil to the task. His brother was a true aficionado at the tedious sport. Zor, on the other hand, preferred them already broken in, or he had leastways, before mating. Now he wanted none save Kyra. "I would talk with you brother."

Kil glanced up to where Zor stood. He settled comfortably into the servant's breasts that were pillowing him, then nodded. "For a certainty." Waving his hand at the blonde to get off his rod, he gestured toward a brunette, indicating 'twas her turn.

Zor strolled up to where his brother lay, paying the riding, groaning servant no more attention than was Kil. "Is Kyra all right?"

"You have yet to see her?" Kil looked surprised.

"Aye," Zor admitted, chagrined. "I fear she will be sore angry with me for not telling her of the gentling."

"Why did you not prepare her for it?"

"Arrogance, I suppose. I thought my way best. I thought she should learn everything of Tryston by discovering it for herself." Zor shrugged his massive shoulders. Absently, more out of habit than anything else, he reached for the breasts of the blonde servant that had just ridden Kil to peak, toying with her nipples while he confided in his brother. "I just hope Kyra will forgive me."

"Your *nee'ka* loves you. She will forgive you."

"How can you know?"

Kil shrugged. In reaction to the brunette's first orgasm whilst riding him, he automatically rubbed her clit as reward, but paid her no more attention than that. "It took me many hours to gentle her."

"Really?" Zor's heart lightened a considerable degree. He stood up straighter, gently setting the blonde away from him, who was currently trying to free his penis for a suckling.

"Aye." Kil grinned, a rarity for Zor's brother. "Her mind was fierce set against me, brother, hated me she did."

"Harrumph."

"'Tis true, for a certainty." Kil shook his head. "By the goddess I swear to you I was gentled long before Kyra."

Zor couldn't help it. He threw his head back and laughed. He could see his Kyra doing that to a warrior, driving him nigh unto daft. He shook his head and grinned. "Thank-you, brother."

Kil grunted. "Let us speak no more of it, aye?"

"Aye." Zor inclined his head to Kil, flicked a nipple on the blonde one last time, and strolled from his brother's rooms.

Kil returned his attention to the task set before him. The majority of these bound servants were to be given away as gifts, so he wanted them broken in the soonest. Mayhap, though, he would keep one or two for himself. The brunette was a lusty rider for a certainty, but of course, the blonde was as well. Mayhap the other ten initiates would prove just as wanton.

"Come Myn," Kil beckoned to her, gesturing with his hand, "show these wenches how to suckle again." He motioned for the brunette to end her ride. "You did well, Frey. Now move to the side and watch Myn. Gret, show them how to suckle from my man sac whilst Myn administers to my staff."

Kil sucked in his breath, groaning. "The rest of you watch whilst contemplating new ways to please me."

* * * * *

Zor's long, heavy strides toward his bedchamber indicated just how much he needed to see his *nee'ka*. The talk with Kil had lightened his mood considerably. Somehow, he would coax his wee one into forgiving him and they would get on with their lives.

It was troubling to the spirits indeed when Zor found their bedchamber empty. Kyra always awaited him here upon the moon-rising, as eager for his physical affection as he was for hers. He put his hands to his hips and took a deep breath. Where could she be? Was she that angry with him?

Grunting, Zor stalked briskly from their apartments, heading first for Cam's quarters. He knew Kyra had taken a liking to the young warrior. Mayhap she would visit with him if her spirits were unduly sullen. Feeling guilty, he pounded on Cam's door.

No answer.

Ever a High King, Zor took the liberty of allowing himself into Cam's suite. Come to think of it, the young warrior hadn't been at training this morn, the first time ever that he had missed a practice of the warring arts.

Then Zor knew why.

Shaking his head at the scene before him, he grinned knowingly. Cam was snoring as loudly as a malfunctioning conveyance, stretched out on his back, thoroughly spent. Muta was still administering to Cam's semi-flaccid shaft, asleep or no. Zor had been able to hear the familiar sucking sounds before he'd even seen her. "Wake up, Cam. 'Tis your High King."

Cam's eyes opened slowly. When he registered who it was that was standing above him, he made a move to sit up, then remembered Muta when he was unable to do so.

Zor held up a palm. "Do not get up. I thought to ask you if you had seen your High Queen, but 'tis obvious you have been otherwise occupied."

"I'm sorry." Cam flushed. As spent as he was, his flag still rose full mast for Muta's mouth. She mewled. He whimpered, then turned to face Zor. "She is missing?" he asked anxiously.

"Nay, not exactly, but should she come here, tell her I needs speak with her."

"For a certainty, Your Majesty."

Zor nodded, then made to leave. He hesitated. "One more thing, Cam."

"Aye?"

"Be at practice on the morrow."

Cam's face flushed scarlet. "Aye, Your Majesty," he mumbled.

When the door closed behind Zor, Cam craned his neck to gaze at Muta. She was such lovely, blue perfection. He could still scarcely believe she belonged to him for all times.

"You are still hungry, my sweet?" At Muta's mewling sound, he settled himself back upon the *vesha* hides and closed his eyes in bliss. "Then feed, my lovely. Milk me of all that I have. 'Tis yours."

Chapter 18

It was another hour before Zor had his worst suspicions confirmed: Kyra was nowhere within the perimeter of the palace.

"We are sorry, Excellent One," a fierce looking warrior guardsman demurred to him. "We had no orders to stop the High Queen from leaving and she refused to tell us her destination."

"In the future you are to tail her does she leave without me!" Zor roared, his nostrils flaring. "Am I clear?"

"Aye, Your Majesty. Again, I apologize for all of-"

"Save it." Zor held up a large hand. "I haven't the time for words. Sound the alarm. Send out as many hunters as can be spared."

Moments later, a shrill blaze of horns rang throughout the castle. The warriors scattered throughout the palace suites alighted from their beds, quickly donned their leathers, and ran full speed to the conveyance hatch. Zor waited until he spotted both Kil and Cam amongst the throng, knowing they were the last he waited on. From their disheveled looks, 'twas apparent they had both converged upon the conveyance hatch with all due haste.

Zor came right to the point, his bellow loud, carrying throughout the gigantic launching pad. "The High Queen is missing." At the sound of disbelieving rumbles, he hastened to add, "'tis possible she seeks to flee Tryston, which of course, cannot be allowed." He paced back and forth atop the raised launching pad, his features grim. "I want all of you to go hunting. You are to check in with the tower and let my man know the very moment she is spotted.

"Have a care not to harm her whilst bringing her back, but no matter what she says to you, what threats she delivers to you, you are to bring her back. You answer to me above all others, aye?"

"Aye," the warriors repeated.

Zor took a deep, steadying breath. He needed these men-the finest warriors in existence, the finest hunters in any known dimension-to leave the soonest, yet he also needed them to understand the gravity of the situation. "The insurrectionists on Tron have been brought to heel for the most part, yet are there a few foolhardy enough amongst them to attempt a kidnapping if they were able to smuggle themselves into Sand City, spotting your Empress unawares."

A rumble of outrage swept throughout the conveyance hatch, to which Zor held up a silencing hand. "Each squadron leader is responsible for assembling and dispersing his men to various points throughout Sand City and beyond." He stopped his pacing and came to a halt in the very middle of the din, looking every inch the feared, proud warrior he was. "Whoever amongst you is the one to bring my *nee'ka* back to me will be richly rewarded, no matter your rank."

"What will you give us?" one bold young buck called out, inciting bouts of lusty laughter to ring throughout the hatch.

Zor had to smile back. Then he very seriously raised his voice and bellowed, "a suite of honor your very own in the south wing"-He held up a palm for silence when the warriors began to whistle through their teeth-"Plus five of my favored *Kefas* to see to your needs."

Kil's lips curled wryly as the sound of enthusiastic shouts and boasts rippled throughout the conveyance hatch. Feeling an unexpected and unfamiliar rush of guilt for the part he had unwittingly played in Kyra's disappearance, he jumped up onto the raised launching pad where Zor stood. Whistling shrilly to garner everyone's attention, he then bellowed, "I would add to my brother's booty, men."

That got their attention.

"To the warrior that finds my brother's *nee'ka,* two bound servants each owing five Yessat years worth of duty will be yours."

Zor clapped him on the back as a series of stunned murmurs echoed throughout the hatch. "They are freshly broken in, recently captured on Tron," Kil boasted, "and are much starved for a warrior's ministrations."

Pandemonium broke out amongst the gathering. Warriors ran to catch up to their squadron leaders. Bound servants were even more costly than *Kefas* and everyone knew it. Since they were typically given as goodwill gifts to lesser kings and high lords, the average warrior on Tryston rarely owned such a prize.

"Now go," Kil bellowed, slashing his hand tersely through the air. "The hunt is on!"

* * * * *

Kyra took another swig from the bottle of moonshine matpow, then swiped her arm across her mouth. Belching, she put her fingers to her lips and hiccupped. "Sorry."

"Do not apologize, Empress." An extremely large, heavily tattooed ex-convict who went by the name "Death" saluted her with his bottle of moonshine. Kyra stared at the large skull tattooed on his forehead, thinking it the most fascinating thing she'd ever seen. Of course, she was also stone drunk.

Death nodded. "This moonshine is sweeter than the tit of a *heeka-beast,* is it not?"

Kyra clicked her teeth shut when she realized how moronic she probably looked, her mouth drooped open as she listened to Death speak. She was having a difficult time hanging onto a single thought though. "I don't know," she admitted, "I've never tasted one."

Laughter roared throughout the smoke-filled room of Pika's Place, an establishment catering to the lowest class of clientele on the outskirts of Sand City. Bruisers, thugs, and men who made less than respectable livings made up the majority of the bar's patronage. The blue crystal structure of the shabby bar had more holes in it than a piece of Swiss cheese. The ventilation system could have been better, but a fan overhead served to cool the room's atmosphere to an acceptable level.

"I never knew royal wenches could be so much fun," another shady character named Glok called out. Apparently this one made his living importing illegal moonshine, or some such thing. Kyra licked her lips, deciding that the outlawing of moonshine was a dumb law. Almost as dumb as that gentling business was.

"I wasn't raised royal," Kyra admitted to the men gathered about. "I was a tax accountant on the planet I came from."

"Oh yeah?" Death asked, his mammoth biceps flexing as he handed a lit mooka, a cigar-like smoking device, to Kyra. "Sounds to me like a good thing. The big house needs a hot piece of art like you to shake things up a bit."

Kyra sucked on the end of the mooka, swaying back and forth on the cheap crystal barstool in time with the blues-like music playing in the background. "They don't want me to shake things up, Death. They want me to conform."

"Fuck the establishment!" Glok cried, slapping his fist on the bar. "How could they not see you for the fine woman you are?"

"Aye," a barrel of a man named Hod concurred, shaking his head. "By the goddess, I would want you just the way you are."

Kyra's hand flew to her throat. She whimpered. "That's the sweetest thing a man has ever said to me," she sobbed, drunk and emotional. "I think I'm going to cry again."

"Don't do that, little fire-berry," Death gruffly ordered her, clearly glad they had gotten past that. He patted her on the back in an awkward attempt to comfort her, nearly knocking her off the barstool in the process. "'Twill make your eyes go blotchy and send your nose off into running fits again."

Kyra considered that for a drawn out moment as she sucked on the end of her mooka. "You're probably right. Can we sing another song together then?"

"Aye," Glok answered for the lot of them. "I've a special liking to that ditty you taught us, what was it called again, Your Majesty?"

"YMCA."

"Aye, the YMCA. Let us partake of that ditty."

"Okay." Kyra took another swig of moonshine, then jumped from her barstool to the ground. "Would you like me to teach you the dance that accom*pani*es it?"

"For a certainty," Hod beamed, jumping up to join her on the dance floor.

Kyra swung around, looking Death up and down. "Aren't you going to join us?"

"Aye," Death grumbled as he stood up and headed her way. "But you best be easy with me this time, little fire-berry."

* * * * *

Cam and two others from the same squadron were the first to arrive at Pika's Place, having spotted the High Queen's golden crystal conveyance from the air. The team was the youngest at the palace and therefore a randy bunch. Cam was the only among them to possess a *Kefa* and he had obtained Muta only the day prior.

The trio of friends had agreed amongst each other before beginning the hunt to share in their spoils. Since one suite in the south wing was nigh as big as ten suites in the common barracks put together, they had decided prior to the hunt that should they stick together and win, all of them would move into the honored rooms of the new suite, sharing in the delights of their new *Kefas* and bound servants.

"By the sands," Mik whispered to Cam, "my staff is nigh unto bursting just thinking of what awaits us upon our return to the palace."

"Your staff is always close to bursting," Cam retorted affably.

"As was yours," Mik countered with a grin, "before you were nigh unto suckled to death by your *Kefa* last moon-rising."

Cam smiled as a vision of Muta came to mind. "She is sore talented," he mused, missing the feel of her warm mouth moving up and down his cock already. "Muta was a gift from the High Queen, you will remember. Gladly will I share with you her charms, but if ever I leave the palace, she is mine to take with me."

"Of course." Mik nodded, realizing that was a given conclusion. Anxious to return to the palace, he looked around for their friend. "Has Gio returned yet from signaling to the tower?"

"Nay, he-ah, here he comes now."

Gio's seven-foot, three hundred and thirty pound frame, which was fashioned of the same raw muscle and handsome looks Cam and Mik were carved of, jogged up to their sides smiling. "The hunt is over, my friends. We win."

Clapping each other on the back, the three of them grinned like green boys attending their first consummation feast.

"Tell us our orders then," Mik urged Gio, careful to keep his tone hushed, lest those inside Pika's Place call out a warning to the High Queen.

"The High King wishes for us not to alert his *nee'ka* of our presence. We are not to go in unless it sounds like things are getting out of hand in yon bar." Gio shrugged. "Otherwise, we are to remain outside. The High King and his brother are on their way."

"We did it then!" Mik laughed, clapping his friends on the back. "We've six *Kefas* between the three of us, including Muta, plus two bound servants and an honored suite!"

Gio was grinning from ear to ear. Unfortunately, Cam wasn't. His smile faltering a bit, Gio turned to him. "What is it, my friend? What ails you?"

Cam shrugged, uncomfortable discussing his feelings with other warriors. "'Tis just..." He sighed, running a hand through his golden locks. "The High Queen has been naught but good to me. I cannot help but to feel I have betrayed her in some fundamental way."

"You speak untruths," Mik consoled him, clapping him on the back. "What if she had been ill-used by an insurrectionist from Tron? Would you say this then?"

"Nay, but..."

"Then don't feel that way now," Gio cut in. "Someone had to find her. Why feel guilty for proving ourselves able hunters?"

Cam sighed, but eventually relented with a nod. "You are right. 'Twas necessary to find the High Queen."

He just hoped the Empress saw it that way.

* * * * *

Zor had never been so relieved in his life as when his man in the tower put the call through to his high-speed conveyance that Kyra had been located by Cam and two other warriors. He felt so much joy upon hearing she was well and unharmed that he decided to throw another bound servant into the booty, so each of the randy young warriors would possess two *Kefas* and a bound servant apiece.

Gio had told the tower guard that Kyra was inside of Pika's Place, a seedy establishment on the outskirts of Sand City. The sordid bar having gained something of a reputation from its disreputable goings on, Zor wouldn't be completely relieved until his *nee'ka* was safely ensconced within the palace perimeter. He could only imagine what sorts of cutthroats and swindlers frequented a place such as Pika's.

"We are here," Zor called out to Kil as he landed the conveyance.

Kil alighted from the conveyance alongside Zor, his features harsher than normal. "What goes on in there?" he asked the three younger warriors as they approached.

Cam stepped forward to bring them up to par. "We have heard no shouts, no screams, only music and laughter. We could not know for a certainty what transpires without alerting them to our presence, but we have been listening through holes in the shabby crystal walls and find naught amiss."

Zor nodded. "You have done well. Accompany us inside as back-up, for we know not what we are up against."

"Aye, sire."

A minute later, the front doors of Pika's Place were kicked in and five warriors armed to the teeth rushed into the decrepit crystal bar. 'Twas so noisy inside, not even one of the patrons heard them.

The warriors stood there, mouths agape, unable to believe what it was they were seeing. The High Queen was perched atop the shoulder of some mammoth-sized man sporting the markings of a skull across his forehead. She had a bottle of illegal moonshine in one hand and a lit mooka in the other.

The Empress appeared to be directing the two score of patrons in the bar in some sort of primitive dancing rite. The criminal element in Pika's was currently contorting their arms and bodies to make odd shapes as they chanted something about Ys, Ms, and a CA character.

Zor caught his brother's eye to gage his reaction. Clearly, Kil was as stunned as he.

Kyra's laughter forced Zor's attention back to her. The big man with the tattoo was now twirling her around, apparently much to his *nee'ka's* delight. The man's hands were clamped around Kyra, one of them right on her creamy *sekta* pearl thigh.

His nostrils flaring, Zor bellowed his war cry.

Chapter 19

"Forget it!" Kyra announced in slurred tones. "I'm not going anywhere with you, you jerk!"

Zor tried to hold onto his temper as his *nee'ka* out and out defied him, in front of a chamber filled with people no less. "Kyra," he snarled, the muscle in his cheek ticking, "we will discuss our troubles at home. You will come with me now that there might be no bloodshed."

"Nope." Kyra crossed her arms under her breasts and raised her eyebrows defiantly. "Death here says I can stay with him." She patted the huge man gently on top of his shiny head, an act that elicited a grunt of approval from the towering eight-foot giant. "He's niiiice"-she slurred the word-"to me. He cares about my...my...uh..."

"Feelings," Death supplied.

"That's right," Kyra announced, her chin set at a stubborn angle. "He cares about my feelings." During a series of hiccups, she studied the wicked tic in her husband's jaw, noted the grim size of his flaring nostrils, but decided she didn't care. "Death would never send me to another man's bed."

Zor flushed at the sounds of Cam, Gio, and Mik sucking in affronted breaths. "She speaks of the gentling," he heard Kil murmur in explanation.

"Kyra," Zor bit out, spacing his words evenly, "I give you one minute to come to me, else will I come to you." He shook his head and smiled without humor. "'Twill not be pretty if I needs take you, that I can promise."

Glok and Hod pulled out some sort of weapons, the kind of which Kyra had never seen. They were long, black, and sleek, and had a pulsing of neon colors running through them.

"Pretty," she announced, running her fingertips over the barrel of Glok's weapon.

The warriors retaliated at once, training their weapons on the men aiding Kyra. Kil aimed his site directly for the skull on Death's forehead. "If you care at all for your friend, Kyra," he murmured, "you will keep him from dying this moon-rising."

That announcement sent a shiver down her spine, sobering her up a bit. She didn't know what to do. She was drunk, emotional, and knew little beyond the fact that she wanted to go nowhere near that prison of a palace. "I cannot live with you, Zor!" she yelled, hoping to draw Kil's attention away from Death. "Leave me be. Go away. Do you hear me?" she shrieked. "Go away!"

Zor heard her loud and clear. He felt every word cut straight to his hearts. His features remained impassive, yet like a mortally wounded animal, he made a small dying sound in the back of his throat.

"Your *nee'ka* is sotted," Kil reminded him quietly, his weapon still trained on Death. "Do not listen to her words, brother."

"Don't let these men scare you!" an outlaw next to Hod snarled, aiming his zykif at Kil. "We have them outnumbered."

Faster than Kyra thought was possible, Kil snatched a second weapon from his leather pants and without even taking his eyes off of Death, sent it whirling across the room until it met its mark. The outlaw released his weapon and grabbed his throat, dead before he hit the ground.

Kyra's hand flew to her throat as she gasped. She couldn't believe it. She was too stunned to believe it. A man had died for aiding her.

Kyra looked into the face of the giant that had befriended her, the same man who had kept her from harm's way and cared for her, and knew she couldn't do anything to jeopardize his life. Holding a palm up, she surrendered, tears coursing down her cheeks. "You win, damn you! Just like always! I'll go with you!"

"Are you certain, little fire-berry?" Death asked calmly, not willing to let Kyra go without a fight unless it was of her own choosing.

"Do not," Zor bit out through clenched teeth, "call my *nee'ka* by that name."

Death paid the High King no attention. All of his focus was centered on Kyra.

"I'm certain," Kyra told him quietly. "Please let me down. I would not repay your kindness this way." She motioned to the warriors, emphasizing her meaning.

"We will fight do you desire it," Hod called out. "Do not go if 'tis only for thoughts of us."

"Aye," Glok seconded.

"No." Kyra shook her head. Glancing first at Zor and then at Kil, she realized who the winners would be in this skirmish regardless to the numbers in the opposition's favor. Meeting first her husband's gaze and then her brother-in-law's, she said in a hiss, "they are both merciless."

Zor flinched inwardly, but made no motion to correct her. Where Kyra was concerned, he was merciless. He watched with grim satisfaction as she slid from Death's shoulder and took to her feet.

Kyra marched stoically across the bar, not stopping to speak to any of the warriors until she noticed Cam. Her jaw dropped open in surprise to see him there. Disbelieving, she sucked in her breath.

"Your Majesty," Cam began, clearly upset to have her thinking he betrayed her.

Kyra held up a palm. "What did you get for this?"

Cam's gaze fell to the floor of the bar. "Your Majesty please," he murmured.

"What," she bit out, "did you get?"

"Five *Kefas* and two bound servants."

Kyra swiped at the tear that fell from her eye. "Well," she said shakily, "congratulations." Turning on her heel, she walked from the bar.

* * * * *

Kyra took to her rooms, barring Zor from their suites for three full moon-risings. Originally, her plan had been to lock herself in and, like a martyr from some tragic novel, let herself die a violent, morbid death when her bridal necklace strangled her from lack of replenishment of Zor's life-force.

When she woke up the next morning alive and well, Kyra realized that the two-hearted scumbag had lied about that as well. Furious, she kept to her rooms another two days, refusing to admit anybody, Tia included.

On the third moon-rising of her self-imposed exile in the royal suites, Kyra grabbed a bottle of bootlegged moonshine and went out to sit on the balcony. Cam had smuggled the outlawed matpow into her rooms while she had slept, along with a note of apology begging her to forgive him.

Donned in a transparent purple *qi'ka,* she fell onto a reclining cot out on the balcony and laid back to watch the glowing green moon shine down. She was a little surprised when, a few minutes later, Kil dropped down from the roof and landed on two feet before her.

"What do you want?" she snapped, scowling at him angrily. "Can't you see I'm busy?"

Kil lifted a pompous brow. "Doing what? Drinking matpow guaranteed to eat through your stomach lining?"

"If I want to," she responded petulantly, knowing she sounded like a child, but not caring.

"You are acting like a spoiled little girl, not at all like an Empress."

Kyra arched a fire-berry brow. "Is Zor dead?"

"No."

"Then fuck off. I don't have to answer to you."

Kil's mouth dropped open in shock. For many moments, he was too stunned to respond. Finally, he threw his head back and laughed.

"That was supposed to be an insult, you idiot!" Kyra snapped, affronted. She sat up on the reclining cot with a harrumph, throwing a pillow behind her back for support.

Kil grabbed the bottle of moonshine from the floor beside her and took a long swallow. Sighing lustily, he swiped his arm across his mouth and grinned. "I know." Dropping onto the cot beside Kyra, he jested, "I think I gentled you too well do you speak to me with such disrespect."

She snorted at that.

They were quiet for long moments until Kil at last broke the silence. "You are hurting him, Kyra."

She flinched, but refused to budge from her stance. "And what of me?" she asked. "Oh never mind, my feelings don't matter. I forgot." She grabbed the bottle of moonshine from Kil and drank a sip.

"Of course they matter," Kil argued, taking the bottle back at first opportunity. "But you won't permit him anywhere near you to give his apologies."

"He wants to apologize?" she asked, hoping she didn't sound overly curious.

"Aye." Kil took a drink from the bottle, then passed it back to her. "He has been haunting my rooms for three moon-risings, nigh unto driving me daft." Rolling his eyes, he pressed on. "The man is punishing himself, refusing his pleasures even."

"Pardon me?"

"He takes no *Kefas* to bath, refusing release of his life-force."

Kyra disliked how good that made her feel. She scowled when instead she wanted to smile. "And no bound servants?"

"Nay!" Kil denied, clearly affronted, "the man is joined with you!" He shook his head. "I have ten brazen, lusty servants awaiting their transfer to their new masters-not to mention the ever ready Myn-begging every hour upon the hour for Zor to give them their woman's joy." He shook his head again. "My brother barely notices their presence, let alone responds to them."

"Really?" Kyra asked quietly, hopefully.

"Aye, really."

They sat in silence for a moment or two until Kyra sighed, gesturing toward Kil. "Why did you come here?" she asked simply.

"Because I love my brother," Kil answered without hesitation, "and because my brother loves you." He craned his neck down to her, surveying her expression. "You believe otherwise?" At Kyra's shrug, he prodded her to reveal more. "Why do you think this?"

Kyra inhaled deeply, throwing her head back and gazing up at the low hanging green moon. "Where I come from, a man in love would never let a brother do what you did to me. Never."

"And you think Zor didn't hurt from it?"

"Did he?"

"Aye." Kil slashed a hand through the air. "He did his duty, though it tore him to pieces, not knowing what it was I was up here doing to you. Aye, 'tis against the laws of succession for a lesser husband to stick his rod into his elder brother's *nee'ka*, but think you there are not some who would do it anyway, caught up in the frenzy of the gentling?"

Kil's lips curled into a snarl, twisting his scar menacingly. "Think you my brother was at training, passing a fair day?" he growled. "He took to the bottle, so overset he was."

Kyra bit her lip. "Then why allow it-insist upon it-in the first place?"

"'Tis the holy law."

"He's an Emperor, a High King. He can change the law."

Kil shook his head. "Nay. How can I make you understand?" Taking a deep breath and muttering something about primitive first dimension notions, he began again. "For all of Tryston's pleasure-seeking, we are also a people steeped in tradition, many of them so ancient we don't remember when or where they began. The laws of succession are amongst those ancient ways. What you, Kyra, have likened to a smack in the face, was the very same tradition that Zor used to prove his caring of you."

Kyra rolled her eyes, not believing it for a moment.

Kil grabbed her by the chin, his nostrils flaring. "Do not," he said quietly, "do that." He made a gentle rubbing motion on her cheeks to soften the fierceness of his words, then released her. "I am being very serious," he said as he settled back upon the cot.

"How so?" she asked in a small voice, feeling somewhat contrite.

"When a woman here is *nee'ka* to the eldest of a line, but no longer has a warrior to command her, be that man a husband or a son, she can be given unto another as a bound servant or worse to protect the line from infiltration of another king's seed. You might not agree with the law, but it is still the law and not even the High King can change it."

Kil held her gaze, forcing Kyra to listen to him. "The laws of succession prevent that from happening."

"And the gentling?" she asked quietly.

"'Tis a warrior proving he cares more for his Sacred Mate's happiness than for his own. 'Tis a man showing his *nee'ka* that she would never have to fear for her future were anything to happen to him, for she would be looked after and well cared for."

Kyra bit her lip. She nibbled on it for a moment. "I see."

She sat quietly for a while, then, deciding to change the subject, asked Kil about what had transpired at Pika's. "Was it necessary to kill that man?" she inquired, studying the floor.

"Aye."

Her head snapped up. "Why?"

"He was not like the others there. I recognized him immediately as an insurrectionist I encountered whilst on Tron."

Kyra nodded. She tipped the bottle of moonshine up to her lips and drank deeply of it. Sighing, she contemplated the matter for a drawn out moment. "Okay. I'll go to him."

"Good." Kil patted her on the knee, then stood up, holding out his hand to give her a lift up. "And one more thing."

"Yes?"

Kil looked her up and down. "I said nothing this moon-rising because of your ignorance of our ways, but now that you have been informed, I expect you to honor your duties."

Kyra blushed, knowing he referred to the removal of her *qi'ka* while alone with him. She nodded slowly, relenting. "All right." She shook her head. "But I don't see the difference," she muttered under her breath. "The damn things are see-through."

Kil smiled unapologetically. "I plan to insure that my brother lives a long and lusty life. You would deny me what little reward I can claim by the law?"

Kyra shook her head and grinned. "Can I ask you a question? Just out of curiosity."

"Aye."

"What would happen if Zor died and you had already claimed a Sacred Mate? We would both be your wives?" she asked stiffly.

Kil shook his head slowly, meeting her gaze. "I cannot even begin to search for a *nee'ka,* if indeed I have one out there, until you breed an heir. Were Zor to die, your bridal necklace would bond us for all time when we joined. Somehow the fates would know and, mystical though it might be, any potential *nee'ka* I might have otherwise claimed would find a true match with another."

"Wow," Kyra breathed out, "how strange."

Kil shrugged negligently. "To you, mayhap, not to us."

She nodded, then took a deep breath. "I'm going to go find Zor." She smiled up to him, hesitantly. "Thank-you, Kil."

He nodded, then turned on his heel and left the way he'd came.

Chapter 20

Kyra found Zor in the blue crystal chamber where she had bathed with Ari upon her arrival in Sand City. He was alone in the bathing pool, laying on his back on a soft jewel rock, without a *Kefa* in sight.

Dropping her purple *qi'ka* to the floor, Kyra waded into the cool silvery waters and walked to where he lay. Zor's head snapped to the side when he realized he wasn't alone.

"Kyra," he whispered hoarsely, his normally glowing eyes dimmed in pain, "what do you here?"

"Is it okay that I'm here?" she asked gently, moving closer.

"For a certainty."

When Zor made a move to sit up, Kyra poked him in the chest and bade him to remain lying down. She scanned every inch of his hard, muscled body, watching with appreciation as he grew aroused at the mere sight of her. "Let me wash you."

"You would do that?" Zor asked in a choked voice.

"You're my husband," she said simply, "and I love you."

"Kyra-oh *pani,* I-"

"Shh. I know." She used her hands to cup up the enchanted water, releasing it over his chest. "You don't have to say anything." She placed her palms on the massive expanse, then ran them soothingly over it. His flat nipples grew hard at her touch, causing him to suck in his breath.

"*Nee'ka,*" he whispered, his erection growing thicker and longer. "I have missed you."

"I know. I missed you too."

Kyra spent the next twenty minutes cleaning every part of Zor's body with her bare hands, touching and rubbing everything but his erection. By the time she finally touched him there, he nearly came up off of the rock. "You best not clean me there, wee one, or I'm liable to spurt."

"It's my duty to make certain every part of you is thoroughly washed," Kyra said wickedly. "Don't fight me."

Zor sucked in his breath when she began to massage his man sac. "Oh *pani*," he groaned. Closing his eyes, he gave up the fight and enjoyed every moment of his wife's attention. "'Tis tight for need of you," he whispered thickly.

"It needs me?" Kyra asked coyly as she bent her head to lick his balls. At Zor's bellow, she figured it did. Sucking his scrotum into her mouth, she stroked her hands up and down her husband's cock while she suckled from his man sac.

"By the goddess," Zor sighed, his head falling back on the rock. Breathing deeply, he sat up, hoisted Kyra into his arms and waded toward the middle of the pool. "I can take no more tortures, woman."

Splaying her body wide on a flat, soft jewel rock that put her channel at the perfect angle to accept his shaft, Zor lifted her hips and thrust into her. "*Nee'ka*." He pounded into her, hard and violently, needing to be one with her. "Do you see what you do to me, lusty wench? Do you see how my body demands yours?"

"Zor." Kyra met his thrusts eagerly, her vaginal muscles milking his cock. "Harder," she begged. "I need all of you."

Zor pummeled her cunt fast and hard, long and deep. When Kyra arched her back and climaxed, he grabbed her proffered breasts, kneading them and tugging at her jutting nipples. "Give me more, *nee'ka*. I command from you more." Grinding his hips into her, he took her ferociously, making up for his abstinence.

When again Kyra peaked, Zor went from ferocious to animalistic. Releasing his hold on one of her nipples, he continued to pound away at her slick, flooded channel while he expertly massaged her drenched clit with his thumb. "Is this what you want?" he asked arrogantly.

"Oh god-oh yes." Kyra climaxed violently, her hips thrashing out for more. "Please, Zor. I'll do anything-just do it."

"What would you have me do?" Zor growled through clenched teeth, hammering into her. "Spurt my life-force? Are you lusty for my seed?"

"Yes-oh god-yes."

When Kyra peaked again, her husband rewarded her with the reward she'd asked for. Spurting deep into her channel, the stones in her necklace pulsed. Zor closed his eyes, the muscles in his neck corded tightly.

"Mine," he roared, his bellow carrying throughout the bathing chamber. "All mine."

He continued to thrust deeply as Kyra screamed and the ceaseless waves brought peak after peak of mind-numbing climax.

* * * * *

No one in the palace heard from nor saw heads or tails of the High King and High Queen for three more moon-risings. Finally, feeling somewhat worried, Kil let himself into their apartments to make certain all was well.

His lips kicked up into a semi-grin when he reached the raised bed and knew for a certainty his brother was in good spirits. 'Twas obvious the poor warrior was sorely besotted with his *nee'ka*.

Kyra was asleep, her arms thrown up over her head, her breasts thrust upward, pink nipples jutting up deliciously. One of her legs was bent at the knee, giving an explicit view of her swollen labia and clit. Zor was snoring the sleep of the dead, stretched out half on top of her, his head resting on her breasts, his mouth latched onto one of her distended nipples. One of

Zor's hands rested near his *nee'ka's* pelt of fire-berry hair, his fingers occasionally grazing the wisp of curls.

Kil shook his head and grinned. His brother had the worn out, utterly contented look of a green warrior just given his first plaything to see to his pleasures. He remembered so many years past when first his father had given him three *Kefas* to see to his baths. Kil had no doubt been the cleanest lad in all of Tryston. And when the *Kefas* were later given to him in truth, permitted to accompany him back to his rooms, none had seen Kil for a sennight or longer.

"Wake up sleepy heads," Kil said, kicking his foot against the red crystal bed's foundation. "You have company."

Zor grumbled something imperceptible as he half opened his eyes, then upon seeing his brother, closed them again. "Go away. I am nigh unto dead."

"Such bad manners," Kil commented with mock hurt. "And when I have traveled all the way from the great hall just to see your handsome face."

Zor sat up and rubbed his eyes. His hair was disheveled and he looked to have the markings of love bites spotting his chest. Kil wanted to laugh, but figured his brother wouldn't appreciate it. "Your *nee'ka* sleeps well too, I see."

At the mention of Kyra, Zor's eyes lit up to their usual glowing blue. Lying back on his elbow, he craned his neck to gaze down at her slumbering form. He smiled, so sweet and innocent his wee one looked in slumber. Not at all the she-beast in heat she had been at last moon-rising. "Aye."

He bent his head and licked his tongue up the length of her pussy, starting at her channel's opening and ending at her swollen clit. "She has been loved well these past moon-risings." Squinting, he looked up to Kil. "How many moon-risings has it been anyway?"

Kil snorted. "Three."

"For a certainty?"

"Aye."

Zor sat up, stretched his muscles and yawned. "Call for some *Kefas*. We've a blessed need for a bath. You will bathe with us, brother?"

"Twill be an honor." Kil inclined his head formally, then turned to summon the slaves.

* * * * *

Kyra lay naked on her side, propped up on one elbow, partaking of breakfast with Zor and Kil. Fresh out of the bath, she felt languid and dreamy as she lay in a bed of soft *vesha* hides on the floor. The men were naked as well, as was the norm when breakfasting together after bathing.

Kyra smiled secretly, bemused by the fact that after the *Kefas* had brought her to peak for the men's viewing pleasure, it had taken Kil five climaxes before he felt sated enough to dine. Poor guy. When she looked at the situation from his perspective, it must be difficult to be forced by the law to observe all the formalities of a husband, but receive none of the benefits of it.

They dined on vintage matpow, creamy cheeses, and thick loaves of fragrant bread. Not to mention sweet fruits-fire-berries included-and a delicious stew of some sort. It was the only full meal she and Zor had partaken of in days.

Leha, a beautiful topless servant with tanned skin, silky blonde hair, and large breasts that sported perfectly rounded nipples, came flying into the bedchamber, her breasts bobbing up and down. Kyra happened to like the woman a lot and was therefore secretly plotting to cajole Zor into setting her up financially when her five Yessat years worth of service were up.

"Your Majesty!" she beamed, smiling at Kyra as she ran toward her. "I have excellent news!"

Kyra smiled, sitting upright. There was something about the glow in Leha's eyes that told her she wasn't exaggerating. "What is it?"

"'Tis King Dak!"

Kyra's eyes widened. "He's here?!" She took to her feet, smiling from ear to ear.

"What's this?" Zor frowned, a scowl smothering his features. "I do not think that I care o'er much for your excitement over seeing my brother, *nee'ka*."

"Aye," Kil seconded. He winked at Kyra. "Most especially when she treats me with disrespect."

"Hush you two." Kyra waved her hand, indicating they were to be quiet. The brothers looked at each other and grinned. Kyra turned back to Leha. "Well. Tell me!"

Leha laughed. "He has brought his Sacred Mate!"

That caused a murmur amongst the men. Kyra held up a hand to silence them. "And?!" she prodded, grabbing the servant by the arms. "Is it Geris? Is it my best friend?"

"Aye!"

Kyra squealed, jumping up and down in her excitement-an action that caused both warriors a painful erection. "Oh my god!" she beamed. "Leha, please help me find a *qi'ka*. I want to go to her right now!"

"What's this?" Zor asked, somewhat bewildered. "Do you speak of the comely onyx wench who was with you when I claimed you?"

Kil sat up, clearly intrigued. Two of his brothers had found their women in the first dimension? Hmm.

"Yes!" Kyra clapped her hands together and jumped up and down again. Both men groaned. "Dak said because of the fact he was too busy scanning for threats, he didn't test Geris to see if she was his Sacred Mate. We talked the other day, a week ago I guess, and he told me he planned to return to first dimension earth to see if she was his!" Her words were tripping out over each other in her excitement. "And she is!"

Leha bounded over, a black *qi'ka* in her arms. She helped Kyra put it on. "'Tis for a certainty Queen Geris seems not at all pleased with King Dak's insistence that she belongs to him. Nor does she have a care for the wearing of her *qi'ka*."

Kyra grinned. "I'll just bet."

"She has been ranting in the great hall about certain unalienable rights-whatever in the sands those are-and demands to speak to the 'mutha fucka' in charge." Leha blushed, turning to Zor. "That t'would be you, Your Majesty."

Zor grunted. "Your best friend is daft, *nee'ka,* does she think I will let her forsake Dak and leave."

Kyra waved dismissively. "I remember being just as angry, Zor. She'll get over it. Besides,"-she turned and grinned-"they must not have joined yet."

Chapter 21

Kyra, Zor, and Kil entered the great hall in time to witness Queen Geris having a royal fit of temper. She was standing on top of the raised table, preparing to throw an extremely expensive bottle of vintage matpow to the ground. Her bridal necklace was glowing an ominous red, indicating that her husband was pissed.

"Ger-is," Dak reprimanded in his most chastising tone, "you will put my brother's bottle of matpow down anon, else will you be grounded from your woman's joy for a full sennight after the joining." He crossed his arms over his chest and frowned formidably.

Kyra was amused to note that her best friend actually hesitated. Then, scowling, Geris hoisted the bottle higher into the air, preparing to render it to shards.

"Please don't," Kyra grinned, making her presence known, "that happens to be my favorite label."

Stunned, after having thought she'd been tricked into coming to Tryston by Dak, Geris whirled around. "Kyra?" she asked quietly, disbelieving what she was seeing.

"Ger?" Kyra took a step forward.

"Kyra!" Geris beamed, smiling from ear to ear.

"Ger!"

The two women squealed, running toward each other at top speed. When they met, they danced around in a circle, hugging and laughing. Dak grabbed the bottle of matpow out of his recalcitrant wife's hand while she was distracted.

"Kyra!" Geris laughed, running her hand down the side of her best friend's face to make certain she was really there. "It is you, girl!"

"And it's you!" Kyra beamed, tears streaming down her face. "I missed you so much!"

The two women chattered nonstop, taking seats by the raised table. Dak turned to his two brothers, and strolling toward them, rolled his eyes. "If you thought the taming of Kyra was a trial, then would your head have the ache whilst taming my *nee'ka*."

Zor chuckled low in his throat. "She is, uh, tenacious."

"Aye."

"But lovely," Kil added, his glowing blue eyes flicking over her dark, statuesque form. "Quite lovely."

"Aye," Dak replied dreamily, hugging the brother he hadn't seen in well over a Yessat year. "My wee one is a beauty for a certainty."

Kil clapped him on the back, shaking his head. "Do all women of first dimension earth possess such rare skins?"

"Nay," Zor supplied for his brother, "though many do."

"'Tis true," Dak expounded, ruminating over what he'd seen. "Even the beauties whose hues lie somewhere between the *sekta* and the onyx have a coloring much different from the bronzed women here."

"Interesting," Kil murmured.

At Dak's sigh, both brothers turned questioningly, prodding him for information.

"What ails you?" Zor asked.

"We needs have a consummation feast tonight."

Zor scowled, knowing that meant that non-mated warriors would be touching his *nee'ka*. He hadn't thought he'd have to endure this so soon after the last one.

Kil, on the other hand, was licking his lips and rubbing his palms together. "And this is a problem how?"

"I fear telling my *nee'ka* what transpires at one. You have seen her in a temper." Dak groaned, clapping a hand to his forehead. "And that 'twas but a mild one."

Kil chuckled. "Then do not tell her. Leave Kyra to prepare her."

"Or Ari," Zor mused. "Ari will no doubt be here the soonest to bathe with her. Ah," he grinned, "here comes the Chief Priestess now."

* * * * *

Kyra had thought to tell Geris of what was going to happen tonight at the consummation feast when she spotted Ari strolling toward them. Having forgotten about that part of the ritual, she wetted her lips, getting nervous as to how she should proceed. In truth, she didn't know what Geris would think about peaking with a priestess while being intimately massaged by slaves. She decided the reaction would not be a good one if she knew what was coming before it actually transpired.

Kyra could sense that Geris already harbored attached feelings toward Dak. Her best friend repeatedly denied them, of course, even as her gaze would seek the golden-haired warrior out and flick over him dreamily. Kyra understood exactly what she was feeling and, because she did, could empathize with her best friend wholeheartedly. Of course, she also knew that once Geris joined with Dak, she would never again seek to leave him. Kill him, perhaps, but never leave him.

Whether out of a selfishness to keep her here or out of an altruistic desire to see her best friend happy, Kyra decided not to do anything that might rock the boat. If they could just get through this day and Geris and Dak became successfully joined, all would be well.

So, rather than say anything that might caused Geris to put out her prickles like a porcupine, she simply patted her hand and smiled at her, figuring she'd leave the rest up to Ari. "Here comes the Chief Priestess." Kyra cleared her throat. "I believe she'll want to speak with you in private."

* * * * *

Kyra grimaced when she saw the look of rampage on Geris's face as she came charging toward her. Feigning ignorance, she pretended not to see her, whistling as she looked around the cavernous great hall.

The consummation ceremony had just begun, but nothing had transpired yet, as they had all been waiting on the guest of honor to arrive. Now here she was, huffing as she took her seat next to Kyra.

Kyra couldn't hold it in any longer. She gave up the fight and giggled. "Ger!" She grinned mischievously. "Have a nice bath?"

Geris harrumphed. Crossing her arms under her breasts, she set her chin at a stubborn angle. "How," she asked as she leaned in toward Kyra and whispered through set teeth, "could you not prepare me for that?"

Kyra had the good grace to blush. "I was afraid you wouldn't take it well."

"Wouldn't take it well?" she squeaked. "Girl, you know I'm a Southern Baptist. My mama would roll over in her grave if she knew what I did in there with that priestess woman!"

Kyra's mind flicked ahead to what Geris might possibly end up doing with Ari tonight during the joining. Telling herself she was remaining silent for Geris's own good and not because she was chickening out, she decided not to mention it. "Yes, well, that's the last time you'll have to bathe with Ari." That much was true.

"Is it true about those slaves? They are enchanted women? They don't have brains or emotions?"

"It's true." Kyra nodded succinctly.

Geris let out a breath, relaxing somewhat. "Thank God for that. But what about them?" Her hand waved toward the other side of the dining hall where the topless bound servants were beginning to file in to see to the warriors, mated and non-mated alike. "You can't tell me they aren't real."

Kyra briefly explained what a bound servant was. Geris either accepted her answer better than Kyra had thought she would, or the new bride was feeling too overwhelmed by the enormity of it all to question her further.

Kyra turned Geris's attention by introducing her to Tia, as well as to some of the other royal *nee'kas* of her acquaintance. Most of the bridal party was already mated, though a few non-mated women took part in the festivities as well. Once Geris's attention was thoroughly ensconced in conversation, Kyra's eyes flicked towards the groom's party across the room.

All of the men had *Kefas* and bound servants administering to them. Zor, of course, was the one Kyra's attention was focused on, taking in the sight of him through semi-narrowed eyes. She was jealous. Not to mention turned on. Two volatile emotions when brought together.

Zor had no *Kefas* administering to him, only bound women tonight. A brunette was pillowing him from behind, her hands massaging his expansive shoulders, while Leha sat in his lap and giggled. Zor smiled back at her, then sucked on her nipples, leaving a popping sound echoing in its wake when he released them.

Parting her *qi'ka*, he showed off her nest of blonde curls to Kil. "Fair tempting," he grinned, running his hands through her intimate hair. Bidding her to part her thighs, Zor rubbed Leha's labia and clit until she moaned, climaxing on his hand.

Kyra couldn't believe how aroused she was getting, watching the scene unfold. Actually, she could believe it, having discovered her lust for watching the night she and Zor had joined. She felt jealousy as well, but it was growing less and less acute, washing away as pleasure took over.

Leha was passed over to Kil, Kil having wanted her since first he saw her and her bobbing breasts running into the royal bedchamber this morn. Leha lay in his arms with her legs spread, smiling up at him, as the warrior fondled her woman's bud, pressing on it with the pad of his thumb. She groaned, peaking for him three times before he next spoke to her.

"I vow, beautiful Leha, you are a comely wench. Would you like to be mine for the remainder of my stay here, sharing the *vesha* hides with me?" he rumbled.

"Aye," she breathed out. "If you would have me, 'twill be you I call master whilst you are here."

"Then call me master," Kil growled, stroking her swollen labia. "And attend to my staff before I spill my life-force in my pants."

Leha giggled, then did as she was bade.

Zor was currently holding two sensuous twins on his lap, taking turns sucking at their nipples while they stroked his freed shaft. It was Kyra's understanding that the duo had been obtained by Kil while warring on Tron.

Kyra felt the familiar heat in her belly pooling as Zor closed his eyes and lay his head back on the brunette who was pillowing him. The twins were now taking to their knees, one of them sucking up and down the length of his cock while the other one attended to his scrotum. "Mmm," he purred, "'tis bliss, your mouths."

The brunette that was pillowing Zor began stroking his chest, running her fingertips across his hard nipples as the twins continued to suck. A few minutes later, Zor was climaxing and the voracious twins were switching who got to do what. "Do not be too greedy for my seed," he teased, "I needs have some left for my *nee'ka*."

"What in the hell," Geris intoned in a hiss, "is going on over there?"

Startled out of her arousal, Kyra craned her neck to study Geris. Her best friend was currently watching the scene across the dining hall with a look of fascinated horror on her face.

"It's a part of the consummation ceremony," Kyra murmured. "The warriors are brought to climax by the servants and slaves."

"Sweet Jesus. Are those the warriors with no mates?"

"Uh, no."

Geris squinted, then realized it was Zor she was watching spurt his orgasm into the mouth of a servant. "Girl, your husband just...just...just..." When Geris's jaw dropped open, Kyra bit her lip, knowing her best friend had spotted Dak.

"Bastard!" Geris snapped, jumping to her feet. "Two-timing dog!"

Dak paled, grimacing even as he climaxed. "'Tis naught but tradition, my hearts!" he called out on a moan from across the great hall.

"Tradition my ass!" Geris screamed, her eyes smoldering him where he sat. "Get that blue bitch off you now!"

Kyra and Tia pulled Geris back down into her seat. "'Twill be all right," Tia informed her soothingly. "Kyra did have much the same reaction, though one not quite so loud." At Geris's frown, Tia hastened to add, "you will get your revenge the soonest."

"Oh really?" Geris scowled, crossing her arms under her breasts. "How?"

Kyra and Tia looked at each other and then at Geris, giggled and simultaneously informed her, "you'll see."

Chapter 22

Geris, it seemed, took the revenge business very seriously. Whereas most new brides would be content trysting with the non-mated warriors on a reclining cot, Geris had demanded that the table be cleared so she could lie up there, making certain Dak and every other warrior across the great hall had an excellent view of her, Jek, Mik, Gio, and another warrior unfamiliar to Kyra, going at it.

Dak was standing across the chamber, his hands folded across his massive chest, a tic in his cheek working furiously. Smiling to herself, Kyra turned on her heel to go back to her seat and instead found herself being lifted up into Cam's massive arms.

Laying her down on a reclining cot, he deposited himself next to Kyra and propped up on one elbow to gaze down at her. "Do not be angry with me any longer," Cam pleaded in a sad, quiet tone. Parting the skirt of her *qi'ka,* he ran his fingers through her pelt of fire-berry hair and groaned. "'Tis killing me inside."

"Is it?" she breathed out, inhaling sharply when Cam began to stroke her intimately, massaging her clit.

"Do you like that?" he whispered thickly. "By the goddess, how I wish I could stick my rod into you. You've no idea how many moon-risings I have brought myself to peak thinking only of you."

"Oh, Cam." Kyra ran her hand over his handsome jaw, not certain what to say. This was evidently the Trystonni version of a first crush and he was obviously taking it seriously.

Spreading her legs wide to accept his questing fingers inside, they both groaned when she gyrated her hips. "Have you made love with your new servants yet?" she asked breathlessly.

"Nay. We are supposed to go pick out the ones we want in a few moon-risings, yet can I not work up an appetite for it with you mad at me." His fingers still exploring the inside of her pussy, Cam used his other hand to remove the fragile *qi'ka* top and throw it away from them. He groaned. "I have thought of these hard berries every moon-rising since last I suckled from them." Inclining his head, he closed his eyes and curled his tongue around one erect nipple, sucking from her chest like a weaning babe.

Kyra bit her lip. Cam really did have it bad for her. He was such a sweetheart that the last thing she wanted was for him to walk around pining away for her. The realist in her argued that Cam's crush no doubt stemmed from the fact that she was the only humanoid female in constant contact with him. Prancing around all but naked while being near him couldn't have helped matters much. Cam definitely needed to go pick out his servants.

"I'm not mad at you, Cam," Kyra admitted, sucking in her breath as the warrior drew harder from her breast, his fingers thrashing frantically inside of her. "Oh-Cam." She climaxed, her hard nipple jutting up into his mouth.

Cam groaned, sucking harder at the rigid peak. Raising his head a minute later, he removed his fingers from her passage and licked them clean. "You promise?"

"Yes."

"Good." His eyes feasted on Kyra's aroused body as he grabbed a breast and squeezed. "Let me attend to you again, Your Majesty. Your body drives me nigh unto daft."

Kyra grinned. "With lines like that, you'll go far with the women."

"'Tis the truth," Cam said, grinning back but nevertheless serious. "I chose not to dally o'er much at your consummation feast because I had not Muta for relief back then, but now"-he wiggled his golden eyebrows mischievously-"I am ready to gorge."

"Go feast on the other wenches," a familiar voice commanded him softly, "I would have this time with the High Queen."

Kyra was stunned to see Kil lowering himself down beside her. Not wanting to make a scene, she turned to Cam and nudged him with a smile. "Go on. I know you want to. Enjoy yourself with the other mated women here."

"For a certainty?"

"Yes. Go on."

Cam smiled, then stood up to defer to the lesser husband's wishes. When he was out of earshot, Kyra turned to Kil and searched his face. "What are you doing over here?"

"What does it look like?" Kil took the spot Cam's departure had opened up. Running his fingers over Kyra's engorged labia, he began to massage her clit. "I see the young buck has prepared you for my ministrations."

"Actually," Kyra admitted on a gasp, "I've already peaked twice, so I should probably go to Zor."

"I didn't hear you peak."

"Well I still did."

"If you say so." Kil grinned. Thrusting two fingers into her tight channel, he continued to rub her swollen clit, something the much younger Cam hadn't been experienced enough to automatically know to do. "But Zor will not leave the warrior's side of the chamber until he hears you climax."

"He came for me the last time."

"'Tis my understanding that you screamed the last time."

"Yes," Kyra breathed out, rotating her hips as a natural reaction to pleasure-seeking. "But last time I was in Geris's position on center stage. I had hands all over me."

Kil thrust his fingers deeper, continuing to massage her sensitive bud. "Believe me, lusty one, I will be able to accomplish alone what it takes four and five of these young bucks to do."

Kyra didn't doubt that, and that's what worried her. Placing her hand on his wrist to stop him, she was irritated when it didn't work. "Kil," she moaned, "please stop. This doesn't seem right."

"What doesn't seem right to me," Kil said brazenly, massaging her as her channel flooded, "is having a tradition that forces me to sample of your charms, but not allowing me to taste of them." His lips curled unrepentantly. "So I'm going to remedy that just a wee bit."

Kyra was about to climax when Kil brought his ministrations to an abrupt halt. Her eyelids fluttered open questioningly.

"You do not get off the hook that easy," Kil informed her mockingly, "because as I said, I would taste of you first."

"But-"

He held up a silencing palm. "'Tis my right as a lesser husband to do this at consummation feasts should I desire it." He situated his body between Kyra's splayed legs and feasted his eyes on her heavy breasts. She could feel his fierce erection. "Do you deny me my rights?"

Kyra flushed, remembering the promise he had extracted from her a few days past out on the balcony. Now she had to wonder how mapped out this situation had been on her plotting brother-in-law's part. "No, of course not."

Kil grunted, satisfied. "Grab both of your breasts for me, then hold up your nipples for my inspection. Come now, let me see you do it."

Kyra did as she was bade, the arousal in her belly knotting. She felt guilty for a moment, but let the feeling pass when she heard Zor climax for what had to be the fifth time across the room.

"Leha," he was crooning, "had I known of your talent for suckling, I would have availed myself of you before."

Nostrils flaring, Kyra thrust her elongated nipples up to Kil's mouth. "Suck them."

Kil grinned down at her, the scar on his right cheek twisting. "If you plan to have a happy life on Tryston, 'tis important to learn that lust and love do not always go hand-in-hand. Leastways, not at consummation feasts." He bent his neck, laving at both rosy peaks, then raised his head to meet her gaze again. "But, aye, I will be happy to make Zor jealous for you."

With a growl, Kil lowered his mouth to Kyra's plumped up nipples and feasted. She inhaled sharply, grinding her hips against him. Kil ground his hips back, simulating the act of joining.

"Mmm," he said on a low moan over and over, as he continued to draw from her nipples and rock back and forth between her thighs. "Mmm."

Kyra moaned. "Oh god-oh Kil."

"Mmm." Kil rotated his hips, steering Kyra closer and closer to peak. And just when she almost reached it, he stopped-again.

Kyra hit him on the back. "That's twice! Stop it!"

He lifted his face from her breasts and grinned unabashedly. "Getting frustrated, lusty one?" He craned his neck to brush his tongue over both nipples in one long swipe, then raised his head again. "I would taste more of you before giving you your woman's joy."

"Such as?"

Kyra sucked in her breath as Kil moved down her body, raining wet kisses in his path. Behind her she heard Geris scream out her release, then heard Dak snarling at the warriors who had caused it as he picked her up and carried her from the room.

"Are you ready to scream like that?" Kil asked arrogantly, splaying Kyra's legs wide and settling his face between them. He teased her with a quick lap to her cunt, inducing her to moan. "Answer me."

"Yes."

"Is my brother watching?"

Kyra grinned without looking away from Kil. "Yes."

"How do you know?"

"My bride's necklace is glowing a red-green."

"Ah." Kil took another lick, savoring the sweet, clean taste of her flesh. "He's pissed and he's lusty-an excellent combination."

Kyra rotated her hips, swiping her labia across Kil's mouth. Now it was her brother-in-law who was groaning. "Pinch my nipples while you taste me," she breathed out on a thick whisper.

"By the goddess, you are a lusty piece." Kil reached up and grabbed both of Kyra's nipples, rolling them between his fingers.

"Oh god-yes." Kyra's neck went limp, her head falling back on the reclining cot. When Kil growled low in his throat and his mouth dove to feast on her wet cunt, she actually came up off of the cot a little. "Ohhh." Knowing that her husband was watching, that later he would fuck her mindless, only heightened the effect Kil's stellar skill had on her. "Yes. Kil. Suck harder-oh yes, there."

Kil dined on her swollen pink flesh like a hungry animal. Still pulling on her nipples, he licked and sucked on her labia and clit, slurping sounds echoing throughout the great hall.

"God." Kyra wrapped a leg around Kil's neck without thinking, smashing his face into her slippery folds.

"Mmmmm," Kil rumbled, vibrating Kyra's clit with the sound. "Mmmmmm."

It was all she could stand. Arching her hips, Kyra wrapped both legs around his neck, smashed his face into her trembling flesh, threw her head back, and let out a scream that brought the rafters down.

A few moments later, Kil sat up, breathing harshly. Kyra rolled onto her stomach, then got up on all fours, doing the same. Expecting for Zor to lift her up and take her to their bedchamber, she was surprised when instead she felt his hands grab a hold of her hips and his large, thick cock surge into her from behind. "Zor-what are you-ohhhhhh!"

Kyra's eyes rolled back into her head as a swift, ferocious climax overpowered her thinking. Moaning, she met her husband's thrusts eagerly and wantonly.

Kil stretched out on his side, propped himself up on one elbow, and his lips curling wryly, watched the show. More warriors gathered around until there was a huge circle formed about Kyra and Zor.

It wasn't everyday they would be given the chance to watch a royal mating and well they knew it. A High King only put his *nee'ka* on public display when he wanted to demonstrate his dominance over her, when he wanted to prove to his warriors that 'twas him that held all dominion over her pleasures.

Zor thrust his cock into Kyra from behind, over and over, again and again. When she climaxed, he pumped harder. When she begged for more, he pummeled relentlessly. When she pleaded for him to make the bridal stones pulse, he denied her.

He made her beg for it.

He made her plead for it.

He made her grovel for it.

And still, Zor denied her. After Kyra's next shattering climax convulsed her, Zor pounded into her flesh as he arrogantly asked, "who owns this lusty piece of flesh between your thighs?" She peaked again, sobbing for his seed. "Who?" he barked.

"You do. Oh god-you do."

Zor shifted his hips, grinding into Kyra's cunt until she screamed. Rotating again, he hammered her mercilessly from behind, her breasts jiggling in time with his thrusts. "What warrior has fucked this sweet channel but me?" he possessively growled.

"No one."

"Say it again."

"No one."

"Shall I show these men why?" Zor asked arrogantly, thrusting harder, pounding faster.

"Yes-oh god yes."

The non-mated warriors grew still, eyes wide, penises erect, all of them eager to see what happened when a bride's necklace pulsed. Even Kil, jaded as he was, couldn't squelch his brewing restlessness. They had all heard stories. None had seen it firsthand.

Muscles tense and corded, Zor grabbed Kyra's hips and pounded into her. Hard. Fast. Relentless. Over and over. Again and again. She bucked and arched, screamed and begged, pleaded and sobbed. And just when she thought she wouldn't be able to stand it anymore, Zor's nostrils flared and he bellowed, "then take my seed."

The bridal necklace pulsed.

Kyra screamed.

Zor bellowed.

The spectators blanched.

Kyra and Zor convulsed and shook-her keening, him roaring-both of them riding peak after peak after peak of ceaseless, never-ending, soul-shattering climax. It went on and on, wave after wave, mind-numbing in its intensity.

When at last the waves ebbed, Kyra fell to the ground, depleted. Zor gentled himself on top of her, breathing harshly.

Kil was the first to come out of the trance-like state and regain some semblance of reason. Inhaling deeply, he stood up and shuffled the warriors from the great hall to give his brother and sister-within-the-law their privacy.

"Find a lusty wench and take to your rooms, men," Kil directed as he blew out a breath of air. "I know I'll be finding a few."

* * * * *

Dak dragged his gaze back from where the naked Chief Priestess sat next to him and leveled it onto his bride. He took in the sight of her tempting onyx body stretched out and splayed wide, ready to accommodate him, and his nostrils flared with the satisfaction of an accomplished hunter. His breathing was choppy, his control stretched.

'Twas time.

Dak summoned the clothes from his body, one golden eyebrow arching arrogantly when he heard his *nee'ka's* drawn-in breath at the sight of his fierce erection. "Aye?"

Geris licked her lips. Her almond-shaped eyes rounded disbelievingly. "Sweet Jesus," she muttered.

Dak grinned. "You know what they say, my hearts."

"W-What's that?"

"Once you go Dak, you never go back."

Chapter 23

The following morning, Kyra left her rooms to go down to breakfast only to discover that not only had last night's performance managed to reaffirm Cam's crush on her, but she also had a few more recruits to add to his number. Mik, Gio, and two more warriors she hadn't been introduced to until just now, followed in her wake like puppies clamoring for attention.

"'Tis I who should escort her to breakfast," Cam declared.

"Nay," Mik scowled, "you escort her nigh unto every morn."

"Think you that 'tis you who should do it?" Gio snapped at Mik.

And so went the conversation until Kyra held up a palm and bade them all to escort her to breakfast. When they then almost came to blows over who would stand on what side of her, she'd had enough.

Making them flip a credit, she then assigned Cam to her left, Gio to her right, and the remaining three to the rear of her. At first the "losers" of the credit toss had thought to complain, but then they had gotten a close-up view of what losing offered and clamped their mouths shut.

Cam and Gio were the happiest, though, for being to either side of the wee High Queen made it easy for them to gaze down and watch her breasts jiggle as she walked.

Smiling sweetly and just as falsely, Kyra gently asked her escorts if they had yet been moved into their new suite.

"Nay," Gio pouted, his handsome brow furrowing. "It could mayhap be another sennight before the suite has been made ready for us."

"So that means you haven't had your women yet?"

"Nay," all answered in unison.

"Except Cam," Gio added, "who has Muta."

Kyra nodded, figuring as much. She decided to make her next project a magician's trick-she would figure out how to turn a sennight into a day. Please, she sighed to herself, let it be possible.

* * * * *

"Ah," Kil teased Zor. "Here comes your *nee'ka* now. And look, five hard warriors are with her." Bellowing in laughter at his own pun, he grabbed his stomach and guffawed.

Zor rolled his eyes, clearly not impressed with his brother's warped wit, though 'twas good to see him laughing more and more these days. "Cease your bellowing, dunce. They seek only to escort her to the table."

"Uh huh. That explains their leathers being stretched at the crotch then."

"Harrumph. They are not...they are n-harrumph. I see your point."

Zor's eyes trailed possessively up and down the length of his wee *nee'ka's* form. She looked resplendent today in a *qi'ka* of green that set off the fire-berry of her hair, both atop her head and between her thighs. 'Twas almost nonexistent, the *qi'ka* was so transparent, so he could understand the reaction it had on the randy young warriors. 'Twas having the same effect on him were he honest.

"'Tis I who shall hold out her chair for her."

"Nay, lackwit, 'tis I."

"Ha! I don't think 'tis either of you. I think-"

"Enough." Zor scowled at his quibbling warriors as he surged to his feet. "I will hold the chair for my *nee'ka* this morn." When they knew enough to flush awkwardly on their feet and cast their gazes to the ground, he realized that they understood him well. "Which of you has seen to the High Queen thus far?"

"Cam," Gio answered begrudgingly.

"Then Cam will see to her from now on, aye?"

"Aye," they answered in unison.

"Be gone and take to the fields. Kil will teach you more offensive maneuverings this day."

When the warriors had gone and Zor still hadn't made a motion to seat her, Kyra delicately cleared her throat, garnering her husband's attention. He was staring at her territorially, and if she hadn't missed her mark, he wanted to couple. But there was something else there too. Some glint in his eye Kyra didn't recognize.

"Aye?" Zor asked in a thick whisper.

"My chair," she whispered.

"Ah. Of course, *pani*."

Zor telekinetically summoned the chair to move out. When Kyra sat down, he flicked his wrist to send it back in. "So," he said stiffly, as he took his own seat, "what 'twas that sorry scene all about?"

Kyra shrugged, motioning toward Kil to pass her the *taka* juice. "Beats me. Where are Geris and Dak?"

"They have not yet emerged from their rooms. Why were those bucks trailing after you that way?"

Kyra threw Kil a "gee-I-wonder-why" glance. "I don't know. Has anyone seen them? The joining went well then?"

"They are fucking like two *maki* beasts in full rut. Why were they following you?" Zor bellowed.

The great hall grew very quiet. Servants tried not to stare as they passed by the raised table with foodstuffs and drink.

Kyra's face colored. She shifted her gaze to her goblet of juice. "They have crushes on me, I suppose."

"I see. And why would that be?" Zor asked viciously. "Were you letting them touch you before you came down? Did you part your *qi'ka* and let them fondle your channel?"

"Brother," Kil murmured, "you are embarrassing your *nee'ka*."

"Stay out!" Zor held up a palm to silence Kil without removing his gaze from Kyra. "So tell me, devoted *nee'ka* of mine. Tell me why. Tell me which of them has been giving you your woman's joy, or has it been all of them?"

"Fuck you!"

Kyra surged to her feet, spun on her heel, and fled from the great hall.

Kil took a calming breath before laying into Zor. "Way to go, brother. I take it you enjoy having your *nee'ka* out of sorts with you. It seems to me you just got back in her good graces and here you are already back out of them."

Zor pounded his fist on the tabletop, sending goblets and crystal dishes flying. "How dare you defend her!"

"She has done nothing!"

"Oh? And you know this how? Because she saves all of her charms for you?"

"You," Kil bit out, "go too far."

"Not nearly as far as you went with her last night."

"'Twas a consummation feast!"

Zor slashed his hand tersely through the air. "I care not what it was. You did everything but fuck her right there on the floor!"

"I did no more to Kyra, and mayhap far less, than what you did to our brother Rem's *nee'ka* during her consummation feast. And since only the *nee'ka* of the eldest in the line needs be gentled, we both know you were no lesser husband to her." When Zor flushed, Kil smiled without humor. "I see now what your temper is about."

"I know not what you mean," he growled defensively.

"Aye brother, you do." Kil stood up, preparing to take to the fields. "You're feeling lower than a *heeka-beast* for splaying your woman out and fucking her like a dog before common warriors." Kil shook his head and sighed. "You should have been grateful your *nee'ka* was still speaking to you, but because she was forgiving enough to do so, you punish her for it rather than thanking her."

Zor closed his eyes and lowered his head into his hands. "She will never forgive me now," he whispered. "Never. I know it."

Kil sighed deeply. "You are wrong, brother." He clapped Zor on the back. "If you would but open your fool eyes, you might just realize how much the wee wench loves you."

* * * * *

Zor found Kyra at Pika's Place, sitting dejectedly on a barstool trying to get sotted. Thankfully, Death and Glok were nowhere in sight, else Zor wasn't certain he could have held his temper. Actually, not many were in sight this time of the day, save a couple of stragglers scattered about.

When Kyra looked up from her bottle of moonshine and saw him, she quickly averted her gaze, muttering something about all the gin joints in the world and the luck of him walking into hers. He couldn't be certain, but Zor sensed 'twas her first dimension sarcasm at work again.

"What are you doing here, Zor?" Kyra put the question to him with a sigh, rubbing her temples, as if she was too tired to fight with him.

"I came for you, *nee'ka*."

"Why?"

"You belong with me," Zor said softly.

Kyra snorted. "And with everybody else, to hear you tell it," she grumbled.

Zor flinched, hating himself for what he'd said in the great hall. "*Pani*, please. I did not mean it. I was just...just..."

"Just what?"

"Furious with myself."

Kyra swung around on the barstool. She eyed him up and down curiously. Opening her mouth to say something, she clicked her teeth shut, thinking better of it. Swinging back around, she was about to take another swig of moonshine, but hesitated when a strange flutter went through her belly. It was the fourth or fifth time she'd felt it in the past couple of weeks.

"Please, my hearts," Zor pleaded quietly from behind her. Wrapping his thickly muscled arms around her tightly, he rubbed Kyra's baby-smooth cheek with his own gruff one. "Please just take a ride in my conveyance and let us talk. I would apologize. And I would explain my behavior."

"Zor..." Kyra hesitated, clearly indecisive. "I don't know. I-"

"Please." He squeezed her, hugging her as if afraid to let go. "I cannot," he admitted hoarsely, "spend even one more moon-rising like I did when you barred me from our rooms." Rocking her back and forth gently on the barstool, Zor implored her once more. "Please wee one," he whispered thickly, "I'll grant you any boon save leaving me do you come with me now."

Kyra didn't have to guess whether or not Zor felt as bad as he sounded, for her bridal stones told her he probably felt even worse. He was scared she wouldn't forgive him, frightened that he'd damaged their relationship beyond repair, and utterly terrified that she would seek to find a way to leave him.

"Oh all right." She sighed, deciding to give in a bit and hear him out. "I'll ride with you in your conveyance and hear what you have to say."

"Thank-you," Zor replied in soft tones. Giving Kyra no time to change her mind, he picked her up and cradled her into his arms, leaving Pika's in long strides.

* * * * *

"I thought you wanted to talk."

Zor hadn't said a word since the moment they took their seats in the Q'an Tal conveyance. What he had done instead was proving to be far more effective to Kyra, however: her back against his chest, he was simply holding her.

Divested of her *qi'ka* with Zor's massive penis firmly embedded within her, Kyra had been surprised at first when he'd made no attempt to pleasure himself within her. He made no movements, nothing that would bring him release, simply sat there and held Kyra tightly, as if afraid to let her go.

It was affecting her.

Just sitting on his lap, being held by this primal male who needed to get as physically close to his mate as possible, was chipping away at her defenses. It was as if he couldn't bear the thought of being removed from her even enough to allow her to sit on the seat next to him.

Zor embraced her body tightly as the black crystal conveyance meandered aimlessly about Sand City. He breathed in the scent of her hair, rested his chin on her shoulder, closed his eyes, and held her possessively. He said nothing, made no motions, no movements.

Kyra was beginning to think Zor would never get around to speaking, not even to answer her question, but eventually he did.

"I see no point in words, my hearts, except to say I'm sorry, for 'twas my words that hurt you in the first." He sighed, his tone unnaturally subdued. "But 'sorry' hardly sets the hurt to rights, does it now?"

"I don't know," Kyra murmured in a dulcet voice, "but I'd like to hear the words anyway and know that you mean them."

"Ah *pani*, of course I am sorry, and of course I mean it." He breathed in deeply, the scent of Kyra's hair reaching his nostrils. "I was angry with myself, but never did I have the right to take it out on you."

"I don't get it." Kyra shook her head slightly, not comprehending. "Why were you angry with yourself?"

"Why?" Zor's mouth fell agape. Stunned, he blinked twice before responding. "For allowing jealousy to rot my brain, for being a bestial Sacred Mate who needed to prove I could pleasure you better than any other in front of my men last rising."

"You were upset by that?" Kyra bit her lip. "Really?"

"Weren't you?" he asked incredulously.

"Actually, no." At his sharp intake of breath, she couldn't help but to giggle.

"What is so amusing?" he bellowed.

"You just have to understand where it is I come from." Kyra laid her head back against Zor's chest and waxed sentimental over her upbringing. "On earth, sexual pleasure is viewed in a negative light. Even some types of erotic acts shared between committed mates are viewed as amoral. In fact, in my own country-uh, colony-there are several states-I mean, sectors-in which oral stimulation is illegal."

"By the goddess," Zor groused, "I would have been locked up the very day my sire brought my first *Kefa* to me."

"We don't have *Kefas* on earth, but I take your point." Kyra absently surveyed the beautiful crystal homes they were passing over as she continued her explanation. "When I came here to Tryston, I felt the same way that you must have felt when your father first gifted you with a *Kefa*." She shook her head and grinned. "I wanted to try everything, make up for all the time I'd missed, discover for myself what turned me on and what didn't."

Zor found his first smile. "You are turning out to be more than a warrior can hope for. A wanton baggage, you are," he said teasingly.

Kyra reached behind her and ran her hand over his jaw. He turned into it, nuzzling her palm contentedly. "But I love it, Zor. Every day I learn something more about myself sexually. I'm coming to understand my needs in a way I never did before you came into my life, or should I say, charged into my life."

He smiled at the memory of the claiming. "I'm glad 'twas I who gave you this time for experiences, then." He grabbed her hand and kissed it gently.

"So am I," Kyra admitted.

Zor squeezed her tightly. "So what you are saying then, is that you looked upon our coupling at the consummation feast last moon-rising as another of these experiences?"

"Yes."

He grunted. "I wish I could see it that way and mayhap I would if I had taken you for the right reasons." Bending his neck, he kissed her sweetly on the shoulder. "But I thank you for not hating me because of it," he said in low tones.

"I could never hate you." Kyra shook her head. "Never."

"Ah *nee'ka.*" Zor kissed her cheek, then turned her face slightly to kiss the tip of her nose. "I do not deserve one so fine as you."

When Kyra indicated that she wanted to turn around on his lap, Zor somehow managed it without breaking their intimate bond. Giggling at his outrageous ability, she reached up and cupped his face in her hands. Kissing him first on the lips, then slipping her tongue inside of his mouth, she began to rock her hips back and forth on top of him.

"Ah, *nee'ka.*" Zor broke away from the kiss momentarily and grabbed a buttock in either hand. "Be still, my sweet, and I will use my powers to rock you."

"Mmmm." Eyes closed, Kyra smiled at the familiar feel of her husband's jutting erection buried inside of her, giving her pleasure. She kissed him again before adding, "by the way..."

"Aye?"

"I discovered something else about myself last night."

"Oh?" Zor summoned her body, rocking her faster. She moaned hedonistically, sucking in her breath. "And what was that, my lusty one?"

Kyra grinned without opening her eyes. "I'm an exhibitionist."

Chapter 24

"Would you just admit it already?" Kyra grinned at Geris, who was currently reclining next to her on the royal bed. She continued to needle away at her best friend to get her to confess the truth. "You're in love with your husband. There's no crime in that. Just say it!"

Lying propped up on one elbow, Geris puckered her lips into a frown. "And how do you know if I'm in love with the man?"

"Hmm...let me think." Buoyed up on an elbow facing Geris, Kyra tapped her chin and pretended to give the matter serious consideration. "Could it be because this is the first time anyone has seen you in seven"-she held up her fingers-"days? It's not, however, the first time anyone has heard you," she answered smugly.

Geris gasped. Her hand flew to her heart. "People were listening at the door?"

"Servants talk."

"Sweet Jesus. What did they say?"

Kyra batted her eyelashes rapidly and fell onto her back, arms thrust over her head. "Oh Dak," she mimicked in her best impression of Geris, "make the stones sing to me, daddy, make them siiiiing."

"Oh God." Mortified, Geris clapped an elegant hand over her eyes. "I am so embarrassed."

Laughing, Kyra pulled Geris's hand away from her face. "Don't be. That's the beauty of Tryston, don't you see?" She shrugged. "If it makes you feel any better, I did it with Zor in front of a room full of warriors and begged him for it."

"Ooohh girl, you didn't."

"I sure did."

"Why do I get the feeling you're proud of it?"

Kyra grinned. "Because I am." Propping herself back up on her elbow, she gestured toward her best friend with her other hand. "Back on earth, I never would have had the nerve to do something like that, even though I had fantasized about doing it in front of others like a zillion times. But here, it's different. No one thinks less of you for indulging your fantasies. On Tryston, I feel..."

"Beautiful."

"Sexy."

"Sinful."

"Wicked."

The two women laughed, enjoying the feminine banter they had missed during their separation.

"Oh fine, I admit it." Geris groaned comically, falling on her back and flinging her hands dramatically over her head. "I'm in love with the man. All right? Happy now?"

"Uh huh." Kyra grinned. "I couldn't be..." Eyes rounding, her smile faltered a bit. "I couldn't be..."

Geris sat up quickly, the pained look on Kyra's face alarming her. "Girl, what is it?" When Kyra's only response was to blanch and clutch her stomach, Geris went from alarmed to frantic. "Kyra!" she yelled. "Please baby-talk to me!"

Kyra grabbed her stomach and dragged herself to the middle of the bed. "Ger," she gasped between breaths, "Help...Please."

"What do you want me to do!"

Kyra shook her head, not really knowing what she needed, but realizing she needed something. "Hold me," she gasped out.

Geris cradled Kyra's head in her lap and stroked her hair soothingly. She did this for about fifteen more minutes, hoping the pains would go away. Unfortunately, Kyra's moaning only intensified. "What's the matter, baby? Was it something you ate?"

Kyra's breathing grew more and more labored. Moaning, she clutched Geris's arm.

"Girl, I'm going for help!"

"No!" Kyra closed her eyes and cried out as a sharp pain twisted her belly. "Don't leave me." Unable to restrain herself, Kyra moaned like a dying animal as she felt a rush of warm liquid burst from her insides and pour down her legs.

Geris screamed as a glowing blue plasma-like substance soaked them both. "Sweet Jesus! Kyra, I have to get help! Now!"

Kyra shook her head even as she moaned, struggling for breath. "Don't. Leave. Alone. To. Die...Please," she wheezed out between sobs.

Geris set Kyra away from her and jumped up from the bed, flying toward the doors. "I won't leave you!" she screamed, tears streaming down her cheeks. "I'll just tell a guard to call Zor!"

Geris threw the doors wide and ran out into the black crystal corridor. Spotting Cam and Gio stationed a ways down the hall, she yelled at the top of her lungs, "Get help! Kyra is dying!"

Cam and Gio went pale. Gawking at the queen of Ti Q'won and then at each other, then took off. "We shall alert the High King!" Cam called out over his shoulder. Wasting no time, he and Gio sprinted at top speed toward the great hall.

Geris dashed back into the bedchamber, coming at a dead halt in front of the raised bed. "Sweet lord in heaven," she muttered, clutching her throat, her eyes bulging.

"Geris help me!" Kyra sobbed, clutching her stomach and spreading her legs as she began to work a mammoth-sized oval structure out of her body.

Feeling faint, Geris clapped a hand to her forehead. "Girl, you're laying an egg!"

Frantic, and having never seen anybody lay an egg before, Geris started screaming hysterically, running for the chamber doors again. Throwing the doors wide, she shrieked, "Help! We need help! She's laying eggs in here! Oh my god, she's laying eggs!"

* * * * *

Zor, Kil, and Dak had been sharing a bottle of vintage matpow in the great hall when all three simultaneously spotted Cam and Gio running at top speed toward them. Instinctively realizing that something was very wrong, the trio of brothers shot to their feet. "What is it?" Zor bellowed.

Cam reached the raised table first. Panting heavily, he clutched it to steady himself, even as Gio appeared at his side. "Queen Geris says..." Cam grabbed his stomach, trying to catch his breath.

"What?" Dak roared. "What does my *nee'ka* say?"

"'Tis the High Queen," Gio gasped out.

"Aye," Cam confirmed between pants. "She is dying."

* * * * *

Zor and his brothers had no idea what they would find upon arriving at the royal suites. Thoughts so grim that they had brought tears to his eyes had flitted through Zor's mind, but nothing-nothing-could have prepared him for this.

Dak's *nee'ka* was standing next to the raised bed screaming hysterically, clutching a *pani* sac to her breasts as Kyra moaned and sobbed, in the process of hatching another one. His hearts flooding with relief and elation, Zor took a deep breath to steady himself. "By the goddess," he murmured, overcome with emotion.

"You're about to become a sire!" Kil grinned, slapping him on the back.

"To two babes!" Dak enthused, even as he clapped a hand over his *nee'ka's* wailing mouth and took the first *pani* sac from her. "'Tis fine, my hearts." Dak smiled down to his wife. "These are naught but babes, silly wench."

Geris's eyes rounded. After Dak handed the *pani* sac over to a beaming Zor, she threw his hand from her mouth and stomped on his foot.

"Ouch!"

"B-Babies!" Geris sputtered. "I thought she was dying! Why didn't anybody tell us you hatch eggs for babies around here? Sweet Jesus in heaven," she sobbed, "I'm never having one! I-"

"Enough, *nee'ka,*" Dak commanded, his nostrils flaring. "You will hatch my babes for a certainty!"

"Well," she sniffed, her chin notching up stubbornly, "we'll just see about that!"

"Aye, we will for a certainty! We'll see to it as you lie in the bed and hatch!"

"Enough, you two." Kil waved a hand in their general vicinity. "Kyra is still laboring the other *pani* sac."

Immediately contrite, Geris leaned over the bed and clutched Kyra's hand. Kyra took the time to smile at her best friend in between moans of pain and curse words leveled at her husband. "This is the most despicable thing you've ever done!" she wailed. "How could you not prepare me! How could you not tell me I was carrying eggs!"

"But my hearts, I did not know. You should have told me when first you felt the belly flutters."

"Oh my god!" Kyra cried hysterically, clapping a hand to her forehead. "I'm laying eggs. Geris, I'm laying eggs!"

Dak saw his *nee'ka's* eyes widen in sympathetic, frenzied horror. He waylaid her inevitable scream by clamping a hand over her mouth again.

"Oh my god!" Kyra screamed, clutching onto Zor's free arm. Images of the movie Alien ran through her mind. Suddenly, she was more than shocked and frightened, she was out and out terrified. "Will they be human?" she wailed.

Wide-eyed, Geris rapidly flapped her hands up and down and screamed behind Dak's hand. Then finally, unable to bear any more surprises, her eyes rolled back into her head and she fell limp against her husband, fainting in his arms.

"Praise the goddess," Dak muttered. Shaking his head, he picked his wee *nee'ka* up and cradled her in his arms. "She was nigh unto driving me daft."

"Will they be human?" Kyra cried out again.

"Nay," Zor boasted arrogantly, his jaw rigid with the pride of the Q'an Tal line. "My life-force makes naught but Trystonni."

Kil clapped Zor on the back, careful not to disturb the *pani* sac his brother was clutching reverently to his chest. "I think what she means is will the babe look like us, not like a *pugmuff*, or a heeka beast, or some other creature."

"Oh, aye." Zor waved dismissively.

Kyra let out a relieved breath even as she sucked in a pained one. "Oh god," she moaned, "the blue stuff is coming again!"

"Kil!" Zor bellowed.

"Aye?"

"Catch it."

* * * * *

Two hours later, Geris sat perched on the freshly made royal bed next to Kyra and Zor, crooning to the baby girls each parent held in their arms. Dak stood behind her, grinning. "My nieces are adorable!" she exclaimed, rubbing a soft finger over the thatch of fire-berry curls atop both of their heads.

Kyra, who was still marveling over the fact that she'd given birth to two beautiful daughters after having carried them no more than a few weeks, shook her head and grinned down at her babies. "They are. Just look at them," she boasted like a true mother, a tear forming in her eye.

"They are sweet perfection," Zor admitted on a contented sigh, rubbing his chin gently atop little Zora's fluffy head.

"Let me hold her, brother." Kil plopped down next to Geris and held out his large hands.

Zor scowled, fixing a lordly look on his brother. "I just now managed to wrestle her away from her auntie, dunce. Besides, wee Zora needs spend time with her papa." He glanced over to Kyra and frowned. "Now that I think on it, wee Zara has not had her fill of me just yet. *Nee'ka,* give her back."

Kyra huffed, throwing her husband an outraged look that made him back down immediately.

Geris, on the other hand, wasn't taking no for an answer. She figured guilt would work where Zor's autocratic orders had not. "After all the worry you put me through, girl, the least you can do is let me hold Zara for a minute."

Kyra rolled her eyes and grinned. "The last time you said that, you hogged Zora for an hour."

Zor grunted his agreement, but didn't look up from the baby in question.

"It wasn't just me," Geris regally intoned, "Dak held her too."

"Aye," Dak waxed sentimentally, embracing Geris from behind. "When I cradled wee Zora in my arms, it made me want to take my *nee'ka* back to the *vesha* hides and not let her up 'til she hatches."

Kil cleared his throat. "Must I remind everyone, that I haven't held either one of my nieces yet?" He rolled his eyes. "By the goddess, Zor would not even let me hold the *pani* sacs whilst they incubated for the hour after the hatching. He held onto them like a miser hoarding credits."

Zor snorted arrogantly. "A man has the right to hold the fruit his fertile loins produced."

Kyra groaned, rolling her eyes at his egotism.

"You see there!" Geris used the opportunity to her advantage, gently snatching tiny Zara up into her arms. Kyra smiled, giving up. "Her uncle Kil hasn't held her yet," Geris crooned as she cradled the baby in her arms, making cooing sounds.

"'Tis odd, Geris, but I'm still not holding a babe." Grinning at his sister-in-law's antics, Kil scooted closer to her, then rubbed the tuft of soft hair atop Zara's head. Geris smiled up to Kil, then showed him how to hold a tiny baby before placing his niece in his massive arms. Zara took to the gruff warrior immediately, cooing.

Kil smiled down to his niece. "They've both got our eyes, brothers," he informed the Q'an Tal men boastfully.

"Aye," Dak answered, crouching down to stroke Zara's cheek. "And Kyra's fire-berry hair."

Zor groaned as if pained. "By the goddess, I shall be batting off warriors left and right when they come of age."

"They needs must wed with only lesser kings of ample means," Kil announced with an incline of his head.

"Aye," Dak groused, "no dandy high lords, scarce able to control their own sectors."

"Please." Kyra rolled her eyes and groaned. "The girls are two hours old!"

"It never hurts," Zor said stiffly, "to prepare for these things well in advance."

"Aye," Kil and Dak grumbled in agreement.

"This is amazing." Geris leaned closer to Kil and bent her neck to place a kiss atop Zara's tiny head. "Where we come from, women carry their babies nine months before giving birth."

"Nine months!" Kil grimaced. "By the goddess, the eggs must be exceedingly large."

"We don't hatch eggs," Geris said haughtily. "We give birth to pre-incubated babies." She puckered her lips into a frown.

"Though in retrospect I admit," she conceded, "that I prefer it this way."

Kil grunted. "'Tis best you do. Dak will set you to hatching the soonest for a certainty." His lips kicked up into an ironic grin. "After seeing you in action at Kyra's hatching, I wouldn't miss yours for all the kingdoms in Tryston." Kil only laughed when Dak groaned and Geris shot him a "very funny" look.

"Speaking of the way we do things on earth..." Kyra bit her lip, looking first to one daughter and then to the other. Alarm beat through her as she considered something she hadn't thought of before. Grabbing at one of her nipples and tweaking it, she *pani*cked when her suspicion was confirmed.

"Girl, what are you doin'?" Geris asked.

"I don't have any milk in my breasts," Kyra murmured, horrified.

"Oh no!" Geris patted her on the knee, then looked to Zor. "How will she feed them?"

"Milk?" Zor looked up from Zora, his brow furrowed. "What's this of milk?"

"I said," Kyra repeated, "I don't have any milk in my breasts to feed the girls with."

"Yeeck!" Dak shuddered, his lips curling in disgust. "I should pray to the goddess not."

Kil looked horrified. "You mean to say that when you bear the fruit of a human man, your breasts gorge with milk?" When the women both nodded, he shook his head. "By the sands, that is nigh unto disgusting."

"It's nutritious!" Kyra screeched, affronted. Still worried, she turned to Zor. "How will I feed our daughters then?"

Zor rolled his eyes as if the answer was obvious. "The same as what they suckled from in your womb before hatching. Sweet juice."

"Sweet juice?"

"Aye."

Geris's lips pinched into one of her famous scowls. "You mean that glowing blue junk that came pourin' out of her like something in a horror movie?"

"Aye."

When Zor didn't expound upon his answer, Kyra waved a hand toward him. "They don't breast feed from me then?"

"Of course you will breast feed them, *nee'ka*." Zor shook his head and sighed, as if he was being forced to turn away from the important task of cuddling Zora to explain the way of things to a simpleton. "But when you bear the fruit of a Trystonni warrior," he boasted proudly, "your breasts gorge with sweet juice, not with milk." He made a face, mirroring his brothers' reactions. "Who in the sands ever heard of such a blasted thing? Milk-yeeck."

Kyra and Geris shared a puzzled frown. Huffing and out of patience, Kyra crossed her arms over her breasts and scowled at her husband. "When does this sweet juice come in, Zor? I don't have any."

"Do not fear, *nee'ka*. Zora and Zara are my firsts, yet have I heard it said by other warriors 'tis usually a few hours past the hatching before the mani's breasts gorge."

Mani-Trystonni for mommy, Kyra thought. "But it will come in?"

"For a certainty." Kil nodded succinctly. Then casting his gaze to Zor, he licked his lips and grinned. "How I envy you, brother."

Zor and Dak chuckled lecherously, causing Kyra and Geris to look at each other and furrow their brows. "Why?" Geris asked bluntly.

Kil wiggled his eyebrows mischievously, his eyes flicking over Geris's form. "'Tis said that a warrior has a difficult time not mounting his *nee'ka* every hour of the day whilst she's gorged of the sweet juice."

Geris clapped a hand to her forehead. "Y'all are giving me a headache."

"Ditto," Kyra sniffed. "Can nobody around here give a straight answer? All this talking in riddles is nonsense."

Kil's lips curled wryly. "Look at yourself in a holo-mirror in a few hours time and half your riddle will be solved."

"And the other half?"

"Hmm," Kil murmured. "'Tis up to my brother to show you."

Chapter 25

Kyra stood with her hands on her hips, tapping her sandaled foot with much irritation, as Geris rolled around on the royal high bed, pointing at Kyra's breasts and howling with laughter. "It's not funny, Ger!" Scowling at her best friend, she huffed. "Now that the girls are asleep, I'd like to go to the great hall for breakfast." She raised a fire-berry brow. "If you can control your laughter that long."

"Oh my." Geris wiped the tears of laughter from her eyes as she sat up. "I've already eaten."

"Well I haven't."

Her face threatening to break into another grin, Geris forcefully puckered her lips into a frown. "Has Zor seen"-she gestured toward Kyra's chest-"those yet?"

"No," Kyra answered tightly. "My sweet juice came in a little late. We fed the girls *taka* juice last night."

"It mighta come in late, honey," Geris replied with a grin, "but when it came in, it came in with a bang!"

Kyra crossed her arms under her mammoth bazooms and frowned. "Yes, well, the girls seem to like the sweet juice better than the *taka*."

"Thank God for that." Geris shook her head, growing serious. "I'd hate to see how big those things get if you didn't have Zora and Zara to relieve you a few times a day."

Kyra grimaced, not caring to ponder the truth behind that musing. Her breasts were the size of medium watermelons as it was. She couldn't imagine them being any bigger. Suddenly feeling embarrassed by the thought of anybody seeing them, she sat down on the bed next to Geris and bit her lip. "Perhaps I'll just have my breakfast sent up here," she said quietly.

Shamefaced for laughing at Kyra's obvious discomfort, Geris patted her on the knee. "I'm sorry I teased you, baby. Don't let your breasts dictate your life."

"Oh god." Kyra's head dropped into her hands. "I look like that stripper our friend Mike used to date. What was her stage name again?"

Geris nibbled at her lower lip. "Nancy Knockers."

"Oh god."

"Perhaps this was what Kil was talking about last night." Geris smoothed Kyra's hair back from her face. "Maybe Zor will really like these, uh, changes."

Kyra's head shot up. "You think so?" she asked hopefully.

"It wouldn't surprise me on Tryston."

"True." Kyra nodded, then waved her hand toward Geris, wanting to change the subject. "Are you sure you don't want to come down for breakfast?"

"No, you go ahead on." Geris sighed. "Dak wants us to leave for Ti Q'won tomorrow, so I need to pack."

"That's a moon, right? How cool! You're the queen of a moon, Ger!" Kyra scrunched her face up thoughtfully. "Which moon is yours?"

Geris took a deep breath, then blew it out. "It's the low-hanging green one."

Kyra reached for her hand and squeezed it. "Are you nervous?"

"A little."

"Don't be." Kyra studied Geris's face. Her best friend looked more than a little nervous, she looked very nervous. "I'll get Zor to bring us there for a visit real soon."

"You promise?"

"Definitely."

Geris blew out a relieved breath. "Good." Patting Kyra on the knee, she made to stand up and leave. "You go eat, I'll go pack, and we'll hang out later."

Kyra grinned. "You got it."

* * * * *

Zor sat pompously at the raised table in the great hall, still feeling arrogant over the fact that his life-force had been so potent. Not only had it beget two babes, but his wee *panis* were both females. On a planet where female hatchlings were a rarity, 'twas often a boast among warriors with girl babes that their seed was the superior to other warriors. Indeed, not even the almighty Q'an Tal line had sired a female hatchling in nigh unto a hundred Yessat years.

"Look at him, brother." Speaking to Dak, Kil gestured toward Zor. "You would think he was the first warrior to ever sire a female *pani*."

"Aye." Dak crossed his arms over his chest and grinned. "'Twill not surprise me does he have his staff gilded after this feat."

"Harrumph." Zor waved arrogantly. "Though it deserves to be for a certainty, I think my *nee'ka* prefers it the way it is."

Kil rolled his eyes, groaning. "By the sands, you are driving me daft with your claims to superior prowess."

"Two." Zor held up two fingers, emphasizing his words. "Two female *panis*. And," he sniffed, "they are not even identical, not of the same sac." He sat up straighter in his seat, telekinetically summoning his crystal fork-spoon. "Now tell me whose seed can boast of that, besides the High King of Tryston and the Emperor of Trek Mi Q'an?" Throwing his brothers a haughty look and swiveling his neck back and forth in such a way as he had learned from Geris, he said, "I am waiting."

Kil and Dak merely rolled their eyes and groaned.

"Harrumph." Zor stabbed at a fire-berry fruit and raised it to his lips. "As I thought."

Dak grinned at Kil as he raised his goblet of *taka* juice and took a large swallow. Sighing lustily, he asked, "Did Kyra's sweet juice ever come in? She seemed worried about it last moon-rising."

"Hopefully by now," Zor replied in earnest. "I had to leave our apartments early to go bark at the crystal guildsman this morn. Finally, will he and his craftsmen have that promised suite ready in the south wing for the young bucks."

Kil grunted. "'Tis about time. I will have to leave to see to my colonies the soonest and would like the warriors to come choose their servants anon."

"For a certainty would the bucks like it as well." Dak shook his head. "I overheard Gio complain to Cam that if he did not share of Muta's charms with him, he feared his rod would fall off."

Zor chuckled. "The master guildsman did vow their suite would be ready by this very moon-rising."

"Thank the goddess," Kil grumbled. "I've enough of my own servants to see to without listening to the constant lusty petitions of the new ones."

"You would even give up Myn without qualm?" Zor asked bemusedly.

"Aye." Kil rolled his eyes. "She can all but put luscious Muta to shame."

Dak's eyebrows shot up. He turned to Zor. "I did not know you gave Myn to Kil."

"Aye," Zor answered dismissively. "Kyra would not have her in our suites."

"Where is your *nee'ka* anyway?" Kil asked. "I've yet to see her this morn."

Zor shrugged. "I sent Cam to fetch her, which of course, the randy warrior was more than eager to do."

Dak chuckled wryly. "Think you 'tis true that a *nee'ka's* breasts gorge bigger than moosoos whilst suckling *panis?*" He shook his head. "I fear Cam will spill his life-force at the very sight of Kyra if it is."

Zor grunted.

"Is it true?" Kil sat up straighter in his chair, licking his lips unconsciously as he regarded Zor.

"How would I know?" Zor mused, his voice a rumble. "Zora and Zara are my first hatchlings." Pondering the matter somewhat, he shook his head in the negative. "Leastways, I doubt it. 'Twould be a foul trick of the goddess Aparna did a *nee'ka's* breasts nigh unto burst whilst her Sacred Mate is left without his pleasures for the first fortnight of it."

Kil shuddered. "I do not know how you will manage without coupling for a full two weeks."

"*Kefas,*" Dak grinned. "Zor will be the cleanest High King ever to rule Tryston."

* * * * *

Kyra and her breasts walked over to the bedchamber door to open it up for Cam. He was knocking loudly, calling from the other side of it that the High King desired her company over the morning repast.

Sporting a transparent white *qi'ka* in honor of Dak and Geris's last night in Sand City, Kyra stopped long enough to do a quick inspection of the image she presented in the holo-mirror. Good grief.

Kyra didn't know whether to laugh or cry over her new, and thankfully temporary, watermelon jugs. She had always been chesty, but this was on the far side of obscene. Her breasts could put Ana Nicole Smith to shame. And her cleavage-good lord! As if it wasn't enough of a show walking around in a *qi'ka* that left absolutely nothing to the imagination, she now had enough cleavage to drown ten men in.

Cam knocked louder, snapping Kyra out of her musings. Sighing, she walked quickly to the chamber doors, not wanting the girls to get jarred awake from their naps before she had a chance to eat. Throwing the doors open wide, she smiled up to Cam.

"Good morn," Cam said affably, "I came to congratulate you on the hatching of the High Princesses and to escort you to...to..." Noticing the High Queen's chest for the first time, Cam swallowed-roughly. "By the sands," he groaned.

Flushing scarlet, Kyra pretended not to notice his regard, or his fierce erection. "Thank you," she replied brightly. "Shall we go?" When the warrior only stood there, gawking at her breasts and making no move to escort her, she tapped him on the arm. "Cam?"

"What? Oh, aye." Shaking his head to clear it, Cam forced his gaze from Kyra's chest to her face. "We, uh, should go. I, uh..." He sighed, taking her by the arm. "Let us go," he groaned.

Kyra, Cam, and her gargantuan breasts walked down the black crystal corridor that led to the great hall. Kyra held her head high, her spine erect, even as she wanted to shrivel up and die from the wide-eyed, aroused looks the warriors they passed by were throwing her way.

When finally they made it into the great hall, the first one to spot her was Kil. Kyra grimaced as she watched her brother-in-law do a double take, and then, eyes round with disbelief, awe, or both, he mumbled something that made Zor and Dak turn their heads to look at her.

Kyra was infuriated by their open-jawed, glazed-eyed expressions, but said nothing. Sniffing regally, she sauntered toward the table, Cam and her breasts in tow.

* * * * *

"What's for breakfast?" Kyra asked the question as nonchalantly as she could manage, hoping to discourage her husband and his two brothers from staring at her like some sort of an erotic arts performer. "Anything good?"

They merely continued to gape. Flushing, she picked up a crystal dish and served herself from a selection of sweet breads and fruits. "It's a beautiful day today," she said in the way of conversation. "Isn't it?"

They said nothing.

Her nostrils flaring, Kyra arched a brow and scowled at her husband. "Isn't it?" she shrieked.

"What?" Zor asked thickly. The glow of his eyes said without words that he wanted to couple. "Oh aye, *pani,* uh, I mean-aye, mani."

"I'm not your *pani* anymore?" she teased, hoping to change the topic.

"A mani is much better," he said hoarsely. "By the goddess, 'tis better for a certainty."

"I must go." Dak surged to his feet, his eyes never straying from Kyra's chest. Ever the brother to come straight to the point, he bluntly confessed, "I needs take my *nee'ka* to the *vesha* hides to work on our hatchlings."

Kyra rolled her eyes-not than anyone noticed.

Ten minutes after Dak departed, not a single word had yet been spoken at the raised table. Furious, Kyra threw down her crystal fork-spoon, crossed her arms under her behemoth breasts, and scowled. "Stop it!"

Kil had the decency to look chagrined, but Zor tried to play it off. "Stop what, my hearts? I was but admiring your lovely *qi'ka*. 'Tis new, aye?"

Kil snorted.

"You were not!" Kyra fumed, slapping her hand on the table. "You were staring at my hideous breasts!"

"Hideous?" Kil repeated incredulously. He shook his head. "Many words do come to mind to describe them, yet 'hideous' is not amongst them."

"They are filled with sweet juice to feed your babies," Kyra charged, shaking her finger at her husband. "How dare you two make me feel like I'm on display!" Surging to her feet, she placed her hands on her hips, glowering at the odious men. "I'm going to my rooms!"

And with that, Kyra and her breasts bounced away.

Zor and Kil groaned.

* * * * *

"Come in." Kil inclined his head to Cam, Mik, and Gio, letting them into his rooms. "You may pick one servant apiece from any amongst them," he called out over his shoulder as he led them down a corridor. "I have them situated within the parlor according to how many years of Yessat service they have left. On the left side of the chamber are wenches owing five, in the middle four, and on the right three." He threw them a wry look as he continued to walk. "None owe less than three."

The younger warriors glanced at each other, grinning from ear to ear. "You even let us pick of your own stock?" Cam asked.

"Aye." Kil shrugged. "I have too many to care."

Gio blew out a breath, throwing a glimpse toward his comrades that clearly said he hoped to be so wealthy one day. "I hope 'tis not too difficult a decision," he muttered. "I imagine you would like us to take leave of your suites the soonest, Your Majesty."

When the group made it to the doors of the parlor, Kil turned around to regard the younger warriors. His lips kicked up into a knowing half-grin, the scar on his face twisting. "'Twill be difficult for a certainty, but I am giving you the rest of the moon-rising to choose." He inclined his head, then turned to stroll into his own bedchamber where his favorites awaited him. "Sample of their charms and enjoy," he called from over his shoulder.

"Praise the goddess," Mik whispered enthusiastically, rubbing his palms together. "Let us see how many we've to choose from."

Gio clapped him on the back. "'Twill be nigh unto bliss if there are mayhap ten or twenty."

"Aye," Cam confirmed, grinning. "Let us go in and sample away."

Opening the parlor doors, the jaws of the three warriors went slack as their eyes feasted on the bounty before them. There had to be a hundred bound servants within-all of them beautiful, all of them busty, all of them completely divested of their *qi'ka* skirts, and all of them lying down with their legs spread wide for a sampling.

"By the sands," Gio murmured. "By the holy sands."

For the next five hours, the warriors had the time of their lives. Gio ended up choosing Myn for himself, having been blown away-literally-by her charms. And Mik chose Frey, a freshly broken in brunette who proved herself voraciously accommodating to his desires. Cam was the only one who hadn't yet decided.

Laying naked, stretched out on his back to ponder the matter, Cam was stunned when he felt yet another hand wrap around his jutting staff. Glancing down, he studied the face of the gorgeous servant as if remembering her from somewhere. "Have we met?"

"Aye." Propping herself up on an elbow, the blonde beauty stroked up and down the length of his cock. Cam sucked in his breath. "My name is Mara. 'Twas I who brought Muta to you as a gift from the High Queen."

Cam's breathing grew choppier and choppier. "Are you not bound to the High King?"

"Aye," she answered softly, her eyelashes fluttering coyly, "but I was given permission to come here today. If you want me, I will call you master."

Cam's hand reached out to cup one of Mara's large breasts. He bent his head and drew from her nipple, causing the servant to groan. Enjoying the feel of the turgid bulb in his mouth, he tasted of it awhile before lifting his head to regard her. "I've seen you many times in passing," he whispered thickly, "and always are you watching me. Why?"

"I've wanted to couple with you forever," Mara admitted, grinning. "And I would that I could couple with you now."

Cam smiled back. "You would like to prove your desire to pleasure me?"

"Aye." Mara climbed up on top of the warrior's massive frame and impaled herself in one fluid stroke on his long, thick penis. Cam groaned, inhaling sharply. "Do you choose me for your own," Mara whispered, "I would spend my every moment thinking of new ways to pleasure you." She rode up and down the length of him, her breasts jiggling deliciously. "When you return from the training fields, tired and in need, I would suckle from your staff until you fall asleep, then be ready for your thrusts when you wake lusty."

Cam groaned, thrusting his hips upward for deeper access of her channel. "You would desire this above all things, Mara?" He grabbed her hips and embedded himself further, causing her to moan wantonly.

"Aye," she admitted on a climax, "Oh-aye."

Cam thrust harder, gritting his teeth. "You would not give access of your channel to another without my permission whilst I train or escort the High Queen about?"

"Nay."

"How many Yessat years do you owe?"

Mara closed her eyes, welcoming his deep thrusts. "Four."

"Oh?" Cam flipped her onto her back and plunged into her again, pounding Mara's pussy relentlessly toward climax. "And why should I choose a servant owing but four years when I can have another owing five?"

Mara's eyes rolled back into her head as she peaked once, twice, three times more under Cam. "Because I am willing to pledge five more years to you, giving you nine Yessat years of service."

Cam's eyes went wide as he pummeled mercilessly into her flooded cunt. "You are that lusty for my cock?" he growled.

"Aye. Oh-aye."

Cam thrust deeper, harder, faster-rewarding Mara for her answer. "Then call me master, lusty wench, for you are mine."

Chapter 26

After feeding the babies their dinner, Kyra fell onto the bed, exhausted. It had been a long day.

Zor was currently in the nursery tucking the girls in, something he planned to do each night. "'Tis for a certainty my face is the last my hatchlings will desire to see each moon-rising," he had boasted.

Yawning, Kyra threw her arms above her head and closed her eyes. Thinking back on the day's events, she let herself smile. It was amusing indeed to see Mr. Tough Guy brought to heel by two little sweetpeas. From the way he'd held Zora and Zara in his thickly muscled arms, rocking back and forth to soothe them, to the way he'd smiled down at them crooning, "hello ty'kas, papa loves you," Zor was making her fall in love with him all the harder.

Kyra must have briefly fallen asleep while waiting on her husband to come to bed, because she awoke not much later to the feel of her nipples being suckled. Only this time there were no *panis* drinking from her, but a warrior. Her warrior. It gave the experience a new, erotic twist. "Zor?" she asked breathlessly.

"Shh, *nee'ka*," he murmured, stroking his tongue soothingly across her swollen pink nipples. Taking one erect bud into his mouth, he sipped from it, then groaned. "'Tis my time now, mani." Settling his body between her legs and his head between her breasts, he took turns kissing each nipple. "'Tis my right as your High King and Sacred Mate to relieve your swelling each moon-rising."

Kyra groaned, arching into him. "I wish we could couple," she admitted between gasps. "Oh Zor, that feels so good. Do I taste good?" she asked wickedly.

"Mmm, never have I tasted of anything better, wee one." He closed his eyes, curling his tongue around a tight peak and drawing from it. Kyra inhaled deeply, rotating her hips under him. "Kyra my hearts," Zor whispered gruffly, "'tis naught better to a warrior than the taste of his mani's gorged breasts."

"I'm not your mommy," she teased.

Zor looked up from his work long enough to grin down at her. "'Tis an interchangeable word and well you know it, nefarious wench."

She giggled.

"You are my hatchlings' mommy," he said reverently as he bent to lick her nipples, "but you are my possession."

"Hmm. That seems a little demeaning," Kyra said, "to use the same word for mommy and possession."

Zor grunted. "'Tis an injustice of the galaxies to be pondered over later."

Kyra scowled, slapping him on the back. "So I'm your possession, am I?"

"Mmm." He bent his head, tasting of her sweet juice. "Always. Never would I allow your absence."

She sucked in her breath, closing her eyes on a moan. The way Zor drew from her chest was liable to send her flying through the roof. "I love you," she sighed out.

"Ah *nee'ka*." Zor raised his head from her breasts long enough to place a sweet kiss on her lips. "I love you more than words can say, my hearts."

Lowering his head to Kyra's chest, he then gorged.

* * * * *

Zor didn't know how much longer he could go on without joining with Kyra's body, but 'twas for a certainty he would be atop her, sliding into her luscious cunt the very moment a fortnight was over. Gorging upon her sweet juice during the moon-risings was making his ever-plaguing erection naught but worse.

Even taking to the bathing chamber was fast losing its ability to relieve the agony of his lust. Zor wanted, nay needed, to have his staff attended to inside of a hot, lusty channel. But of course, not just any channel. No passage appealed to him save Kyra's and the ecstasy their joining produced.

A few of the more brazen servants had tried him, hoping to tempt him into the *vesha* hides whilst Kyra's body recuperated. They had all accepted his answer gracefully, though, when he'd gently set them away from him, denying them.

Zor needed Kyra, only his *nee'ka*. She had three days left of her confinement and he all but feared he'd be as daft as a crazed *heeka-beast* by the time she spread her legs and invited him to sample of her charms.

So when Zor let himself into Kil's apartments to speak to him, 'twas not the sight he had desired to see, watching his brother rut atop a servant the way he needed to rut atop his wife.

Sighing, Zor shook his head. For the first time in all of his forty-two Yessat years, he was beginning to believe that Trystonni warriors availed themselves of hot channels far too often. Of course, he was intelligent enough to realize that he would probably not be feeling this way had he been getting any channel himself.

Kil was currently thrusting his staff into a whimpering, moaning Leha whilst licking at the cunt of another bound servant. Zor allowed him the release of his life-force into Leha's passage before making his presence known. "I would that I could speak with you, brother."

Kil's gaze shot over to where Zor stood. "For a certainty." The muscles in his arms and back flexing, he hoisted himself up from between Leha's splayed thighs. "'Twas an excellent fuck you gave me, sweetling," he murmured in a low tone. "Stay spread and ready for me whilst I speak to my brother."

Kil alighted from the bed, but not before tickling the giggling Leha's pussy lips with a lap of his tongue. "What can I do for you?" One black brow rose up a notch as he crossed to the side of his bedchamber where Zor stood. "And why in the sands do you look so grim?"

Zor grunted. Hands placed arrogantly at either hip, he frowned at Kil. "Why do you think, dunce? I cannot share of the *vesha* hides for three more moon-risings." He groaned, shaking his head. "One-hundred-thirty-five Yessat hours, ten nuba-minutes, and two nuba-seconds, to be precise."

Kil didn't smile, but his eyes were dancing with amusement. "Is it as they say? Does gorging of the sweet juice make it worse?"

"By the sands, aye." Zor closed his eyes briefly, as if in pain-which he was, at least in the lower region of his anatomy. "'Tis a foul trick of the goddess Aparna," he said wearily, "a foul trick indeed."

Zor groaned, removing one hand from his hip to clutch it into a fist. "Every time I turn around, Kyra and her breasts are there to bedevil me. They go bouncing around the palace as if they had not a care in the world, whilst I am left to suffer the agonies of a tortured man." His teeth clenched as his fist balled tighter. "Those pink nipples laugh up at me from their wicked big perch, luring me in to suckle of them, offering all the temptations of a thousand *Kefas*, yet allowing for no release."

Kil's lips curled into a half-grin. "You speak of your *nee'ka's* breasts as though they are an entity separate from her."

"They are, I tell you." Zor made a dismissive gesture with his hand. "Leastways I believe them to be enchanted, like a sand muse luring an unsuspecting traveler to his death."

Kil shook his head. That was the most ridiculous analogy he had ever had to endure the telling of. Praise the goddess he had no *nee'ka* to torment himself with. He had always been, as he was now, a man who walked alone, able to find his pleasures between any number of thighs.

Still, he doubted 'twas Kyra's intention to bedevil the poor lout. His brother was apparently given to the dramatic whilst forced into celibacy.

"I believe I am dying." Zor clapped a hand to his forehead and groaned. "Feel my head, brother. Tell me do I have the feel of a man coming down with a life-threatening ague."

Kil rolled his eyes, but clapped his hand to Zor's forehead anyway. "Nay. You have the feel of a man not getting any channel."

"'Tis true," he answered grimly. "I remember a warrior from our childhood who went by the name Old Og. Og died of this very condition, his staff erupting from lack of use. 'Tis an omen to be repeated, for a certainty."

Kil closed his eyes, pinching the bridge of his nose. He took two deep breaths before answering Zor. "Og died because his high-born mistress found him coupling with ten of her bound servants. She blew his staff to pieces with a zykif."

Zor grimaced. "For a certainty?"

"Aye."

He grunted. "Never mind." Zor made an impatient gesture with his hand. "I have not come here this morn to speak of coupling. I came to inform you that our brother Rem and his *nee'ka* are here."

Kil frowned. "He brought Jera with him?"

"Aye." Zor sighed, shaking his head. "And my *nee'ka* does not like her for a certainty."

Kil crossed his arms over his chest. "I fear I already know the answer, yet will I ask. Why?"

"Jera is acting the rabid she-beast she is infamous for being. She made insinuations to Kyra at the morning repast, informing her without words of our past dalliances together before she mated with Rem."

Kil rolled his eyes. "The bitch never changes." His thoughts switching to Rem, he grimaced. "Has our brother seen Zora and Zara yet?"

"Nay." Zor's eyebrows shot up. "Why do you ask?"

"Why do I ask?" Kil repeated in an incredulous tone. Stunned, he shook his head. "'Twill no doubt be hard on the man, knowing he will never sire any hatchlings of his own."

"What's this? Has he some sort of rare malady no one informed me of?"

Kil's eyes widened as his jaw went slack. "You really don't know, do you?"

"Know what?" Zor grunted, scowling at his brother. "Mayhap if you would quit speaking in riddles I could find out."

"Mayhap Rem does not want you or Dak awares." Kil sighed, thinking back on the moon-rising he'd discovered their youngest brother's secret. "I found out by sheer fortune of having overhead him and Jera arguing."

"Kil," Zor bit out, his teeth clenching, "as your High King, I command for you to tell me of what it is you speak."

Kil peered into Zor's eyes, not wanting to miss his reaction. "Rem and Jera," he said in distinct tones, "are not true mates."

"What?"

"'Tis true." Kil waved a hand, shaking his head. He had never had a care for Rem's *nee'ka.* "Jera got Rem sotted with matpow to the point of barely being able to stand, then did lure him to the *vesha* hides, tricking him into clasping his bride's necklace about her cunning neck."

"By the goddess," Zor murmured, dazed. "Whatever would she do this for? By cheating Rem of his true Sacred Mate, she has cheated herself of her own as well."

Kil laughed without humor. "Think you Jera has a care for love of the hearts and bonds of the flesh? Nay. She wanted naught but to advance her own riches."

"By the goddess," Zor murmured. He was too stunned to say more.

"I am willing to bet fifty of my most lusty *Kefas* that she had lured you to the *vesha* hides with much the same intent." Kil scowled, his lips curling into a snarl. "When trickery didn't work with you, she turned her sights to our youngest brother, who, although he may be a warrior to be reckoned with now, was a gullible green lad at the time, lusty for the bed sport."

"Poor Rem." Zor drew in a deep breath, his eyes steadily trained on his brother. "To be sentenced to a lifetime with no hope for a true mate. By the sands, I could not want for a life without Kyra and my *panis*."

"Aye, 'tis sad for a certainty. His only hope would be Jera's death, but Rem is far too noble to wish for something like that, even on her."

"Not even then, Kil. A bridal necklace does not unclasp in death."

"It remains bound on a true mate," Kil amended, "but it will unclasp on mates that are false."

"For a certainty?"

"Aye." Kil shrugged. "When first I heard this disgusting tale, I went to the priestesses for guidance. They informed me that I could do naught but pray to Aparna, saying Rem would only be released by Jera's death." He went on to explain. "So you see, 'tis why I asked whether or not he had yet seen the little fire-berry-headed imps."

Zor scratched his chin. "Think you I should keep Zora and Zara from his sights?"

"I cannot say." Kil drew in a deep breath. "I do not know."

Whatever Zor had been about to say on the subject of his hatchlings came to a sudden halt as Kyra and her breasts came bouncing into the bedchamber, her face red with fury. Zor frowned. "Ah, here comes my *nee'ka* and her wicked henchmen now."

Kil smiled at Zor's term for his wife's breasts. "You look out of sorts, sister. Whatever is it that ails you?" he called out in mock innocence.

Kyra frowned as her and her breasts came to a halt in front of the two warriors. "Kil, you're naked." Glancing over to the raised bed where Leha and another servant lay in wait, she rolled her eyes, pinching her lips with disapproval.

"As you should be whilst alone in our presence, with naught but bound servants as witness. Remove your *qi'ka.*"

Kyra thought to argue with Kil, but didn't waste her breath. Where Trystonni custom was concerned, these warriors weren't malleable. Especially when said custom involved seeing naked women.

She did as she was bade, throwing her *qi'ka* to the ground with a huff. That accomplished, she got back to the point of her visit. "Zor!" she screeched, turning to glare up at her husband. "I want that woman gone from my palace and I want her gone now!"

"But she is Rem's *nee'ka,* my hearts. How can I make Jera leave without forcing my brother to go as well?"

"I don't care!" she wailed, stomping a foot-an action that caused her breasts to jiggle wantonly and the two warriors to groan. "Think of something! In the short time that she has been here, she has managed to infuriate the cook, knock an expensive bottle of vintage matpow from its perch, and insult Jik and Tia-two of our very best friends! Friends, by the way, who are being kind enough to watch our girls for me while I came over here to have it out with you because Kil is busy getting it on with the nanny who should be watching them!"

Her nostrils flaring, Kyra then turned to go another round with Kil. "*Kefas* and bound servants included, you have over two hundred here to see to your needs and God only knows how many more back at your own palace! Why do you insist on coupling with the one I need?"

When Kil opened his mouth to speak, Kyra held up a silencing hand. "I want Leha back, end of story. If you and Leha want to get it on, do it after hours, when I'm not in need of her assistance to get your nieces"-she shook an accusing finger up at him-"your nieces situated on my mammoth breasts." Kyra clapped a hand to her forehead, closing her eyes, ready to lose it totally. "If I try to do it without help, I sometimes lose my balance," she choked out.

"Ah, *nee'ka,*" Zor crooned soothingly, feeling somewhat guilty over not having considered how Kyra must feel lugging her two wicked temptresses around. "I will come help you feed our wee *panis*. But she is right, Kil, we needs have Leha during the days for I shall be at training most of the time."

Kil nodded his ready agreement. His eyes flicked over Kyra's enchantingly fertile form, lingering overlong on the best parts. "I regret any discomfort I may have unwittingly caused you or your, uh"-he coughed into his hand-"breasts."

"I don't know how much longer I can stand them," she sobbed, falling down into the chair behind her. "They ache and they're swollen." She unconsciously massaged them, seeking to lessen the pain. Her brow shot up when she heard both men groan. "What's the matter? Are you two all right?"

"Do you see now of what I speak?" Zor muttered to Kil. "See you how her moosoos sing the song of the sand siren, luring me to my doom?"

"Aye," Kil croaked out, his erection fast and fierce.

"Good grief, Kil, put that thing away." Kyra shook her head, frowning at his erection. "I need to get back to the girls. Somebody help me up and help me get dressed."

Both men groaned. When Zor refused to do it, mumbling something about having the ague, that left only Kil to care for her. Kyra accepted his aid as she dictated her needs to him. "Be careful placing the *qi'ka* top over my nipples. They feel especially tender this morning."

"Of course," Kil bit out, wanting to get this session in torture over and done with so he could work out his lust on a servant. When all was said and done and Kyra took her leave of his bedchamber, Kil turned on his heel and headed straight for the raised bed without detour. "Tell Rem I will see him at the evening meal," he threw out over his shoulder to Zor. "I needs relieve myself anon."

Zor grunted. He glanced up at the holo-clock on the wall. "One-hundred-thirty-four Yessat hours, fifty nuba-minutes, and fifteen nuba-seconds," he mumbled on a dejected sigh.

Chapter 27

Bolstered up on one elbow, Kyra lay on the raised bed, crooning down to a smiling Zora and Zara, both getting ready for their feeding. "Hello my sweethearts." She craned her neck and blew her lips against both of their lightly tanned bellies, inducing giggles to erupt. "Give mani a kiss, Zora. And now you, Zara."

It still amazed Kyra that at a day shy of two-weeks-old, the girls had the size, motor coordination, and alertness of six-month-old babies back on earth. When Ari had stopped in to see the newly hatched princesses and give them her blessing the day after their birth, she had warned Kyra of this, preparing her for how swiftly the twins would develop throughout their first year.

Ari had definitely not exaggerated the truth. Zora and Zara were growing by leaps and bounds. The Chief Priestess had informed Kyra that unlike on "primitive" worlds such as earth where babies were at their most vulnerable during their first year, Trystonni hatchlings evolved differently, growing out of their defenseless first year within six fortnights, or three months. After that, they aged like normal earth children until the aging process slowed to almost a complete standstill, right around the time when they reached the height of their physical beauty.

"Who are the prettiest girls in all of Tryston?" Kyra beamed a huge smile down to her babies, then tickled them again. Zora giggled, clasping her tiny hand around one of Kyra's fingers. Zara blew out spit bubbles, then made a gummy grin.

"And who is the prettiest mani in all of Tryston?"

Kyra smiled, cocking her head to study Zor. "I didn't know you were here. When did you get in from training?"

Zor plopped down onto the raised bed next to Kyra. He craned his neck to kiss her lips, then turned to look down at his daughters. "Papa just got back," he crooned in the voice he used only for his *panis*. Picking them both up, he cradled each one in a Herculean arm.

Zor placed sweet kisses atop both their fluffy heads, then, his voice returning to normal, his gaze flicked to Kyra. "Leastways, I wasn't at training today. Kil and I spent our time with Rem." He inclined his head. "He is aware now that I know of his secret."

"You're kidding?" Kyra's eyebrows shot up. Zor had told her the story of how Jera had tricked Rem into mating with her the very day he had found out about it from Kil. "What did he say?"

He shrugged. "What could be said? He admitted to it, but asked that the story never be repeated to outsiders for fear of looking the fool."

"I can't blame him for that." Kyra sighed, shaking her head. "It's really a shame, Zor. Rem's a very good-looking, not to mention genuinely nice man. He deserves better than Jera. The woman gives me the creeps."

Zor grunted. "You think him handsome?"

Kyra rolled her eyes. "Out of all that I just said, that is what you choose to comment on?" She grinned. "You'll never change, will you?"

Zor took a moment to place more kisses atop wee Zora and Zara's fire-berry tufts. "'Tis unlikely." He narrowed his gaze at Kyra. "You have changed the subject, wench, and well you know it. You think my brother handsome, aye?"

"Yes, I do. He's the image of Dak, just as Kil is the image of you."

"Who is most winsome of the brothers, I ask you?"

Kyra ran her fingers over Zor's upper lip. "Fishing for compliments?"

"Aye."

She giggled. "At least you're honest." Sitting up on her knees, she leaned into him and ran her tongue along the outline of his mouth. He growled low in his throat. "You are the most handsome man I've ever laid eyes on, and that's a vow between Sacred Mates."

He grunted. 'Tis good eyesight you have, mani."

Kyra shook her head at his egotism. "Speaking of mani, it's time for this one to feed her *panis*. Can you help me?"

"For a certainty, my hearts."

Zor watched as Kyra settled herself in comfortably for the last feeding of the moon-rising, propping a few pillows behind her back in the process. He sucked in his breath when she removed her *qi'ka* top. "We've but thirty hours left," he whispered thickly, his eyes feasting on her fertile chest. "Will you invite me to sample of your charms whilst gorging on your sweet juice?"

"Zor," Kyra whispered back throatily, her eyes glazing over, "let's discuss this after you tuck the girls in and I can better appreciate the conversation."

His eyes flicked over Kyra, taking in everything. "Aye."

Clearing his brain of its lusty thoughts, he settled Zora at one of his *nee'ka's* nipples. When his hatchling latched on and started drinking of her mommy's sweet juice, he then settled Zara at the other one, helping his other hatchling latch her tiny rosebud mouth around it.

And then Zor simply watched his *panis* feed. 'Twas the most beautiful sight in the goddess' creation.

* * * * *

By the next morning, word had spread throughout all of Sand City, as well as within the perimeters of the Palace of the Dunes, that insurrectionists on Tron had managed to breach Trystonni airspace. Zor had sent word to Dak, and after the King of Ti Q'won had arrogantly informed him that Geris had begun her belly flutters, Zor had commanded him to return to Tryston immediately with his queen, fearing for the safety of any babes she was to hatch. He would take no chances with any of the Q'an Tal bloodline until the insurrectionists had either surrendered or been annihilated.

Over breakfast with Zor, Kil, and Rem, plus her sister-in-law Jera-a woman she couldn't stand even after many attempts to warm up to her-Kyra was to learn that Tron was a planet on the outskirts of Trek Mi Q'an galaxy. For over twenty Yessat years, the insurrectionists there had been staging terrorist activities, sometimes going so far as to incinerate entire sectors to make a point.

"I don't understand why you simply don't give the rebels what they're after and be done with it." Jera aired herself with an ornate hand-held fan. Why she did this when the great hall was kept at such a comfortable temperature, Kyra couldn't say. But it annoyed her. Everything about the blonde, voluptuous woman annoyed her. She might have been beautiful, but Jera was also mean. The haughty woman seemed to have a malicious gleam in her eyes all the time.

"Jera," Rem murmured, "that is enough. You know not of what you speak."

Rem was golden-haired and possessed the same glowing blue eyes as his brothers. He was as big and formidable looking as his brothers as well, but harbored a sternness about him that Zor and Dak didn't.

Not even Kil was so serious and stern-looking. Of course, Kyra had come to realize that as harsh and merciless as Kil could be, it was mostly bluster, at least where family was concerned. The man had scars, physical as well as emotional-scars that Zor had refused to speak of to her.

But whereas Kil had proven he was more bark than bite, especially where his two adored nieces were concerned, Rem looked to be more bite than bark. He had a sadness to him, a deep melancholy that had been channeled into an implacable grimness. It was something Kyra hadn't noticed the first few times she'd spoken with him, but it was getting harder and harder not to observe it.

At first, Kyra had thought her brother-in-law's roughness had come as a result of being a warrior and a formidable lesser king. But as she spent more time with him, and saw firsthand how he reacted to the closeness between Zor and herself, Kyra realized Rem was the way he was simply because he had given up all hope for a future with happiness in it. Never would Rem experience the kind of intense emotional and physical bonds that Kyra and Zor shared. And because of that, he would never know what it was to hold his own babies in his arms.

"I know perfectly well of what I speak!" Jera fumed, slapping her fan down onto the raised table. "I think all of you need to open your eyes. The rebels have breached Trystonni airspace. Think you they will stop at that?" She waved her hand in a gesture of regal disdain. "Give them what they seek and be done with it."

Kyra noticed the flush on Zor's cheeks. He was trying to hold on to his temper. "The insurrectionists are naught but high-born lords wishing to reclaim sectors that were forcibly taken from them after they abused the people living within them." He spoke in a low voice as he picked up his goblet, turning it round and round between his fingers. "I cannot turn over the lives of innocents to monsters."

"They tortured women and their *panis*," Kil bit out, his tone deadly. He was visibly fighting for control, as if trying to extinguish a memory that ate at him relentlessly. "Including the Empress who was our mother."

And suddenly Kyra knew. At last she comprehended the anguish that had consumed Kil, driving him off to walk alone for what Zor had said would sometimes equate to years at a time. Kil had been there. He had witnessed his mother's murder. And he hadn't been able to protect her. She wondered if that was where he had earned his scar-on Tron, trying to aid his mother.

Kyra didn't know if Zor was letting his emotions spill over without realizing it, transferring them through to her bridal necklace, or how it was that she knew what she knew. But she was certain. Kil had suffered much. And worse yet, he blamed himself for it.

Kyra reached out and placed her hand over Kil's and squeezed gently, letting him know she was there for him. Kil closed his eyes as if warding off pain, then when he was steadied, looked up to her and nodded his thanks. She lifted her hand and patted him on the back, a token of affection amongst two people who had grown into friends.

The action hadn't gone unnoticed by Rem. He turned to Jera, fixing her with his grim gaze. "I said that's enough. Hold your tongue or be sent to your rooms."

"Well," Jera fumed, shooting up to her feet. "Mayhap I was feeling fatigued anyway. The goddess knows my sleep was much disturbed last moon-rising by the cries of her"-she threw a hand toward Kyra-"recently hatched little brats!"

Before he could react, Kyra clutched Zor's fist with her other hand and squeezed. "Don't," she murmured, "she isn't worth it."

Kyra didn't know whether or not she had helped matters, but one thing was for certain-her husband was furious. Nobody but nobody could speak of his daughters that way and get away with it, she was soon to find out. Even Kil's eyes had widened, waiting to see how this scene would play out.

"Remove yourself from my presence anon," Zor bit out, each word distinct and precise as his gaze blazed into Jera. "You will keep to your rooms whilst you are here, barred as you now are from my sight."

Jera flushed, clearly realizing she had gone beyond too far. And yet she continued to make demands. Kyra couldn't get over the woman's nerve. She was either brazen as all hell or stupider than Kyra didn't know what. She guessed it was a combination of both.

"You can't possibly expect me to stay to my rooms during the whole of our stay!" she wailed. "I needs must come out sometime!"

"Make certain I see you not," Zor replied in a low rumble, and then he emphasized, "at all."

Jera scowled, but nodded her consent, then made to leave the great hall.

"And Jera," Zor called out, his tone cool and remote. "If you speak of my *nee'ka* or *panis* again in such treasonous terms you will be sentenced as any betrayer would." At her gasp, he said simply, "remember who holds all power over life and death in this world, indeed in the whole of the galaxy, before any more words next leak from your black-hearted lips."

Rem watched as his wife stomped off to their suite, then turned to Zor and blew out a breath. "I apologize, brother, for Jera's words. She is not a kind soul, as you must have surmised."

"Zor does not hold you responsible for Jera's tongue," Kil gently informed their youngest brother.

Zor grunted his agreement. "If I did that, both of you would have been sent down to the gulch pits many moon-risings ago." He shook his head sadly. "The goddess knows I have bit my tongue on more than one occasion, telling myself to leave it be out of respect for the fact that she is your *nee'ka*. Leastways, I did before learning of how she came to be your *nee'ka*."

Rem's eyes strayed toward Kyra. His gaze flicked over her form, lingering at her engorged breasts. "'Twas my own fool-headedness and for that I needs pay."

"No warrior needs pay for a lifetime, Rem," Kil argued. "I vow, why have you not sent the she-bitch to a different palace, that you need not look upon her wily face?"

Rem sighed, his eyes shuffling from Kyra's breasts to Kil's face. "The main palace on Sypar is huge. I rarely see her. She keeps to her rooms with her lovers and I keep to mine with my bound servants and *Kefas*."

Zor shook his head and sighed. "'Tis sad, that."

Rem shrugged absently. "'Tis life." And then he added with a sarcastic grin. "'Tis my life leastways."

As the great hall grew silent while the men finished their meal, Kyra gnawed at her bottom lip and thought about Rem's situation from every angle. Sighing, and praying her husband didn't try to throttle her for what she was about to say without asking his permission first, she did as she thought was best and plowed onward. "Rem?"

"Aye?" He looked up from his meal.

"Would you like to meet Zora and Zara?"

Kil stopped chewing mid-bite, his eyes widening. And yes, Zor definitely looked like he wanted to throttle her. Kyra's belly clenched. Perhaps she had misread Rem. Maybe he didn't want to get to know any children, even those of his own brother. She really should have spoken to Zor first.

"*Nee'ka,*" Zor began in a chastising tone, "I think-"

"Aye."

Jaws agape, Zor and Kil turned to Rem. "You-you do?" Zor asked hesitantly.

"Aye." Rem inclined his head, offering Kyra a grin. "I was beginning to wonder if ever you would ask."

Kyra expelled a breath of air she suspected she'd been holding in for a while. "Would you escort me to my apartments, then?" She smiled, trying to lessen the intensity of the moment. "Perhaps you can visit with the girls while I take care of a few things. I want to get ready for Geris's arrival tomorrow so she can have a more comfortable hatching than I did." She shot a look over to Zor that clearly said she still held him responsible for her own horrific hatching experience.

Zor grimaced, not caring to argue with his *nee'ka* when he had but a few hours more before he could sample of her charms.

"I would be honored to escort you," Rem answered her in gallant tones as he rose to his feet. "I am given to understand by servant talk that my nieces possess your rare mane of hair, but are of Q'an Tal eyes and bronzed coloring."

"A light bronze, but yeah." Kyra grinned. "They're gorgeous."

"I'll go see the babes as well," Kil announced, rising to stand. "Wee Zara gets a temper with me if I stay from her sights o'er long."

Zor chuckled. "'Tis true, she does." He inclined his head in a lordly gesture. "Although both of my hatchlings prefer their papa's handsome face above all others,"-Kyra rolled her eyes at his arrogant claim, the truth or not-"'tis for a certainty wee Zara sees something in the dunce none other is able to glean."

Kil grunted.

Kyra giggled. "You're just jealous because, unlike Zora, you have competition where Zara is concerned."

Zor scoffed at the notion. "From this lackwit? Harrumph."

Twenty minutes later, Zor was crossing his arms over his chest and scowling formidably at his turncoat hatchlings. Both of them. Where Zara had taken an affectation toward Kil, Zora had also found a favored uncle in Rem. "Ingrates," he muttered, though he was grinning when he said it.

Zor knew his *panis* preferred him above all others, so there was naught but goodness that could come of sharing their love with two hardened warriors who desperately needed it.

Chapter 28

When the final countdown was over and a full fortnight had passed, Zor was more than a little disgruntled not to find his *nee'ka* on the royal bed, naked and waiting for him, her legs spread wide open, and her channel eager to accept his thrusts. Every muscle in his body was clenched in anticipation, his jaw was rigid, his erection painful. And Kyra and her wicked breasts were not in the one place they should be.

Zor sighed, groaning as he fell onto the bed. He had made it to the final moments of the tortuous two weeks, only to be lured by the sand muse to his death. He clapped a hand to his forehead and moaned. He was dying for a certainty.

"All that moaning sounds like you're starting without me."

Zor's eyes shot open to the delicious sight of his *nee'ka* climbing up onto the raised bed, settling her and her two jiggling moosoos astride him. "Ah, wee one," he sighed, "how I have dreamed of this moon-rising."

Kyra smiled coyly down to him, feeling utterly feminine and carnal. She loved this new erotic power that she held over Zor. It never failed to amaze her that so powerful a warrior would want her...plain old Kyra the tax accountant. Plain old Kyra with, uh, the big bazooms.

Rubbing her wet labia back and forth over the erection bulging from her husband's leather pants, she felt her belly knot with arousal at the sound of his deep growl. "Do you like that?" she whispered thickly.

"Oh-*pani*, aye."

She smiled. "I've missed you calling me that."

Zor sucked in his breath when Kyra rotated her hips, grinding her pelvis deeper into his. "You don't like mani, my hearts?"

"Yes, but not in bed." Kyra ground harder, while simultaneously rubbing her hands over her engorged breasts. She closed her eyes and massaged them all over, secreting away a smile when she heard his breathing grow choppier. "In bed," she admitted breathlessly, "I like for you to make me feel dirty and wicked, submissive and dominated."

"Play with your nipples," Zor commanded her in a low murmur.

"Mmm. You like that?" Kyra took each nipple between her thumbs and forefingers, expertly massaging them as she continued to grind her hips into Zor's stiff arousal. He sucked in his breath and ground back. "You're always so quick to summon away my clothes, husband. Why don't you summon away yours?"

As quick as a flash, their positions were reversed, with Kyra flat on her back and Zor's fully clothed form settled between her splayed thighs. He returned the torture Kyra had dealt him in spades, grinding his erection against her drenched labia, offering her enough friction on her clit to become aroused, but not enough for release. Kyra threw her head back and moaned in delicious agony.

"You are greedy for my cock, wench?" Zor asked the question in a dark, commanding rumble. Rotating his hips, he ground them enough to deepen the friction against her clit. She gasped. "Answer me."

"Yes. Oh god-please."

"Are you begging me to sample of your charms?"

"Yes."

Zor ground his hips into her again, the leather of his pants getting drenched from her arousal. "I am not convinced. Beg me again."

"Please." She clutched at his forearms as she writhed in need underneath him, her nails digging into his skin. "Please. Please. Please."

Zor used but one massive hand to hold both of Kyra's smaller ones captive over her head. She tried to break free, desperate to tear at his clothing.

Zor smiled with a predator's satisfaction as his wee *nee'ka* tried to loosen his grip on her hands. 'Twas like the hands of a babe trying to dislodge him. He rotated his hips again and reveled in her pleading moans. "Do you deserve to feel my rod thrusting into your tight little channel?" he asked arrogantly. "Have all of your thoughts this day been of how to please me?"

"Yes! Zor please-I can't take it!" Kyra moaned in agony.

Zor bent his head to lick away a stray tear, summoning his clothes away in the process. He positioned his stiff erection at the juncture of her channel, still holding her hands prisoner above her head. "Is this what you want, *nee'ka*?" he asked thickly.

"Yes." Kyra groaned when Zor bent his head again, this time to swipe his tongue across her jutting nipples. "Please."

"Then 'tis yours." Clenching his jaw, Zor embedded himself into Kyra's cunt in one long thrust. She climaxed instantly. "Mmm. Aye, *pani*. Milk my cock with your woman's tremors." Offering her body a series of hard, deep thrusts, his breathing grew labored at the exquisite tightness. "Kyra."

Kyra thrust her hips up, eager for more. "Oh yes-oh god, yes." Needing to feel him embedded deeper within her, Kyra wrapped her legs around his waist and settled in for a hard ride.

"Is this what you want?" Zor growled, thrusting into her pussy faster and faster, pounding into her channel possessively. He craned his neck and took one plumped up nipple into his mouth to draw from. Groaning, he gorged of it.

"Oh god-YES!" Kyra peaked violently, moaning loud enough to be heard throughout the palace corridors. She rotated her hips, meeting every stroke he gave her with a primitive need. "I need more," she gasped. "Do it. You know what I want."

Zor pounded into her flooded channel faster, harder, mercilessly. His strokes were primal and territorial, branding her of him. The sound of perspiration-soaked skin slapping against perspiration-soaked skin sounded throughout the bedchamber. "Do you beg for my seed, *nee'ka*? Do you want the High King who owns this lusty channel to give you another of his hatchlings?"

"Yes. Oh please. Give it to me!"

Gritting his teeth, Zor thrust into Kyra like an animal. He took her ruthlessly, binding her flesh to his as the bridal necklace had bound their emotions and lives together. "Your pleasure is mine, *nee'ka*." Lowering his head to gorge of her breasts, Zor spurt his life-force deep within her womb, inducing the stones in the necklace to pulse.

Kyra threw her head back and screamed, convulsing with the ceaseless climaxes that her husband's gorging made even more ferocious than usual. Zor roared low in his throat, his body peaking violently while he continued to gorge.

As the intensity of the joining wound down, Zor grunted with the satisfaction of a male *maki* beast that had caught his prey and feasted well. He kept himself firmly embedded within his Sacred Mate as he rolled onto his back and bade Kyra to rest on top of him.

"Mmm." Kyra grinned, propping herself up on her elbows to gaze down at him. "That was wonderful." Zor kneaded her *sekta* pearl buttocks as he studied Kyra's face with an intensity that almost frightened her. His nostrils were flaring, the muscles in his neck tightly corded. "Zor? What is it? What's wrong?"

"Do not ever think to leave me, *nee'ka*. I will not allow it. I would hunt you down and return you to my bed always. Tell me you would not ever make me do this."

Kyra was startled by his fiercely impassioned plea. Although it had been issued in Zor's typically autocratic fashion, she recognized it for what it was...insecurity. Why he would feel this way, she hadn't any notion, but she refused to allow him to worry over something that would never come to pass. "Zor," she whispered, running a hand over his jaw, "I would never, ever leave you. Never."

He grunted, somewhat appeased. "Tell me then that you love me."

"I love you. Very, very much." Kyra scowled when his only reply was another egotistical grunt. "And?" she wailed.

Zor found his first grin. "You'll do."

"I'll do?" Kyra punched him in the arm, huffing.

Laughing, Zor grabbed her fist, clutching it in his massive one. Growing serious, he whispered very meaningfully, "I love you, *nee'ka*. Now and forever, there is only you."

"Oh, Zor." Kyra craned her neck, bending down to kiss him full on the mouth. Sighing her content, she thrust her tongue between his lips and kissed him languidly. They tasted of each other for long minutes, then Zor began to use his powers to move her up and down the length of his shaft. "Mmm. On earth we have an expression for this, you know."

"Aye?"

Kyra nodded. "Uh huh."

"What is it?"

"'A hard man is good to find.'"

Zor grinned. "'Tis lucky for you then that I shall be availing myself of your lusty channel every day and every moon-rising for the next three weeks."

Kyra's brow wrinkled. "Only for the next three weeks?"

He sighed like a martyr. "Aye." Zor resumed his kneading of her buttocks as a thoughtful look permeated his features. "After you hatch this time, though, I want to wait mayhap another six months or so before getting you with another *pani*."

"W-What?" Kyra shot up. Still impaled, she sat fully astride him. "You gave me another baby?" she shrieked.

"Aye." Zor nodded arrogantly. "What think you of ten or eleven more?"

"Ten or elev-Zor! I just gave birth two weeks ago!"

"'Twas bliss, aye?"

"No!" she screeched. "It hurt like hell!" Kyra huffed, her arms crossing under her breasts. "Good grief. Why didn't you ask me?"

"I did!" Zor bellowed, hurt by what he perceived as a rejection of his hatchling. "I asked you did you want another, you said aye, and so I gorged whilst I gave to you my life-force."

"I thought it was a rhetorical question to get me hot!" Kyra clapped a hand to her forehead. She was getting a headache. "Wait a minute. Are you saying that you got me pregnant by gorging while you came inside of me?"

"Aye."

"Then how did you get me pregnant the first time?"

Zor sighed. 'Twas the only time he resented his *nee'ka's* primitive upbringing, when forced to answer such lackwitted questions. "We coupled, *pani*."

"I know that!" Kyra fumed, huffing her disgruntlement. She held up a palm like a talisman for sanity. "What I mean is, how did I get pregnant if you need to gorge to do it?"

"Ah, that." Zor waved a hand dismissively. "There is no controlling the first time, leastways none that I know of. You simply get with a *pani* sac when you do, much like on your earth I would imagine." At Kyra's nod, he continued. "'Tis after you've hatched and are gorged that we can control how many more *panis* you hatch and when you hatch them."

Kyra was curious despite herself. Her brow furrowed curiously. "How so?"

Zor shrugged absently. "'Tis simple, really. If I gorge whilst giving you my life-force, you will get with another *pani* sac. If I don't, you won't."

"Fascinating," she murmured.

"And when we decide we want no more hatchlings"-Zor slashed his hand tersely through the air-"which will not happen for many, many *pani* sacs yet to come"-He ignored Kyra's frown-"then I simply cease gorging whilst mating altogether until the time comes when your sweet juice has dried up."

Kyra was so astounded that she forgot to be angry. "That's amazing! That's incred-hey wait!" Her hand flew to her throat as a horrific thought occurred to her. "Does that mean I'll have these humungous breasts until we quit making babies altogether?"

A lecherous purring sound emitted from Zor's throat. "Mmm...aye, mani."

"Oh god." Kyra's hand flew back to her forehead. She really was getting a headache. "Zor! We have to quit after I have the next one. I can't stand these breasts much longer!"

He grunted. "On Tryston, we have an expression for this, *nee'ka*."

"Really, Zor? What is it?"

"'Too bad.'"

* * * * *

The strutting Dak, who had been swaggering around Ti Q'won ever since Geris's belly flutters first began, arrived with his queen the following morning.

After escorting his *nee'ka* to Kyra's apartments, Dak settled in at the raised table in the great hall with his brothers, bringing with him news that a few of his most trusted warriors had recently gleaned from a Tron insurrectionist they had captured within Trek Mi Q'an airspace. "They seek to kidnap the High Queen."

Dak pulled out a communicator, a small device that projected holographic images, and set it to replay a stored memory. "Here is the message the leader of the rebels has been passing amongst his followers."

Zor, Kil, and Rem watched in fury as the holographic message of the leader of the insurrectionists known only as Ty played back for them. He was a large man, though not so large as the average warrior. He was of a stocky build, sinewy in his strength and musculature. The hair had been shaved from his head and he sported only a closely cropped beard.

Greetings unto you, my fellow anarchists. The time has at last come upon us to reclaim what is rightfully ours by virtue of birth. No longer will we succumb to the unjust dictates of the unholy Emperor Q'an Tal, fleeing from our sectors for fear of his reprisals. There is naught to fear, my friends. The Emperor is but a man... Ty smiled savagely. And like any man, can be killed...

Zor listened to Ty's deranged spewing for a few minutes more before putting a question to Dak. "Were your warriors able to find out where this rebel leader heralds from? We know not much of Ty besides the fact that he is not native to Tron."

"Nay." Dak shook his head. "But 'tis not Tryston for a certainty."

"How do you know?" Kil asked curiously.

"Watch this part coming up," Dak murmured, gesturing to the holographic image of Ty. "Notice that he refers to Kyra as 'the Empress', but never as 'the High Queen'."

When the part of the recorded memory Dak had referred to finished playing, Rem was the first to comment. "I take your point, brother. Had Ty been a Trystonni by birth, his first inclination would be to refer to her as the High Queen. That he calls her only the Empress, insinuates that he is of somewhere within Trek Mi Q'an, but not of Tryston."

Zor inclined his head, agreeing. "'Tis not much more to go on, but leastways it rules out this planet and its seventeen moons."

"'Tis a start," Kil rumbled in low tones.

Dak turned off the communicator and regarded his brothers. "So now the question becomes, do we sit back and wait for the madman to make a move, or do we go hunting?"

Zor took a long, deep swallow from his matpow. His nostrils flaring, he slammed the goblet down upon the raised table, inducing the glowing turquoise liquid to spill out over the sides. "We hunt."

Chapter 29

On the next moon-rising, Geris was safely delivered of a golden-haired, glowing blue-eyed baby girl who was the spitting image of her father. Dak was prouder than Kyra didn't know what, strutting around like a peacock, his female *pani* cradled into his massive arms.

Kil, who had immensely enjoyed watching Geris hatch-he'd never heard so many dirty swear words at once-was now sitting on the bed next to the new mani, trying to get her to calm down, as Zor, Rem, and Kyra looked on.

"Forget it, Kil!" Geris's lips puckered into a frown. "I don't care what my husband wants, and furthermore I don't give a damn if it was your grandmama's name. I refuse to name my daughter Pyg!"

"'Tis a fine Trystonni name!" Dak bellowed as he paced back and forth with his hatchling.

"It's stupid is what it is." Geris crossed her arms over her still normal-sized breasts and scowled. "Kyra, tell him girl!"

Kyra-trying desperately not to laugh-glanced over to where Dak was pacing and nodded. "On earth, that name refers to a small, fat animal that snorts like Kita and eats a lot."

"On Tryston," Dak countered with a sniff, "'tis the name of the ancient mystic who is credited as the discoverer of the healing sands."

"Forget it!" Geris's frown went from puckered to pinched in a nuba-second. "I won't have it." Turning to Kil-the brother-in-law that had let her beat on his chest while she was pushing the *pani* sac out-she grabbed his shoulders and turned pleading eyes up to him. "Please talk to him. I couldn't bear to name my daughter Pyg!"

Kil sighed. It hadn't escaped his notice that where his two first-dimension sisters-within-the-law were concerned, he was turning out to be a royal pushover. "Dak, cannot you settle on a name both of you like? Why must you upset your *nee'ka* so?"

"'Tis a fine name, Pyg!" He threw a heavily muscled arm toward Zor and Rem. "Aye?"

Both brothers grumbled something, refusing to get in the middle of it.

Sighing, Dak turned to Geris and relented enough to hear some of her suggestions. "What name do you wish for, my hearts?"

Geris beamed. Smiling brightly, she admitted, "well, I've always been partial to Helena." At Dak's growl, she harrumphed. "Okay, then name another name. But no damn Pyg!"

"What think you of Mif?"

"Mif?" Geris clapped a hand to her forehead. "It's butt-ugly is what I think!"

Dak grunted. "Sig?"

"No!"

"What think you of Suka?"

"Arrg!"

Kyra held up a palm to silence their argument. She turned toward her brother-in-law and thrust her hands to her hips. "Dak, all of your suggestions have been truly atrocious. I can hardly blame Ger for hating those names."

"They are fine Trystonni names, the lot of them." He slashed his hand through the air, his nostrils flaring. "'Tis better for a certainty than Palena!"

"Helena," Geris corrected. She frowned. "And no it's not!"

He merely grunted.

Unable to take much more of their banter, and desperately desiring to take a tumble with his *nee'ka* in the *vesha* hides, Zor stepped in between his quibbling brother and sister-within-the-law to render his verdict. "As the High King of Tryston and the Emperor of Trek Mi Q'an, I am claiming my right by the holy law." He glared daggers at both of them before bellowing out his decision. "I give you five nuba-minutes to choose a name for my niece that is agreeable to you both, else will I name her myself."

Geris's swift intake of breath deterred Dak from any further outbursts of stubbornness, precisely what Zor had hoped for. Dak did not want his *nee'ka* hurt could it be helped.

"All right, all right." Sighing, the new papa handed his *pani* over to a grinning Rem and made his way toward the bed to sit next to Geris. Grasping her hand in his, he searched her eyes. "Let us settle on a name together, my hearts. What like you besides Helena?"

Geris contemplated that for a suspended moment. The silence in the chamber was deafening. "Hmm." She tapped a finger against Dak's arm as she considered the question. And then she smiled. "I like your mother's name," she said softly.

Kil's head shot up. A pained expression crossed his face. He looked to his niece and then to Geris. And then slowly, his lips kicked up into a smile. "She does have our mani's fair hair."

Zor grunted. "Aye. And 'tis from mani that we get our eyes."

"She has her golden brown skin color too," Rem murmured.

"Well then!" Kyra clapped her hands together and grinned. "It's settled."

"Aye." Dak drew his *nee'ka's* hand up to his lips for a kiss. "We will call her Jana."

* * * * *

The next several weeks passed swiftly and without incident. Four hunting parties had been sent to scout throughout Trek Mi Q'an for any signs of Ty and his insurrectionists. All four hunting squadrons had come back with no new word.

The women soon grew weary of being cloistered up within the confines of the palace, both of them wanting an excursion of any kind to alleviate the monotony of what had become, in effect, a royal prison.

The men were having none of that.

Kyra was safely delivered of a third girl child almost three weeks to the day of Geris's hatching. This one they called Kara, naming her after Kyra's missing, beloved sister.

Whereas Zora and Zara possessed their mani's mane of fireberry hair, Kara was the image of her papa, sporting jet black tresses and glowing blue eyes. The new little High Princess was well-loved and joyously received by all, including her two older sisters who were still developing at a rapid rate, both of them now the physical and mental equivalent of year old earth children.

When Zor's sentence of celibacy ended two weeks after Kara's hatching, he vehemently agreed with his *nee'ka* that they should wait several months more before getting her with another *pani* sac. No matter how erotic and stimulating the experience was, gorging whilst joining was shied away from, giving the couple time for themselves and for furthering the bonds they shared with the three daughters they had already made together.

As Kyra saw it, the only downside to postponing further hatchings was that the decision forced Kil to remain bound to his duties as a lesser husband, as she had yet to give birth to a son. Until Kyra beget an heir, Kil was unable to search for his own *nee'ka,* a situation that distressed her sorely.

Kil, however, assured her that he didn't care. "I have far too much to see to," he had said, "without the distraction of a *nee'ka*."

When Kyra had thought to press the issue, Zor had kissed her into silence. "Leave it be," he had whispered in her ear. "My brother prefers to walk alone."

Kyra had deferred to Zor's wishes, especially since he was getting better and better at deferring to hers as of late. Except for on the issue of allowing her and Geris to have an excursion outside of the palace perimeters. On that, he was proving to be far less than accommodating. And so, Kyra had decided, she needed someone to help persuade her husband to her way of thinking.

One morning, after feeding the babies their sweet juice, Kyra made her way to Kil's apartments to speak to him.

Kil raised a curious brow when he opened his doors to Kyra, but bade her to come inside. Showing her into the parlor, he motioned for her to have a seat. He was pleased when she removed her *qi'ka* before availing herself of a chair, not having to remind her-for once-of her duty to do so. He had to wonder at this sudden observance to tradition. The woman wanted something for a certainty.

Kyra let the gold *qi'ka* shimmer to the ground, then took her seat and faced Kil. "How are you feeling today?"

Kil's eyes trailed over Kyra's engorged breasts, then made its way down to the fire-berry thatch of hair between her thighs before finally flicking upwards to meet her gaze. "I am well. And you?"

She sighed. "I am restless, Kil. Very restless."

"Forget it, Kyra."

She harrumphed. Scowling, Kyra crossed her arms under her breasts and glared daggers at him. "Why does Jera get to go shopping at the stalls," she whined, "when Geris and I have become virtual prisoners here?"

Kil's eyes narrowed speculatively. "Jera has left the palace before?"

"Of course." Kyra waved dismissively. "Even I can't blame the horrid woman for sneaking off. The palace becomes boring when it's all you see for weeks on end!"

Kil ignored that. "How many times has she left? When did you see her leave?"

Kyra sighed. Clearly her brother-in-law had no intention of aiding her. "I don't know how many times. I'm not her shadow for goodness sake."

"Try," he said gently, "to remember."

Her arms resting at either side of the chair, Kyra crossed one leg over the other and rocked it back and forth. She bit her lip as she searched her memory. "Let me think." Scrunching up her face, she began to tap her cheek absently with her index finger. "Oh, of course!" She smiled up to Kil. "I know for a fact that she sneaked out the afternoon Kara was hatched."

"For a certainty?"

"Yes." Kyra nodded. "I remember happening upon her on my way to the kitchens. Cook had made me some of those maza candies I love, so I went to fetch them. I distinctly remembering feeling a bit hurt because here Jera was planning to sneak out for a shopping spree when she couldn't even take a second to congratulate me on Kara's birth."

Kil snorted. "As if you can expect common courtesy from one so cruel."

She shrugged. "Perhaps not."

"And what of the other times?" He leaned forward, placing his elbows on his knees. He steepled his fingertips together. "Can you remember them?"

Kyra sighed morosely. "You're not going to help me convince Zor to let us leave the palace, are you?"

"Nay."

She harrumphed. "Fine. Then I don't remember," she stated petulantly, her chin thrusting up a notch.

"Kyra," Kil growled. "You will tell me what you know anon."

She took a moment to huff out her annoyance before relenting. "There were at least two other incidents, but the only one I can place within a time frame was the day Zora and Zara took their first steps." She gave him a date in Yessat years.

Kil nodded. As with Kara's hatching, it was reasonable for a mani to remember the moments surrounding such an event well. "Go on."

"I was with the girls in the main atrium off the great hall. We were looking at the flowers and plant-life there."

Kyra uncrossed her legs, momentarily distracting Kil. His vision was again snagged by the tuft of dark red curls at the apex of her thighs. He flicked his gaze upward, noting the large pink areolas circling her distended rouged nipples. He sighed. At times, being a lesser husband was more annoyance than honor. "Go on."

"You know how the atrium has a path that shortcuts to the conveyance launch pad?" At his nod, Kyra continued ruminating. "Jera came running toward the atrium from that direction, looking, um,"-she coughed discreetly into her hand-"disheveled."

"Recently joined with?"

Kyra blushed. "Yes." She re-crossed her legs and absently rocked one of them back and forth. "I asked her where she had been and she informed me that it wasn't really my business, but if I had to know, she had been out for another shopping excursion."

"Interesting," Kil murmured.

"What was that?"

"Nothing." Standing up, Kil held out his hand for Kyra. "Come. I needs leave to see to an errand."

Kyra frowned up at her brother-in-law, but stood nonetheless. "You're not going to relent at all, are you?"

He shook his head slowly. His lips curled into a slight grin. "Nay."

Kil decided he didn't like the menacing look that shone of a sudden in Kyra's eyes. "What?" he asked warily.

"Nothing." She turned around and, keeping her legs splayed apart on the floor, bent over slowly to pick up her removed *qi'ka*, exposing everything to him. Kyra felt somewhat vindicated when she heard Kil suck in his breath. Turning around with a cunning smile on her face, she batted her eyelashes and held out her *qi'ka* to him. "Be careful," she announced a little too sweetly as she ran her hands over her engorged breasts, "they're very tender this morning."

"Of course," Kil bit out, his gaze narrowed. "Tender."

* * * * *

Kil found his brothers on the training field. As Zor looked on, his hands splayed at either hip, Dak and Rem were instructing the warriors in hand-to-hand combat, a weaponless strategy used only when telekinetic combat was rendered ineffective due to head wounds or breaks in the atmospheric conditions of the battle environment.

It was a perfect day for defensive weaponless instruction, as the shimmering gold of Tryston's air was very light. For the past fortnight they had been plagued with dense glitter, making it difficult to see your hand even if held before your own face.

Today the western sun hung a proud golden red, casting off clear, pure rays of light. Gulch beasts flew by overhead, coming out of the swamps to find their prey within the pits.

Kil smiled a warrior's satisfaction. 'Twas a day made for the warring arts.

Strolling over to where Zor stood, Kil inclined his head upon reaching his side. "I would that I could speak with you, brother. And for that matter with Dak and Rem as well." And then he emphasized, "privately."

Zor studied him curiously, but relented with a grunt. Cupping his hands around his mouth, he bellowed for the warriors to take a break, then ordered Dak and Rem to his side. When all of the Q'an Tal line was present, Zor nodded to Kil. "Now what was it you wished to speak to us of?"

"'Tis Jera."

As three sets of brows raised in speculation, Kil inhaled deeply, hoping what he was about to say wasn't on the far side of paranoid. He wasn't a man to trust easily, after all, so suspicion of others came natural to one such as himself. He glanced toward Rem as he crossed his arms over his chest. "Did you know that Jera has left the palace a few times in the past several weeks?"

Rem's eyes widened. "Nay. 'Tis not possible. She has been guarded."

Kil sighed. Not one to dance around an issue, he came straight to the point. "Is it possible Jera is fucking her guard?"

Rem grunted. Smiling sarcastically, he admitted the truth. "Anything is possible whilst speaking of my beloved *nee'ka*."

"What is this about, Kil?" Zor regarded his brother thoughtfully. "Why think you that Jera has been coming and going from the palace at will?"

"Kyra." At Zor's raised eyebrows, Kil grinned. "Your crafty *nee'ka* came to my rooms this morn, seeking to garner my aid. 'Twas her hope I would dissuade you in your rigid stance, that you might allow she and Geris to leave the palace for a spell."

"I assume you told her nay?" Zor bellowed. He shook his head and sighed. "By the sands, the wee woman is but a constant trial. Forever is she bedeviling me."

"You know not a trial," Dak muttered, "until you have displeased my *nee'ka*. The woman's frown alone could nigh unto turn your man parts to stone, and let us not even consider the shrieks that accompany those bedamned frowns."

Rem chuckled, a dimple so much like Dak's popping out. "Her tempers are worse than she was whilst hatching?"

"Aye." Dak groaned. "The fortnight after Jana hatched was naught but a wicked nightmare. I couldn't even mount her to get her to shut-up."

Zor couldn't stop the reluctant grin that broke out onto his face. "Do not feel o'er bad, brother. Kyra does much the same thing to me. She merely does it in a different way."

"What does she do?" Rem asked. He was slightly jealous of the relationships his elder brothers had with their Sacred Mates, but not so much so that he couldn't enjoy this banter.

"If she is especially out of sorts, she does just the opposite as Geris." Zor snorted incredulously, as if even the memories agitated him sorely. "My *nee'ka* will refuse to speak to me, or even acknowledge my presence if I enter a chamber whilst she's in it." He gritted his teeth and clutched his fist. "Once when she asked me if I thought she looked fat and I told her I liked for my woman to be fleshy, she refused to couple for two moon-risings, claiming I was a 'dickhead'-whatever in the sands that is."

The Q'an Tal men looked horrified. "She denied you the right of a husband to join with his mate?" Dak asked disbelievingly.

"Aye." Zor shook his head, looking every inch the familial martyr. "'Twas torture, I tell you."

Kil snorted, shaking his head. "'Twas torture for me as well. You haunted my rooms much as you did the time she banned you after the gentling." He rolled his eyes. "I could have lived without getting channel those moon-risings had you not subjected me to having to feel your bedamned forehead to see if you were dying of the ague every few minutes."

"'Twas possible," Zor insisted, his spine rigid with defensiveness. "I was seeing spots before my eyes and hearing the voices of fallen warriors whispering to me of my doom."

Kil grunted, waving his hand in irritation at the memory. "We have strayed much from the point."

Dak scratched his head. His smile was chagrined. "What was the point again? I forget of what we were speaking."

"Jera."

After his three brothers muttered their "oh"s, Kil flicked a hand toward Zor. "Leastways, when your *nee'ka* came to speak with me and I told her nay, that I would not help"-he ignored Zor's grunt of approval-"she complained that it wasn't fair that

Jera could go shopping whilst she and Geris were confined to the palace."

"Shopping?" Rem intoned. "What's this of shopping?"

Kil repeated verbatim all that Kyra had said, then eyed his brothers questioningly. "Think you I am being paranoid, or is it too much coincidence that on both of the occasions Jera disappeared, Tron insurrectionists were spotted near the market, trysting with a high-born woman no less?"

Zor ran a hand over his jaw. He craned his neck back and looked absently up to the golden sky. Sighing, he returned his gaze to Kil. "Nay, I do not think you paranoid."

"Nor do I," Rem murmured. He noticed the pitying glances his brothers were throwing him and scowled. "Do not," he bit out, "feel sorrow for my fate. 'Tis done."

"I want her watched by trusted warriors at all times," Zor said in a low, conspiratorial tone. "The next time Jera thinks to leave, let her go, but have her followed."

Kil nodded slowly, regretfully. He wished none of this burden to be Rem's to bear. "'Tis done."

Chapter 30

Kyra couldn't stop thinking of her sister. Every time she looked into Zora or Zara's faces-who were both her sister's spitting image save their eye color and golden skin tones-and every time she spoke her daughter Kara's name aloud, memories of the woman she had been named for would weigh heavily on her mind until it was all she could think about.

After a sennight of watching his *nee'ka* suffer from depressed spirits, Zor could no longer bear to see her in pain. He insisted that she visit with Ari, who, as Chief Priestess, was the personal spiritual advisor to the throne.

Kyra agreed immediately. Not only did seeing Ari mean spending time with a wizened friend, but it also meant leaving the palace. Or so she had thought. Zor had taken great pleasure in announcing to his *nee'ka* that there was an enchanted barrier she could pass through-right there in the royal apartments-that once crossed, spit her out inside of the dune where the priestesses and their male slaves resided.

Instead of reacting badly to Zor's announcement, Kyra had been elated. She might not be getting directly out of the palace during her visit with Ari, but she'd never actually seen a mystical barrier before either and therefore couldn't wait to get a move out.

Zor, who was well used to the evidence of magic, had thought her excitement naïve, but had decided against commenting upon it. He simply counted himself fortunate, relieved that he and his *nee'ka* would not have yet another argument about the restrictive life that the insurrectionists were forcing her to lead. He felt bad enough about her confinement as it was, unsuccessful as his hunters had been so far in apprehending Ty and his goons.

And so here Kyra stood, her heart pounding in anticipation, as she prepared to unlock a door within the royal chambers that she had never even noticed before. Unlike the majority of the heavy crystal and bejeweled doors within the palace, which opened and closed like the ones seen on earth-though here there were warriors aplenty to summon them open and closed for you-the door that led to the enchanted barrier was like the ones aboard the gastrolight cruiser, opening and closing automatically when they sensed the arrival and departure of your body heat.

Taking a deep breath, Kyra raised her palm to the recognition scanner and waited with wide eyes as the door's lock clicked open. A moment later, the sensory door slid wide, bidding her entrance to the other side.

Kyra stepped inside slowly, giddy with anticipation. She felt like she was in the middle of a Nancy Drew mystery, where she herself was starring in the lead role.

The room was dark, slightly cold, much like the temperature in the stomach of a cave. Noting the twisting staircase of shimmering gold crystal that led to another floor below, Kyra crept toward it, realizing this had to be the way since she could see no other method for exiting the chamber.

As she made her way down the winding, corkscrew stairs, the faint sounds of female moaning could be heard as if from a distance. Kyra followed it, curious, and if she was honest, slightly aroused by it.

At the bottom of the stairs there lay a glowing golden circle where the floor should have been, but nothing else. It was as if the twisting staircase and the shimmering circle laying at its end were perched in a vacuum where nothing else existed.

Kyra shivered, her nipples thrusting out, as she ran her hands up and down her arms to ward off the chills. The scene before her had gone from feeling like a Nancy Drew mystery to looking like an episode out of The Twilight Zone.

Ridiculously afraid that a vampire or a ghoul or something of that nature was about to pop out at her, Kyra picked up her pace and made her way to the glowing, pulsing orb of gold that lie in wait. Warily, she placed first one sandaled foot and then the other upon the large, flat, disk-like structure.

Another door appeared.

Constructed of a pulsing red crystal, the door was encrusted with glittering Trystonni jewels around its frame. Reaching out for the round, protruding diamond-esque structure that could only be a knob, Kyra's teeth sank into her lip as she slowly turned it, then snatched her hand back when the door began to open of its own volition.

The door swung wide.

The moaning grew louder.

She stepped through the threshold and followed the sounds.

Kyra caught her breath at the opulence of what was, in effect, Ari's personal kingdom. Everything inside of it, from the ceiling to the floors to the walls, was made of shimmering golden sand. With one exception, she silently amended, after reaching a fork within the dune where one had to decide which path they would take. Every road was paved of golden *trelli,* except for one paved of glittering red sand. Instinctively, Kyra knew that this path would take her to the Chief Priestess of Tryston.

Kyra grinned. She had gone from feeling like she was in the middle of a Nancy Drew novel, to fearing that she'd walked into The Twilight Zone. Now she was following the yellow brick road-or red sand road-that led straight to the Chief Priestess of Oz. As long as no flying monkeys obstructed her path, she figured she could handle the rest of her adventure.

Kyra strolled down the red road at a cautious pace, in awe of her surroundings despite herself. The path was long, shimmering, and narrow. The sounds of females being pleasured grew louder and louder.

When at last she reached the end of the trail, Kyra was deposited at the mouth of a massive golden cave. Wide-eyed, her gaze took in its every detail until at last it settled at the top. Ancient Trystonni writing similar to hieroglyphics was firmly embedded into the sparkling tunnel.

Q'i Liko Aki Jiq-She Who Is Born of the Goddess.

Suddenly feeling very trite and unworthy of being in a place that carried such an omnipotent air about it, Kyra hesitated at the mouth of the dune, wary of continuing onward.

She took a deep breath and expelled it. Telling herself to quit acting like a behemoth-breasted chicken, she straightened her spine and walked through the cave's threshold.

In the belly of the dune lay paradise.

Nude priestesses were scattered about everywhere, reclining in grooves within the dune that were each thatched with colorful silken pillows. Naked male slaves sporting perfect physiques and enormous penises attended to their whims. Some priestesses were being fed, others made love to, and still others both simultaneously.

Kyra's gaze was snagged by the largest of the grooves that lay in the center of the dune, directly where the red path dead-ended. This groove was raised above the others by a formation of *trelli* sand, clearly stating that the priestess within it was exalted above all others. And, of course, she was. For within the colorful pillows littered about the groove reclined Ari, being serviced even now by several slaves.

The closer Kyra got to the erotic scene before her, the more aroused she became.

Ari lay on her back moaning. Her legs were splayed wide, her pink nipples jutting seductively upward with arousal. A slave's mouth closed over one nipple, clamping around it and drawing from it. Another mouth descended on Ari's other nipple, latching onto the protrusion and sucking.

Desire surged through Kyra's body, growing more and more acute as the scene continued to unfold.

Ari's cunt was as as pink as her nipples, puffed up and swollen with need. Two tongues slithered around her sleek folds while a third tongue flicked at her clit. The Chief Priestess's eyes were closed in her passion and a look of pure, carnal bliss etched her features.

Through a haze of desire, it occurred to Kyra that She Who Is Born of the Goddess was erotica incarnate.

Kyra's steps were light and methodical as she continued to walk toward where Ari lay. The rhythmic rise and fall of the Chief Priestess's breasts beneath suckling mouths signaled that her climax was drawing nearer. Her back arched and her head fell back upon the massive, pillowing breasts of a beautiful golden *Kefa* that was obviously enchanted of *trelli* sand, rather than the colored sands found in the borderlands.

The *Kefa's* gentle hands massaged Ari's temples, soothing the Chief Priestess even as her peak neared. Ari's moaning grew louder, her breathing choppier. She splayed her legs wider, giving her male slaves as much access to her genitalia as was possible.

The slaves continued to suckle from every intimate part of her body. Mouths were clamped onto her nipples, drawing harder now that Ari's climax loomed over the horizon. Tongues slithered faster about her glossy pussy lips. The possessor of the tongue attending to her clit drew the swollen bud into his mouth and suckled vigorously.

Ari moaned louder, her head thrashing about upon the *Kefa's* breasts. The *Kefa* gentled her, turning her perfect face toward one plumped up golden nipple. The Chief Priestess's mouth latched onto it and suckled from it.

Ari's orgasmic convulsions began a moment later. Her body trembled violently, quaking out its relief as she moaned into the *Kefa's* golden breast.

Ever the voyeur, Kyra's eyes took in everything, spellbound and aroused that she was.

"Come, Kyra. Remove your *qi'ka* and lie with me."

Kyra's head snapped to attention. She hadn't realized that the Chief Priestess knew of her arrival, but then again, Ari seemed to know of everything. Doing as she had been instructed to do, Kyra removed her black *qi'ka,* allowing it to drop to the floor of the dune, before making her way up the golden steps that led to Ari's lair.

The Chief Priestess smiled serenely as her male slaves and *Kefa* continued to massage her all over. "Lie down upon the pillows next to me and allow my slaves to see to your need."

Kyra shook her head no. She couldn't imagine that Zor would care for male hands rubbing and caressing her intimately. It was true that they both took *Kefas* to bath, but they were not real people. These male slaves were quite real, their skin tones that of flesh and blood men.

Ari grinned, her dimples popping out. "They are enchanted like the *Kefa,* my High Queen." When Kyra's eyes widened questioningly, the Chief Priestess smiled fully, her white teeth flashing against her tanned skin. "My men are of the sands."

"Then how is that they look so..."

"Real?" At Kyra's nod, Ari explained unabashedly. "The spell of their enchantment is more powerful, giving them the look of pure Trystonni warriors. I love the look of a warrior." She shrugged absently. "I've the powers to enslave real ones-the younger ones leastways-if I chose to do so, yet do I not believe in binding the humanoid spirit. Even possessing bound servants goes against my beliefs."

A wrinkle of disgruntlement appeared on Kyra's forehead. "I agree with you wholeheartedly!" Settling herself down upon the pillows, she propped herself up on an elbow, turning to meet Ari's gaze. "I've tried to tell my husband a thousand times that I don't like having women bound to us, but it falls on deaf ears. He won't even speak of the issue with me any longer," she admitted.

Ari chuckled softly. "Somehow, this does not surprise me."

Kyra sighed. "Yes, well, that doesn't mean I won't keep try-oohhh." She sucked in her breath, briefly closing her eyes as four male slaves appeared out of virtual thin air and began to massage her everywhere.

"It's all right," the Chief Priestess murmured. "Take your pleasure and we can talk freely after."

But Kyra barely heard her. Already she had fallen to her back, her thighs opening, accepting the intimate caresses the slaves gave her. Large warrior hands massaged each engorged breast, plucking and plumping up her nipples. She moaned, delirious with arousal.

Through glazed over eyes, Kyra gazed up into the face of one of the male slaves massaging her. His eyes were the only part of him that gave away the fact that he was enchanted. Although crafted of a beautiful azure, the slave's eyes were as lifeless as a doll's-the same as a *Kefa.*

As if the knowing granted her a license for lasciviousness, Kyra closed her eyes and allowed the erotic feelings to overwhelm her, now that she was certain no life dwelled within the slaves' bodies.

Sand. They were but enchanted sand. Yesss.

Kyra raised her arms over her head and rested them on the silken pillows behind her. Hands caressed her everywhere. Her breasts. Her thighs. Her belly. Her labia. Even her toes. She moaned in need and desire as the liquid flame that had been pooling dormant in her belly flared to life.

Splaying her legs wider, Kyra sucked in her breath as male fingers retreated and tongues replaced them. Wet, hard, insistent tongues swirled everywhere within her pussy folds. A slave's mouth latched onto her swollen clit and drew moans from her with his intimate play.

On a groan, Kyra's back arched and her legs went unbelievably wider, giving the handsome, lifeless creatures full access to the center of her need. A feminine tongue curled around one of her jutting nipples, drawing from her. She didn't have to open her eyes to know it was the beautiful, provocative Ari sucking on her nipple, nursing from the base of her erect peak to its swollen tip. Over and over. Again and again.

Kyra's moans grew louder. She needed to climax, but didn't want the sexy, urgent feeling of dangling over an erotic precipice to end.

After a few more delicious stolen moments, her body took the decision from her mind and pounded ferociously toward climax. Kyra's cry of release sounded throughout the cavernous den, as every cell in her body tingled with ecstasy. Hot blood surged to her face and her nipples thrust temptingly upward. Her whole body felt alive.

As the intensity of the peaking winded down and the soothing, languid calm stole throughout her body, Kyra sighed dreamily, then turned back to face Ari. The Chief Priestess was laying on her side facing her, grinning unashamedly, her body buoyed up by an elbow.

Kyra grinned back. With a moan of fatigue, she shifted onto her stomach and situated her breasts beneath her in such a way that made reclining possible. "Mmm." She smiled slowly, her eyes semi-closed, as the slaves began running their hands over her back and buttocks. "That's nice."

"I know." Ari did the same, flopping over onto her belly and allowing her enchanted men to administer to her. "Of what did you wish to speak to me?"

"Hmm?" Kyra furrowed her brow, unable to remember for a moment. The non-sexual touching felt good, the perfect after-climax elixir. For these few precious minutes, she had forgotten all of her worries and sorrow. But eventually she remembered.

"It's my sister. Kara." Kyra shook her head slightly and sighed. Briefly describing the events surrounding her sister's disappearance to the Chief Priestess, she then voiced the question most prominent in her mind. "It's the not knowing that kills me, Ari. Was Kara murdered? Or is she still alive and well?

Will I ever see her again?" Her eyes grew moist at the thought. "I miss her so much," she choked out.

Ari reached out and tenderly rubbed her hand up and down the length of Kyra's arm. "She is not dead," she said quietly.

"What? Really?" Kyra's head shot up. Her eyes were hopeful, her smile wistful. "Will I see her again?"

Ari's eyes shuttered, concealing them briefly as she drew in a deep breath. "I would that I could tell you that which you long to hear, my beautiful High Queen, yet I simply do not know for a certainty. I see her swept through a time vortex, much as you were. But is she in this dimension or another?" She sighed. "I simply do not know."

The Chief Priestess closed her eyes completely as she rolled over onto her back, putting herself closer to Kyra. Ari placed her hands behind her, cradling her neck, which served to thrust her nipples upward. Kyra couldn't seem to resist running one of her hands over Ari's plumped up breast, her finger tracing over the peak of her nipple.

Kyra snatched her hand away as if she'd been burned the moment she became fully cognizant of what she had just done. She had touched another woman. Privately. Intimately. In desire. Mortified, color stole into her cheeks.

"There is naught to be embarrassed of," Ari murmured, taking Kyra's hand and gently placing it back upon her breast. "Do not be embarrassed," she whispered.

Kyra bit her lip. She hesitated for a moment, then took her time, feeling, exploring, knowing what it was to hold a desirable woman's breast in her hand and feel the nipple tighten under her touch. The pink bud jutted up, stabbing her palm. The woman it belonged to exhaled shakily, enjoying it.

Slowly, tentatively, Kyra lowered her mouth to Ari's nipple and curled her tongue around it. She drew it in and sipped of it, sucking and laving, aroused by the Chief Priestess's moans.

"You're so beautiful," Ari murmured. "So beautiful..."

She'd never really thought so, but the Chief Priestess was making her feel that way. She knew she should stop, but there was one more thing she wanted to experience before she did.

"Not half as beautiful as you are," Kyra whispered as her mouth unlatched from Ari's nipple. Her head came up and she smiled down to her, their gazes clashing, as she slowly lowered her mouth to the mystic's.

Their lips met in a soft kiss. Kyra cupped Ari's breast and ran her palm over an erect nipple as she thrust her tongue between the Chief Priestess's lips. Ari moaned into her mouth, her hand running over Kyra's belly, finding its way down to her aroused pussy. She played with her clit, rubbing it in knowing circles until Kyra groaned, coming.

Kyra tore her lips away, panting heavily, thoughts of burying her face between Ari's legs overwhelming her. Instinctively realizing that she was not ready for that lesson in carnal indulgence yet, she decided to stop now rather than further lead this woman on, a woman whom she called friend. She bent her face and placed a soft kiss on the tip of Ari's nipple. "I'm sorry," she softly murmured, raising her face from Ari's breast. "So sorry."

Ari smiled, her eyes hazy with desire. "There is naught to apologize for," she whispered thickly. "We have many Yessat years left to love each other."

Kyra smiled back, at peace once again. Her eyelids were heavy, tired. The feel of male hands roaming over her back and legs, neck and buttocks, had a balmy effect. Slowly, unthinkingly, she lowered her face onto Ari's breasts and fell into a deep, sated sleep.

Chapter 31

Kyra woke up to the feel of her body climaxing. Disoriented and breathing harshly, it took her a few moments to figure out where she was and what was going on.

She was still laying on her belly, the pillows making it so her breasts fit comfortably beneath her. She was highly aroused, but Ari and her slaves were nowhere within her sights.

Kyra was about to draw herself up to her knees, when a long, thick cock slid into her pussy from behind. Sucking in her breath, she expelled it on a moan. "Mmm. I missed you," she whispered provocatively.

"Did you?" Zor thrust into her slowly, taking his time gliding in and out of her wet channel.

"Mmmm."

He rotated his hips, grinding into his *nee'ka's* flesh from behind. When Kyra groaned appreciatively, he rewarded her with deeper thrusts, reaching up and around her at the same time to rub both of her nipples between his fingers. Her moans grew louder. His thrusts became faster.

"I could sense your arousal whilst training," Zor gritted out, his breathing becoming labored. Kyra shifted her hips, slamming backwards to meet his plunges. He groaned. "Aye, *pani*-give me that lusty channel. Just like that, my hearts."

"Oh-yes. Oh god-Zor."

"Did Ari's slaves bring you to your woman's joy?" He pounded into her harder, faster. She moaned louder, thrusting back eagerly. "Answer me," he growled. "Never think to lie to me."

"Yes," Kyra admitted, her worry cutting through her haze of desire somewhat, "they did."

Zor ground his hips until she moaned again, worry forgotten. "And did you like it?" he demanded. "Did they make you feel as you feel now, *nee'ka*?"

"Yes-no." Kyra closed her eyes and groaned loudly as a delicious climax ripped through her belly. "Yes!" she cried out as it hit her, "I liked it...but no, it was never like this, could never be like this."

Zor's thrusts became fast and merciless, primal and branding. "Who do you belong to?" he asked arrogantly, his jaw rigid from holding back his own release. "Who do you allow to fuck this tight channel?"

"You. Oh god-only you."

"Good answer." He possessively tugged at Kyra's nipples, slamming into her from behind until her cunt began to tremor around his manhood. He allowed her the benefit of his release as a reward for her lusty peaking. "For you, *pani*," he ground out.

Kyra moaned and whimpered, writhing in pleasure-pain, as the delicious, ceaseless climaxes pounded relentlessly throughout her body. Her husband's seed was addicting, the violent peaks it brought her mind-numbing in their intensity. She knew she had spoken the truth when she had told him that no other man could ever make her feel this way.

A few minutes later, while Kyra lay in the fold of Zor's arms, a worry line creased her brow. Propping herself up to study his face, she searched his gaze for the truth. Her husband's glowing eyes were dimmed with...Sadness? Hurt? Betrayal?

"Zor?"

He took a deep breath. "Aye, *nee'ka*?"

"You're not angry with me are you?" She ran a hand over his jaw, her eyes filled with regret. "I swear I would never have let those enchanted men touch me if I had thought it would hurt y-"

"Enchanted?" Zor grabbed Kyra by the chin, careful not to hurt her in the doing. He searched her eyes. Hoping. Praying to the goddess. "They were not of flesh?" he asked hoarsely.

"N-No." Kyra frowned. She thumped her husband on the chest. "You thought I let a man of real flesh touch me?" she screeched. "I think I know the difference between a consummation feast which you are present for and everything else." She huffed out a breath of air. "How could you!"

Zor was too relieved by his *nee'ka's* words to be concerned with her shrewish tongue. He forced her head back down upon his chest and hugged her tightly against him. "Ah, *pani*-forgive me. I was overset with jealousy and grief."

"Oh Zor," she mumbled, her face pressed into his chest, "I-harrumph-let me up."

"Eh? Oh, aye."

"Thank-you." Kyra peered into his eyes, searching for answers she wasn't finding. "You made love to me thinking I had permitted a man to touch me." She shook her head slowly, not understanding. "Why?" she asked softly.

Zor inhaled deeply. Twirling a lock of her fire-berry hair around his index finger, he closed his eyes briefly and sighed. "I couldn't bear to lose you, my hearts, no matter what had transpired in this place. I needed to know you were still mine, that none other had been inside your channel." He placed a kiss atop his wife's head. "I could not bear to lose you," he repeated hoarsely.

"Oh Zor." Kyra studied his features as she rubbed her hand soothingly across his chest. He had the look of a man she'd once met on earth who had thought he'd lost his family in a violent tornado, then was too overcome with relief to so much as speak when he realized that he hadn't. "I need your trust," she said gently. "I love you and I need your trust. May I have it?" She leaned down and kissed the dimple in his chin. "Please?" she murmured.

Zor was quiet for a protracted moment, rubbing Kyra's shoulders and placing loving kisses atop her head. "I trust you more than ever have I trusted another," he admitted in subdued tones, "please give me time, my beloved *nee'ka,* to make that trust a perfect one."

Kyra smiled gently. "You'll work on it?"

"Aye," he admitted, his emotions genuine.

She smiled again. "That's all I can ask."

* * * * *

Two months later, Zor, Kyra, and their three hatchlings strolled down to the main atrium for a bit of fresh air. Zora and Zara took their father by either hand and guided him toward a pizi tree.

"Wook, papa." Zora pointed enthusiastically toward the blue-leafed shrubbery. Her glowing blue eyes lit up. "Wike mani."

Zor laughed aloud. "Aye, my hearts. 'Tis like you and Zara too." He bent down and plucked a fire-berry fruit from the pizi tree, then held it out to his first-born *pani,* the elder by five nuba-minutes. "You and Zara have fire-berry hair too. Is that not the truth, Zara?"

Zara looked up to her father and grinned gamine-like. Where Zora was the more sensitive of the twins, the contemplative and reflective one, Zara was the opposite, light-hearted and bubbly. "Zawa eat it!" Her chubby fingers snatched the fruit from her papa's hand. Ever thoughtful of her twin, she broke the juicy ball into what could have passed for halves, and handed Zora a piece of it.

Zor chuckled softly, rubbing Zara on the head. "You care not what the color looks like, merely what it tastes like, aye?"

Before Zara could answer, he heard Kara squealing behind them. Turning, Zor grinned at the exasperated look on his *nee'ka's* face.

Kara was the royal mischief-maker and had been getting herself into trouble since she first learned to crawl at nigh unto a fortnight of age. Now, at ten weeks since her hatching, the tiny hellion was beginning to walk. Unfortunately, this just gave her further opportunities to get herself into trouble with mani.

"Don't touch that, sweetheart," Kyra chided. "It has sharp fronds."

Zor rolled his eyes. "By the sands, as if the babe knows what a frond is." He stood up and walked to where Kara stood. She was currently reaching out for everything within grabbing distance. "Come see papa, my hearts."

Kara held out her arms and squealed. Her two-toothed grin gave the word ornery new meaning. Zor chuckled, shaking his head. "Wee terror."

Kyra strolled over to Zora and Zara's sides. She plucked two more fire-berries from the pizi tree and handed one to both. "Can mani have a bite?" She laughed when both of them shook their heads no.

"Papa get." Zora looked at her father, instructing him to get their mani a fire-berry fruit. She had being a High Princess down to an art form.

Zor inclined his head solemnly. "But of course, Your Highness." Winking at Kyra, he plucked three fruits, handing one to her and keeping two for Kara and himself. "Think you Kara misses Jana o'er much?" he asked on a serious note. "My niece used to accompany her on her walks."

Since the Tron insurrectionists had up and disappeared from Trek Mi Q'an, Dak, Geris, and Jana had gone back to Ti Q'won a couple of weeks past. Rem and Kil remained in Sand City, hesitant to leave until they were certain the threat was truly over. Although permitted a bit more freedom within the palace perimeters, Kyra was still not allowed to leave for so much as a shopping expedition. And worse yet, Zor refused to explain why-a constant bone of contention between them.

"I know Kara misses Jana," Kyra replied thoughtfully. "But Jana wasn't walking with us for the entire last week of their stay."

"Oh?" Zor raised a brow. "Why not? Where was she?"

"In trouble," Kyra said around a mouthful of fire-berry. She swallowed it down, then grinned. "Jana threw the biggest temper tantrum this side of Trek Mi Q'an, so Dak confined her to her suite."

"Ah." Zor understood immediately. 'Twas already obvious to all that where Zora and Zara were twins by birth, Kara and Jana were twins by mutual love of mischief-making. Those two would forever keep the Q'an Tal men on their toes.

Zara tugged at Zor's hand, effectively snagging his attention. "Aye, my hearts?"

"Mo, papa." Her glowing blue eyes lit up when he handed her another fruit. "Zowa now."

Zor handed Zora another fire-berry. "Now you've both two and no more. 'Twill spoil your noon repast."

Kyra scanned the horizon, her eyes squinting semi-closed as she tried to focus on a particular goings on. The glitter in the air was slightly dense this morning, rendering visibility less than perfect. Eventually, however, recognition struck. Frowning, she jabbed Zor in the side Kara wasn't attached to. "There goes Jera again. I swear, it's not fair that she can leave while me and your daughters are stuck-"

"What?"

"Uh, Jera." Kyra's gaze shot over to her husband. "Leaving. Why are you yelling?"

"Hold Kara."

"Huh? Zor!" Kyra placed Kara on her hip even as she scowled at her retreating husband's back.

"I'll explain later, my hearts!" Zor's bellow carried from over his shoulder, while he sprinted toward the great hall at top speed.

"You better," Kyra murmured. Shaking her head, she took a deep breath and dismissed her husband's bizarre behavior from her mind. "Well sweethearts, where should we walk to today?"

* * * * *

Cam, recently promoted to the rank of Commander, returned with the rest of his hunting party later that moon-rising. He had been gone for a little over eight weeks, scouting out Trek Mi Q'an for signs of the insurrectionists. They had found naught.

His promotion having earned him a suite all his own on the south side, he no longer shared rooms with Gio and Mik, though they were just next door. Cam missed living with his friends at times, but for the most part, he thought the new situation just as well. He was tired, hungry, surly-tempered, and having been away from Mara and his two *Kefas* for so long, he was also especially lusty. 'Twas with great pleasure and much appreciation that he found Mara awaiting him in his bedchamber, naked and legs splayed wide.

Cam gritted his teeth as he thrust into her wet cunt. He closed his eyes and savored the feel of her pulsing flesh enveloping his staff. Rocking back and forth within Mara, he grabbed a plump breast in either hand as he took what he needed.

"Mmm-master. How I have missed the feel of you inside of me."

"Have you?" he asked thickly. "Have you spent your days thinking of new pleasures to bring to me?"

"Aye." Mara wrapped her legs around Cam's waist, getting the most sensation out of the ride he gave her. "Would you like for me to get Muta and Frig to join us in the *vesha* hides?"

"Aye," Cam ground out, thrusting faster. "After I peak, you may bring my beauties to me."

Five hours later, Cam fell asleep on Frig's large green breasts. Muta continued to suckle from him, asleep or no. Her shimmery blue lips worked up and down the length of his staff, which even in sleep remained semi-hard.

Mara retired to her own room within the suite feeling vastly sated, but somewhat apprehensive of the future. She had seduced the handsome golden warrior for a purpose, binding herself to him because she had thought he would be easier to control than the omnipotent High King, whom she'd never wielded any power over since he'd had so many others to see to him and his pleasures before taking a mate.

She'd vowed nine Yessat years of service to Cam, believing him manageable. After all, 'twas no life easier than being a bound servant to a lusty warrior, giving her the free time she hadn't had when forced to work for a living before she had been captured by the High King in war.

Her mother had called her lazy, but Mara didn't care. She was most content when free to do as she willed, answerable to no one. To her way of thinking, being bound to a warrior gave her all of the sensual pleasures of a *nee'ka* with none of the responsibilities associated with such a status. No child bearing or estate management, no political functions or hostess duties. Just fucking. Fucking and freedom.

Mara flopped down onto her bed with a groan. She was sore between her thighs, having brought the master to pleasure many times this moon-rising.

Sighing, she closed her eyes. Had all been going according to plan, Cam should have been more emotionally bonded to her by now, Mara being the only humanoid whose channel he had constant access to. 'Twas necessary to bond in order to retain power.

Mara worried her lip as she lay in the dark, rethinking what she'd done. She was beginning to worry that what the gossips had said was true...only a Sacred Mate could ever have a hope to get a warrior to do her bidding.

Chapter 32

A week later, Cam awoke to a lusty channel riding up and down the length of his shaft. 'Twas a channel he hadn't availed himself of in two moon-risings, favoring Muta's mouth over it.

Mara seemed especially wanton this day. She was riding him hard. He rewarded his bound servant for her appetite by rubbing her clit as she continued to grind down on him, sending her into a series of climaxes that nigh unto milked him of his life-force.

Almost. But not quite.

It took a lot of riding, but eventually Cam was able to spurt his seed deep inside Mara's channel. He patted her on the buttocks for her efforts, then rose to don his warrior's garb.

Cam sighed as he gazed into the holographic mirror in his bathing chamber. He now understood why warriors purchased as many bound servants as finances allowed before finding and claiming their Sacred Mates. He was growing bored with Mara.

And he had thought to keep her nine Yessat years? By the sands, how naïve he had been! He would definitely not make Mara keep that vow.

A *Kefa* was ever able to hold a warrior's attention, but a bound servant was not. 'Twas most likely because *Kefas* were only called to the *vesha* hides once in a rare while, whereas a bound servant's main obligation was to make her self ever-available for a tumble. For the most part, *Kefas* remained relegated to the baths, unless a warrior was unable to purchase his own bound servants, or like Muta, the *Kefa* in question had a particular talent most humanoid servants didn't possess.

Cam almost despised the fates that kept a warrior from being able to harbor any emotion toward females they were sexually intimate with, save that of their Sacred Mate. Mayhap emotion could make a tumble more lusty. 'Twas going to cost Cam a fortune did he wish to purchase another bound servant to alleviate his boredom.

But then again, 'twas no doubt best that his emotions could not become involved. The goddess in all her omnipotent wisdom had probably declared it so, that a *nee'ka* might never have to compete with a rival.

Cam exited his suite and strode toward the royal apartments, gifts for the High Queen and her hatchlings in his arms. He had meant to bring the presents when first he had returned from hunting, but being a recently promoted Commander, he had been too busy training with his squadron to find the time.

When Her Majesty opened the doors and smiled brightly up to him, Cam knew that waiting for his Sacred Mate would be worth it. He could still vividly recall the look of pure, unadulterated ecstasy that had passed over the High King's face after filling the High Queen with his life-force during the last consummation feast. And this from a man so jaded, a warrior who owned over three hundred *Kefas* and three hundred more bound servants.

"Cam!" Kyra greeted him enthusiastically, having not seen him in over two months. "How are you? What's that you're holding?"

"'Tis gifts I brought back for you and the High Princesses." Cam grinned down at the wee High Queen who looked radiant today in a translucent rouge *qi'ka*.

"That's so thoughtful. You didn't have to do that!" Kyra waved her arm toward the inside of the royal apartments. "Come on in."

"Thank you." Cam followed Kyra through the corridor that led into a game parlor, a chamber she no doubt spent a lot of time in now that she had three *panis* to see to. "I've yet to meet your youngest hatchling, Kara I believe it is?"

"Yeah." Kyra threw a wry grin over her shoulder. "Zor has two pet names for her, 'the hellion' and 'wee terror'. She chuckled. "Does that give you any hint as to how exhausted she makes me?"

Cam laughed good-naturedly. "Aye." He shook his head as he continued to follow behind Kyra. "I hope wee Kara likes my gift. I'm a trite fearful of displeasing her now."

Kyra giggled. "I'm sure she will."

As it turned out, Cam didn't have that particular worry to concern himself over, for Kara was fast asleep, apparently napping in her rooms. So for the next fifteen minutes, he passed out his gifts and enjoyed the feeling it gave him to see so many smiles.

Zora and Zara were thrilled with the holographic games he had purchased for them on Myrak, a planet lying between Tryston and Galis within Trek Mi Q'an airspace. He had also acquired them three new kazis apiece, a kazi being the conservative but colorful skirt and top that girl children wore until they had their come-outs at eighteen Yessat Years and were given a mazi.

A mazi had the see-through top of a *qi'ka,* but the protective skirt of the kazi. *Qi'kas* were forbidden until the girl became of claimable age at twenty and five Yessat years.

Kyra was equally thrilled with her gifts. For her, Cam brought back two bejeweled arm bracelets from Tron, as well as a basket filled with assorted sweet candies that a talented confectioner on Galis had concocted.

"These are wonderful," Kyra murmured between a mouthful of migi. Her eyes rolled back into her head in bliss. "Just wonderful."

"What's this? Nothing for me?" Zor grinned at Cam as he strolled into the game parlor and held out his hands for his hatchlings to run into.

Zora and Zara took great delight in showing their papa all that Cam had purchased for them. "They are beautiful kazis for a certainty, my hearts. Mayhap you and Zara should save them for the celebrations during the moon-phasing."

"Oh," Kyra mumbled between a full mouth of candy, "I fowgot abowt that."

"Aye." Cam nodded. "'Tis but three months away, Your Majesty. Then the skies will turn to night and every of the seventeen moons will be visible from Sand City for four full Trystonni days."

Zor clapped Cam on the back, turning the subject. "Congratulations on your promotion, Commander. If you keep proving yourself such a worthy hunter and leader, 'tis my hope to make you a high lord or mayhap even a lesser king someday."

Cam flushed awkwardly on his feet. "'Tis my hope as well," he quietly admitted.

"Well," Zor sighed, "I needs get to the training field. Where is Kara, *nee'ka*? Has she no kisses for me this morn?"

Kyra stood up as she swallowed down the remainder of her migi. "Leha said she woke up early and couldn't fall back to sleep, so she's already nap-ah wait." She grinned. "Here comes the hellion now."

Cam absently glanced toward the doors where a topless Leha was entering the chamber with the youngest Q'ana Tal, then glanced away just as quickly.

He did a double-take.

He sucked in his breath.

Cam's eyes widened as he watched the High Queen pick up wee Kara and cradle her against her chest. He couldn't believe it. He was simply stunned.

Cam stood there for what felt like hours to him, but was probably no more than several seconds, debating with himself over what he should do. And then finally, unable to resist the temptation of knowing what his future held, he scanned Kara's tiny form until he located a small, bejeweled bracelet that dangled from her wrist.

He closed his eyes briefly, then opened them. He fixated all of his attention, all of his powers, on the summoning of the petite bracelet.

Cam heard the High Queen laughing as she kissed a giggling Kara. He heard Zora and Zara enthusing to Leha of their new treasures. He heard it all, yet it seemed a million miles away. As if in slow motion, every fiber of his being, every cell of his body, was fixated upon the chubby wrist of a wee High Princess. He was sweating. His breathing was choppy. His throat felt unbearably parched.

He sent out his summons.

The bracelet responded, unclasping and falling to the ground.

Cam closed his eyes and inhaled deeply. By the holy sands, it was true. How, he did not know. But it was true. In twenty and five Yessat years, the girl child would be a woman grown, and she would belong to him.

"By the goddess," Zor murmured.

Cam's gaze flew to the High King, the only other in the chamber who apparently now knew. His nostrils flaring, he reigned in his temper and regarded him. "I know I am common of birth," he gritted out in a low, private tone, "yet not even a High King has the right to deny a warrior his true mate." When Zor said nothing, merely continued to search his features, Cam inclined his head. "I mean no insolence, Your Majesty, yet will I claim her as is my right by the holy law in twenty and five Yessat years."

Zor didn't speak for a long, suspended moment that seemed to Cam to last an eternity. But finally, the High King murmured in low tones, "Then you will spend the next twenty and five years becoming a hunter who is elite even amongst the elite. I care not what the law says, for I will release my girl child to none but a lesser king." His gaze flicked to Kara and then back to Cam. "Am I clear?"

Cam slowly inclined his head. "Aye, sire," he murmured.

Zor nodded, taking a deep breath. He hadn't thought to be faced with such a situation for many, many moon-risings to come. As much as he wasn't ready to admit it, he did admire the younger warrior. Very few ever made it to the rank of Commander at all and to do so at such young years was no small feat. Cam would prove himself. Of this he was certain.

"You best be on your way, Commander." Zor peered into Cam's eyes. "I give you permission to give Kara your gifts if you so choose, but from this day forward your meetings will be limited."

Cam had expected no less. Kara would be guarded from him even more vigilantly during the years between her come-out and the claiming. "Aye, sire."

Taking a deep breath, Cam strode over to where the High Queen and her *panis* stood. He smiled down to Kyra. "Might I hold her but a moment?" he murmured respectfully.

Kyra's eyebrows shot up. "Of course!" Handing her youngest over to the warrior, she grinned at her daughter. "Kara, be nice. This is Cam."

Cam peered into the wee babe's face, surveying her features. She would have hair the darkest of nights and eyes the glowing blue associated with the Q'an Tal bloodline. 'Twas an odd shade of blue, pale and beautiful, as if it could see right through you and into your soul. "Hello Kara." He smiled. "Mayhap you would like a few new kazis too?"

Kara's pudgy little hands grabbed at either side of Cam's face. She flashed him a two-toothed grin that caused him to chuckle. And then she did something that made him wonder at the goddess' sense of humor.

Wee Kara kicked him in the man sac.

* * * * *

Zor, Kil, and Rem spoke not a word to each other as they surveyed the carnage around them. Women, children, guildsmen, traders, teachers, grandmothers, grandfathers...all dead. The whole of the sector gone, wiped out, completely annihilated, its remains even now incinerating to the ground.

Ty.

The rebel leader's name had been etched in blood, carved into the chest of the sector's high lord, who from the looks of him had been tortured long hours before succumbing to merciful death.

Ty.

The name was scrawled in blood against the barely budding breast of a young girl who had been brutally raped before death came to her.

Ty.

The name was etched in blood across the buttocks of a boy child who had been sodomized repeatedly, then left to die of his injuries.

Ty.

A holographic memory of him had been left behind. The sadistic man smiled venomously as the memory played over and over, the leader of the insurrectionists crossing his arms over his chest and laughing. "'Tis the Empress I now seek...'Tis the Empress I now seek...'Tis the Empress I now seek..."

Kil heard Ty's recorded boast from somewhere in the back of his mind, but paid it no heed. His every attention was focused upon the young girl, lying raped and murdered at his feet, her kazi torn to shreds.

So young. She had been so very young. And had she survived past twelve years, mayhap would have been a great beauty with warriors tripping over their feet to do the lass's bidding.

Kil inhaled sharply, the sight of her wee broken body reminding him of another wee body he had stood over years past, just like this-unable to bring life back to her. Where their tiny mother Jana had at least known many precious years of marriage and child-bearing before meeting so gruesome a demise, this young girl child had not been given even that much reward.

Kil crouched to his knees and bent over the child's body. Fighting back tears, he placed his hand over her face and gently, reverently, closed her eyes.

"'Tis the Empress I now seek...'Tis the Empress I now seek..."

Cam picked up the communicator that the rebels had left behind and disengaged it. Ty's holographic memory faded instantaneously, leaving in its wake an eerie quiet. Walking stoically to where the High King stood, he sighed deeply, handing the disengaged communicator over to him. "I recognize this piece, sire."

Zor took the instrument from Cam's grasp and searched his features. "What say you?" he murmured. It didn't seem respectful of his many dead colonists, people who had depended on him for their protection-people he had failed-to speak in anything above a hushed voice. Anything else would sound like bellowing in a graveyard to his ears.

"They were so certain of themselves this time, so eager to leave behind Ty's memory, that they made a small, but significant tactical error." At the Emperor's raised brow, Cam hastened to explain. "This communicator is of Morak for a certainty."

Zor could hear Kil stiffen from behind him. He sensed his brother's approach before he heard him speak. "Let me see that, Commander."

Zor handed the device over to his brother. "I have it," he said softly, "not Cam."

Kil investigated the communicator from every angle, turning it this way and that, inspecting every groove and indentation. Finally, he closed his eyes and sighed. Nostrils flaring, his hand gripped the communicator until his knuckles went white. "All along," he bit out, "these murderous, sadistic thieves have been hiding away within the confines of Morak, mine own colony."

Rem, who had come upon his brothers when first Cam had given his news, placed a hand gently on Kil's shoulder. If it wasn't for the blood bath surrounding them, the proof that Ty's evilness knew no bounds, he could almost feel sorry for the traitor.

Cam was right...the rebel leader had made a grave tactical error.

Rem understood as readily as the others assembled, that squirreling himself away on Morak, Tryston's dominant red moon, was the most hazardous mistake the murderer could have made. No finer hunter lived than Kil. Nor did a warrior live who despised Ty more. And now, the rebel leader had insulted the King of Morak with his daring. "We will take him," Rem said quietly. "He will be ours by the next moon-rising."

Kil smashed the communicator within his fist, an act of strength that caused the eyebrows of all who had witnessed it to shoot up in disbelief. "He will be mine," Kil growled, stomping off toward his conveyance, "all mine."

Zor watched Kil's retreat with a sense of impending fate. Truly, the madman Ty had just sealed his own destiny. Turning to Rem, he inclined his head. "Call Dak. I would have Geris and Jana within the Palace of the Dunes anon."

Rem nodded, then turned to do as he'd been instructed.

Zor stood quietly in place for a dragged out moment before shifting toward Cam and clapping him on the back. "Good work." He scanned his face. "Keep it up."

On the next moon-rising, the insurrectionists' hiding place on Morak had been completely wiped out. Kil had seen to it personally, just as he'd vowed. Unfortunately, the ever-elusive Ty had managed to elude the ever-vigilant hunter once again.

But no matter. They would meet again. Of this Kil was certain.

Destiny had a way of working itself out. And Ty's destiny, Kil reminded himself with grim satisfaction, was to die at his hands, the same as the Empress Jana had died at the rebel leader's.

Chapter 33

Sporting black leather garb of her husband's that she'd pilfered from the royal closet and taken in-a lot-to accommodate for her smaller size, Kyra tiptoed around the conveyance launching pad, ascertaining whether or not any warrior guardsmen lurked near. She was careful to rein in all of her emotions in the doing, ensuring that none of them would spill over and tip off Zor to her well-laid plans.

The coast was clear. Just as she'd known it would be this time of the day. Yesss.

Kyra turned on her communicator and signaled Geris. When her best friend's holographic image appeared, she was pleased to note that Geris had also been able to raid Dak's wardrobe. Not only that, but she had also taken the time to smear black camouflage paint below her eyes just as Kyra had. Why they had thought to do this, neither could say. The make-up just seemed to go well with the role of prison escapees. "The coast is clear," Kyra whispered. "How are things at the hatch?"

"I just engaged it," Geris whispered back. "I'm on my way to the launching pad as we speak."

"Affirmative." Kyra nodded, her expression serious. She felt every inch the secret operative preparing to outwit the enemy with a brilliant tactical maneuver. Her excitement was evident. They had even created pseudo names to call each other by. This was just too cool. "Over and out, Rambo."

"Over and out, girl-I mean Commando."

Kyra disengaged the communicator. It was time.

She felt a hand on her shoulder. Damn it.

Preparing to come up with a plausible excuse for her attire and for being caught creeping about the launching pad, Kyra whirled around and ended up colliding-thankfully-with none other than her best friend. Geris tried to steady her, but Kyra's sharp turn caused both sets of their mammoth breasts to bounce off of each other, sending the women flying to the ground with an unceremonious thud.

"We'll never pass as warriors," Geris muttered as she and Kyra helped each other back to their feet.

Kyra signaled with her hand for Geris to follow behind her as she crept up the crystal launching pad's steps to alight into the floating Q'ana Tal carriage. "You don't know that for sure."

"We have huge titties!" she whispered harshly. Geris waited until she was safely ensconced next to Kyra in the front seat of the conveyance before puckering her lips into a frown. "And compared to real warriors, we're noticeably short."

"Maybe people will just think we have growth deficiencies or something, kind of like Gary Coleman from Different Strokes, or that Webster kid." She waved her hand dismissively. "As long as we look like them from a distance, we'll be fine, Ger."

Kyra placed her palm on the recognition scanner, inciting the carriage to lurch upwards from the launching pad and transcend the hatch. She clapped her hands together and grinned gleefully. "Here we go!"

Geris forgot her reservations long enough to get caught up in the moment. Just as Zor had done to Kyra, Dak hadn't allowed her to leave the confines of whatever palace she was stowed away in either. Week after week of confinement with no end in sight was getting to her. "We did it!" She jumped up and down in her seat and laughed. "We really did it!"

"I know!"

Geris laughed for a few triumphant moments more before reality began to dawn somewhat. She bit her lip and nibbled on it. The two days Dak had grounded her from her woman's joy for disobeying him last week were still fresh in her mind. Suddenly, she was a little apprehensive. "Are you sure we won't get caught, girl?"

Kyra snorted, dismissing her best friend's worry with another wave of her hand. "I've been watching the schedule at the launching pad for a solid month. Believe me, Ger, so long as we come back in exactly five hours, nobody will be the wiser." She shrugged. "We slip back in and land while the patrolmen are switching shifts, change into our *qi'kas,* wipe the make-up off of our faces, and stroll back inside."

"And we'll have a solid five minutes to land the conveyance?"

"Uh huh. Definitely."

Geris chewed that over for a moment. After a pregnant pause, she nodded her head succinctly and grinned. "Then Pika's Place, here we come!"

* * * * *

The warrior guardsman entered the black crystal warring arts planning chamber and approached the raised table inside of it with heavy steps. He was going to have to confess to the High King that he had allowed the High Queen to escape the palace yet again. On top of that, the Queen of Ti Q'won had gone with her, which wouldn't exactly put him in King Dak's good graces either.

Around the raised table sat the High King, his three brothers, and five hunting commanders. They were drinking matpow together and discussing their plans to capture the rebel leader Ty. "I believe Jera will lead us right to him," Rem stated, his features grim. "'Tis just a matter of time."

"Aye," Kil concurred, "the nefarious she-bitch won't be able to stay away from her lover's *vesha* hides o'er long."

The warrior guardsman was about to make his presence known, when Commander Cam K'al Ra came tearing into the planning chamber, alerting his superiors and comrades to Jera's whereabouts. "She has left again!" he roared as he neared the raised table. "One of the hunters from my squadron has followed her to Kogar, an area of wild terrain outside of Sand City where there is naught but gulch beasts and other assorted predators."

"Home at last," Rem murmured.

"Is she alone?" Zor bellowed, rising to stand.

"Nay." Cam grinned. "She is accom*pani*ed by an insurrectionist fitting Ty's description."

Kil pounded his fist on the table. "By the goddess, 'tis about time."

"Aye." Dak stood up, attaching his zykif to the strap of leather around his waist. "Let us go."

"Your Majesty, I would that I could speak with you." The warrior guardsman waited until he had the chamber's full attention before tamping down his nervousness and confessing the truth. He turned to Zor and nodded grimly. "'Tis the High Queen," he said quietly, "she and Queen Geris have fled."

* * * * *

"I'm going to kill her for a certainty." From the luxury of his high-speed conveyance, Zor and his brothers watched the recorded holographic memory of the devious escape of Kyra and Geris from the Palace of the Dunes. Apparently his wily *nee'ka* hadn't considered the possibility of roaming holo-cams when she'd put together her asinine plot to leave the palace perimeters without him finding out about it. "The wench's arse will bear the print of my hand for nigh unto a Yessat year," he gritted out.

"As will Geris's." Dak clenched and unclenched his fist, the knuckles of his hand deathly white. "For the love of the sands, I wondered what had happened to that pair of leathers!"

"Why are they sporting those bizarre black slashes beneath their eyes?" Kil asked curiously, slightly bemused by his sisters-within-the-law's escapade.

"I've no notion," Zor bit out, his gaze smoldering. "Mayhap 'tis some primitive first-dimension custom. Mayhap all wenches there thinking to outwit their Sacred Mates don those bizarre black lines."

"They can't possibly think anyone will believe them to be warriors," Rem intoned. He shook his head, stunned by the women's audacity. "They are both engorged of sweet juice."

"They are both engorged of idiocy!" Zor bellowed. He slashed his hand through the air. "Apparently Kyra needs be set to hatching again. 'Tis the only time she doesn't think to bedevil me, when she's freshly delivered of a *pani* sac and too tired to mischief-make."

"Geris hatched my son but a sennight ago," Dak muttered. "Apparently hatching 'twill not work with my *nee'ka*."

"Where are we going?"Rem barked from the backseat next to Kil. "Where think you they went?"

Kil clapped Rem on the back. His lips curled up into a half-smile. "Pika's."

"Pika's?"

"Aye."

Zor switched the communicator's channel, thereby turning off the recorded memory and opening up an unused frequency. "They left over two Yessat hours past," he announced. "If they have returned to Kyra's conveyance yet, 'twill be my pleasure to give them the fright of their lives."

Kil raised an eyebrow. "Kyra does not know that you can turn on the communicator within her conveyance?"

"Kyra doesn't even know that there is a communicator within her conveyance."

Kil and Rem looked to each other and grinned. "Then by all means signal her," Kil encouraged him, trying to keep the laughter from his tone. "See if your *nee'kas* are in the Q'ana Tal conveyance."

* * * * *

Laughing uproariously at a joke Geris had just told, Kyra handed her best friend a lit mooka, then took another swallow from the bottle of moonshine matpow. Death and Glok had assured them both that their sweet juice wouldn't be affected by the drink, for it took no more than "a pissing", as Death had so nicely put it, to work the contents of it out of the system.

Moonshine. Gotta love it.

A little tipsy after just having left Pika's Place, the women were having the time of their lives, floating aimlessly about the outskirts of Sand City, drinking their moonshine and smoking their mookas.

"Oh Ger!" Kyra grinned as she passed the bottle back to her. "That's hilarious!"

"I know. That Hod dude was a trip." Geris shook her head, smiling bemusedly. "By the way, how many hours do we have left?"

"A little over two and a half." Kyra accepted the bottle of moonshine back from Geris and snorted incredulously. "Not that I'm worried. I've been thinking about it and I've decided that I don't care what my husband says."

"Me neither." Geris took a puff from her mooka, then puckered her lips into a frown. "It's time I laid down the law. This girlfriend does whatever in the hell she wants." She followed that pronouncement up with a series of snaps and a neck swivel. "I-eeeeekkk!" Geris's hand flew to her heart as the image of a scowling, furious, enraged Dak appeared before her sotted eyes.

"I know what you mean," Kyra mused, oblivious to her best friend's warning screech. She was too tipsy to register it as significant. "Zor's just going to have to accept the fact that what I say goes." She harrumphed. "I think that-shiiiiiit!" Kyra's eyes bulged noticeably out of their sockets as she stared at the holographic projection before her. Her jaw dropped open.

Zor was pissed.

Both women looked to each other, then to their husbands, then back to each other as they pointed at the other one. "It was her idea!" they simultaneously yelped.

"Kyra!" Zor bellowed. "You will turn your conveyance around anon and go back to the palace to await my return."

"You've the same instructions," Dak bit out to Geris, the tic in his cheek lethal. He followed that announcement up with a mimicking series of snaps and a neck swivel. "Now."

Kyra glared at the images of Kil and Rem who she could clearly see sitting behind Zor and Dak. Both warriors had hands clamped over their mouths, snickering behind them. "Zor, be reasonable. I-oh my god!"

"Kyra?"Zor shouted, concern overriding his anger for the moment. "*Pani*, what is it? What has happened?" When he heard a loud boom and saw both women scream, he bellowed, "Kyra! What is happening?"

Kyra turned back to her husband's holographic image. Her silver-blue eyes were wide with fright. "Help us! We're being shot at!"

"Oh my god!" Geris screamed. "Our conveyance is going down!"

* * * * *

The hearts rate of every Q'an Tal brother sped up rapidly when the frequency went dead. Kil, Rem, and Dak immediately removed their zykifs, preparing to fire back once the Q'ana Tal conveyance and its pursuers were within their sights.

Zor accelerated the high-speed conveyance up to hyper-mode, shooting off and leaving a trail of gastrolight spark in its wake. His stern features grim with worry, he quietly issued his command. "Each of you look to your side of the conveyance. Tell me when you spot Kyra and Geris."

All was deadly calm for a full nuba-minute until Rem bellowed out the women's location.

"Rem has the right of it. There they are!" Kil pointed toward an area of tall forest where the Q'ana Tal conveyance was rapidly descending to. "Geris was right! They are going down!"

"For the love of the goddess," Dak murmured. "Nay. Tell me they are not going down in-"

"I fear 'tis so," Zor choked out. "They are crashing into..."

"Kogar."

Chapter 34

"Are you okay?" Kyra helped Geris to her feet. Both of them were lucky to be alive so far as she could tell. The conveyance had thrown them at least twenty or thirty yards when it crashed. "Are you hurt?"

"No-I'm fine." Geris's eyes went wide with alarm. "But Kyra, where are we? This place looks like the Trystonni version of Jurassic Park."

Kyra took Geris by the hand and squeezed it. She did a thorough scan of their whereabouts and didn't care for what she was seeing. The place was spooky. It gave her the creeps. "More like the Haunted Forest," she muttered.

Tall, gnarled trees as dark as black sackcloth surrounded them for as far as the eye could see. Black, mud-like sand churned sluggishly beneath their feet. Even the winds in this nightmare world seemed to moan.

The women knew it was still daytime on Tryston, but the forested terrain they were lost in was devoid of light. The only reason they could see anything at all was because of an eerie blue sap that oozed down the twisted bark of the trees, casting off a dimmed bluish glow in the process.

A humanoid scream echoed throughout the forest. It was quickly drowned out by the sounds of hissing, a bizarre cackling noise, and a loud crunch. The screaming stopped.

Geris clamped both of her hands over her mouth and whimpered softly.

"Why did it stop?" Kyra whispered hysterically. "Oh god Ger, why did the screaming stop?"

Geris shook her head, indicating that she either didn't know or that she didn't care to examine the reason behind the sudden quiet. Most likely a little-or a lot-of both.

Swallowing nervously, Kyra slowly glanced upward. She caught her breath and clamped a hand over her mouth before she cried out. Nudging Geris in the ribs, she told her with wild eyes to take a look.

Winged beasts of prey loomed menacingly overhead. Their powerful reptilian bodies were thickly armored with a blue-black metallic substance. If the creatures were standing erect, Kyra didn't doubt for a moment that they would be over eight feet in height. Twelve-inch razor-sharp nails protruded from each of the beasts' digits. Like humans, they possessed two hands and five finger-like projectiles on each one. The musculature of the creatures was ominously thick and lithe.

Kyra could only be grateful that the monsters had apparently not picked up their scents...yet. "Ger," she whispered, her body quivering with fright. "We need to start walking, sweetheart. Okay?"

"Y-Yeah." Her eyes darted back and forth restlessly. "But which way do we go?"

Kyra shook her head. "I don't know." She took a deep breath and peered at Geris. In the midst of the black forest, it was impossible to estimate which way lay Sand City and which way would take them further into the bowels of hell. "Rock, paper, scissors?" she choked out.

"Y-Yeah." Geris inclined her head, nodding absently. "Fine. If I win," she whispered, "we head to the west, if you win, we go east."

"Fine. Two out of three?"

"Yeah."

Seconds later, the women headed due west. They both doubted the direction would matter, as they could still make out no evidence of light from either way. If they got out of here, both women realized it would either be because they'd been rescued or because they happen-chanced onto a path that would lead them into a clearing.

A half an hour later, Kyra and Geris rounded a narrow path that led to an even thicker patch of gnarled black trees. The oozing blue sap was denser, illuminating the barely traversed section of the forest to a greater degree.

A flash of red caught Kyra's eye. Her head snapped in the direction she'd seen the flicker of color and motion, but she could no longer discern signs of any life other than black trees and glowing blue sap. Swallowing roughly, she shook her head and continued on.

"I feel like we've been walking forever," Geris muttered, "only we aren't getting any closer to being out of this hellhole."

Another flash of red flitted past. Kyra inhaled sharply and clutched Geris's hand. "Did you see that?" she whispered, eyes wide.

"See what?"

"That flicker of red." Kyra squeezed her hand tighter. "I feel like we're being watched by something." She took a steadying breath. "By something hunting us perhaps."

"Oh sweet Jesus, please don't say that, girl." Geris removed her hand from Kyra's long enough to lace their fingers together and clamp down as tight as humanly possible.

Another flash of red sped by.

"Did you see it that time?" Kyra asked tensely. Eyes wide with terror, her head darted back and forth in a futile effort to locate it.

"Y-Yes." Geris waited for Kyra to look at her before she bore her gaze into hers and gulped nervously. "And d-did you hear that hissing and c-cackling sound it made?"

The winds picked up, moaning like an old man rattling out his last breath of life before succumbing to death. Kyra's free hand flew to her heart. "Y-Yes. I-I heard it. It was just like before when..."

"The screaming stopped," Geris murmured, finishing her thought for her.

"We need to make a run for it, Ger." Kyra felt surreal, her body oddly disjointed from her soul. "Let's start running. Let's just run and-oh my god."

"Sweet Jesus." Geris gripped Kyra's hand harshly even as her other one flew to her mouth, concealing it to keep from crying out.

A body. A very mangled, beheaded body lay at the foot of a twisted black tree, blue ooze absorbing into the murdered man's remains. It was clear now that the sap was some sort of gel-based scavenger, feeding off of what a predator had left behind.

"Ger," Kyra cried out softly, "we need to get out of here."

Geris shook her head up and down, agreeing. "Let's bypass that poor man's body and-"

A high-pitched bleeping sound caused both women to stop talking, and-at least momentarily-breathing. Kyra knew that sound. Although she wasn't exactly a warring arts aficionado, she recognized the shrill bleep of a zykif being turned to engaged mode from her brief fling with Glok's weapon in Pika's when she'd run from Zor. Somehow she wasn't overly surprised when she turned around and saw...

"Jera."

* * * * *

"There's no sign of them." Rem walked to where his brothers stood and nodded implacably. His features were harsh. "This is definitely the Q'ana Tal conveyance, yet are they nowhere within its vicinity."

"Where could they be?" Dak mumbled, scratching his head in agitation and more than a little worry.

"I don't know," Zor rumbled in an undertone, his deep voice quieter than a fading echo. "Though the possibilities don't bear thinking about."

Kil shook his head, sighing. Nay, the possibilities that came to mind didn't bear dwelling upon for a certainty.

And yet no warrior present could keep the horrific thoughts from pounding relentlessly through their minds. Mayhap rebels had taken the women. Or mayhap gulch beasts had dined on them. Or, the goddess forbid, *heeka-beast*s. At least a gulch beast would swoop down and take out his prey mercifully. A *heeka-beast* had no mercy. She enjoyed the killing, enjoyed tearing her prey apart before feeding upon their brains, then leaving them to the gulch sap to dine on.

Zor took a deep breath and refused to succumb to grief just yet. He would continue to hope that Kyra still lived. He assured himself that he would know had she passed onto the goddess' realm. As her Sacred Mate, he would know. "Let us split into groups of two. Kil and Rem, go east and circle back. Dak and I will head west and circle back."

"What of north and south?" Rem asked.

"Kyra wouldn't bother," Zor informed him. "The trees are too dense. They have gone either east or west for a certainty."

"Then let us be off."

* * * * *

"Jera, what are you doing? Are you crazy?"

Kyra held up both palms in the universal sign of surrender before putting the question to her plotting sister-in-law. "I can't imagine Rem would be pleased with you if you killed Geris and me. In fact, I'd say he'd probably have you thrown into the nearest dungeon." The thought that Rem would most likely never know at whose hands they'd died registered in her mind, but she refused to dwell upon it.

Jera gave a pompous snort. "Think you I concern myself with Rem's wants? Nay, when my beloved Ty takes over Sand City I shall be Empress and High Queen, and you"-she waved the zykif menacingly-"will already be dead and dined upon and unable therefore to bear witness." She grinned evilly. "Mores the pity."

"Who is this Ty?" Geris asked, anger overriding any concern for their dilemma, at least for the moment. "And why would you betray your own Sacred Mate for him?"

"Ty is the leader of the insurrectionists," Jera replied proudly, "and he is my true Sacred Mate."

"Somehow that doesn't surprise me," Kyra muttered more to herself than anyone else, though both Jera and Geris had heard her.

"And what's that supposed to mean?" Jera gritted out between clenched teeth.

"It means you're the she-bitch Zor said you were!"

"Just for that," Jera murmured in a tight, agitated tone, "you get to die first."

Kyra gulped. If she ever survived this ordeal by some miracle of fate, she would work on controlling her tongue. "Jera, I-"

A flash of red bolted past, snagging Kyra's attention completely. "Oh god, did you see that?" she whispered hysterically.

"Yes." Geris clutched Kyra's hand and pressed her body closer to hers. "Good lord, yes."

Jera rolled her eyes and chuckled mockingly. "The winged gulch beasts will not look to the pits for their prey for mayhap another two hours. Don't try to outwit me for it shan't happen."

"B-But it didn't look winged," Kyra pleaded desperately, "it was red and it wasn't flying overhead. Jera, I know you hate me for whatever reason, but this has gone far enough. We will all die if we don't get out of here!"

"You'll be dying anyway, my dearest Empress. I daresay..."

Jera continued to ramble on with her venomous spewing, but neither Kyra nor Geris were paying any attention to her words. Wide-eyed and speechless, they were both watching in horror as a hissing red creature with the body of a snake from the navel down and the body of a woman from the navel up slithered behind Jera, inching closer and closer as the madwoman continued to talk.

The creature was long and lithe, red all over, and was slinking up behind Jera on a tail that kept her upper body erect. The beasts' eyes glowed a dull gold that seemed to grow brighter and brighter, apparently in anticipation, as it drew closer to its prey. When the beast opened her mouth, three rows of razor-sharp teeth gleamed the same gold-like color.

As much as Kyra hated Jera, she could not let the woman die like this. She found her voice and screamed out a warning. "Jera! Behind you!"

"I'll not fall for that," Jera bit out. She aimed the zykif's sights for Kyra's forehead. "Say hello to the goddess for me, sweet Empress."

Less than a second later, Jera watched in horror as the hand that held the zykif cocked and ready to murder the High Queen was ripped from her arm.

Jera's scream of agony sounded throughout the cavernous forest. She reached her intact hand out toward Kyra and Geris and sobbed uncontrollably. "Help me!" she cried. "For the love of the goddess, help-"

Kyra and Geris clapped their hands over their ears and shook violently as they watched the cackling woman-snake tear each of Jera's limbs from her body, one by one, as if toying with her and enjoying it. Jera's moans of agony were sounds both of them knew they would never forget. It would haunt them. It didn't matter that Jera was evil. It simply didn't matter.

"Run!" Geris screamed, breaking both of them out of their shock. Then when Jera's decapitated torso flew threw the air and fell at their feet, she screamed again, "run!"

Kyra glanced from the woman-snake to the torso. Preparing to flee, she took but a moment to grab Rem's bridal necklace from the carnage at their feet before bolting from the scene alongside her best friend.

Dear God in heaven, Kyra silently prayed, please let us live.

* * * * *

Kil stood over the dead body of Ty, the very body he had brought death to, and studied it. His nostrils were flaring, his gaze was smoldering.

It was done.

Ty had raped and murdered the Empress Jana and now he had paid the ultimate price. Death had come to him.

"'Tis over," Rem said in low tones as he came up behind his brother. He laid a gentle hand on Kil's shoulder and squeezed softly. "'Tis done."

"Aye."

"Will you be all right?"

Kil drew in a ragged breath. The man whose shell of a body lay before him had been his life's obsession for as long as he could remember. He had lived only to hunt him, risen up whole and healed from many a battlefield deathbed that should have claimed him only to realize this moment.

And now that it 'twas here he felt...empty.

'Twas as if his life no longer held meaning or direction. He was now a nomad, a stranger even unto himself. He had no sons, no daughters, and like as not ever would. Even did Kyra breed an heir to the empire, he could not fathom placing his emotions in another's care, giving her the power to destroy him should she die, just as their father before him had been destroyed following their mother Jana's death.

Nay. He could not and would not conceive of it.

And yet, 'twas only with the thought of obtaining his Sacred Mate that his sorrow was vanquished somewhat. An odd quandary that, and one he chose not to think on just now. Kyra, after all, was yet to hatch a son. He could deal with these odd feelings, premonitions, later.

"Aye," Kil answered at last. "'Twill take some time, but I will be all right."

Rem nodded, though Kil couldn't see it for his back was to him. "Let us go."

Chapter 35

The four brothers met up at the Q'ana Tal conveyance. Neither group had found any sign of either Kyra or Geris. But Zor and Dak had found Jera's remains. They could not help but to wonder had their *nee'kas* met the same fate.

"You are certain 'twas her?" Rem asked, his eyes giving away nothing of his feelings.

"Aye." Dak inclined his head. "Beyond a doubt, brother. Jera is dead."

"And the necklace?"

"We tried to retrieve it," Zor said softly in way of apology, "but 'twas gone. Nary a sign of it anywhere." He wished he could restore his brother's happiness since it seemed that his and Dak's was to be snatched violently away, but there was no help of it. Jera was dead and the necklace was gone. Rem could never find and claim his true Sacred Mate.

Rem closed his eyes and inhaled deeply. When he opened them at last, it disconcerted every of the Q'an Tal warriors to behold the slight evidence of tears within them. Rem was not given to such extreme emotion. Rem was not given to emotion at all. "Thank-you for trying," he murmured.

"You are welcome," Zor offered in a subdued tone.

Silenced ensued for long minutes. Finally, Kil looked up to the black skies within the forest and said what needed to be said. "We have combed the forest, we have left behind no gulch pit or heeka nest without thoroughly searching it first." He took a deep breath and met first Dak's and then Zor's gaze. "They are not here," he said quietly.

Silence prevailed again. And then regretfully, remorsefully, Zor turned to Kil and sighed. "I know."

* * * * *

Kyra and Geris jumped up and down, squealing from both excitement and relief as they saw Death and Glok's revved up, super cool conveyance make a landing at the edge of the forest clearing beside them.

This had been a day made of nightmares. But they had survived it.

Kyra glanced upward toward Tryston's setting dominant sun. As it sank soulfully into the horizon, it shimmered down from the golden-red of day into just plain red. Not necessarily her favorite color after their tangle with the woman-snake, but she was still glad to see it. She'd never thought to see it again.

"Hey there little fire-berry. You and the onyx babe need a lift?"

Kyra and Geris glanced at each other and then at Death and Glok. They were grinning from ear to ear and couldn't seem to help themselves. They had made it. They were alive. "You bet we do!" Geris laughed out. "We've never been so happy to see two handsome faces as we are right now!"

Glok actually blushed. "Then get in, ya hot little piece a art." He wiggled his eyebrows. "Cuz we, as you say, are here."

Five minutes later, Kyra spotted Zor's conveyance at the edge of the forest clearing several miles down from where she and Geris had emerged from it. "Death!" she shouted. "My husband's down there! Can you land this thing and help me find him?"

"Aye, little fire-berry," he rumbled back, throwing the conveyance into hover-mode to prepare for a landing. "But we can only stay mayhap another hour. After that, there will be too many gulch beasts down there."

It occurred to Kyra that Death must be serious, for it was the most words she'd ever heard him utter in one sentence. "Okay," she answered back, "if we don't spot him, we can try the communicator again."

*****

The Q'an Tal brothers walked stoically from the crashed Q'ana Tal conveyance and headed toward the forest's edge. It had taken a good while to make Zor and Dak accept the only logical explanation that existed, but eventually Kil and Rem had talked their brothers into retreating before the forest of Kogar brought death to them all.

Time, simply put, was no longer on their side. The gulch and *heeka-beast*s would be out in full assault within the hour. At daybreak, when the majority of the beasts hibernated, they could begin to search for Kyra and Geris's remains.

Deep in the forest, neither woman could have possibly lasted this long without having succumbed to death. 'Twas not possible. Not even a warrior armed to the nines could have survived it.

"I should have told her my fears," Zor choked out. 'Twas the first he had spoken in many minutes. He halted at the forest's edge, inducing the others to stop as well. "I should have explained why I did not want her to leave the palace, rather than seeking to shield her from worry of Ty's threats."

"Aye." Dak swiped at a tear, then rapidly batted his eyelids opened and closed to ward off any more from falling. "I should have as well."

"Do not do this, brothers." Kil stood between them, clapping a hand on either of their shoulders. "Your *nee'kas* loved you." He sighed, tears of his own threatening to spill. "They would not want for you to do this."

"By the goddess," Rem breathed out. He squinted his eyes to make certain his vision wasn't failing him. And then he knew it wasn't. He smiled slowly. "For the love of the goddess-look!"

The Q'an Tal brothers followed the direction of Rem's pointing finger. Two very short warriors with extremely engorged breasts were alighting from a conveyance that looked to be operated by Death and Glok of Pika's fame. The beautiful warriors were bounding toward them even now, arms outstretched, tears coursing down their cheeks.

"Kyra," Zor murmured. "Kyra."

Running the rest of the way to meet her, Zor took off and sped in the direction of his *nee'ka.* He grabbed her when he caught her, fearful to ever let go again, and swung her up into his embrace as he clutched her to his chest.

Zor could hear Geris sobbing into Dak's arms about winged monsters and red snake women. He could hear Kil and Rem laughing triumphantly behind him. He could hear it all, but he had not a care of it. 'Twas the feel of Kyra in his arms that encompassed the whole of his world. "I thought I had lost you," he said quietly. "By the goddess, I thought I had lost you."

"We made it," Kyra replied, emotion tight in her voice. She drew her husband's face down and kissed him. "We're okay."

"I love you, *nee'ka*."

"I love you too, Zor."

A few minutes later, after Zor and Dak had put their wives down, Kyra and Geris expounded upon their harrowing adventure to all four of the brothers, leaving nothing of it out. They spoke of the gulch beasts overhead, of how Jera had tried to kill them, of the red woman-snake, and of how Jera had eventually died.

"I'll never forget it," Kyra said, her eyes unblinking. "As long as I live, the look on Jera's face will be forever etched in my memories."

"Neither will I," Geris admitted softly, "forget it, that is."

Kil hugged Kyra and Geris simultaneously, rocking back and forth on his feet with them in his embrace. "You two are kind indeed to grieve for one such as Jera. She thought to kill you."

"Aye." Zor shook his head, his teeth clenched. "She got naught but what she deserved for what she did to you, as well as to my brother."

"'Tis over," Rem said simply, not caring to dwell upon Jera or her death any longer. "No more needs be said."

"I'm still regretful that we could not set things to rights for you, Rem." Dak removed Geris from Kil's arms with an indignant huff, inducing his brother to chuckle. He clutched Geris firmly against his side, then nodded to Rem. "We would that we could have brought you peace."

"Oh." Kyra shook her head and grinned. "I almost forgot."

"What did you forget, *nee'ka*?" Zor splayed his hands at his hips and regarded her. "You've more to tell? I hope my hearts can take it," he muttered.

"Well, sort of." Kyra backed out of Kil's embrace and turned to face Rem. She dug into the pocket of her-Zor's-leathers and pulled out a bridal necklace whose stones looked...hopeful. "For you."

Rem's jaw went slack as he studied the proffered piece of jewelry. Stunned, his gaze shot up to meet Kyra's. "But how...?"

Kyra blew out a breath. "I, uh..." Shuddering, she backed up into Zor's embrace, seeking the comfort of her Sacred Mate's arms around her. She took a deep, cathartic breath and told Rem how it happened. "I snatched it from her...her..." She shook her head. "I snatched it from her severed torso before Ger and I ran."

"Oh, *nee'ka*." Zor squeezed her tightly, as if to ward off the bad memories.

"Thank you, sister." Rem searched her eyes, still unable to believe that the necklace was his again, or that during all that had transpired, she had thought to retrieve it for him. "I cannot ever repay you for this."

Kyra smiled. "You can start by taking it from my hand." She shivered tellingly. "No offense, Rem, but the damn thing holds as many fond memories for me as it does for you."

Rem couldn't help it. He laughed. "I hope to remedy that."

Kyra grinned back at him. "Please do."

As Rem was removing his bride's necklace from Kyra's palm, Death and Glok were strolling over to the group to make certain all was well. "You okay, little fire-berry?"

"Yeah." Kyra ran over to Death and Glok and hugged them tightly. Geris joined her moments later, embracing the big men as best as she could manage.

Zor frowned, but said nothing. The men had, in effect, played a part in his *nee'ka's* rescue. Had they not come upon Kyra and Geris, gulch beasts could have devoured the women whole before they'd made it far enough away from Kogar before darkness fell.

Relenting, Zor walked to where the men stood, embracing the women even now. There was something about the giagantic one called Death, some nagging suspicion that told him there was more to him than what meets the eye. Dismissing the feeling, he inclined his head gratefully. "I owe you much."

"Nay." Death shook his head. "'Twas the least we could do, Your Majesty."

"Mayhap," Zor replied thoughtfully, "but I'd still like to repay you."

"Oh yeah?" Glok asked between puffs on his mooka. "How?"

Chapter 36

"Mmmm." Kyra closed her eyes and moaned softly as her husband thrust slowly in and out of her welcoming pussy. There had been many times today when she had never thought to feel this again. "Oh Zor. You feel so good."

"Not even half as good as you feel, my hearts."

Kyra secreted away a smile. She could distinctly remember a time when that endearment had annoyed her mightily, yet now it was one of the sweetest sentiments she'd ever heard tell of. Gliding her hands over his muscled buttocks, she moaned greedily as he continued to ease in and out of her. "I love you, Zor Q'an Tal. High King or common man, there could only be you."

"Ah *nee'ka*."

Kyra smiled fully. She opened her eyes and made a thorough study of his features. "And thanks, by the way, for what you did for Death and Glok."

Zor grunted as he slid into Kyra's channel and ground his hips into hers. "Let us not speak of them whilst we couple, *pani*."

"But I'm serious." Kyra groaned out her praise of Zor's prowess before returning to the topic of her choosing. "That was so nice of you, making them both high lords. I can't believe-mmmm."

Zor silenced her with a long, heady kiss that came complete with tongues, lips, and a whole lot of love. Picking up the pace of their mating, he thrust into Kyra's inviting cunt faster and faster, their mouths never breaking contact.

When the moment of truth grew closer and Zor realized he was but moments from spurting his life-force, he broke off the kiss in favor of gazing into Kyra's eyes. He pounded into her harder, possessively. "Aye or nay," Zor gritted out, his hips slamming into hers. "Aye or nay, *nee'ka*."

Kyra's hips thrashed upwards to meet her husband's, her own thrusts eager and needful. "Aye," she moaned out. "Yes Zor-do it."

"Your pleasure is mine, *nee'ka*."

And with those prophetic words, the High King of Tryston and the Emperor of Trek Mi Q'an lowered his head and gorged.

Epilogue

Three Weeks Later

The High King and High Queen of Tryston threw a small, intimate party to celebrate the arrival of their fourth hatchling, another girl child named Klea. Zor was imminently pleased, as Klea's birth was yet further proof that his seed was fiercely potent. And since Kil had seemed relieved by Klea's hatching-most likely because he wasn't yet ready to deal with the intense emotions a Sacred Mate brings with her-Zor was all around elated, his happiness lessened by naught.

The gathering included all the Q'an Tal brothers and their hatchlings, plus Kyra, Geris, and Cam. Much to Zor's disgruntlement, as he was still not ready to accept the fact that he would be relieved of Kara the very day she turned twenty and five, Kyra had insisted upon inviting Cam to the celebration and would brooch no arguments to the contrary. If he was to become her son-in-law, she had declared, then he was also to be a regular attendee at family functions.

Kyra had more or less persuaded Zor to her way of thinking, debating with him that since family gatherings would be but a couple of times a year, there was no harm in including Cam. She wanted, after all, for Kara not to be afraid of the warrior, a warrior that gossip held would no doubt rise to the rank of high lord within the year.

Speaking of high lords, two more attendees showed up at the Q'an Tal/Q'ana Tal soiree. Kyra smiled brightly as the two men now referred to as Lord Death and Lord Glok made their way to the table.

Already, and they had gained control of their sectors scarcely two weeks past, the two unique high lords were turning out to be quite popular leaders amongst those they protected. Death had displayed a military-like precision while taking control first of his own sector and then aiding with Glok's, which had only further flamed Zor's curiosity regarding the giant's history.

Anyway, the high lords' sectors were now firmly under control. In their sectors, Kyra was pleased to note, moonshine matpow had been declared legal. She planned to visit both of them very soon.

Death had also announced his intention to hunt for his Sacred Mate, much to Kyra and Geris's delight. He'd never given the concept much thought, he had said, but now that he needed heirs, he decided it was past time.

The women had merely nodded, holding back smiles, trying to imagine the look of unadulterated *pani*c that would cross his *nee'ka's* face when Lord Death beat on his tattooed chest and came barreling toward her like a charging predator.

If his bride survived the fright, Kyra thought bemusedly, she would no doubt grow to love the eight-foot giant. For all of Death's grumbling and fierce looks, he was actually quite sweet and masculinely handsome of face and thickly muscled form.

The private dinner party was held near early moon-rising at a rounded crystal table out on the royal balcony. The moon of Sypar hung overhead, casting a magnificent silver-blue light. Crystal gel-lamps had been lit to add further illumination to the get-together.

Death and Glok passed out expensive mookas to the warriors and slipped a couple of them to Kyra and Geris while their husbands weren't looking. Rem, who had witnessed it, merely shook his head and smiled.

Rem was preparing to return to Sypar before heading out on a bridal hunt with Death a sennight hence. Like Death, claiming his true Sacred Mate was something he didn't wish to put off, though his reasons were different from his new-found friend's.

Rem had never thought to have this opportunity; he had never thought he would be given the chance to realize the joy of having a true bride or the contentment of holding his own *panis* in his arms. Now that said events were looming just over the horizon, Rem was eager to find his Sacred Mate and claim her as Q'ana Tal.

Kyra could almost feel sorry for whatever woman her brother-in-law was to claim. Rem would be too overcome with possessiveness to let the as of yet unknown *nee'ka* from his sights once he found her. Now that would be an interesting marriage to watch blossom, she thought wryly. But the bride would come around, she was certain. Rem, after all, would allow for nothing less.

Kil was planning to leave the Palace of the Dunes the following morning as well. He needed to return to Morak and meet with the high lords that controlled his various sectors to establish that all was well and to insure himself that no new signs of insurrectionist activity had been found. But his leave-taking was more than a desire for governing and everyone knew it.

Kil needed time, he needed to walk alone again. He needed to gather himself together and figure out what direction he wanted to take in life now that his obsession with Ty had come to an abrupt end. Kyra suspected that even when she did hatch a son, her stubborn brother-in-law would not deign to begin a bridal hunt. That one would have to happen across his Sacred Mate accidentally to find her.

But once the fates brought her to him...lord help the woman! Kyra understood that in many ways Kil was like a dog with a bone. Once he sunk his teeth into something, it was his and his alone. She couldn't imagine a warrior the likes of Kil being able to sit back and stew while he watched younger warriors paw all over his Sacred Mate at a consummation feast. He would feel the need to brand her for all times, possessing her body and soul, killing any who dared to touch his bone, or uh, *nee'ka*.

Dak and Geris were staying in Sand City until Geris hatched next week. Since both husbands realized that Kyra would demand to be there for her best friend's hatching, both Dak and Zor thought it pointless for them to leave for Ti Q'won until Geris was safely delivered of the *pani* sac.

Zor and Dak chuckled as they watched Kara and Jana bedevil Cam, shrieking in laughter as the Commander chased them around the balcony pretending to be a gulch beast. Dak's youngest hatchling, his son Dar, was sitting on Dak's lap, displaying a winsome, gummy grin as he watched his sister and cousin dart past Cam.

Zor waited for Kyra to kiss Klea's mop of dark hair before he passed his sleeping hatchling off to Leha and bade her to put the wee one abed. Thinking to snuggle up with another of his *panis,* he grunted when he noticed that all were busy.

Kara was still playing the gulch beast game with Cam and Jana, and Zora and Zara were cuddled up in the laps of their favored uncles. Zora was showing "Unca Wem" her new arm bracelet, whilst Zara was placing kisses on "Unca Kee-wil's" nose. Why Zara threw the extra "w" sound into Kil's name, none could say, but 'twas apparent that "Unca Kee-wil" was too bedeviled with the imp to care.

Zor shook his head in amusement and turned his attention to his *nee'ka.* Kyra and Geris were busy jabbering a mile a minute with Death and Glok. Death was demonstrating how 'twas possible to make the skull on his forehead wink when he wrinkled his forehead just so. Glok was "discreetly" slipping Kyra some of his homemade moonshine, certain as he was that none were watching. Zor could only chuckle at that.

Kyra, Zor was happy to say, was much more content now that Ty was dead and she was free to head for the shopping stalls whenever the mood struck. Four times in the past two weeks his *nee'ka* had bade Gio and Mik to escort her, Geris, and their brood of hatchlings to the marketplace.

The women and *panis* had come back with a hoard of treasures each time, forcing the Q'an Tal brothers to watch as the girls tried on their new kazis and modeled them individually, one by one, for their papas and uncles. 'Twas an amusingly torturous process, long and drawn out as it was. Yet somehow the girls managed to make the forced sittings fun, their excitement bubbling over to bedevil everyone.

Zor caught Kyra's eye when she glanced up at him. She bit her lip and smiled seductively, recognizing that look within his glowing blue eyes that clearly announced he wished to couple. But of course, coupling was forbidden for the next fortnight, so he would have to settle for gorging this moon-rising. Not that gorging wasn't bliss. 'Twas just that Zor much preferred spurting his life-force within Kyra's welcoming body as opposed to within the confines of his leathers.

Aye, he could take *Kefas* to bath did he desire it, but even that no longer held appeal. Zor thought it interesting that the longer he was mated, the less he was able to stomach the thought of anyone but Kyra touching him, even when that someone was composed of naught but enchanted sand.

And so it had been since Kara's hatching that Zor would only take a *Kefa* to the bathing chamber when Kyra was with him. Even then it was solely for the delight of watching his beloved *nee'ka* peak, as it had become his desire to not participate. Dak had confessed to the same, making Zor feel better, for he'd never heard tell of this bizarre need to abstain from other warriors before.

Zor smiled at Kyra, then crooked his finger, telekinetically summoning her to his lap. She gave out a muffled shriek, but grinned good-naturedly, then settled herself into his embrace

Much better.

If he could not cuddle with one of his *panis*, then Zor would at least know the joy of snuggling with mani. "You've hatched yet another beautiful daughter to bedevil me with," he murmured in a private tone. He placed a sweet kiss at Kyra's temple. "Thank-you, *nee'ka*."

"You're welcome." Kyra took a long, thorough look around the balcony, relishing the sight of everyone she loved smiling and having such a good time, before her gaze strayed back to Zor and stayed there. "You're very welcome."

"I love you, my hearts."

She smiled. "And I love you. Now and forever, there is only you."

About the author:

Critically acclaimed and highly prolific, Jaid Black is the best-selling author of numerous erotic romance tales. Her first title, The Empress' New Clothes, was recognized as a readers' favorite in women's erotica by Romantic Times magazine. A full-time writer, Jaid lives in a cozy little village in the northeastern United States with her two children. In her spare time, she enjoys traveling, horseback riding, and furthering her collection of African and Egyptian art.

She welcomes mail from readers. You can write to her c/o Ellora's Cave Publishing at P.O. Box 787, Hudson, Ohio 44236-0787.

Why an electronic book?

We live in the Information Age—an exciting time in the history of human civilization in which technology rules supreme and continues to progress in leaps and bounds every minute of every hour of every day. For a multitude of reasons, more and more avid literary fans are opting to purchase e-books instead of paperbacks. The question to those not yet initiated to the world of electronic reading is simply: *why?*

1. *Price.* An electronic title at Ellora's Cave Publishing runs anywhere from 40-75% less than the cover price of the exact same title in paperback format. Why? Cold mathematics. It is less expensive to publish an e-book than it is to publish a paperback, so the savings are passed along to the consumer.
2. *Space.* Running out of room to house your paperback books? That is one worry you will never have with electronic novels. For a low one-time cost, you can purchase a handheld computer designed specifically for e-reading purposes. Many e-readers are larger than the average handheld, giving you plenty of screen room. Better yet, hundreds of titles can be stored within your new library—a single microchip. (Please note that Ellora's Cave does not endorse any specific brands. You can check our website at *www.ellorascave.com* for customer recommendations we make available to new consumers.)
3. *Mobility.* Because your new library now consists of only a microchip, your entire cache of books can be taken with you wherever you go.

4. *Personal preferences are accounted for.* Are the words you are currently reading too small? Too large? Too...**ANNOYING**? Paperback books cannot be modified according to personal preferences, but e-books can.
5. *Innovation.* The *way* you read a book is not the only advancement the Information Age has gifted the literary community with. There is also the factor of *what* you can read. Ellora's Cave Publishing will be introducing a new line of interactive titles that are available in e-book format only.
6. *Instant gratification.* Is it the middle of the night and all the bookstores are closed? Are you tired of waiting days—sometimes weeks—for online and offline bookstores to ship the novels you bought? Ellora's Cave Publishing sells instantaneous downloads 24 hours a day, 7 days a week, 365 days a year. Our e-book delivery system is 100% automated, meaning your order is filled as soon as you pay for it.

Those are a few of the top reasons why electronic novels are displacing paperbacks for many an avid reader. As always, Ellora's Cave Publishing welcomes your questions and comments. We invite you to email us at service@ellorascave.com or write to us directly at: P.O. Box 787, Hudson, Ohio 44236-0787.

9 780972 437707

Printed in the United States
29334LVS00001B/49-2010

9 780972 437707